April Showers

Anne Maisy Scott

PublishAmerica
Baltimore

© 2007 by Anne Maisy Scott.
All rights reserved. No part of this book may be reproduced, stored in a retrieval system or transmitted in any form or by any means without the prior written permission of the publishers, except by a reviewer who may quote brief passages in a review to be printed in a newspaper, magazine or journal.

First printing

All characters appearing in this work are fictitious. Any resemblance to real persons, living or dead, is purely coincidental.

ISBN: 1-4241-7136-9
PUBLISHED BY PUBLISHAMERICA, LLLP
www.publishamerica.com
Baltimore

Printed in the United States of America

This book is dedicated to my mother with
a lifetime of love, despite the weather.

Acknowledgments

I have the utmost gratitude and respect for my hero, my sister, Shell. I don't know where I'd be today if it wasn't for you. Thank you for everything, sis, and I love you with all my heart.

Thank you, Dad, for all your support. I will never forget the encouragement you gave to me during the construction of this story. Thanks for being there for me and I love you very much!

Thanks to my loving husband for all your support during many sleepless nights. You had to suffer through many of my thoughts and were forced to listen to all my revisions. I appreciate your spicing up some of my vocabulary. I love you dearly.

This book is a reference for you, my Triple "J" children, of how life can go so terribly wrong. It is so important to listen to *your* children and keep them safe. However, faith, hope, and forgiveness are an important combination to survival. Thanks for cheering me on and I love you all!

I cannot forget to thank the matriarch of our family, L.H. I respect and thank you for reading my manuscript and sharing old stories of an era I didn't know much about. Thank you for all your support. I hold lots of love and respect for you.

Many thanks go out to A.S. and N.S. Thanks for the stories and support. Thank you for the laughs and for being an inspiration to me. You are very special to me and I love you both dearly.

Thanks to our dear friend Lee, from Kokomo, Indiana. Thanks for reading the first draft of *April Showers*. I appreciate all your input and encouragement to finish this project. I will always be thankful!

I need to thank my aunt, D.R.T., for listening to my crazy stories through countless, long-distance hours on the phone. I appreciate your support, which means a lot to me. I love ya bunches!

I have to thank my cousin, Steve, for daring me to dream. Thanks for the push I needed to pursue a path I had never traveled, but I had always wanted. Thanks to you, I am now an author!

Many, many thanks to PublishAmerica for this exciting opportunity to share my story! Thank you all for everything!

Chapter 1

It was 3 AM when she was suddenly awakened by the piercing rings of the telephone, which echoed off the walls and rattled every fiber in her nervous system. As she fumbled in the dark to answer the phone, she accidentally knocked the lamp off the nightstand and sent it crashing to the floor. She managed to grab the phone just before the answering machine was about to kick in. This seemed to be a ritual in her family as if it were some kind of contest to be able to *beat* the machine.

As she picked up the phone, she covered the receiver with her hand and practiced a few hellos with hopes of lessening the harshness of her morning voice. She had been accused of being a man on more than one occasion during early morning phone conversations. Despite her best attempt, she did not manage to pull it off as her voice sounded like a blues singer who smoked three packs of cigarettes a day.

"I'm sorry to have wakened you, sir. I must have dialed the wrong number," said a familiar voice on the other end.

After clearing her voice a few times, she asked, "Who are you trying to reach?" Her voice was starting to sound more normal and less gruff.

"Maggie, is that you?" asked the woman on the other end.

Being half asleep, she wondered how anyone knew that Maggie was her childhood name. When she was born, her sister could not pronounce Megan, so she called her baby sister Maggie, and the name forever stuck within her family back in Ohio. Her husband, Alec, called her Maggie because he thought it was cute. She thought with pride, *I'm Megan Graham, sales person of the year!* She was known by local people due to real-estate advertisements and billboards throughout Indianapolis.

She suddenly realized it was her big sister, Maddie, on the other end of the line. "Oh, my gosh, Maddie! How are you? How are the kids? How's Chase?" She was so surprised to hear from her sister that it never occurred to her that the phone call was taken in the middle of the night. Maggie was always happy to hear from her family, but with her living out of state also kept her out of the loop with her family in Toledo. It had been at least six months since she had heard from Maddie. She loved her sister, but they did not always see eye to eye.

"This is not a social call, Maggie," said Maddie as her voice dropped and became unusually serious and monotone. "It's Mom. She passed away an hour ago."

There was a long pause on the phone. Maggie felt her whole body instantly go numb. Her initial thought was that this must be some sort of sick joke. Maddie was always good for a joke no matter what the cost. "Madelyn Rose! This better not be a joke or I will *kill* you!" warned Maggie. If nothing else, Maddie was always able to bring the juvenile spirit out of her kid sister.

"This is no joke, I'm afraid. Kenneth called me and told me about it. He asked me to call you because he had to sign papers or whatever other death things he was called upon to do. You know that was Mother's wishes. *He's* the one to dictate orders at the time of her death. She appointed *him* to her throne years ago when she and Dad did their wills. Kenneth, the *good* son!" said Maddie sarcastically. She had painfully labeled him that for years out of spite.

Maggie was overcome by many different emotions, which was why she forced herself to ignore Maddie's insults against their brother as she abruptly derailed the topic by asking, "How did this happen? Was there an accident? Was there someone involved?" with a tone of desperation in her voice.

"Hold on a minute," said Maddie. She dropped the phone and Maggie could hear her scurry on the other end. Maggie listened carefully out of concern for her sister. She then heard a loud slurping noise that hurt her ear. Maddie returned to the phone a few seconds later.

"Sorry about that," said Maddie unsympathetically, "I spilled my beer."

"What happened to Mom?" cried Maggie. "I'm stunned because I believed with all my heart that she would outlive us all!"

Maddie let out a little chuckle and said, "It's so funny to me that she was found dead at home on the toilet. Don't you find humor in that too? The queen was sitting on her throne," she laughed. Maggie could hear her sister open another beer.

"Who found her that way? She lives all alone!"

"Kenneth to the rescue!" said Maddie as if she were announcing a superhero. "He's always been kind of a *grunt* man," she laughed. She paused briefly and her voice dropped and became serious again. "No. I don't really mean that. Even though he *is* Mom's favorite, he's still my little brother and I do love him. I'm just letting off some nervous tension, as Dad would say. But we all know that Kenneth *is* a butt-kisser."

"Does Kobe know yet?" asked Maggie.

"Of course he knows. He got the call from Kenneth before 911 was even dialed. It must be a twin's bond or something," Maddie scoffed.

"What was Kenneth doing at Mom's house at that hour anyway?" asked Maggie while trying to set the scene in her mind.

"You know how the neighborhood is in the north end. They've got the Crime Stoppers program in full motion, thanks to Dad. Neighbors know *everything* in the north end. I guess Mom was on the toilet and must have had a heart attack or something. Her lights were still on at such a late hour and it attracted the attention of the nosey old Widow Dooley from next door. The old fossil tried phoning Mom to check on her. After fifteen minutes of her not getting any answer, she decided to notify Kenneth right away."

"How awful!" exclaimed Maggie with such sorrow. Maggie sensed the preoccupation on Maddie's end of the conversation. It was obvious that Maddie had just slammed her beer. There was an awkward moment of silence, which prompted Maggie to ask with uncertainty, "So, you think it was her heart?"

Without hesitation, Maddie blurted, "You have to first have a heart to have a heart attack!"

"Maddie!" exclaimed Maggie with great surprise.

"I've always believed that she's had a big black hole that pumped poisonous blood."

Maggie shook her head with disbelief after hearing such harsh words at what should have been a tender moment. "You're in shock, Maddie," she said softly. "Try to calm down. I know that you don't mean that."

Maddie cried, "Maggie, she is the reason for so many hurts in our lives. The biggest disappointment is when she drove Dad out of the house. Well, *one* of the biggest. *You* of all people know *exactly* what I mean by that!"

The girls spoke on the phone for two hours. Maggie worried about Maddie being home alone. Her husband, Chase, was on his way home from a business trip in Milwaukee. His firm was flying him back home on their company jet after he received the news about his mother-in-law. Chase knew things would not be good for Maddie, especially *after* April's death. He knew that ill, dormant feelings would soon surface and flood their lives as if a dam broke.

As it was, the whole family struggled to keep their heads above the flood waters created by their mother's torrential rains of disappointments and ridicule, which had become known as April Showers. Their father, Michael, was also a victim of such harsh and violent storms. There was not much they could do to protect themselves from the ugliness except to huddle together and weather the storm. They found their strength through unity and humor—lots of humor.

Maggie did her best to stay on the line with Maddie until Chase got home. Maddie was getting groggy and conversation kept circulating back to how their mother, April, despised Maddie and their father, Michael, the most out of the Getman family. Maggie was so relieved to hear in the distance, "Doll! Where are you?" Chase had made it home. He raced through the house to comfort his grieving, intoxicated wife. Maggie listened sympathetically as Chased embraced her sister while she sobbed on his shoulder. When Maddie began to quiet down, he retrieved the phone and thanked Maggie for keeping his wife company.

"I'll be there sometime tomorrow," promised Maggie. She ended her conversation with the famous "I love you guys."

Maddie was the one who introduced "I love you" as a family ritual when she was about ten years old. She always envied her best friend's family because they always said it without shame or embarrassment. Since then, the Getman family always said it along with a hug whether they meant it or not.

Maddie always warned, "We just never know if that might be the last thing we might ever say to one another." She would always follow up that statement by teasing, "I know that what I *really* want to say would be safely spoken behind your back!"

Maggie had been sitting in the dark since 3 AM. Daylight would soon be arriving along with her husband, Alec, who was a third shift supervisor for General Motors. Still being in a state of shock and disbelief about her mother's death, she decided to make a positive out of her negative tension. She was just too wound up to go back to sleep. She was certain to have her house cleaned before Alec got home. The first place she needed to start was picking up the broken pieces of her lamp that rested at her feet.

She carefully walked across the room to turn on the overhead light so that she could see just how badly damaged the lamp was. She was hoping that it sounded worse than it actually was and her perpetual optimism kept her hoping against the odds, but the loud crash was a sure indication that the lamp was demolished. With a quick flip of the light switch on the wall, her suspicions were confirmed and she grabbed the wastebasket from the master bathroom. As she stooped over to pick up a large piece of jagged glass, it suddenly dawned on her that the shattered lamp was a metaphor of her life.

Maggie pondered that thought for a moment. She interpreted it as her needing to pick up the broken pieces of her past by freeing her incarcerated ghosts from her closet by way of assessing the damage, consider discarding or repairing it, and then move on with her life. With a newfound confidence, she thought to herself, *If I can survive the clean-up duties of a messy past, then I will never be broken nor in the dark again*, as she cleaned the mess from her bedroom floor.

Chapter 2

Alec arrived home at 7:30 AM, which was just in time for Allie to drive to school. Maggie could not bear the thought of spoiling Allie's special day with news that couldn't wait another seven hours. She was running for class president and it was Election Day. Maggie could hear Allie singing in the shower earlier as she prepared for her big day. Maggie fought back the tears as she prepared her daughter's breakfast with mixed emotions of excitement for her daughter and sorrow for the death of her mother.

Maggie shook off such thoughts as she concentrated on how Allie had really grown comfortable in her skin this year and that she was more of a wonderful, energetic, and beautiful young lady. She had numerous friends at school, which made her feel confident that she would win the election. She wanted this kind of victory added to her Purdue University application next year. She enjoyed razzing her father for his misfortune of being an Indiana University graduate, which fueled the ongoing rivalry in just one of many Indiana families.

Despite their differences of opinions on who supported the better college, Alec did support his daughter in all she set forth to accomplish as well. Maggie helped her create a catchy campaign slogan while Alec used his computer graphic skills to create posters that she proudly displayed throughout the school. Alec was just getting out of his truck as Allie was about to walk out the door.

"Bye, Mom. I wish you a million dollar sale today so my college tuition will be paid in full," said Allie with a big cheeky grin. Maggie giggled and handed Allie her lunch at the door.

"Don't get too mouthy, little miss sassy pants," teased Maggie.

This little joke had been going on for the past few years between the two since Maggie earned her real-estate license. Her employer sponsored her continuing education classes, which had really paid off because it helped her become sales person of the year. Maggie's career was a perfect fit for her personality. She had always been a people person and she enjoyed meeting individuals from all walks of life. She traditionally baked a homemade loaf of bread for her clients the night before each closing.

Allie would say on a regular basis, "Oh! Did you hear that? Twenty minutes had past and Mom must have sold another house. Cha-ching!" She would say that in church, at a restaurant, and she'd even said it in her sleep! Maggie was just happy that Allie had been focusing on college since her junior year was quickly coming to a close.

Maggie never had the opportunity to attend a university, even though she graduated sixth out of two hundred students in her class. Her inner-city high school had been rumored to close while the teachers and counselors were more concerned for their futures rather than for the students' well-being. She studied diversified health occupations and graduated with honors. She was voted most likely to succeed by her class.

The closest Maggie came to college right after her high school graduation was when April's father, Bo, offered to pay her tuition for nursing school at Providence Hospital in Sandusky, Ohio. He invited Maggie to live in Port Clinton with him and he even offered to buy her a car to commute back and forth to school. She had to decline his generous offer because her mother was furious with that idea and said to Maggie, "You are *my* problem, not his!"

On most occasions she would hear her mother say, "College isn't for everybody" or "If any of my kids want to attend college, they can indulge in the burden of paying for it themselves!" All three of Maggie's siblings were offered college tuition from her parents, she was the only one that was not. April knew that Maddie wasn't interested and the twins would also decline the offer. Maggie later discovered that her father purchased vehicles for her brothers in lieu of paying for college tuition.

Maggie looked at her daughter with admiration as she wished

Allie all the luck in the world with the election. She even offered some motherly encouragement to allow her daughter to walk a little taller.

"Don't sweat it, Allie. You are the perfect person for the job. If your peers can't see that, then it will be a big mistake for them. Regardless if you make it or not, you will always be special to me and I will love you with or without the title of Ms. Class President. Have some faith, Allie. Let's sit back and watch how it will all unfold for you today. Remember that everything has its own time and place. I believe in my heart that this time is yours."

"Thanks, Mom. I hope that you said a few prayers for me just in case. This election really means a lot to me. You know that bossing people around is the *one* thing that I excel in!"

Maggie pulled Allie into her arms and gave her a big hug. "I know you will be a wonderful president for your class, Sergeant! I love you and have a wonderful day!" Maggie patted her on the back and out the door she went.

Alec came in from getting the newspaper from the driveway. He had a grin on his face and said, "You just couldn't resist, could you?"

Maggie looked as innocent as she could and said, "Who? Me? Why whatever do you mean?"

He let out a chuckle and said that he saw the note taped to Allie's back that read, "Victory is sweet and I have big smelly feet!"

Maggie always played little tricks on her family. Her favorite prank was when she wrote on the back of the tailgate of Alec's black truck with white shoe polish, "Honk! I'm 30 today!" On his drive to work he couldn't figure out why people were honking at him. He was a bit self-conscious because his speedometer didn't work and he felt he might have been driving too slowly.

He finally became irritated to the point of flipping those poor Hoosiers the finger! He never knew about his personal announcement on the back of his truck until his shift was finished. It was then he realized how his co-workers knew it was his birthday. He just figured that he was a popular guy!

Maggie laughed out loud and claimed not to be a very good poet. "What can I say? I just simply could not resist!" she said as she waved her hands up in the air and knocked a coffee mug to the floor.

"Ugh! I am on a roll today!" she growled.

Alec looked at her with concern. "Are you okay this morning? You look a bit pale to me. Did you not sleep well last night?"

Maggie couldn't answer right away. Alec knelt down to help her pick up the broken glass. She kept her silence and avoided eye contact with him.

"Maggie? What's wrong?" he asked with concern.

He gently lifted her chin so that he could look into her eyes. She looked like a small child about to be scolded. Her soft auburn hair was falling out of her hair clip. Her hair looked as if it were beyond a modest repair at that moment. Her green eyes were heavy and weighted down with tears. As her eyes met Alec's exuberant, bright blue eyes, he witnessed huge crocodile tears stream effortlessly down her cheeks. He took her by the hand and led her away from the mess on the floor. He embraced her in his arms tightly against his chest to where she felt as if she could hardly breathe.

"Talk to me, baby," he said softly. "What's got you feeling so down?"

She cried for what seemed like an eternity. He grabbed a napkin that was within his reach and gently dried her tears. She looked like a child within his arms. Alec stood six feet three inches tall with a muscular physique compared to her petite, five feet two inches and slender frame.

Maggie began to settle down. Alec was gently swaying back and forth with her feeling secure within his arms. He removed her hair clip and gently stroked her hair with his fingertips. He kissed her softly on the forehead.

"Are you ready to tell me what's wrong?" he asked as her eyes met his.

She nodded and said in a raspy voice, "Maddie called me in the middle of the night to tell me that my mother passed away."

Alec was so surprised by the unexpected news about April that he could not find the words to console his wife. He stood in the kitchen feeling stunned and in disbelief as she told him that they didn't know for sure the cause of death, but an autopsy should solve any mystery. There was an awkward moment of silence. Maggie stood there staring into space as if she were in a trance. With the combination of shock and the lack of sleep, it appeared that Maggie was taking a mental nap.

"I'm so sorry, baby," said Alec.

Maggie jumped as if she were awakened from a sound sleep. She pulled away from him and announced that she was going to start packing right away. As she reached the stairway, she forgot what it was she was going to do. Her head was spinning and she felt as if she spent the whole night drinking. She then heard the alarm clocks going off in Mark and Missy's bedrooms.

"Oh, my gosh! My kids! How could I forget about them? I'm losing my mind!" she cried. "Just call me April!"

"Whoa! Calm down, Maggie!"

"What am I going to do? I totally forgot! I can't leave today because Missy has a field trip to the apple orchard, which I took the day off to spend with her, and Mark has a soccer game after school! I can't disappoint them, Alec."

Alec reassured her that he would take care of the children while she went to Toledo. He would bring the kids for the funeral later.

"We will be fine here. You have a lot to tend to there, which is more than just making funeral arrangements. You need to bury old ghosts from your mother once and for all. Not just your ghosts, but ones that have been haunting the rest of your family as well. I will tell the kids about their grandmother after school today. What I need for you to do is to march upstairs and go back to bed because you are in no condition to drive. You need your strength! All of the ugliness and tears will be waiting for you in Toledo, nothing *too* unfamiliar," he said. "Go upstairs and get some sleep. A few winks will do you some good."

Mark and Missy greeted their mother on the stairway. "Good morning, my little monkeys," Maggie said with a rehearsed smile. She gave them both a hug and kissed them on top of their little heads. "Did you have sweet dreams?" she asked like she did every morning.

"Mom, I don't dream because I'm too busy sleeping," said Mark candidly.

Missy smiled and said, "I dreamed that I was a princess and everybody did *exactly* what I told them!"

Maggie laughed out loud and said, "Yep! The women in this family carry the bossy gene that bears April's name all over it."

Alec told the children to get dressed before going to the breakfast table so that he could clean the broken glass.

"Mommy's going to bed because she's not feeling well," he said.

Before Missy could open her little mouth, Alec said, "I will be taking you to your field trip today. I look forward to being your date this afternoon. Now go get dressed and don't wear anything that will embarrass me."

Missy rolled her eyes and said, "Oh, Daddy."

He tucked Maggie into bed. She was nearly asleep when her head hit the pillow. He gently kissed her good night. He sat by her side for a moment and was taken by her beauty. His heart ached for his wife with thoughts of the unspeakable things April had done to her. If her mental scars would be visible, she would still be beautiful to him. In his eyes, she was a survivor. She was much stronger than what she credited herself for. She was so beautiful, but she didn't see it. Maggie's self-worth was near nonexistent from growing up in a household where she lived in her sister's shadow and took a backseat to the spotlight of attention for her brothers. Everyone else's needs somehow came before her needs were met.

He continued to watch his wife with admiration. He thought about how she'd survived abandonment, a loss of innocence, repeated dangers, and robbed of any decent childhood at the hands of her own mother. His train of thought was derailed when he heard his kids finishing up in their rooms. He knew he needed to beat them downstairs before they injured themselves on the broken glass that awaited them on the kitchen floor.

As he rose from the bed, Maggie whispered, "Thank you, Alec. I love you so much," as she reached for his arm. "You *are* my knight in shining armor," she said with a sleepy smile.

Alec smiled and kissed her tenderly on the lips. "And *you* are me lady," he said as he kissed the back of her hand. He giggled and teased, "I am in love with Megan Graham, sales person of the year! And don't you forget it!"

She responded with a half-hearted smile. As he walked toward the door, he turned to look at her and said, "And for the record, you could *never* be like your mother! Don't bother wasting your time worrying about that nonsense. Try to get some rest."

He stifled a yawn and met the kids at the top of the stairs. "Stand back!" he joked. "Dad needs to get some coffee to make it through my exciting apple orchard date today."

While Alec tended to the children, Maggie fell quickly into a dream. She dreamed that she was walking through a crowded smoky room filled with people. Everyone was talking amongst themselves and she didn't recognize any faces as she passed through the room. She was quick to notice that there was no color and everything looked dull and lifeless. Just as she reached the door, she looked over her left shoulder and saw her great uncle standing alone in the corner of the room.

In her dreams, she saw her Uncle Doug wearing a white Zoot-Suit that looked ten sizes too large on him. He looked as if he were a small child playing dress-up. His physical appearance was small and his color was nothing but that of a shadow. He never spoke a word, but he carried an expression of sadness upon his shaded face and he could never look Maggie in the eye.

Maggie saw him in her dreams from time to time and he always appeared to be lurking in the background, but she had done the right thing and kept moving along without so much as a single word. From what should have been a pitiful sight, she never gave him a second glance or an ounce of sympathy, which contradicted her compassionate and giving nature. She exited the room and entered a new phase of her dream.

She found herself dining in a charming little restaurant with April and Maddie. They were seated at a table towards the back of the room and enjoyed the warmth of the sunshine as it illuminated the restaurant. The atmosphere was pleasant and cheerful. The little round table had a white pressed tablecloth decorated with a single yellow rose placed in a jelly jar, which sat in the center of the table.

The yellow rose was symbolic of the Getman family. It was adopted because that was the flower of choice at Michael and April's wedding. That was the only wedding detail that Michael insisted upon. It was the first flower he ever gave to his beloved April. When they were dating, he would often send yellow roses to April and then finally, decades later, he did the same for their children on special occasions.

Nothing was out of the ordinary with the dream until a stranger entered the establishment and scanned the crowded room. Maggie became extremely alarmed because she felt there was something evil about this person. She couldn't make out the features of his face because it was a blur to her. He carried an essence about him of a man with a mission—an evil mission. In Maggie's heart she knew that he meant to inflict harm. And for whatever the reason, she knew that he was after no one other than her.

It was obvious to her that she was the only one who could sense his presence because the patrons remained unnerved. She didn't have time to study his face because she feared that he would find her in the crowd. She quickly got up from the table and snuck out the rear exit. The feeling of fear tightened across her chest to where she found it harder and harder to breathe.

There was something familiar about this man as if she had seen him before. Her fear intensified to the point to where she wanted to scream. Maggie could see the man through the window as she hid behind a parked car in the rear parking lot. When the man approached the table and inquired about Maggie, she assumed that her mother would protect her daughter's identity for safety reasons. She was alarmed when she saw April quickly point to the back of the restaurant where Maggie had escaped only a brief moment ago.

As Maggie ran from the restaurant, the scenery began to grow noticeably cold and dark. She realized that she had been running through the streets of a neighborhood in the north end of Toledo, which happened to be near her childhood home. She desperately tried to reach her Ontario Street home, where her parents still resided. She ran as fast as she could while still looking over her shoulder.

She came to the corner of Ash and Erie Streets; she thought it would be safe to rest a bit to catch her breath. All the streetlights were on and it appeared to be sometime after midnight. She knew that no one in their right mind would be wandering around at that time of the night, especially alone in that neighborhood! She thought it would be easier for her to cross Ash Street, the overpass of I-280, to get closer to home. She was constantly looking over her shoulder and shaking uncontrollably from fright.

When she neared the bridge, it suddenly became a tunnel. The tunnel was as black as night. She could see Ontario Street on the other side of the tunnel, but she could not see what lurked within its darkness. She hesitated for a moment. The feeling of fear began to tighten in her chest again. She felt that it was impossible to take one more step closer to that tunnel. She was so scared that her legs couldn't move another step forward even if she wanted to. Her heart was pounding so loud that she thought it would beat right out of her chest.

Suddenly, out of the darkness, stepped the man in black! This was the same man who had haunted Maggie's dreams for years. Everything about this person was draped in black leather. She never saw his face because he was masked. He was holding something in his hand. Maggie was speechless and she felt paralyzed. He held the object over his head so the light of the moon might help Maggie realize what it was that he was showing her.

The reflection of the streetlight danced off of a shiny narrow object. It suddenly occurred to Maggie that he was holding a knife! The man in black leaned his back against the tunnel with one foot perched on the wall. It appeared that he was enjoying the torment and fear he had inflicted upon her, yet again. She felt so helpless and weak. Her perpetual fear only fueled his power.

"Leave me alone!" cried Maggie.

"Come with me, Maggie, and get it over with," he said. She felt as if her legs weighed a metric ton. "There are no shortcuts with me," he said as the streetlight continued to dance from his blade.

Maggie let out a scream and was able to break free from her paralyzed state. She ran down Erie Street as fast as she could. She could hear the footsteps of the man in black running behind her. She tried to think logically, as she always attempted to do in her dreams and in the real world, but she felt that it was forbidden for her to seek refuge with anyone she knew. She possessed an undying fear that they would be severely punished for trying to protect her.

She was running out of options and was about to an old friend's house on Buckeye Street. As luck would have it, Billy was sitting on his front porch. Maggie ran to him in a panic.

"Oh, thank God! Hide me, Billy! He's after me again!" she cried. "Oh, please help me," she pleaded desperately.

Without question, Billy told Maggie to hide in his basement. "You'll be safe with me, Maggie. I won't let him hurt you," he promised.

She flew down his basement stairs and hid behind a large sofa. Being in the dark, she noticed that there were not any windows. Ever since she was a child, she had a fear of not being able to escape if she had to. She could hear a loud pounding on Billy's front door. She could not make out what was being said, but voices began to rise. She could hear a scuffle upstairs. She heard the scream of a man, who was quickly silenced. The ghostly sound of silence only intensified her fear.

Something suddenly came crashing down the stairs and ended with a loud thud. Maggie never moved or gave away her position. The lights came on and there stood the man in black. "Look at your hero now, Maggie. Look what *you* did to your friend," he said. Billy lay at the bottom of the stairs bloody and stabbed to death. He was the eldest brother of her childhood friend Krista.

Maggie felt helpless and ashamed for the death of her friend. She felt responsible for the tragedy since she went to a friend for help. She knew there would be consequences if she disobeyed her instincts, but Maggie was desperate and had nowhere else to run. She had no one to help her. She screamed and cried. "Please leave me alone," she begged as she buried her face into her hands. She cowered behind the couch like a frightened animal.

As the man in black attempted to approach her, she found the strength from deep within herself to stand up and face him. She pointed with a stern finger and vowed, "You will *never* win with me! You cannot have me!" she exclaimed. He raised his bloody knife over his head and lunged at her.

Maggie quickly sat straight up in her bed with a start! She had a wild and confused look in her eyes. Her nails were embedded tightly in her sheets as the sweat rolled down her face. As she began to regain a normal respiration, she sighed with relief that it was just another silly dream. "If it's not the man in black, then it would be me falling off a decrepit bridge sending me plummeting into the Maumee River," said Maggie as she wiped the sweat from her brow. Such nightmares were the only reoccurring dreams that she would suffer from time to time. The man in black dreams seemed to be more frequent than ever before.

Since she was a small child, her dreams had always been so vivid. She once dreamed of Jesus walking out of the darkness and kneeling with His arms outstretched calling for Maggie to come to Him. She ran away screaming because her father had once told her that if she saw Jesus, then she must be dead. She also had a dream about a demon that captured her mother in their fiery driveway as he asked Maggie to join them. She was about two or three then.

When they moved to Toledo, Maggie dreamed that a strange woman grabbed Maddie by the hand and escorted her into their new house. She looked like a sweet and innocent woman who could not harm anyone, much less a child. Maggie listened in horror as she heard the pounding of the hammer as Maddie screamed in pain. Maddie came out with nails pounded all over her body! She found Maggie hiding behind a large tree in front of the house. She tried to convince Maggie to go inside the house for her turn because the woman with the hammer was waiting for her. Maggie was then four years old.

The clock read noon and Maggie couldn't believe that she slept that long. "I need to grab a quick shower and hit the road!" she said aloud as she tried to get motivated. The warm water felt so relaxing to her. She imagined that the heat of the water was melting away her stress and anguish. She washed her hair and watched the suds swirl down the drain as if she had the power to flush her negative energies and rid herself of such unpleasant thoughts and dreams. Maggie forced herself to hurry because she had a lot of ground to cover today.

She got dressed as quickly as she could. She pulled her hair up into a ponytail and put on a dark green jogging suit for her five-hour drive. She did take the time to perfect her makeup. Because of her career, she always needed to look presentable in public no matter what the occasion. She slipped into her Reebok tennis shoes and ran for the door. She grabbed her purse and jumped into her brand-new silver Cadillac. As she backed out of the driveway, she suddenly realized that she forgot to pack!

"Get a grip on yourself, Megan!" she said as her car came to a screeching halt. She drove the car into the garage and ran in the house. She threw a few things in a bag, she took a moment to write, "I love you," on the bathroom mirror with her lipstick, and out the door she went. She finally left her home in Fishers, which was a suburb northeast of Indianapolis. "Holy Toledo! I'm actually on the road," she said as she raced from her driveway.

Chapter 3

Maggie had encountered some rain along with the notorious springtime construction near Fort Wayne, Indiana. *Great!* she thought. *This is so typical.* Every time Maggie passed through this city it was either raining cats and dogs or there was a mini-blizzard. Fort Wayne reminded her of a smaller version of Toledo. It left her with a feeling of home, storms and all.

The mere mention of Fort Wayne took Maggie back to the memory of one Christmas Eve while driving back home from Toledo during a mini-blizzard. What would normally be a five-hour drive, took an additional three hours to get home on account of poor road conditions. Fort Wayne was the worst area by far. The Graham family witnessed numerous cars slide off the expressway. Alec helped stranded motorists when he could until he slipped and fell on the black ice on the pavement of the expressway. He cracked two ribs as his body slammed into the side of his opened door when he attempted to board his truck.

Maggie shuttered at that memory because April refused to have Christmas Eve sooner than 6 PM because that had always been the tradition at Grandpa Getman's house for years. Now that he was deceased, she took on the tradition for her family and she refused to make any exceptions to the rule. It was an inconvenience for Maggie's family because they lived out of state while everyone else resided locally. April suggested that Maggie's family stay overnight, knowing that they would decline the offer. Alec and Maggie made their feelings known that their children would be home to find their presents under their tree Christmas morning at their Indiana home. April ignored their family traditions and showed no concern for their safety.

Michael had done his best to hurry along the gift exchange because the weather was getting bad. Even though their visit was brief, they still got home at 4 AM Christmas morning. Maggie remembered her children crying in the back seat of the truck for hours. Mark wished that Santa could drive them home safely in his magic sleigh. They tried to sing Christmas songs to distract them from the slippery roads, but it had not lasted very long. That was the last Christmas Eve spent in Toledo for Maggie's family. April's selfishness ruined Christmas for them that year. Of course, there were no apologies from April.

As three lanes bottlenecked into one, the traffic came to a standstill. Traffic was backed up for miles. "Oh great!" she said. She was only a few miles away from her exit. As she remained parked on interstate 69 with the other motorists, she stared at the sign that read Toledo Highway 24 East, which was just a few short exits away. She inched her way along and kept staring at the sign. She found herself deep in thought as she reminisced about when she first moved into the house on Ontario Street.

Maddie was seven and Maggie was four and a half. These two little girls were so excited to be living in Grandma Ruby's old house. Grandma's house came complete with an upstairs and another bathroom to boot. It was a three-bedroom home with a possible fourth on the main level. It even had a small basement, which would offer more hiding places for hide-and-seek.

The Getmans moved from a small country house in Perrysburg, which happened to be next door to Michael's parents. April insisted that they move because they needed more space due to the anticipated arrival of the twins. She told the girls that they would be able to walk to school since it was only a block away from the house. She also told them that it was closer to work for their father, which was only a ten-mile drive from the country in the first place. In reality, the in-laws were just too close!

Grandma Ruby's half-sister, Paula, was the previous owner of their new house. Aunt Paula sold the house to April for one dollar. She wanted to just give it to April, but there had to be an actual dollar amount on the deed. The Getman family also had to take over payments of the newly constructed garage out back, which was the sum of five thousand dollars.

Ruby and Cami, April's younger sister, had been renting the house from Paula just weeks before the house was sold. April complained constantly to Paula about how awful it was living next to Michael's parents. Paula sympathized with her niece and she wanted to help her if she could. It was then that Paula decided that it was time for Ruby to start fending for herself, so she evicted her sister and niece so that April and her young family could move in immediately. Paula had no regrets about her abrupt decision because Ruby had been late on her rent for the past few months.

These young country girls traded in grassy acreage for the city's concrete beneath their feet. The sounds of roosters crowing on a country morning were soon replaced with sounds of sirens in the city all hours of the day and night. Maggie was still not over her fear of hearing sirens. She used to run and hide behind a chair along with her trusty blanket in hand and with a thumb wedged tightly in her mouth. A short time before the move, she had an uncle tell her when the noon whistle would sound, "Here they come, Maggie. The police are coming to take you away forever!"

They had been in their new house just under a week and the neighborhood buzzed with commotion. Sirens were screaming down the streets while Maggie had been doing some screaming of her own. It was early afternoon and Michael grabbed his daughter before she went into hiding.

"Come with me, Maggie," said Michael as he reached for her hand. "I want to show you that these sirens you hear are filled with good people. They could be police officers, firemen, or even ambulance drivers who take sick people to the hospital. They help people, they do *not* hurt them!"

"Hurry, Daddy! We're going to miss the show!" Maddie said anxiously as she yelled through the screen door.

"Relax, Maddie. They sound pretty close. We will investigate just as soon as Maggie is ready," said Michael.

After Maggie saw how anxious Maddie was, curiosity got the better of her and she grabbed her father's hand without hesitation. Michael briskly walked hand in hand with his daughters as with the many spectators heading a few blocks south. As they approached the intersection, they could see a large crowd of people huddled around a car parked on the front lawn. Maggie held on to her father's hand tight as she proceeded with caution, especially when she saw all the police cars lit up on the street. Maddie grabbed Maggie by the hand, which forced her little hand apart from Michael's hand, and maneuvered their way to the front of the crowd. Michael made his way through the crowd and stood close behind his girls.

They found themselves standing with a bird's-eye view of a car that crashed through the side of a red brick colored duplex. Apparently, witnesses said that the driver was drunk and he left the scene on foot. Trapped inside was a woman on the passenger side of the vehicle with her face embedded in the windshield. The girls could see blood oozing down on to her bare legs, just missing her cut-off denim shorts. The woman's bottom hovered above the seat while bracing herself on the dashboard with her elbows. She was screaming in pain. Pieces of glass was scattered throughout her hair.

A police officer was sitting beside her with his hand in the back of her head. Her bushy brown hair was entangled tightly within his fist while he was yelling, "Don't move! Don't f-ing move!" She was becoming hysterical. It looked as if he was hurting her, but in reality he was keeping her from ripping her face from her skull.

Michael grabbed his girls and said, "We've seen enough. Let's allow these officers to help that poor woman." They headed back home in silence. Michael treated the girls to a snack at the candy store on the corner of Buckeye and Ontario. He felt bad for the blunt introduction into the neighborhood, but Maggie's fear of sirens disappeared on that afternoon. Even though she witnessed the officer screaming at the woman, Maggie realized that he was helping her for her own good.

Maggie could see that traffic was trying to move along, but she could not justify the prolonged congestion. "Wow! I think I moved a mile in about twenty minutes," she said. She was so close to her exit that she was beginning to become anxious and irritated. She wanted to lay on her horn, but she knew that would not get her anywhere any faster. She just took a deep breath and attempted to preoccupy herself by looking at the vehicles around her.

The semi-truck in front of her was fairly dirty. Someone wrote in the dirt on the back of the trailer, "Home is where the heart is," which made her think of Ohio. She looked in her rearview mirror and saw a Jeep Liberty, which triggered stories that she had not thought of in years. Her mind drifted to her great-aunt, Paula.

Aunt Paula was like a mother to Ruby, since she was sixteen years her senior. Ruby was born to elderly parents and she was treated like an only child. Their mother had several husbands over the years, all of which died of illnesses. Maggie thought it was strange that no one ever questioned their deaths. There were children with each marriage. One sister died in her early twenties and they had a half-brother, as a teenager, who was sent away for violent criminal behavior. Ruby was the only family member that Paula remained closest with throughout life. They especially remained close after the death of their mother. Paula vowed to watch over Ruby even though the child went to live with an elderly aunt.

Paula adored Ruby's father, Will, as if he were her own father. He, too, died of a brief illness at the age of sixty-three. Everyone was devastated, especially Ruby at the loss of her father at the young age of five. Their mother never remarried and died two years later. Paula always said that Will was a fine example of the perfect father. He loved his step-children as if they were his own. He was overjoyed with the surprise birth of his daughter and only offspring, for he named Ruby after his sister, who died at birth. He hoped that his daughter would have a blessed life and live it to the fullest. In his mind his daughter would be living for her namesake as well. Ruby was his prized treasure.

It was unfortunate that after his death, Ruby lived her life with no boundaries and got pregnant at an early age of fifteen. Ruby married Bo Connolly at the Lucas County Courthouse in 1944, which was a few short months before the birth of their first daughter, Kathleen. April was born thirteen months later in 1945. Ruby was now a sixteen-year-old wife and mother of two while Bo was proudly serving his country as a Marine. Cami and Ginny were soon to follow April's birth, which would complete the family.

Aunt Paula financially supported Ruby and her young family for years. Paula never had a family of her own. It was assumed that she was infertile. She took great pride in her job as a supervisor at Overland, which the old building had recently been demolished, and the new Jeep plant was up and running a few miles away. She was married to a Canadian born native, an only child, named Douglas Carr. He served in the army during World War II and he worked for a pharmacy, in East Toledo, making home deliveries to the terminally ill and the elderly.

The couple always took goodies out to the farm when April and her sisters were young. Money was never a problem for the couple. The girls always looked forward to seeing their aunt and uncle because they knew that it would be a feast. The geese on the farm would chase the car up to the house because they had a sack of stale bread waiting for them with every visit.

Bo and Ruby's relationship was not what it used to be. After the military, he kept odd jobs and would come home late at night. He had a sweet tooth and he was not one to share his sweets with anyone. April once said that her father protected his ice cream by hooking up an electric shock so that if the girls should attempt to sneak his stash from the freezer, they would get an electric poke.

Kathleen was the smart one who decided to wear her rubber boots for the deed. They all took one spoonful out of the carton. Needless to say, Bo did notice the lower level of ice cream. He summonsed his four girls into the kitchen for questioning. He was a man of few words. "Who stole my ice cream?" he asked, looking as if he stood ten feet tall. Without saying a word, their expressions of guilt spoke for them.

When one child got whipped, they all got it because they never snitched on one another throughout their childhood. It was a strong bond of sisterhood that was sacred to each girl. This was one act of their childhood that remained true. Besides, they figured it was best for everyone to remain silent because no one would believe them anyhow. It was a family pact that was developed early in life. Their punishments were rare, but when it happened, they would remember it for a long time.

One day Cami removed the numbers from the front of the house and Bo paddled them all for that too. He was so mad because he missed an important in-house interview from the sheriff's department because the man couldn't find the right house. The interview was rescheduled, but Bo, being discredited by Cami's mischievous behavior, did not earn the deputy sheriff's position that he wanted so badly.

There was a lot he didn't know about his girls. He was gone most of the time and when he was home, all he did was yell or spank them. He never knew of them jumping off the chicken-coop with umbrellas imitating Mary Poppins or about them smoking cigarette butts that they collected throughout the week from ashtrays. Sometimes they would pocket butts from the sidewalks when visiting their Aunt Paula in the city.

On one particular afternoon, Ruby was doing some spring-cleaning while Bo was working. She was standing on the countertop in the kitchen and came across a large paper sack hidden in the very top cupboard. Her words caught in her throat when she discovered it was a sack full of candy. She was so angry at the thought of her ogre husband not sharing candy with his girls that it made her feel ill. Bo already made Ruby feel unimportant, but it killed her to see him treat their girls like that too.

She stood on the countertop for a moment thinking of what she really wanted to do with the candy and her husband, but she called her four girls into the kitchen instead as she emptied the bag onto the table. The girls' eyes were aglow as they watched candy spill out and scatter across the table.

"Have at it, girls! Enjoy your dinner. Just make sure you eat it all," she said with disgust.

"Wow! This is better than the holidays," exclaimed Ginny.

"What about Dad?" asked Kathleen.

"What about him?" snarled Ruby as she threw her apron on the counter and stormed out of the kitchen.

Ruby soon found comfort in alcohol when Bo had an affair with a family friend. She was soon a divorced woman at the age of twenty-eight. He and Ruby decided to divide custody of the girls and that he would take Kathleen and April while she kept Cami and Ginny. Bo and his two eldest girls lived with his parents, Katherine and Herbert, for two years.

Kathleen, being the eldest grandchild, was also the prize possession of Katherine. She doted over the child, who was her namesake and only joy in the world. The woman detested April more than anyone. Her hatred towards the child was obvious to many people inside and outside of the family.

April swore that Katherine had done all she could to make her life unpleasant. One example of her grandmother's harshness was when she put too much food on April's plate to where it was impossible for her to finish, which would result in some sort of punishment. Bo would protect his daughter from such nonsense by saying at every meal, "You are excused, April." She would carry her plate to the kitchen and start her nightly duty of dishes without fail.

April heard threats of being placed in an orphanage, which was what happened to Katherine. "Ugly and unwanted children go there," she would say on occasions to April. She always had odd tasks for April to finish before she could participate in any kind of social engagements. She was never allowed to sit on the white sofa with her sister and she was often ordered to clean the bathtub after her grandmother would use it. If April would laugh too loud, Katherine would give her more chores for having too much time on her hands. Kathleen always claimed that she suffered from migraine headaches and got out of doing her chores while April dared not to complain.

At an early age she feared the wrath of her grandmother. At the age of nine, April claimed that Katherine stopped in for a visit just before the girls got home from school. April was nervous because she was wearing a dress that Katherine purchased for Kathleen. She hated the ugly dress and secretly gave it to April. As soon as April stepped inside the house, her grandmother ripped the dress off the child! "That's Kathleen's dress, not yours!" she growled.

Katherine threw April and Bo out of her house on Thanksgiving because Bo had confronted his mother about April, Kathleen, and Joe, their cousin, went for a joyride one afternoon during Katherine's watch. They all were to take turns driving. Not one child had their license, but Kathleen talked April into driving their grandmother's car while she was home napping. She knew that it was wrong, but she enjoyed the attention she was getting by them cheering her on to do so.

April misjudged the distance of a narrow country driveway that was bridged over a steep ditch. She accidentally put the front passenger tire off the wooden bridge when she attempted to get turned around. A friend of Bo's happened to drive by and bailed them out. "Could we keep this our little secret, Mr. Bryan?" they asked, being hopeful. After they paid him with every penny they could scrounge, he just smiled and winked.

This Good Samaritan later teased Bo at the garage about him rescuing his hoodlum kids. Bo confronted his mother about her being careless while caring for his daughters. Katherine wasn't going to be talked down to by no one. The kids were watching TV in the living room while they could hear arguing from the basement. They were all petrified as they heard Katherine stomping up the stairs.

She grabbed April by her arm and said, "You get out of this house and you are never welcomed back here again! I know it was you who was driving. You are nothing but trouble!" The other two children were in total fear of the woman. They attempted to admit their guilt in the matter, but Grandma's fury was more than they could humanly bear.

April went to her room to collect her things. The child was devastated. She was fifteen and homeless.

Katherine followed the frightened girl and said, "There is nothing for you in this room. Everything you see I purchased! These things are all mine! In fact, the clothes on your back are mine, too!" She implied that April leave the house naked.

"That is quite enough!" exclaimed Bo. "April, get in the truck. We are out of here!"

April went to stay with her mother while Bo married the family friend, Donna, whom shared the responsibility of their affair. Her divorce was finalized and her twin boys were now three. He had a new family and forgot all about his four girls, according to April. When they did visit their father, it was on rare occasions. They spent most of their teen years roller-skating at the Roller Ranch in Perrysburg. Cousin Joe enjoyed meeting up with his cousins at the rink and he was enthralled by their skating talents. It was a utopia for teens—especially for the Connolly children.

Kathleen continued to stay with her grandmother. She soon became pregnant and married at the age of seventeen. Katherine stayed by her side and remained closely associated with her granddaughter and her young family. Kathleen was treated differently, not only by her grandmother, but her sisters always regarded her as the princess of the family, which nourished the animosity between she and her three sisters.

Ruby continued to go from job to job. She needed help supporting her girls. Her sister, Paula, and brother-in-law, Doug, took the girls in months at a time. April and Cami would walk two miles to Waite High School, which was located in East Toledo, while Ginny got a ride with a friend to the junior high. They enjoyed their visits with Aunt Paula, but there was something not quite right with Uncle Doug. He was the family secret that would not be revealed until the birth of the next generation.

Maggie moved along through traffic and made it to her ramp. She was finally motoring along. She grabbed her cell phone and called her brother, Kenneth. He answered on the first ring.

"Maggie! What's happening, sis?" he said in an upbeat voice.

"I wanted to ask if there was anything that you need for me to pick up on my way in?" she asked. Michael always asked April that question every day before he came home from the bank. All four of his children adopted that little ritual of his.

"I believe that we are all set on this end. Mom had all of her arrangements made years ago down to the very detail of what she would be laid out in. You know Mother, she always had to have the last word," he said.

"Are you doing alright? Do your little girls understand about their grandma?" asked Maggie.

"I don't even understand their grandma!" he said with a laugh.

During their conversation, Maggie noticed that he was a bit humble now that everyone had no choice but to accept the fact that he was the executor of the will. Maggie reassured him that no one held any grudge against him because that was what their mother wanted. She could not help but feel that may have been April's plan for such tension all along. Besides, April took great pleasure in telling each of them that they weren't even in the running to handle her affairs except for Kenneth.

Kenneth was birth order number three. Maddie was ruled out because she and April got along like cats and dogs. Maggie was ruled out because she lived out of state, which April claimed the lawyer suggested. Poor Kobe wasn't even in the running because of his wicked wife, according to April, who coincidentally shared a similar temperament with her. Maddie, being the protective eldest sister, did not get along with Kobe's wife either.

"Do I understand correctly that you will be staying with Maddie and Chase?"

"Yes. Maddie isn't doing very well. She told me she had something to tell me that was very important. It irritated me that she wouldn't tell me over the phone. I should be arriving at her house in about an hour and a half," she said.

"I'll be catching up with you both later. I'm supposed to pick up Kobe later this afternoon. Please drive safely and thanks for calling. Love ya."

"I love you, too, Kenneth. I'll see you soon."

Maddie resided in Napoleon, Ohio, which was about an hour south from Toledo. Kenneth and Kobe remained in Toledo. Michael, since his retirement five years ago, was on the road taking in the sights. He had his checks directly deposited in his private savings account and he lived off his debit card. He traveled the country and checked in with his kids often. He sent his grandkids post cards regularly. April would *never* travel, especially with Michael.

It was funny how both boys married women who were very similar to their mother. Kenneth was lucky to have survived his divorce, which he recently realized was worth *every* penny. Kobe's wife might kill him before they would ever see the inside of a courtroom. Hazel once pushed him through a window, which about cost him two fingers and a kidney. They had six children together. The youngest looked just like April.

Maggie could feel her heart sink as she drove past the state's sign, which read, "Ohio Welcomes You…A Lot to Discover." Her heart began to pound as the anxiety kicked in. *What's the big hurry?* she asked herself. The realization of seeing her mother dead was nothing she ever imagined; maybe not as often as some people would. She felt nauseous as her stomach began to knot up tight.

"Dear God, I don't want to do this," she said aloud. She felt as if she were that small, insecure child she left behind years ago. She thought she buried little Maggie Getman years ago, but at times she felt as if that little girl still lingered just beneath the surface. She had to pull over at the next stop to clear her head. She made it to a little town called Antwerp, which was about a half-hour away from Maddie.

She stopped at a little park next to the A&W restaurant. The rain had stopped and the sun peeked out from behind the clouds briefly as if it were saying good night. She walked around to stretch her legs. She noticed the time was nearly 6:30 PM and she decided to call Alec.

The phone rang three times. Alec answered the phone winded. He and Mark raced to the phone.

"Hey, handsome!" she said.

"Hey yourself, Monica. Or is this Amanda? My wife's out of town for a few nights and it is safe for you to come over," he teased. They always joked like that. It was just a rule not to use a name that either of them knew, an important rule to follow.

Seventeen years earlier, Maggie met Alec for lunch at the Burger Joint. She was about eight months pregnant for Allie. Being in her third trimester, she couldn't wear her wedding ring because of her weight gain. Two nosy elderly women watched the couple inside the restaurant the whole time, which annoyed Maggie terribly. The women followed the couple outside with disgust as Alec kissed Maggie good-bye in the parking lot.

Maggie could see them standing over Alec's shoulder gawking and whispering. This made Maggie furious. She could no longer tolerate such rude behavior. As Alec pulled away from her, Maggie quickly pulled him in for another kiss. This time she poured more juice into it than normal. Poor Alec never knew what was happening, but he never complained. In fact, it was obvious to Maggie that he really enjoyed himself. As Alec reached his car with weakened knees, Maggie yelled from her car across the parking lot, "Be sure to tell your wife that I said hello!" The two old biddies about choked! Maggie went back to work with a cheeky, yet victorious, smile.

"Yeah, in your dreams you might wish you had a hot babe," she said with a chuckle.

"Come on, Maggie, you know you are all the woman I need," he said with a grin.

"Yeah, maybe the only woman you can handle being more like it."

"Hey! You said it, not me," he laughed.

"How was your day? Did you survive your apple orchard date?"

"We had a blast! Missy made the group laugh when the grumpy farmer held up a gallon of apple cider and asked the kindergarten kids to identify the beverage he was holding in his hand. Sitting in the back of the room, Missy promptly shouted, in a hopeful voice, that it was chocolate milk! The crotchety old man was furious! He corrected her by barking that it was apple cider. His abrupt actions made us adults laugh even harder."

"That's my girl!" she chuckled. "I'm sorry I missed it."

"Mark assisted in two goals for his team. He is really improving on his skills. They sure work hard for being fifth graders."

"Give him a big hug for me and tell him I said good job! I'm so proud of him! How did Allie make out today?"

"Oh, you mean Ms. President? Her feet have not touched the ground all day long! I gave her some cash and sent her and her cabinet out for pizza to celebrate. I'm surprised that her head could fit through the door!"

"I am so proud of her! I knew she could do it! Please give her a huge hug and my congratulations. So I take it that you have not had the opportunity to tell them about their grandmother?"

"I was thinking that maybe tomorrow would be a more convenient day. Everyone has had such a good day that I don't want to see them crash. I'll tell them when they get up for school. Of course, they will not be going to school tomorrow so that we can get to Toledo quicker. I suppose I'll have to ruin their weekend instead," he said humbly.

"However you want to handle it is fine with me. I will call you tomorrow when I know the funeral details. I hope that you can finally get some sleep."

"Yes, that's in my near future. We are ordering in tonight and Missy is watching for the pizza man as we speak. I will crash on the couch as soon as we finish eating. We rented videos tonight. That should keep them entertained for a while."

"Thanks, babe," she said sincerely. "I love you, Sir Alec."

"I love you too, me lady, and try to get some sleep tonight. I'll see you tonight in my dreams, just don't wear anything too complicated," he snickered. That was all the evidence Maggie needed that proved that he had been up too long.

"Pizza guy is here!" shouted Missy.

"Pay the man and don't forget to tip him," he ordered.

"Do I really tell him not to take any wooden nickels?" she asked innocently.

"Alec Graham! You better not be teaching them to be disrespectful!"

"Maggie, I've got to go! She's running for the door! I love you! Bye." He barely got the words out as he slammed down the phone.

Maggie only hoped that he beat Missy to the door. Alec might have to tip the poor man well, very well.

Maggie thought of just how lucky she was to have such a wonderful family. She had a loving and supportive husband at home along with three wonderful children who are bright and loaded with a keen sense of humor. *Laughter has masked so many hurts in my lifetime that I thank God for the joy that spilled over onto my kids*, she thought with a heavy heart.

She felt recharged after speaking with Alec. She got back into her car and hit the road. Maddie had been anticipating her arrival all day long. Maggie decided to fuel her gas tank since she saw the best price for gas all week. She grabbed a bottle of water and some crackers to help soothe her upset stomach.

She felt like this when she was pregnant, which April would insist that something was wrong with each pregnancy since she never suffered from morning sickness. "You are the only female in our family history to complain of such symptoms. Something must be wrong!" April would insist. Maggie learned to ignore her motherly put-downs. Poor Maggie was the only woman to have ten-pound babies, breaking birth weight records in both sides of the family. Alas, a record she had no desire to set in the first place.

After her little pit stop, Maggie called her boss, John Jones, to inform him of her absence for Friday and possibly the following week. Even though the agents covered for one another, Megan Graham would continue to keep in contact with her clients at all costs. She had millions of numbers stored in her phone and she was comforted by the thought of them being only a push-button away from her. However, she was going to feel naked without her laptop computer.

Chapter 4

Maggie turned on to Lake Liberty Road, a narrow country road on which her sister resided. As she approached Maddie's driveway, she saw a sign that read "Mad Rosie's Ranch." The sign was Chase's idea. He said he named their place after his lovely Madelyn Rose because she was just *mad* about him when they first met. He did that ten years ago and he still took great pride in that title today.

Chase had three boys who adored Maddie and considered her their first class second mother. Chase's two boys were grown and his youngest, Jordon, stayed with his mother most of the time. Maddie had three children of her own. A daughter and son were from her first marriage and the youngest boy was from a brief encounter of a second marriage. Her girl was the eldest child and there was an eight-year age difference between her two boys. Trey, the youngest, was eleven years old.

Maddie told her sister over the phone that they would have the house to themselves for the majority of the evening because Trey was staying with his siblings, Kelsey and Kyle, for the night at their apartment. He had trouble adjusting to their absences, so they invited him over as much as they could. Now that they were out of the house, they all seemed to appreciate one another better. Not only that, but Trey had always had trouble fitting in with his stepbrothers. It was a relief to Maddie that her kids shared such a close bond.

Maddie was sitting on her porch swing when Maggie arrived. She was wearing her denim bibs and a pink shirt underneath. She was holding a beer in her hand as she dashed from the swing to greet her kid sister. She hobbled through the yard trying to dodge the stones because she was barefoot. Maggie hardly had her Caddie in park when she sprang from the vehicle like a flash. They nearly tackled one another as they embraced. Maddie's face was worn and tired. It looked as if she never went to sleep.

"My gosh, Maggie! I thought you'd never get here!"

"I know. Alec made me go back to bed this morning."

"Now *that's* what I'm talking about!" said Maddie with a mischievous grin.

"Madelyn Rose! You sicko! But I like the way you think," she said with a smile.

"Are you hungry? We've got some chili in the fridge. We made it today. You don't have to worry about food being older than a few days around here; unlike at Mom's house. That woman never threw anything away. She grew mold cultures like no one I've ever seen."

"Because of that woman I smell everything I eat as it comes out of the fridge to this very day!"

"Seriously, are you hungry?"

"Thanks anyway, but I couldn't touch a bite. My stomach feels full of knots, but I will take a beer," said Maggie with a hopeful smile.

When at home, Maddie carried her six-pack with her like a charm bracelet. The German-Irish blood that flowed in her veins refused to let her discriminate against warm beer. Maddie grinned and gladly yanked a brew from her wrist.

"I know what you mean, sister! Let's walk around a bit so that you can stretch your legs. We need to catch up! First thing is first, you need to shut off that rapper mobile of yours," said Maddie with a touch of sarcasm.

"Hey, I don't see spinners for rims; who can afford it? We'll just have to wait and see if I can be sales person of the year again next year, then *maybe* we'll talk," replied Maggie.

Chase was working on his vegetable garden. He recently added a new flowerbed to their twenty-acre property to honor Maddie's favorite flower, the rose. He worked very hard to woo his wife over the years and always attempted to keep things fresh in their marriage. She respected his attempts at being romantic, but she swore that she married him for his hot bod. Maddie waved for him to come in to say hello. He gave a quick wave and drove his tractor inside the barn. He ran back out and greeted Maggie with a hug.

"Maggie! It's good to see you. I hope you had a good drive. I'm just sorry that this reunion is under such circumstances," he said as he put his arm around Maddie. "Maybe you ladies would like to join me at the racetrack tonight. A client gave me four tickets the other day and it might be a great way of getting your mind off your mother for a while."

"You go without us tonight, honey. We've got a lot to catch up on here," said Maddie.

"Are you two going to be okay?" he asked nervously. "I don't have to go, you know."

"Thanks for the offer, but I'll take a rain check," said Maggie.

"Yeah, me too. But I will cash in on my rain check tonight! I like to keep mine tucked safely in his front pocket," said Maddie with a devilish laugh as she groped her man. She kissed her hubby good-bye and gave him a friendly swat on the bottom. Maggie let out a giggle when she saw a cloud of dust rise from the seat of his pants.

"I love you, baby, and come back to me safe tonight," she yelled across the yard. Chase just waved without turning around as if to conceal his blushing face. Chase pulled out of his driveway screeching his tires when he hit the pavement. He left a cloud of smoke from the burning rubber.

Maddie said with pride, "That's my baby. He always does that when he's on his way to the races. It gets him in the mood. We call it fifth gear foreplay!" Maggie responded by rolling her eyes.

The girls went inside for the evening. Maddie turned the radio on low and invited Maggie to join her in the living room. Her home had a rustic flavor and it possessed a cozy atmosphere. Chase had his twelve-point buck's head mounted over his fireplace. He called it George. Maddie collected handmade wooden furniture over the years to enhance Chase's hunting trophies.

She enjoyed visiting the Amish village of Shipshewana, Indiana, during the summer. One year, the girls chose a day to spend an afternoon of power shopping. Maggie made a quilt for her sister's birthday that resembled the one Maddie fell in love with, the one she refused to purchase on account of its two hundred dollar price tag, at one vender's tent. Maddie had kept it thrown over the back of her rustic couch. Maggie thought her sister's charming house not only matched the couple's personalities, but it should also be featured in a home décor magazine.

They each sat in a wooden rocking chair and Maggie kicked off her shoes. Maddie opened another beer as she turned to speak to her sister when the phone rang. It was Kobe on the line. He told Maddie that the funeral would be held on Saturday at 10 AM. They would be showing April all day on Friday at Kingston's Mortuary in Toledo.

"What's the skinny on the autopsy? Has Kenneth heard yet or does it take forever for the results?"

"The coroner confirmed that Mom died of an anterior aneurysm of an artery located in the frontal lobe of her brain. He asked if she suffered from mood swings, and if so, then he wanted to know how long. Kenneth told him that Mom was always moody for as far back as he could remember. Ken told him that Mom was a recovering alcoholic because he wasn't sure if that would explain her temperament."

"Wow! I'll drink to that," said Maddie, trying to keep a light heart.

"The coroner said that aneurysms could happen from numerous causes and most go unnoticed until it's too late. The bottom line is that he's positive about the cause of death."

"So that's it then," she said.

"There's not much else to report," said Kobe.

"What are your plans for the evening?"

"Kenneth and I are at Mom's house for the night. The neighbors have been bringing us food by the truck loads!" exclaimed Kobe.

"Good. Now I won't have to worry about you going hungry tonight. Witch Hazel won't be around to ruin your appetite," she scoffed while referring to his wife, Angie.

Clearly ignoring her comment, Kobe said, "We'll see you girls some time tomorrow. We dropped Mom's clothes off at the funeral home this afternoon."

"Oh, lord! I hope you didn't forget her bloomers!"

"No, I just grabbed one of Hazel's thongs," he joked.

"Yuck!" she said with a gag.

"I'll end on that note. I love ya, sis," he said with a chuckle.

"I love you, too, little brother. We'll see you some time tomorrow.

We have plans in the morning, but I promise we *will* be there before the funeral home closes," she said half-jokingly just before she hung up the phone.

Maggie picked out bits and pieces of information about the funeral, but she wanted nothing to do with knowing what had grossed out her sister. Maddie told her that their mother died from a blowout inside of her head. Maddie tried to act unnerved about the whole situation, but Maggie could see that she was torn up inside despite her armored exterior.

She was humble for a moment and finally said, "They believe she died from an aneurysm in the front of her brain. I'm curious if alcoholism may be a factor."

"Really?" asked Maggie somewhat perplexed.

"I don't know what I'm talking about. Mom hasn't had a drink in over twenty years!"

"Maybe it's like smoking. Once the damage is done, it's damaged for life," said Maggie sympathetically.

"Maybe she was blocked up and she strained too hard on the toilet," Maddie said lightly.

Maggie thought for a moment and recollected helping Allie with her anatomy project of the brain her freshman year. They reconstructed a human brain out of clay. They used a different color for each lobe. Allie typed the names and functions of the lobes on colored paper, which each color represented a specific lobe. She did a great job and she learned a lot from the assignment. Maggie even learned a thing or two.

"Maddie, do you realize that the personality is present in the frontal lobe of the brain?"

"I guess. I don't really remember because I've slept since high school, Maggie."

"I'm not making excuses for Mom, but I would do anything to understand her or make sense of her actions over the years," said Maggie with desperation in her voice.

"Mom drank for nearly twenty years. Well, that might be when she made it known to us. She could have been drinking *years* before then. I remember her wanting to sleep all the time. She overindulged on the weekends the most."

"Maybe she slept all the time because she was depressed. Do you think it was possible she might have had a tumor or insufficient blood flow to the frontal lobe of the brain back then?" asked Maggie.

"Maybe she was just a bitch!" snapped Maddie. "She always had to be superior over *everyone*. I wonder who would even attend her funeral. She's chased us all away over the years," said Maddie with resentment.

Maggie was stunned by her sister's outburst. There was a moment of silence between the two of them. Maggie was desperate to change the subject.

"I wonder if Kenneth had gotten a hold of Dad yet. I had not seen him in a long while, but it was refreshing to me knowing that he was enjoying his life since he had been free from Mom's wrath. He once told me that he never realized that the sun could shine so brightly and he had actually acquired an appetite for life."

"I don't think it is possible to survive from her wrath!" growled Maddie. "We may be living and breathing, but did we *really* survive?"

"I would like to think about something other than Mom for five minutes. Is that possible?" said Maggie without expecting much of a reply. "How do you think Dad is holding up?"

The girls were silent for a moment reflecting on their father. Michael was always the comic relief in the family. Everyone loved Michael. When he and April first got married he had a job at the Toledo Savings and Loan as a painter. He also worked at a garage in the evenings as a tow truck driver. He had done lawns on the weekends to provide for his young wife and first child on the way.

"Maddie, do you remember the story about how Dad got his position as bank manager?"

"I remember when he had to trade his work uniforms in for business suits. I also remember how those black nylon socks made his feet stink up the whole house! I still gag at the very thought of it!" she said with a modest gag. "I guess the answer to your question is no. I don't remember any details of his promotion."

"The year was 1977 and Dad had his yearly evaluation with his boss, Richard Stiff." Maggie giggled at the very thought of that name.

"I recognize that name!" Maddie said with excitement. "Dad said that Richard got teased endlessly when he was in the military because they say the last name first and first name last. That poor man was known as Stiff Dick!" Maddie laughed out loud at her recollection.

"Back to Dad's evaluation," said Maggie with hopes of keeping her easily distracted sister focused on the story. "Richard asked Dad where it was he saw himself in another year. Dad said that he saw himself sitting behind Richard's desk and sitting in Richard's chair. Richard laughed and warned that Dad better watch what he wished for because it might happen. Shortly after that interview, Richard was in the hospital to have his right leg amputated because of an infection that would not heal. The poor man had diabetes and his leg, just below the knee, was turning black."

"I remember him now! Dad took us over to his house a few times when Mom needed time away from us. He had two teenage girls who always walked us to the park. Their mother would always give us milk and cookies," said Maddie.

Maggie nodded and said, "Poor Mr. Stiff was pleading and begging in the pre-op room for them not to take his leg while the orderly tried to prep him for surgery. He fought and screamed. He became downright hysterical! Richard's wife, Millie, called for Dad to come to the hospital and try to calm him down. Dad was in good standing with his boss and she thought it might help soothe her husband to see a friend during his crisis. Dad called his colleague, George Thomas, who was a known drunk, for backup."

Maggie told the story as it was relayed to her by Michael years earlier. Maddie listened intently as her sister told the story with such emotion and pity.

"Oh, thank God you came, Michael! He's hysterical! Please calm him down, please," begged Millie.

"Oh, Michael! Listen to me! Don't let them take my leg, please!" begged Richard as perspiration beaded on top of his baldhead. Michael watched the sweat roll down his forehead and disappearing into his bushy unibrow. His round crimson face glistened as his breathing became more and more labored. He looked like a scared rabbit.

"Richard, you need to calm down. They are trying to save your life. The infection could travel from your leg and kill you if it gets to your heart. Please cooperate with them Rich. They are trying to help you," said Michael in a calm, soothing voice.

George just stood there concentrating on not staggering or falling in the presence of their boss. Michael took great pity on his boss and tried to remain optimistic and upbeat. Millie was crying and Richard was still worked up. He had made a mess of his room, when the orderly was there earlier, by knocking the shaving kit across the room and tipping over a nightstand. The surgeon walked into the room and Richard became more hysterical than before!

"Don't let them take my leg, Michael!" he said as he grabbed Michael by the lapel. Just then the man stiffened in pain and died right on the spot while still clinging to Michael!

"Jesus Christ! Jesus Christ!" yelled George as he spun in a circle as if he didn't know where to go or what to do. The whole room fell apart. Poor Michael stood there in shock and disbelief. He couldn't stop feeling responsible in some way for his boss' massive heart attack.

At the funeral, Michael was holding the side of the casket as he gazed down at his friend. He felt such sorrow and pity for Richard's family. Millie walked up to Michael and whispered into his ear, "If you're not doing anything later, come over to my place for a nightcap, if you know what I mean," she said with a wink as he turned to look at her with surprise. Michael was in shock over her actions! He never saw that side of her before and he instantly felt ill. In a small way he was hoping that it was a form of temporary insanity due to such emotional grief. That was his way to justify her inappropriate actions.

Michael was immediately appointed as the new bank manager for Toledo Savings and Loan. He eased into his new position surprisingly well and before he knew it, it was the first anniversary of Richard's death. Michael and his former painting crew were sitting in a huddle after work, knocking back a few beers, reminiscing about the man. He finally shared his story with the guys about what Millie said to him at the funeral home. All five men could not look him in the eye. They acted distracted and uncomfortable as he told his story.

George finally said, "Damn, Michael! Who hasn't tapped that keg?"

"Yeah, Michael. We all know Millie *real* well," said Harry with his eyes looking as wide as humanly possible.

Michael had a stunned look upon his face as the guys all broke into a gut-splitting laughter. They all had admitted to sleeping with her on numerous occasions. They teased Michael and claimed that was why he got the promotion. He was the *only* employee of Dick Stiff's blue collar crew that didn't nail his wife! Maggie and Maddie were laughing so hard after the story that tears streamed down their cheeks.

Michael was well-liked and respected by all who knew him at the bank. However, he was also an uptight kind of guy, which made the story more amusing to his girls. His motto was, "Be nice to *everyone* as you climb up the ladder of success because they will be the same faces you will see on your way back down." He just didn't think that being *that* friendly with a boss' spouse was mentioned in his job description.

All who knew him called him Michael. Those who didn't know him called him Mr. Getman, which he allowed to be called only once. He would say, "My name is Michael Getman, but you may call me Michael." He never answered to Mike because of a reason he would not elaborate on other than he did *not* like it.

Maggie made sandwiches while Maddie answered the call of nature. Maggie saw that her sister adopted the famous snack drawer like back home. She fell deep in thought about when the snack drawer came into their lives and how it revolved around her.

Initially, it was a bread drawer with a hinged wooden lid to keep the mice out, but April started to fill it with cakes, fruit pies, and candy bars when Maggie was a nine-year-old child with a weight problem. April informed Maggie that she could not have any sweets because she was too fat.

"I want you to know the pains of dieting. If it tastes good to you, then it must be bad for you," April would say with a smirk. "You are getting so fat that it is getting embarrassing to say you are my daughter. I should change your name to Nikki," she would threaten. Maggie never said anything in her own defense. The more depressed Maggie became, the more sweets April would buy.

Nikki was an overweight cousin who later discovered that she had hypothyroidism. Maggie would watch the others indulge in their treats, but hers would be done behind their backs. One day April smelled chocolate on Maggie's breath. "You are going to be fat forever and no one will want you, so eat all you want. I hope that you enjoy being ugly for the rest of your life," she would say. Maggie hated herself and eventually fell victim to an eating disorder during her junior high school years.

Maddie came to the kitchen table surprised to be waited on by her houseguest. Maggie made five-sided peanut butter and jelly sandwiches cut into the shape of a house. Maggie always did that when they were young. She would cut out a small door and turn it sideways to where it looked as if someone were coming or going.

She grabbed some veggies from the refrigerator and had a fresh beer waiting for her sister while she treated herself to some ice water. After the birth of Missy, her body underwent some changes such as being physically and mentally intolerant to alcohol. She could only handle certain beers and never any more than two. She would become ill for a few days or severely depressed for a week. Maggie did treat herself once in a while, but she had to be careful when drinking because the effects might not be the same every time. Some moments were more severe than others, which left the after-effects unpredictable.

The girls nibbled on their sandwiches and made small talk as they listened to the music playing on the radio. A song came on the radio that mentally took Maggie to 1983. She laughed out loud as she thought about her memory.

"Do you remember before your graduation party when Dad replaced the carpeting?" asked Maggie.

"Yeah, it was because of a large, very large, stain in front of the TV. Mom couldn't even cover it with a throw rug because it was near the floor vent. I never knew how that got there in the first place," said Maddie, pondering that thought.

"I know how it got there. One night Mom challenged me, at fifteen, to drink her under the table. She pulled all the liquor out of the cupboard and made me drink from each bottle. She drank too, but she was already drunk. Kenneth, being ten at the time, was also challenged to drink."

"So, who stained the carpet, you or Kenneth?"

"I fell out of my chair and hit my head so hard that I watched everything blur before my eyes, but I never felt a thing! I made my way into the living room where Mom and Kenneth were arm wrestling on the floor. I fell backwards and my head just missed hitting the TV. I passed out cold."

Maggie recalled the rest of the story as she felt the familiar feeling of betrayal of her mother not looking out for her children's safety or best interest. She wondered what her mother's intentions were for even challenging her underage children to drink in the first place. She figured that maybe April wanted to teach them a lesson about the dangers of alcohol abuse or maybe she was just sizing up her competition. Maggie shivered at the thought of the remainder of the story.

"Where's that water coming from?" Kenneth asked April.

"Did someone leave the bathroom sink on full blast?" asked April as she looked over her shoulder.

Maddie sat in disbelief as she listened to her sister's story. She had no idea what was going on around the house at that stage of life because of her being a rebellious teenager. As she listened to Maggie, she felt a feeling of guilt for not being there to stop their mother's reckless and damaging behavior. Being the eldest child, she had the feeling that she should have been there to be the protector for her siblings. Maggie continued with the story as Maddie struggled with her conscience on how her sister could recollect that time frame, but she could not. A large part of her felt just as guilty of neglect as April.

"You vomited? Who helped you?" asked Maddie with concern.

"Kenneth told me that they turned around to see me sprawled out on the floor looking like a water fountain. He said that I had a stream shooting out of my mouth that reached about three feet into the air as I lay on my back! He said that they even heard me gurgle, which made them both laugh hysterically."

"My gosh! You could have drowned. You've got to tell me how Mom took care of you. This is going to be classic!" said Maddie.

"She dragged me upstairs and threw me in bed with my shoes on and all. The least she could have done was cover me up. She never even cleaned my face! I woke up with my hair plastered to my forehead and cheeks. I was forced to take care of myself throughout the night. Luckily, I had a wastepaper basket next to my bed, which I used all night long."

The next morning Michael confronted Maggie about the mess on the carpet, which was still waiting to be cleaned. He was extremely disappointed by her actions. He was going to ground her for being so irresponsible until Maggie interjected by saying, "Hey! Mom gave it to me. She also gave it to Kenneth. It was a contest we were having and I just so happened to lose." He appeared furious with that tidbit of information, but said nothing more on the matter.

The carpet was replaced two days before the graduation party to save the family more humiliation in front of Grandma and Grandpa Getman, who rarely visited the city. The Getman family residing in the country shared the idea of people who live in the city are involved in drugs or crime in general. Family members living in the city were not exempt from such stereotypes.

The girls finished their sandwiches and cleaned up the kitchen. Maddie asked, "Are you a neat freak at home?"

"When I do clean my house, which is more on a weekly or bi-monthly basis, I like it to be a deep clean. However, between cleanings I might not open my door to anyone due to the embarrassment of my house being in shambles," admitted Maggie.

"There are times when I become obsessed with a clean house that all I do is yell at the boys. I then hate myself for sounding and acting just like Mom. Sometimes I cry at a drop of a hat because of it. There are times I want to rip my face from my skull because I'm looking more and more like her every day!" said Maddie.

"I can relate. Sometimes I find that I can't help such rage that bubbles beneath the surface, but I've always been good at suppressing; you know that," said Maggie while nudging Maddie in the arm.

"When I clean, I feel like a finger to a bulimic. You know, it's all or nothing! There are days I let it be messy on purpose. I call those days therapy."

"Well, like an eating disorder, these obsessions are put into our heads by the demands of society, or in our case, by our mother. We need to learn how to undo what has been done."

"Do you remember Mom locking us out of the house when she cleaned?"

"I remember when we first moved to Toledo she did that to us while she was cutting Grandma Ruby's hair. I remember that as soon as we heard the door lock behind us I had the sudden urge to poop," laughed Maggie.

"She also did that to us in Perrysburg. You might have been too young to remember that, but I always wondered if Grandma Getman knew what she did to us and that might be the real reason behind our moving to the city."

"I remember crying through the screen for Mom to let me in to use the bathroom. I heard Grandma Ruby yell at me to behave myself. Mom stomped her way to the window and threatened to spank me if I interrupted her once more," said Maggie.

The girls reminisced about their shared memory that seemed like only yesterday.

Maddie took Maggie by the hand and said, "Come on, Maggie, I will find you a potty!" Maddie's first stop was to visit the little elderly woman next door. She was a wonderful woman with a very strong German accent. She was stunned to see two little girls standing on her porch unsupervised in such a rough neighborhood. She answered the door thinking something was wrong.

"Hey, lady, can my sister use your potty? She has to poop," announced Maddie.

"Where are your mother and father? You girls need to know the rules of the neighborhood. You *never* go away from your home without your parents!" She then invited them into her house so Maggie could use the bathroom.

Maddie told the woman the whole story. When Maggie returned, she had cookies and milk waiting for her too. She insisted that the girls call her Heidi and that she would speak to their father when he got home. After they ate their snack, she sent them back home because she thought their mother would worry about their absence.

"I can see that event so clearly in my memory," said Maddie.

"I also remember that we were *never* locked out of the house again after that," said Maggie with a smile. "Heidi was a small woman, but her words must have been very powerful to Dad."

"That was when Dad established boundaries for us. We couldn't play or ride our bikes past Heidi's house and the Smiths' driveway. He gave us the talk about strangers and that the neighborhood had some bad people living in it with us."

"Do you remember when Aunt Cami lived with the Peters family?" asked Maggie.

"Yes. There was Tammy, Bruce, and Tim Peters who took her in for a short while after she and Grandma Ruby moved out of the house. Tim ended up doing hard time for murder later on and

Tammy was the mother figure who turned Aunt Cami lesbian," stated Maddie boldly.

"When I was in first grade, I walked home alone for the first time. You were sent home sick from school earlier that day. Mom must have been napping with the twins because I wasn't going to wait around for her to help me cross Galena Street. As I crossed, I heard an alarm sounding from the corner grocery store. As I reached the alley I saw a man running towards me carrying a brown grocery bag. I realized that it was Tim Peters and I shouted a friendly hello to him. He nearly knocked me down as he ran past me. He stopped cold in his tracks and I could see he had a butcher knife in his belt. He hesitated for a moment as he stared in my eyes. He finally ran off down the alley," Maggie said with goose bumps on her arms.

"You could have been kidnapped or worse that day, Maggie! What were you thinking?"

"Yeah. I was just a dumb kid. I said hello because he was not a stranger to me. I didn't understand that he did anything wrong."

"You weren't a dumb kid; you were just a very lucky little girl!"

"I had a different idea of what a bad guy should look like and he was not wearing a black cowboy hat like in the movies. Besides, we knew him and we didn't associate with bad people. Only strangers were bad people, right?"

Chapter 5

The girls ventured onto the porch swing to chat awhile longer. It was getting late, but both girls were far from being sleepy. They were still worked up and their chatter jumped from topic to topic. It was a clear night and the glow of the stars illuminated the sky. Someone down the road had lit a bonfire, which the ambiance of the evening was cozy and relaxing despite their heavyhearted conversations.

They reminisced about times when they would be picked up by their favorite aunt, Aunt Cami, when their mother would be in one of her moods. Michael worked longer hours since his promotion, even on weekends and holidays. Cami loved the girls and her nieces simply adored her too. She owned a 1965 Corvette convertible that was so fast that she had the girls believing that it could fly! Maggie always burned her little legs on its side-pipes.

"I remember when Aunt Cami's visits started to diminish. Mom's temper grew out of control!" said Maggie.

"Which time? There are too many incidences to count."

"Remember when we first moved in and we were both afraid to go upstairs alone regardless of the time of day or night? We were always together, even in the bathroom!" laughed Maggie.

"I remember when I got out of the bathtub and you were getting ready to get in. I was sitting on the clothes hamper getting into my pajamas when I accidentally fell."

"And I was sitting on the toilet when you fell. I can still hear the sounds of thunder rolling up those stairs," said Maggie with a look of surprise on her face.

April came crashing into the bathroom and saw two surprised little girls. They already knew when she was furious by the sounds and vibrations of her thunderous footsteps! Maddie repeatedly said, "I'm sorry, Mom, I'm sorry." She bent over to pick up the hamper and said, "See, it's fine." Being half dressed, Maddie was nude from the waist down and her bottom was beet red from soaking in a warm tub.

April picked up Maggie's pink hand mirror that Aunt Ginny gave her and began to beat Maddie with it on her bare bottom and thighs! Broken glass was *everywhere*. She continued to beat her about ten times as her claws were dug deep into her arm! Maggie witnessed this horror with such a feeling of helplessness. She could still hear the screams in her head along with visions of broken glass flying across the room.

Maddie and Maggie were both screaming. Maggie found herself wedged in a tiny corner of the bathroom next to the toilet without any recollection of her doing so. April then threw the mirror against the wall with a wild look in her eyes. She ran downstairs crying aloud. Luckily for Maddie she was hit with the plastic side of the mirror. Shards of glass were everywhere along with the pink plastic shell of April's weapon. Maddie's bottom was red and swollen with welts.

Both girls were trembling as they picked up the broken glass without a single word. Glass even found its way into the bathwater that Maggie intended to use. They could hear April sobbing while running down the stairs saying, "I can't take this anymore! I just can't!" Maggie never got her bath that night. After the glass was cleaned off the floor, they quietly tucked themselves into bed. They were both afraid to be alone that evening. The sun had not yet set as the girls quietly cried themselves to sleep. Michael was at the office late that evening.

"I remember the phone ringing just as Mom made it to the bottom of the stairs. I have always wondered who it was that she was crying to on the phone," said Maggie.

"Well, it could have been Dad because after that incident was when he would take us to work with him after supper on those late-night evenings. Do you remember the fun we had?" asked Maddie.

"I remember playing secretary and typing memos," said Maggie with a smile. "I learned years later that Dad would bring us home for bed and then return to the office until two or three in the morning," she said as the smile faded from her face. "That job was killing him."

"Who ever Mom was talking to on the phone I can bet never knew what it was she did exactly," said Maddie with certainty.

"Yeah, if Dad only knew half the things she did to us I think he might have left her decades earlier."

"When I was twelve, I can remember begging Dad to leave her and take me with him. I told him that I would cook all the meals and even do dishes! You know how much I hated doing dishes," said Maddie.

"Mom always told me that you had Dad wrapped around your little finger ever since you were a baby. Sometimes she would say that and drift away deep in thought, which I can only imagine what she was thinking," said Maggie.

"Yeah, something on the lines of her knowing why tigers eat their young!"

April ran a strict household and her body English spoke louder than her words. She would walk with very heavy, yet rapid, steps when she was going after one of the girls. They could always expect to be grabbed by the arm with April's long nails buried deep into their flesh. She sometimes grabbed them by the face and would say; "Look at me, Toots!" as the young children would stare at the metal clasps of her 1950s dental bridgework, which later became a family joke amongst all four of her kids.

They only saw that when she was really mad! Her grandchildren also knew to beware of April's bridgework. Kobe would be the one to announce, "Uh-oh, you really pissed off Grandma now. I can see her bridgework!" He was the one who openly called her "The Old Gray Mare." Michael finally stopped demanding respect for the woman after the first dozen of times he had heard it. April went completely gray at the age of thirty-five. That is also the time when she claimed to be going through menopause, which was the excuse she later used for her drinking problem.

When Maddie turned eight, she assumed the duties of motherhood while April slept. Kobe was the one who would wake up in the middle of the night for a feeding. Maddie would quietly get him out of his crib and take him downstairs for his bottle. She did that on the nights when it was obvious that April was not going to get out of bed. It was second nature for her to bathe, dress, and diaper the babies using cloth diapers and pins. Being a child herself, Maddie was an excellent mother to her baby brothers.

On the weekends she would tend to the twins during the early morning hours with hopes that April would be well-rested and in a more pleasant mood. One morning Maggie came downstairs early and found Maddie crying while holding baby Kenneth. She was forcing a bottle filled with water into his mouth with a shaky hand saying, "Drink, baby, drink."

Maggie noticed Kenneth's face was red and blotchy. She figured that he had been crying. Maggie innocently asked, "What's wrong, Maddie?" She looked up with surprise, not realizing anyone came into the kitchen. Kenneth latched on to the bottle and Maddie had an instant look of relief on her face.

"I was going to warm Kenneth's bottle on the stove, so I strapped him on to the bassinette in case he decided to roll over," said Maddie in a shaky voice.

"Did you burn yourself?" she asked as she was looking her sister over.

"I was just getting water into the pan and I heard Kenneth gasping and choking. I looked over at him and I saw that baby swinging from his neck off the side of his bassinette!" she cried.

Maggie listened with horror as Maddie said, "He apparently rolled over for the first time and right off the table he went. His face looked purple and he couldn't breathe! I ran over to him and picked him up right away. He was gasping. So, I ran him to the sink and quickly filled a bottle with water to make sure that his throat wasn't broken."

Maggie had a stunned look upon her face and Maddie looked up nervously and said, "Please don't tell Mom! Don't tell Mom." Maggie kept her promise and never told a soul. Maggie could hear Kobe stirring upstairs. She promptly went upstairs and woke April to tend to her motherly duties.

"Mom never knew how good she had it," said Maggie.

"I think that was because in her little world it was all about her. There was no room in her life for us. Do you remember how she used to play on the floor with the boys when they were little?" asked Maddie.

"I don't remember Mom ever playing anything with us except for making clay animals one time when Jenny came over, which was just for show. I remember Dad being the one who played rough and tumble with us. I also remember him taking us with him all the time sledding, to the park, or even to work. He would tell us that Mommy needed a little break from all of us. Of course, the boys would be home napping."

On one particular afternoon, the girls were punished for playing too loud in the house. They were made to sit quietly on the purple crushed-velvet couch for an hour. It was a bright sunny day, too nice of a day to be stuck inside the house. April was playing on the floor with the twins. She was tickling and kissing them. The trio were all laughing and having a great time. The girls sat on the sidelines and witnessed the rare display of affection.

"Mom, why is it that you love the boys more than us?" asked Maddie frankly.

"That's because I never had brothers," she replied with a smirk.

That statement confirmed their suspicions of *feeling* like a burden to their mother as to now being a reality. Maddie was always the outspoken child and would challenge April with her thoughts and opinions, while Maggie never said a word. She was the child who was terribly shy and would hide behind her sister. In Maggie's eyes, Maddie was not only her best friend, but she was her voice as well.

April had always made her feelings known that Michael loved Maddie more than his own wife. She claimed that Maddie manipulated their relationship since she was a toddler. It was assumed that this was why Maddie was the one who received April's wrath more so than the others. Michael tried to pick up the slack with his girls as best as he could. He knew he had to fix the problems at home and decided to come home after 5 PM every evening to spend time with the family. He would then go back to the office after the kids went to bed to finish his projects or get a head start on others in the making.

That worked for a short while, but April didn't appreciate his sacrifice as much as his employer and she lost out to the bank's demands of him putting in more hours for the good of the company. He had more out of town business meetings and social engagements that he was expected to attend. Meanwhile, April felt more and more overwhelmed at home with the never-ending demands of motherhood.

"Do you remember one Saturday morning when Mom insisted that we clean our bedroom?" asked Maggie.

"Oh, yeah. That's when we shared the back bedroom. We divided up the duties, if I remember correctly."

"You took the bedroom while I cleaned the closet. Both places were a real pigsty! I organized all the toys on the bookshelves that Dad made for us while you cleaned the bedroom," said Maggie.

"We were having a great time because we kept singing songs and laughing. We hated cleaning, but we tried to make it fun so that we could finish quickly and get outside to play."

The girls worked together for about an hour. They opened their window to allow the smell of the springtime air to circulate in their bedroom. Maddie was making piles of clean clothes on each bed while Maggie was busy matching missing playing pieces of games to their rightful boxes. They were nearly finished when they heard the heavy footsteps of April marching up the stairs.

She entered the room with a scowl on her face. She scanned the room as if she were hoping to find something to yell at them about. Maddie stood tall at attention. April immediately looked beneath the beds and found a clean floor. Luckily for Maddie, she had pulled the messes out from beneath the beds and piled them on top. Maddie passed her inspection without a single word of praise. April then stormed into the closet.

"Hi, Mom," said Maggie nervously.

"Do you call this room clean?" growled April, baring her bridgework.

Maggie looked around the nearly organized and cleaned up closet with pride and said with an innocent smile, "Yes, it is almost finished." April held her arm out and walked down each row of toys, slowly knocking them off the shelf one by one. Maggie stood there covering her ears as she witnessed the toys crashing to the floor. April then emptied the board games that Maggie took so much time organizing and scattered them around the room.

"If you call this clean, then I think you need to look at it again," April said coolly as she threw the box to the floor and then exited the room with a final comment, "Clean it up!"

Both girls stood in disbelief at what had just happened. They heard the doorbell ring, which must have been the neighbor kids wanting to play. Maddie reassured her little sister not to worry and that she would help her clean the closet. The two girls helped each other without a word. They cleaned the bedroom first, and then they organized the closet.

Jenny, from next door, yelled up to their room from her own back yard. Maddie and Maggie raced to the bedroom window. They felt as if they were two princesses and a wicked witch, like in the fairy tale *Rapunzel*, locked them in a tower.

"What did you two do to get yourselves grounded?"

"Who said we were grounded?" insisted Maddie.

"Me and the gang came to the door awhile ago and April said that you cannot play today because you and Maggie were grounded."

"We are *not* grounded!" growled Maddie. "She's a liar! We'll be out as soon as our room is cleaned," promised Maddie.

The girls worked as fast as they could to finish the job. After the bedding was changed, Maddie vacuumed while Maggie dusted the baseboards and furniture. The girls even moved the beds and dressers to clean underneath knowing April would be doing the white glove inspection. They did their best to outsmart her and they were determined not to let her win!

Michael came home early that Saturday morning and came upstairs to inspect the girls' progress in motion. He complimented them on their cooperation skills and congratulated them on doing such a fine job.

"As soon as you girls are finished, Jenny will be waiting for both of you at her house," he said with a smile. April never stopped them as they walked around her to go out the front door.

Maddie went into the house to grab herself another beer. Maggie sat on the swing feeling a bit homesick for her family. Alec was such a wonderful husband and her children were the very air she breathed. She thought of them as her strength and her weakness. Maggie would protect and defend her children to the very death. She pondered that thought and wondered why her mother was the complete opposite of her own maternal instincts.

Maggie about jumped out of her skin when Maddie cracked open her beer. She was so deep in thought that she never realized her sister's return. "Easy, Maggie. You act as if someone just walked on your grave." Maddie sat down on the swing and looked at her sister with concern. Maggie's mind wandered as if the word grave drove her to a specific place in time.

"Go on, Maggie. Touch her and feel how cold she is," said April, while holding Maggie on her hip in a funeral home. Little Maggie had a look of confusion on her face. She was nearly three years old when she saw her first corpse. April explained that Lizzy was dead and to prove it was to feel how cold her hands were because of her having no more blood. Maggie let out a scream when April forced her tiny hand upon the dead woman's hand.

The deceased woman was Uncle Doug's mother. She was the original owner of the house on Ontario Street. April went against Michael's reservations about bringing his young daughters to a funeral home. "Everybody dies some time and there is no time like the present to teach them that lesson," said April sharply. Michael took his terrified daughter from her mother and tried to explain that Lizzy was just taking a nap in a special bed.

"Maggie, earth to Maggie, come in Maggie," said Maddie.

Maggie shared her memory with her sister. Maddie thought back as far as she could, but was having trouble remembering. Maggie described the funeral home to the best of her ability. All that she remembered was green carpeting and a stairway next to the casket, which looked like a small hole cut in the floor. At least she thought it was green carpeting because she might not have known her colors at that time.

"Oh, yeah! I remember that now. Aunt Paula kept yelling at me for running between the rows of chairs. She told me that we were supposed to act sad in a place like that. I figured it was playtime since no one other than us were there. I decided to play on the stairs until Uncle Doug told me that the boogeyman lived down there."

Maggie laughed and said, "Missy was three when she viewed her first dead body, which was Grandpa Getman's funeral. Dad waited for all of his kids and grandkids to arrive so we would walk up to the casket together as a family. I was a bit apprehensive about the reactions of my kids, especially Missy, for being so young. Do you remember that?"

The little girl was secure on Maggie's hip as she leaned in for a closer look. Everyone in the room watched in silence as the young child announced out loud, "Yep! He's dead!" Maggie was stunned by her daughter's calloused remark and she tried desperately to send Missy off with Alec. Missy motioned for her father to move away from her as she said, "Go away! I'm busy looking at this, Papa G-man."

Maggie and Maddie broke out into laughter over such a statement. Missy studied the body with great interest. Maggie figured that because of television today, children have become desensitized to such things more so than her generation. The child noticed the dollar bill sticking out from the pocket on his jacket, which was the family tradition of tipping Saint Peter at the gate; just in case. Maggie knew not to even touch that topic with such a bright young lady.

"Why does it have to be my kids to have such outbursts?" asked Maggie.

"Because that's what makes it even more hilarious! You have *always* been the quiet and uptight one in the family. Your kids must get their outbursts from Alec's side of the family," laughed Maddie.

"I know, I know. It is always funnier when it happens to someone else!"

Maggie's mind trailed off to a conversation Missy had with Michael. It was only a month after Grandpa Getman's funeral when Missy had a serious conversation with her grandfather while visiting in Toledo. Michael held her by the hand as they walked back to the house from the corner grocery store and had their little heart-to-heart conversation.

"Grandpa, why aren't you dead yet?"

"Well, maybe it isn't my time yet, baby doll. Why do you ask?" he asked, trying not to sound stunned or offended.

"Because you're old *and* you smoke!"

"You've been talking to your grandmother!" was all he could muster to say.

Maggie was shocked and embarrassed when Michael shared that conversation with her. Michael admitted that he thought it was hilarious and that he appreciated such juvenile honesty.

Chapter 6

After laughing so hard, it was Maggie's turn to answer the call of nature. Maddie decided to sit in the living room to finish up the night's conversation. When Maggie returned, she saw that Maddie had a tape recorder sitting on her lap. Maggie looked surprised by that because no one listened to cassettes today.

"What's that?" she asked.

"When I talked to you last night, more like *early* this morning, I told you that I had something to tell you. I've been waiting for the right moment to arrive so I can share this with you. I hope I'm doing the right thing because I'm not too sure what to think anymore about a certain topic," said Maddie in a more serious and sober tone.

Maggie sat down in the wooden rocker and said, "Let's have it. What's this about?" Maddie continued to tell her that she and Jenny, their childhood friend, celebrated their mutual friend Tanya's fortieth birthday on Wednesday night. For each milestone birthday, they had planned something different and outrageous to mark the occasion. They had all been friends since childhood and they all turned forty this year.

For Jenny's birthday, in February, they went to ride a mechanical bull and then went out for dinner afterwards. This year Tanya wanted to go out for dinner and have a psychic reading. There was a famous psychic in Toledo who was very accurate. People in small circles really credit this psychic. April once had her palm read during a psychic show from this same woman, who told her that she saw a mean streak in her a mile wide. April called her a fraud and walked out. Madam Zoë had helped so many people with her controversial gift. Her accuracy on April's reading proved sufficient credibility in Maddie's opinion.

"You went to a psychic?" asked Maggie with great surprise.

"Yes. She read Tanya first and then Jenny. She saved me for last. The readings were a half-hour each. No one could be in the room but the psychic and the client. She had a room for us to chat in while we anxiously awaited our turn. The one rule was that we could not discuss our readings with anyone inside the building at all."

"What was it like? I've always been curious. I always enjoy watching Sylvia Brown and John Edward on TV," said Maggie.

"It was creepy. When I read your e-mail, a month ago, you asked me if I ever had an opportunity to ask a renowned psychic any one question to put a nagging thought or curiosity to rest, what would that one question be? I personally could not answer that question right away, but I would give it a great deal of thought so I wouldn't waste such a golden opportunity."

"So, are you saying that I inspired you to see a psychic? How much money did I cost you?" laughed Maggie in an uncomfortable manner. She was starting to remember the letter she sent Maddie. She suddenly lost her forced smile and began to feel a bit queasy.

"Do you remember what you said to me exactly?" asked Maddie.

"Of course I remember. This is only a question that has been lingering in my mind for a long time now. I would want to know how far Uncle Doug got with me when I was a child and if he ever drugged me to get what he really wanted. I remember the letter and I told you how I couldn't understand why no adults would help me. I always felt punished for something I did not instigate," said Maggie with a lump in her throat.

Maddie said that she was allowed to record her session with Madam Zoë. The psychic always started each session by saying a few prayers, including the Lord's Prayer. She had Maddie write her full name and birthday on a piece of paper. She had a candle lit on the table and asked Maddie to shuffle her tarot cards. When Maddie finished shuffling, Madam Zoë arranged them on the table. Maddie said that it was a really enjoyable experience until she read the last card.

"I fast-forwarded the tape toward the end of our session. Maggie, I want you to understand that I *never* said anything to this woman about our family. She spoke to me as if she were reading your e-mail back to me verbatim."

Maddie turned on her tape recorder and they could hear Madam Zoë telling her that everything in her life appears to be in order, but there was one card that was alarming to her. "Madelyn Rose, when were you raped?" asked the psychic. Maddie told her that she must have read the card wrong because she would think she would remember something like that. Maddie told Maggie that the candle's flame really grew at that question.

Maggie was sitting on the edge of her chair as she strained to listen. Maddie never took her eyes off her sister. Zoë was insistent that this was no mistake. "You were raped by a man," she said. "The candle began to dance," Maddie narrated to her sister at that point of the taped conversation. The psychic looked at the flame and said, "She tells me that his name was Paul. I believe Paul is what she is telling me. Sometimes I don't hear my spirit guides clearly."

"I don't recall ever coming close to such an encounter. I did wake up once on my couch with my panties on the floor. My back door remained unlocked, but then again I was really drunk," she chuckled nervously.

"No. This happened when you were a child. You were a young girl. My spirit guide insists that the name of the man is Paul. There were drugs involved or maybe alcohol he used to incapacitate his victims. Women in your family knew this was happening and they chose not to do anything about it. He's not in the physical world anymore, but you do see him in your dreams," said Madam Zoë.

Maddie turned off the recorder. Maggie was speechless. "It was then I figured that because of our electronic conversation last month, she was no longer reading me, she was reading you!" said Maddie.

"Dear God! What did you do after hearing all of that, Maddie?"

"When I walked out to the waiting room to get Jenny and Tanya, I simply said that we were going to go somewhere to get a beer to talk about all of this shit. Please forgive me for telling our family secret, but this was just too big for me to handle alone. The girls were in disbelief when I told them. It was Tanya who pointed out the name

Paul might have been mistaken for Paula, as in Aunt Paula and Uncle Doug."

"I don't know how to process all of this," said Maggie as she was rubbing her temples. "I don't know what to think! How could she have known such details? Uncle Doug did have access to drugs because he worked for a pharmacy. All the women, except Aunt Kathleen, in our family knew he couldn't keep his filthy hands off me, yet Mom kept sending me over there!" Maddie walked out to the kitchen and returned with two beers. Maggie did not refuse.

"How could anyone in their right mind send their children to stay with a pedophile?" asked Maddie.

"Back then no one ever spoke openly about such things with their children. We were raised with the belief that we must obey all adults without fail or there would be consequences," said Maggie.

"Do you remember a time when we stayed with the Carrs and they said that we looked ill and we needed to take medicine?"

Maggie thought hard about that question and then she did remember that to be true. There was a period of time where Aunt Paula would give them medicine, in liquid form, with a serving spoon, which Maddie would comment, "Now that's a big spoon!" The girls couldn't understand taking medicine when they were not sick. Paula and Doug were insistent on the girls not giving them a hard time about it.

"Don't you think that's creepy?"

"Shortly after Aunt Cami stopped coming around to collect us, we were shipped over there. It was strange to me that the twins never went over there even as they got older, but it sure seemed as if we lived there most of the time," said Maggie.

"I hated their stupid dog, Max. He always drooled on me and humped my leg!" laughed Maddie.

"At least the dog was the only thing in that household that was humping your leg," said Maggie under her breath as she looked away from her sister.

Both girls were silent for a few moments. Maddie still blamed herself for not being able to protect her little sister from that horrible man. That feeling surfaced years after it all stopped. In fact, Maggie was married and pregnant for Allie when Maddie became haunted by such memories.

She brought this news to the forefront and upset Maggie with such talk, which was when she started to have bad dreams of Uncle Doug trying to hurt her baby. It was strange how she would always be able to save her child in the dreams as she sped away in her car. Doug would never say a word throughout the whole dream. He was alive then, but no one in the family, but April and Ruby, spoke to him.

"I've always blamed myself for you getting hurt because I was the one who was supposed to protect you; that is what big sisters do! That was *my* job," said Maddie.

"No, Madelyn Rose, don't even go there! You need to stop torturing yourself. Even after death, his ugliness found a way to touch us. Don't give him that kind of power! I told you years ago that *you* were my hero. At first I was angry with you for blabbing my shameful secret, but deep down inside I knew you would tell. I believe that was why I chose to tell you. In fact, I was counting on it."

"I remember when you first told me about it and you swore me to secrecy. You were so scared that Mom would find out. I vowed to keep our secret and I wouldn't leave you alone for a second with that man. We even went into the bathroom together like when we were really little. He touched me once and I cried and carried on about it. He insisted on applying a medicated vapor rub on my chest for a cold they insisted that I had. He never touched me again," said Maddie with a shutter.

"He touched me until I was eleven years old. He would tell me not to tell anyone because if he had to go to jail, then no one in my family would like me anymore because I sent the favorite uncle to jail. He said there would be no more toys, presents, or goodies because of me. He told me repeatedly that he was the one who gave us our house and without him we would be living on the streets."

"He worked on you because you were the quiet one. You were an easy target. You were a shy, but a sweet child no less. To him, you were easy to manipulate. He was a monster and you a delicate butterfly in his grasp. How far do you remember him getting with you, Maggie?"

Maggie reflected back as far as she could remember. She remembered her mother packing them in the car and driving them to East Toledo to see Aunt Paula and Uncle Doug. They saw the couple more often than what they visited their Grandma Ruby. "Aunt Paula is more of a mother to me than what my own mother could ever be," April would often say to her girls. The girls felt something was wrong with them because they did not share the same motherly bond with the elderly woman.

They would stay overnight so often that they felt the little green house was their new home. The shades were always drawn and the doors were locked at all times. Their house was filled with antiques and smelled of mothballs. It was a small two-bedroom house with a fenced-in double lot. It was located on Woodville Road, a main drag on the east side, with an alley along the side of their property.

The rules of the house were that the girls could never go outside without permission and they could not speak to *anyone*. The house next door had children the same ages as Maddie and Maggie, but they were forbidden to play together. The girls would watch the other children play through the green fence with their little faces pressed against its mesh.

As soon as a child would attempt to speak, Aunt Paula would call the girls into the house immediately and say, "Come in the house! Come on now; hurry along. What were you talking about? What did they say? Don't speak to those gypsies!" It was always the same predictable speech. When the neighbors moved out, another family moved in and it was always the same story. According to Aunt Paula, everyone was gypsies.

Uncle Doug worked for Vapor's Pharmacy on East Broadway. He delivered medication to the elderly or terminally ill who could not drive. Some days he would take the girls along with him on his deliveries. The girls were made to stay in the vehicle at all times unless it was a trip to The Little Sisters of the Poor.

He stopped at the little nursing home by Pierson Park where nuns ran the establishment. They were the sweetest ladies and they adored the girls. Maddie especially wanted to ride along to see the nuns. At a young age she wanted so much to live anywhere but at home. She enjoyed the attention she received from them and she always hated to leave.

"Come and live with us, girls. We would enjoy your company so much and our residents would enjoy your company too. We have plenty of room for you to run and play. We'll even let you drive our golf cart."

The girls couldn't understand why Uncle Doug would ever tell them that nuns were mean and they enjoyed hitting children across the knuckles with rulers. He would always include the reasons why they had to work with old people, which was because it would spare all the children in the world of them.

One afternoon, he made deliveries to the projects close to his home. He always carried a wad of cash in his front pocket. On that delivery he made the girls roll the windows up and keep the doors locked during a ninety-degree afternoon. People were coming out of their apartments and crowding the car before he had the chance to step out of the vehicle. He met with them in the middle of the street while lots of cash was going deep into his front pocket. It reminded the girls of a swarm of children and an ice cream truck passing out frozen treats on a scorching hot summer's day. However, there were no children, no happy tunes, and no ice cream. It was an old man selling drugs to overly excited adults.

On the way back to the house, Maddie asked if he would treat them to an ice cream cone since it was a hot summer day. "No, I don't have any money," he said. Both girls knew he was lying, but they dared not question him about it. When they got home, Aunt Paula unlocked the deadbolt and other locks; the girls could hear the chains swinging back and forth.

"We had a good time at work and Uncle Doug has a pocket full of money from his job today!" said Maggie proudly.

"Where all did you go? You were gone for a long time," said Aunt Paula, looking at her youngest niece.

"We saw the nuns and we even went to the projects!" said Maggie with excitement.

Uncle Doug was trying to quiet her down behind Aunt Paula's back before she spilled the beans. The girls were too young to recognize an illegal drug deal. Paula was furious with him, but never said a word in front of the girls. She gave them each an ice cream sandwich from the freezer while she had a serious chat with him in the front room. That was the last delivery the girls ever made with him.

Later that evening, Maggie decided to sleep on the couch since Uncle Doug mentioned that it looked as soft as a cloud in the sky and how he wished he could sleep out there. Maggie never slept on a cloud before and she thought it sounded inviting. He bought the girls new pajamas as payment for them helping him make his deliveries. Since Maddie was more of a tomboy, she got ones with racecars on them while Maggie got a frilly pink and white pajama shorts outfit. Maddie looked so tough while Maggie looked like a little doll. That night the girls were separated at bedtime.

"I was sleeping on my stomach on the couch. I was awakened when Uncle Doug crept into the front room and placed his hands down the back of my shorts. He started sliding his hands under my panties, but I acted as if I were waking up and he quickly, yet quietly, moved cautiously out of the room," said Maggie.

"Why didn't you get me?" asked Maddie.

"What could you have done about it? If I were around six, then you would have been about nine. I was so frightened, yet I didn't understand what it was exactly he was doing."

Morning came and Maggie never said a word about the night before. Aunt Paula fixed them a large breakfast. She asked Maddie to help her hang clothes on the line outside after she was dressed. Maggie was told to help Uncle Doug with the dishes. She was disappointed not to be with Maddie, but Aunt Paula told her that everyone had chores to do. Besides, Maddie could reach the clothesline.

"That's when it happened," said Maggie as her eyes met her sister's saddened eyes. "When you and Aunt Paula were outside hanging clothes on the line, he called me into the back bedroom and said that he had something to show me."

"Maggie, look at this. I want to show you a trick!" he said.

Maggie went in unsuspecting of what she was about to see. He was sitting on the bed and he called her over to him. "You look so cute in your new pajamas." He started to rub her bottom with the palm of his hand and then his thumb ran deep across the seam of her pajama bottoms. He could see Paula in the back yard through the bedroom window.

"What are you doing?" she asked innocently as she tried to pull away from him.

"I'm making love to you. This is what happens when someone really loves you. I don't love anyone else like this except for your

Aunt Paula. I now love you as much as her, but it is our little secret. Don't spoil our little secret, Maggie."

"He then removed his handkerchief from his lap to expose his erect penis for me to see!"

"Gross, Maggie! What did you do, besides want to vomit!"

"I began to cry when he grabbed my hand and tried to force me to touch it. He began to panic by my reaction and he told me to get dressed. Aunt Paula was heading towards the porch."

There were many moments when he got Maggie alone. He would always say, "This is our little secret and if you should tell anyone, we will *both* catch hell for it!" Maggie hated being in the same room with that man; especially alone. He always treated her differently in front of adults. He even went out of his way to ignore the child when there were other people in the room. Maggie was too young to understand such behaviors, but she did know that she did not like the way he forced her to touch him. She especially did not want to see his private parts again.

On a few nights when Aunt Paula would be asleep, Uncle Doug and the girls would watch late night TV. Usually it was The Three Stooges or Ma and Pa Kettle. The girls loved comedies, especially when they were on late at night. April would never allow them to stay up late like that at home. Maddie thought it was fun to have such a privilege.

"I remember sitting on the floor on one of those nights with the lights off, which I happened to be right next to Uncle Doug's chair. I heard him unzip his fly slowly when there was a pause in the dialog," recollects Maggie.

"I remember that too! I looked over at you and told you to sit in the rocking chair with me. Your eyes were huge and terrified looking," exclaimed Maddie.

There was one incident in particular when Maggie was about six, she was walking around her house complaining of terrible pain between her legs. This was after another weekend visit from East Toledo. She could hardly walk, as the pain became more intense high up in her inner thighs. Maggie remembered the pains intensifying throughout the day, which inevitably caused her to cry out in pain. She felt as if her legs had succeeded in doing the splits, something she never had any desire to learn, without any knowledge of it ever happening. April ignored Maggie throughout the day until the child cried out in pain later that evening.

As Maggie staggered from the kitchen, April stopped her at the doorway of the dining room. Without hesitation, April pulled Maggie's pants to the floor, underwear and all, and forced her legs apart with her hands. Maggie grabbed the wall to avoid falling. April was looking around down there as an auto mechanic would look under the hood of a car. Young Maggie never saw that coming!

"What on earth are you doing?" insisted Michael.

"Oh, nothing. I think Maggie is suffering from growing pains, that's all," said April as Maggie was pulling up her pants still stunned by her mother's abrupt actions.

Dismissing any thoughts of immoral conduct, April insisted that Maggie visit her aunt and uncle for the following weekend while Maddie had other obligations to honor. Maddie tried to get April to change her mind, but she would say, "When you are the mother, you can make the choices!" Maggie couldn't understand why she could not stay home with her own family. She was homesick before she ever left the house.

Doug picked up young Maggie right after school. April had packed her bag so that he could pick her up from the curb at Riverside School. She hesitated when she saw his station wagon waiting for her. She looked around the schoolyard and saw her peers running and jumping with excitement because it was the weekend, while she dreaded hers with a heavy heart. Her weekend visits were becoming more regular as time went on.

"Here, Maggie. Sit closer to me," he said as he patted the middle of the front seat with his hand. She noticed her bag was sitting in the back seat along with Max drooling over everything.

"Max missed you this week. That's why he insisted on coming to pick up his favorite cousin," said Uncle Doug. As they were driving away from the school, he told Maggie that he had a present for her. She kept her back towards him as she sat in the center of the bench. She was trembling. He grabbed her hand and forced it to his lap.

"What are you doing?" insisted Maggie as she resisted.

"I've got something I want to give to you." He pulled the newspaper away from his lap to expose his erection and said, "Look at my toy. I can make it grow bigger or smaller," as he was thrusting his hips back and forth. Maggie was so frightened because she knew she was trapped inside of a vehicle with the man who was much bigger and stronger than her.

He forced her to touch him. "I want you to tickle me and I will show you how to do it," he said. He forced her little hand on to it. She was terrified to the point of being too afraid to move. She felt like she was about to be sick.

When they reached the house, Aunt Paula was waiting for them. Maggie entered the house and the usual smell of mothballs made her vomit on the rug at the door. Uncle Doug had not even made it into the house yet. Maggie was cleaned up and was told she needed to go home because she was sick. All Maggie cried was, "I want my daddy." Aunt Paula called Michael at the office and he came right away to collect his little girl.

Maddie was so happy to see her little sister come back home. "That was brilliant! How did you ever come up with that idea?" asked Maddie with admiration. Maggie told her sister what had happened and that she was so upset that it was not done on purpose. Weeks had gone by and Maggie decided to fake an illness so that she could stay home. April was furious with the child.

"You better not be lying to me about being sick! You *know* how I hate liars! If I find out that you are lying to me, I will blister your butt to where you cannot sit for a week!" she warned. The clasps of her bridgework were showing themselves behind her snarled lips.

"I just don't want to be there. I don't like it there. I guess I miss my family here at home," she said in a small voice while avoiding eye contact with her mother. "Besides, I hate their stupid dog!" she said as she found the courage to look at her mother.

"I *cannot* believe this! When I was a child, that was the *best* place to be. They always took care of us and treated us to nice things. You need to be more appreciative and respectful! Now I don't want to hear another word about you not liking to be with your Aunt Paula and Uncle Doug! Do you understand me?"

After Maggie responded with a modest nod, April picked up the phone and had Uncle Doug drive to the north end and pick up her daughter. She continued to avoid her Uncle Doug as best as she could. When Aunt Paula was out of the house, Maggie would ignore the repeated calls coming from the back bedroom. Doug soon became irritated with her.

She went outside in the yard with Max and played fetch with him for as long as the dog could tolerate the exercise. Uncle Doug came into the yard as expected. Maggie was sure to move toward the window of the living room so Aunt Paula might catch him harassing her. Much to her horror, the curtains were closed!

Doug forced her to lie in the grass with him beneath the crabapple tree. He lay on his hip about two feet across from her with his head propped on his hand, speaking to her softly as if they were lovers. He playfully twirled a blade of grass around his finger. Maggie was extremely nervous, but she did not want him to see her tremble.

"Maggie! Get over here right now! Hurry along now!" demanded Aunt Paula. She stood at the corner of the house with her hands on her hips. She took Maggie by the arms and insisted that she tell her what was going on out there. Maggie began to cry, "I want to go home! I want to go home!"

She sent Maggie into the house to sit on the couch and wait for her to return. Paula glared out in the distance where her husband still lay beneath the tree. When Maggie walked into the living room, she noticed that the curtain had been pulled back. "Oh, thank you God!" she said. Aunt Paula happened to peek out of the curtain to check on her young niece. Maggie's plan worked after all!

Maggie was not sent home that night. In fact, Aunt Paula was not angry with her at all. That afternoon marked the time when Uncle Doug slept in the back bedroom, alone, for the remainder of their marriage. Maggie was to sleep with Aunt Paula whenever she stayed overnight. On a few nights, Paula would catch Doug sneaking into the bedroom. It seemed that the more protected Maggie was, the more he wanted her.

"What do *you* want, Doug?" growled Aunt Paula.

"I-I was just checking to see if you were both covered up," he stammered. "I can see that you both look as snug as a bug in a rug," he said with his best attempt at sounding sincere.

"We're fine!" she snapped. "Now get the hell out of here!" she warned as she nearly sprang from her bed.

Needless to say, Doug ran from the room and had not returned to their bedroom that evening. Paula outsized and outweighed the man, which intimidated him. She was more of a man than he could ever be. She used her aggressive nature to earn respect from her workers in the factory. This was how she was made a supervisor for the automotive company. She might have carried a rough exterior, but she was very loyal to all she knew.

Doug's sexual advances were still happening over the years, but not as frequent. Maggie would hear an occasional "I'm going to get your button" from the man when no one else was present. She assumed that he meant her belly button, but there was something in the way he said it that made her think otherwise.

He enjoyed taking Maggie and Maddie to the park on sunny afternoons. Aunt Paula would ride along when she could. She was diagnosed with Parkinson's disease and her health slowly deteriorated. The girls enjoyed it when Uncle Doug would leave Max at the park and he would always find his way back home. It was a three-mile hike, but the dog would come home in a timely manner.

Maddie asked Maggie if she wanted another beer because she was going to grab one more. Maggie declined the offer. It was getting late and Chase would be home soon.

"You can sleep in Trey's room, since it's the cleanest of the boys' bedrooms."

Maggie giggled and said, "Just as long as I won't have to hear you cashing in on your rain check, I don't mind where I sleep." Maddie had already had that in mind when she offered the bedroom, which was located at the far end of the hallway.

It was obvious to Maggie that Maddie was only half listening by her missing a golden opportunity to say something crude or sexual about Chase. The conversation was derailed hastily as Maddie's thought pattern jumped track and said, "I remember when I would spend the weekends with you at Aunt Paula's house. As I got a little older, it was only when my schedule would allow me. At that time, I could never understand why she squeezed both of us in bed with her. I wasn't afraid of that man. I grew strong and bold and I continued to protect you from him, especially while you bathed."

Maddie's visits were rare because April got her involved in roller-skating with Aunt Cami. Maddie had a natural talent with any physical sport. She became very competitive with speed skating, yet she was graceful in the freestyle category. She went to many skating meets over the years and she met fascinating people. She spent so much time with her Aunt Cami that she felt like she was her adopted daughter. Maddie got the attention that she craved when she was with that crowd, unlike the feeling of being a burden at home.

"I remember when Uncle Doug tried to walk in on us while we were bathing and you slammed the door on his fingers!" said Maggie as both girls broke out into laughter.

"Don't lock this door because it will jam and we'd never be able to get you out of there," he would say repeatedly.

"Yeah, we hear you, old man. Now go away!" Maddie would say in her most arrogant tone.

When the girls were dropped off at home, Uncle Doug found one of many wooden paddles April had sitting on the coffee table. He asked Maggie to collect all of them that she could find and bring them to him. She did exactly what he asked of her.

"Now go hide all of these. When your mother is going to beat you with them, she can't do it because she can't find them. Never tell her where they are," he said mischievously.

It took only a day for April to realize that her paddles were missing. It was odd to Maggie how she knew to come to her for the interrogation of the missing weapons. Maddie received spankings more often than Maggie. Maggie wasn't around enough to get on April's nerves like Maddie always managed to do.

"Where are *my* paddles?" asked April while her girls were eating their breakfast.

"I don't know where they are," said Maggie, reflecting on what her uncle suggested for her to do. She figured since he was older than April, then he must outrank her.

April grabbed Maggie by the arm with her claws buried deep, bridgework showing and all, as she dragged Maggie to the kitchen. She grabbed the kitchen stool and forced Maggie over it. She reached into her kitchen drawer and grabbed the wooden paddle Maggie had hidden elsewhere and began to beat her with it. Maggie was confused on how she found it because Uncle Doug was the only person who knew where she hid all of them.

"Don't you *ever* lie to me again!" she said between beatings.

"But Uncle Doug is the one who told me to do it," she cried.

"I should give it to you again for lying to me! You know how I hate liars!"

"He really did, Mom. Uncle Doug did say that to her," said Maddie as she ran into the kitchen.

"Shut up and mind your own business unless you would like the same," warned April.

Both girls really resented April and Uncle Doug more than ever before. This only made the girls more afraid to tell their mother about Uncle Doug and his creepy touches. They felt that she would never believe them and she would beat them both for lying. The girls really had nowhere to turn.

Ever since Maggie was a small child, she would have nightmares of her father being dragged away from the police. She could see the officers being nice to her in the beginning, but that was a trick to keep her calm while they waited for her father to come home in the end. She had suffered this dream for years. This was why she never told Michael about Uncle Doug. He was a wonderful father and she feared he would go to prison for the rest of his life for killing a weirdo. She could *never* do that to her father! She knew in her heart that there must be another way. She prayed for a miracle instead.

Since Ruby married Dennis Connolly, Bo's first cousin, Cami had to work longer hours to pay rent. It was expensive to lose a roommate. She didn't have much time to socialize like before, but she made some time and asked for the girls one weekend. They were ecstatic! This would be one weekend that Maggie would not have to worry about Uncle Doug. Aunt Cami would take the girls to the rink on Saturday morning so that Maddie could have her lessons. Maybe this was the miracle that Maggie prayed for!

Aunt Cami had been busy working at her second job, which was coaching at the rink on the weekends. A few years later, she became engaged to Maddie's skating coach after she learned she was pregnant. Cami felt pressure from other people because she was thirty and never married. She gave birth to a son and a year later she had a daughter. After the baby girl was born, she left her husband and children with a note: "I just can't do this anymore."

The girls always felt safe and comfortable with their Aunt Cami. They knew they could talk to her about anything. While they were waiting in line at a McDonald's drive-thru window, a new concept back then, Maddie took an opportunity to talk to Cami about their little secret. Even though she was easy to talk with, the topic was not.

"What do you think of Uncle Doug?" asked Maddie.

"What do you mean by that?" asked Cami with an unfamiliar tone in her voice. Maddie became nervous and looked over at Maggie, who was getting uneasy.

"Because," she said with hesitation, "he can't keep his hands to himself around Maggie. He's even made her touch his dinky!"

Much to their surprise, Aunt Cami told them that he used to touch her in her sleep. He would slide his hands down the back of her pants. He used to touch Aunt Ginny just like he touched Maggie, but worse. She was his favorite out of the four girls. He lavished her with gifts and money, but he promised it would end if she ever told their secret. Ginny always seemed to take it in stride.

"I told your grandmother about it when it happened to me. She just told me to ignore him because that is what she always did when she was a child. He's harmless, just stay away from him," said Aunt Cami.

Maddie's eyes were huge as she looked at Maggie. After their food was delivered through the window, Maddie said in a desperate voice, "Please don't tell Mom."

"Your secret is safe with me," promised Aunt Cami and they never again spoke about it.

Before Maddie became involved with skating, the girls would look forward to one week out of the summer to stay with their Aunt Ginny for vacation bible school. They did this every year until she moved to Savannah, Georgia. She was very active in her Southern Baptist church. She enjoyed spending time with her nieces, since they were the only little girls in a family filled with boys. She had two boys of her own, just like Kathleen and April, of course. This was long before Cami's marriage.

Before Aunt Cami had her children, she always joked, "I don't have time to raise a family because I'm too busy tending to my mother!" When she and Ruby lived together, Ruby was a bit wild. There were occasions when Cami would come home to find her mother in bed with Cami's old boyfriends or potential new ones. Ruby would just say, "It's all about the love, honey."

When Maddie and Maggie stayed with their Aunt Paula, they enjoyed her telling stories about when April was a young girl. Maddie would intentionally mention the name Katherine just so she would hear Aunt Paula swear. The first person to introduce the "F" word to the girls was Aunt Paula, which was sure to follow after the mere mention of Katherine's name.

"I hated that wench!" exclaimed Aunt Paula. The girls would tune in on her tone and study her body English. Her fists would curl and her eyes would flare with anger. The girls would get excited because they knew the story by heart, but they enjoyed seeing Aunt Paula relive the memory with such emotion. She would only talk about the olden days when Uncle Doug was out making his deliveries.

"That woman was pure demon spawn! She lavished her precious Kathleen and ignored the other girls. She especially hated your mother! There were times when I thought if she had an opportunity, she would have killed that poor child. I never told April this, but I ran into that woman at the grocery store one day after work. I was at my car, loading my groceries, when Katherine rammed into the side of my cart!"

Maddie broke out into a large grin because she knew the language was going to start flying! Aunt Paula proceeded as predicted. The harder the girls laughed at her actions, the more she poured on the effects! Maddie always knew how to push the right buttons with people. Aunt Paula was rocking fast and furious in her rocking chair as profanity filled the air.

When their confrontation in the parking lot ended, Katherine walked away feeling as if she won the war on words. "That bitch walked away from me thinking she was so tough. I kept my composure and remained ladylike; I hocked a loogie on the back of her rotten head! She never knew of the special hair accessory she was walking away with because she was too busy gloating. That wicked, wicked witch!"

The girls were laughing so hard at the story because their Aunt Paula acted as if she still wanted to fight their great-grandmother right then and there. "She might have been Ruby's mother-in-law, but my sister made her own bed with that demon. I became the muscle for my darling niece; your mother. Everyone feared that woman but me! It even took a lot for your tough-guy Grandpa Bo to say anything to his own mother's face."

Usually after that story, she followed it up with the days when she and Uncle Doug used to go to Detroit every weekend to an underground gaming establishment. He was the bartender and she was a cocktail waitress serving a room full of gangsters. She said that one man in particular would ask her to run away with him. Something in her eyes told the girls that there was much more to that story.

She would drift away in memory looking so peaceful and happy. She said that this gentleman would tip her with a one hundred dollar poker chip. Her face would glow when she spoke of the man.

"Run away with me, Paula. I promise to give you a life you've always dreamed of," he would say.

"But I'm married," she would say with a hint of regret.

"I'm in the business of fixing that for you. Just say the word, Paula, and it's done, just like that," he said as he snapped his fingers.

She would stare off into space with a look of sadness. The story always ended when she said that he cornered her in the wine cellar and she mentioned, "His eyes, his beautiful hazel-green eyes." The girls were disappointed in her ending such a juicy story, but they knew to let her keep her special memories close to her heart. She said their trips were short-lived and no explanations were ever given why.

Uncle Doug came home later that afternoon to drive the girls back home. He knew that their Aunt Paula entertained them with old stories, which inspired him to tell them a story of his own. On their way home, he drove off the main route to a vacant deserted area in downtown Toledo.

There were large abandoned buildings along this one particular section of town near the High Level Bridge, with the Maumee River at its backdoor. That was the place many folks would come to fish. He drove the girls towards a small grove of trees. It was a shady area where the river pooled behind the deserted parking lot.

"This is where I used to swim with my friends when I was about your ages," he said.

"Did they even have swimming trunks back in those days?" asked Maggie.

"Yes, but we all skinny-dipped," he said proudly.

"What's a skinny-dip?"

"That's where you get naked with your friends and swim. It's fun. Haven't you ever tried it?"

"Was everyone boys?"

"Yes, we were all boys. No girls were allowed!"

"Yuck! That sounds queer to me," stated Maddie boldly.

The conversation was dropped and never spoken of again. That route soon became routine when the girls were with him. He would tell the girls it was a new shortcut because he didn't have to deal with as much traffic. He drove by that place rain or shine. He never traveled there when Aunt Paula was in the car.

One evening, when Paula accompanied Doug to North Toledo, Maggie innocently asked, "Why don't you take the shortcut home like you normally do?"

"What shortcut would that be?" asked Paula under her breath.

He became antsy with the interrogation and quickly answered, "She's just a child, what does she know?"

Chapter 7

It was May 6, 1979, when Maggie turned eleven. The girls always looked forward to seeing all of their Connolly cousins on such occasions. Aunt Kathleen was coming with Trent and Ronnie, who were like big brothers to the girls. They rarely saw one another, yet they enjoyed every minute they did spend together.

All of April's family came, except Grandpa Bo because Grandma Ruby would be there, like she does every special occasion, with her new husband, Denny Connolly. Bo and Denny never got along in childhood. Bo bullied his cousin, Denny, so much throughout their childhood that Denny finally stood up to the big brute at the Connolly family reunion in 1943. Unfortunately for Denny, Bo broke his cousin's nose with one punch.

Bo and Denny Connolly's fathers were brothers. It was known that Denny's father was a very harsh man. He was known as a minister to some and a tyrant to others. He threw each of his children out of the house on their eighteenth birthdays. He personally drove them to a hotel for street vagrants with only $5 in their pockets and the clothes on their backs. Bo hardly knew his minister uncle because Katherine despised her brother-in-law. She refused to have any dealings with a man who once publicly humiliated her.

It was said that she forbid her husband to have any relationship with the man after they attended a church service he was officiating. After months of Herbert's coaxing, Katherine agreed to attend a special church service as personal guests of the minister. Much to their misfortune, they arrived late to the church. Just as the doors swung open and the Connolly couple made it to the middle of the aisle, Pastor Connolly stopped his sermon and announced, "And here walks the Jezebel!" as he pointed directly at Katherine. She stood there for a moment as all eyes of the congregation were upon her. The minister disapproved of Katherine wearing makeup. That story surfaced when Kathleen had put together the family tree.

Life was not easy for Denny being the son of this man. He was the only boy of three girls. He had a problem with trusting people. His mother died one week before his eighteenth birthday. Even though he was grief-stricken, that was no exception to the rules. He, too, was on the streets. He was a musician for a swing band in the early forties. He was not a very physical man, but music was where he could safely vent his aggressions. Denny claimed that he always loved Ruby and she did not deserve to be saddled with a man like Bo Connolly.

At the party, Maggie was excited to be wearing her new pink skirt and matching top. It was a special day for her and she felt like a princess. Her aunts especially doted over her and she enjoyed every minute of it. April made a cake and fixed Sloppy Joes along with a vegetable tray, chips, and relishes. Sodas, which was very rare in that household, were purchased for the special occasion. It was definitely a day for the little girl to shine.

Doug was a favorite uncle to the boys in the family. He always did fun things with them, unlike what he did with the girls. He just got a brand-new riding lawn mower, which he offered to load all the kids into his station wagon and take them across the river to his house for an hour to take it for a test drive. The adults did not object so they could tell their adult jokes with ease. All six kids piled into the station wagon with excitement. The twins were still too little to come along.

Aunt Paula was a bit hesitant on the idea, but everyone reassured her that the kids would be fine with their favorite uncle. Ruby took her big sister by the arm and said with a slur, "You need to relax, babe. We can catch up while they are doing their thing. Do you want a beer?"

"Don't be too long because April wants to sing happy birthday soon," Paula said to her husband before he left the house.

"Don't you worry, I'll have the birthday girl home before you know it," he said as he turned from her with a sleazy grin.

All of the cousins were having a great time in the double lot with the riding lawn mower and playing with Max. Uncle Doug brought out sodas for his young guests. Cousin Trent was driving the mower first since he was the oldest. Uncle Doug suggested loading as many people on to it as possible. There happened to be five kids total on the mower; two were sitting on the hood, one drove, and two were standing on the ledge on the back of the mower. They had a blast!

"Hey, Uncle Doug, we might run this thing out of gas," said Ronnie with excitement.

"That's okay. Run the tank dry for all I care. Trent, make sure that everyone has a turn driving," he said.

"Okay, Uncle Doug. I'll keep an eye on everyone," promised Trent.

Maggie was the one left behind, but she didn't mind because she needed to take a potty break with hopes it would soon be her turn to ride when she returned. Everyone was having a good time and Maggie was distracted with thoughts of missing out for being in the bathroom. She ran as fast as she could inside the house so that she wouldn't miss her chance on the fun with her sister and cousins.

The tractor continued to race up and down the yard as the kids drove recklessly, sending a few bodies rolling here and there on the lawn. Laughter filled the air. Maggie could hear the mower in the distance as she tried to hurry in the bathroom. She could hardly wait for her turn. Soda always went straight through the child and she felt that she was in there forever. The anticipation of driving the tractor was almost too much for her to bear. She was so excited that the water from the sink hardly touched her hands as she raced towards the bathroom door.

She exited the bathroom as fast as she could, but Uncle Doug was waiting for her in the kitchen. He had that sick look in his eyes that she'd seen on more than one occasion. She tried to avoid him as she cautiously walked around the opposite side of the table. He reached over the table and grabbed her by the arm. He forced her into the living room. Maggie began to cry as she resisted him. He pushed her to the floor and quickly lay on top of her. She tried to get away from him as best as she could. She was terrified and felt powerless. Her whole body trembled as she stared at him with a bone chilling fear she had never known.

As her uncle pulled down his pants with one hand, he used the other to restrain her tiny wrists. Maggie looked aimlessly around the room and noticed the screen window was opened next to the side yard. She began to cry louder and louder!

"Shut up! Just shut up! I've had enough of you!" he growled in a voice she never heard before.

He was hurting her wrists as he had them pinned together over her head. He began a rocking motion on her bare leg as he lay upon her. Maggie began to cry aloud for her sister. Her voice echoed off the walls, which sounded strange to her as if it were someone else crying for help.

"Maddie! Maddie! I want my sister," she cried.

"I said shut up!" he screamed as he leaned in her face and tightened his grasp on her.

Maggie cried out loud and shivered uncontrollably. He became so furious with her that he grabbed her by her shirt and yanked her to her feet. He gave her a shove, which sent her sailing backwards about six feet away from him, forcing her to fall and bounce a few times on her bottom. She was in such a state of shock that she never felt a thing! The look upon his face resembled that of a monster. For the first time in that child's mind she realized that monsters really did exist, just not in that of a Hollywood creature.

She didn't know this man at all! His hair was askew as he was kneeling on the floor, with his pants around his ankles, pointing at her with a stern finger. "Go to your sister you little bitch! Get the hell out of this house!" he yelled in a most threatening voice. She's heard him yell at the dog before, but never with such an enraged tone. Maggie ran as fast as her little legs could carry her out of that house without looking back. She forgot all about taking her turn on the mower.

Maddie met her on the back porch after realizing she was missing. Maggie was trembling and Maddie knew that he got to her and this time it was worse than ever before. Maddie embraced her little sister and continued to protect their little secret from their cousins. The boys noticed the birthday girl had been crying and they were all concerned for her. Maddie simply told them that Maggie fell and that she was fine. She refused a ride on the machine with her cousins because she was ready to go home. Her sister never left her side after the incident.

Maggie kept that tragic event to herself for nearly a week. Every time Maggie would close her eyes, she could still see that man on top of her. Maddie had been working on her to say what it was that the monster had done to her. She finally got Maggie to speak when she pointed out that the following day was Friday and she knew that Uncle Doug would be coming for her. Maggie sang like a bird and told her sister everything.

Being in a state of shock, Maddie said in a stern voice, "It's time to tell Mom."

"Please don't tell, Maddie. Please. I'm scared that she won't believe me and she might get really mad," cried Maggie.

"Don't worry, I will talk for you. That way if she gets mad, then she will be mad at me, not you."

The girls went downstairs to speak with April. She was in one of her cleaning frenzies. The girls knew they were taking a chance of being yelled at by interrupting her, but Maddie was willing to take that risk. The girls were hand in hand as they cautiously confronted their mother. April was in the middle of dusting when the girls approached her. She had her hair in curlers, which were secured with a green chiffon scarf. She turned to the girls with a scowl. Maggie began to pull Maddie away from April, but Maddie was a bit stronger than her sister and she had no intentions of retreating anytime soon.

"What do you want? I'm busy!" snapped April.

"I wanted to tell you something that has been happening between Maggie and Uncle Doug," said Maddie with an agitated tone.

April slammed her dust rag on the coffee table and firmly placed her hands on her hips. She glared down at her girls and said, "What exactly do you mean by that?" The girls were nervous. They both were on the lookout for the bridgework to show itself. Maggie began to cry. April grabbed her by the chin and demanded to hear the accusations against Uncle Doug.

"He makes me touch him in his private places," cried Maggie.

"What!" she yelled as she threw her hands in the air. "Why didn't you tell me sooner?" demanded April, looking angrier than usual.

Maggie was too shaken up to respond to her mother's question. She could see that her mother was furious, which made the child feel that the anger was directed at her. Maggie stood there trembling as she anticipated the beating of her life. Her mind was racing off in a million different directions. She was so terrified of her mother that the child wished that she was dead.

"What do you mean about coming to you sooner?" asked Maddie with contempt in her voice. "Did you know anything about this?" she demanded as she took a step closer to her mother.

April shook her head and seemed to be at a loss for words. She muttered just above a whisper, "He used to do that to me, too," as she turned away from her daughters.

The girls looked at one another with disbelief. They knew their mother was not lying because she hated liars. Maggie was shocked to hear such a confession while her sister held nothing but anger in her eyes. There was a long pause after that statement. The girls stared at one another while April kept her back to her girls.

"He also did that to your Grandma Ruby when she was young. She just told us girls to stay away from him."

"Why would you send us over there if you knew he was a bad man?" demanded Maddie.

"Because he is sixty-three, an old man, and I didn't think an old man would still have those kinds of feelings anymore," stated April.

"Well, Mother, you were wrong!" snapped Maddie.

"Why didn't you tell me sooner? I would have taken care of this a long time ago! I will talk to him and he will *never* touch you again," she promised her little girl when she found the courage to look into Maggie's eyes.

"What about telling Dad?" asked Maddie with a taxing tone.

"I'll take care of your father," said April as she looked Maddie in the eye with a stern and intimidating glare. "For now, let's keep this our little secret. I will have a chat with your father and Uncle Doug. He will never touch you again, Maggie," she said condescendingly. "You girls didn't tell anyone else, did you?" said April.

"We didn't tell a soul, Mother," interjected Maddie with disgust.

"Good. Now that it's all over with, I've got a house to clean, dinner to prepare, and toilets to scrub. You girls are holding me up."

The girls went back to their bedroom and discussed their conversation in private. That was a real turning point between Maddie and April's relationship as mother and daughter. Maggie was crying because she felt April was angry with her and she felt it was somehow her fault. She made Maggie feel as if she had overreacted again, as usual. She never got to tell her mother about her birthday present she received from Uncle Doug a week ago and April never asked for any details. She dismissed it as not being a big deal and there was nothing more to worry about.

Maddie crumpled up her beer can and tossed it into the ash bucket next to the fireplace. Maggie could feel the frustration radiate from her sister.

"Can you believe that she kept that secret?" said Maddie.

"I can't believe that she still sent me over there despite all that I had been through! She still packed my overnight bag every Friday," scoffed Maggie.

The little girl always wondered just what April said to her aunt and uncle. Aunt Paula and Uncle Doug talked to her differently afterwards, which made her feel awkward and ashamed. Maggie felt as if April contracted her out to clean Doug and Paula's house and wait on them hand and foot every weekend. The child even had to wait on the dog! She had to hand feed him his kibble one piece at a time. She felt that was her punishment for telling her dirty secret. She felt like a prisoner with nothing to look forward to on the weekends other than late Sunday evening when it would be time to go home.

"Did he ever touch you again?" asked Maddie.

"It was a few months or so after the birthday incident, I was doing their dishes when he snuck behind me and kissed the back of my neck. I turned sharply with a butcher knife in my hand and ready for business. I asked, with a growl to my voice, if he wanted some of this. He saw the sudsy knife in my hand and he never touched me again. He was stunned and it was over!"

"That's my girl!" said Maddie with pride.

"He made advances before then, but I would simply call for Aunt Paula in a tattletale sort of voice, which would always send him sneaking in the other direction. I just got tired of being scared and pawed at all the time."

Months after April learned of Doug's inappropriate actions, Grandma Ruby called Paula one afternoon to chat. Maggie answered the phone.

"Hello, Carrs' residence, this is Maggie speaking."

"Hi, babe. Are you staying with them *again*?" asked Ruby.

"Hi, Gram! It's so good to hear your voice," she said, sounding a bit desperate. Paula took the phone from Maggie. She and her sister broke out into an argument over Maggie.

Paula would repeatedly say, "She's company for me! She doesn't want to stay with you! Maggie likes it here with us."

After their five minute conversation, Paula handed the phone back to Maggie with a look of desperation. Maggie nervously put the phone to her ear to hear her grandmother say, "Maggie, do you want to stay with me instead? Pack your bags because I'm sending your Grandpa Denny to pick you up. He should be there in twenty minutes."

Doug and Paula tried to lay a guilt trip on the child by looking sad and heartbroken, but she didn't much care because she was too busy collecting her things to leave that hellhole. Maggie felt rescued at last. She looked around the house knowing that she would not be back. She was right because she never stayed with her Aunt Paula ever again!

Maddie stifled a yawn. Maggie realized that it was nearly midnight. She still needed to grab her bag from the car. The girls had established the sleeping arrangements for the evening and Maggie went outside to collect her things while Maddie started to get ready for bed. Chase should be coming home soon from the races.

When Maggie grabbed her bag, she did not have it secured properly and some of its contents spilled onto the seat. She giggled when she saw a few tampons roll down to the floor. As she retrieved her unmentionables, she had a flashback of the time when she got her first monthly visitor from Mother Nature. She was nearly fourteen and she received calls from her Aunt Paula and Grandma Ruby to congratulate her on becoming a woman. Maggie was mortified that April blabbed such a private and personal matter to anyone.

"So you got the curse," said Ruby with a slur.

"Uh, I don't know what you're talking about, Gram." She attempted to preserve her dignity as much as possible. She thought lying was her best defense. Gram was drunk again and Maggie figured she would never suspect her little fib.

"Ah! Don't worry about it, honey. It's not your fault. It was that stupid Eve's fault for biting the fruit in the first place! She single-handedly screwed it up for the rest of us," she scoffed as Maggie wanted to scream obscenities to the world.

Maggie went back inside the house and got ready for bed. Maddie gently knocked on her bedroom door just as Maggie was about to turn off the light.

She entered the room and asked, "Are you alright? I feel bad about initiating such unpleasant conversation tonight. I mean, it's not like we don't have enough on our minds with Mom's death and all."

Maggie smiled at her sister and said, "I'm fine, really. I've always been fine."

Maddie suggested checking out Douglas Carr's criminal record in the morning. The thought had never occurred to Maggie, but she agreed to go along and do some investigating with her sister. April had fibbed about various things in the past, this would be right up her alley. Maggie thought about how much her mother hated liars, which could have been a cover for her being one herself.

"I will understand if you don't want to go, Maggie. This will be like opening up Pandora's Box. We will not know what we might uncover until it's too late."

"There's no time like the present to find the missing pieces of a puzzle from the past. I already know that I am fine now and that I will be fine tomorrow, too. He cannot scare me anymore. I refuse to give him that kind of power ever again. Besides, I would be curious to learn what our judicial system knows of the man our mother forced her little girls to hang out with for years."

"I assumed you'd feel this way. I told Kobe on the phone that we would be late at the funeral home because we had plans in the morning. Try to get some sleep. I love you, sis."

"I love you, too, Maddie. Good night," she said with a smile as she laid her head upon her pillow.

Maddie turned out the light and quietly closed the door behind her. Maggie was deeply touched by such concern coming from her sister. Maggie recalled a painful memory that involved Maddie shortly after her first divorce. Kelsey and Kyle were of preschool age then and Maddie took them over to Uncle Doug's house to cool off in his brand-new in-ground swimming pool. Needless to say, Maggie was stunned when she found out! April had been working on Maddie, Maggie's closest ally, which clouded her judgment. Maggie remembered making the phone call to her sister one afternoon.

"Hello, Maggie. We're on our way to Uncle Doug's to swim. I'll call you later."

"That's not necessary because this won't take long," said a stunned Maggie by her sister's very words.

"What's up?" Maddie asked, sounding hurried.

"How can you send your children over to that man's house like that, Maddie?"

"I think that Uncle Doug is harmless," said Maddie sharply.

"What? After all I suffered through, what are you thinking, Maddie? Are you drunk?"

"My kids never leave my sight, Maggie."

"There will be that one time you will turn your back and it will happen!"

"Do you really want to hear my thoughts?"

"Let's have it!"

"I believe that you misinterpreted Uncle Doug's love and affections for you. Since you were just a child then, I believe that you were confused. I mean, really, what does a child know about love? After all, Mom always called you the paranoid one in the family and I believe that she might be right."

"You think that I misinterpreted Uncle Doug's touches? Answer me this, Madelyn, how could I mistake his affections for me when he was rubbing his exposed private parts on my leg? What does it mean when a grown man grinds his hips behind you as he restrains your arms? Do you think that was the code for pass the salt? I wonder what it was that he was trying to tell me when he forced me to touch him! I would also like to know how it feels, as a mother, to serve your children to a pedophile on a silver platter!"

"You're talking crazy, Maggie!"

"Am I? If you want to hear crazy, how do you think Uncle Doug looks at your daughter in her cute little bathing suit? How does it make you feel that he mentally undresses your little girl? Lord only knows what it is that he is doing to your little girl in that diseased brain of his. Each time you take your children over there, you are condoning it! Does this sound familiar, Maddie?"

Maggie broke through the barrier and Maddie never took her children over to that man's house ever again. The twins followed their big sister's lead and stayed away, too. April, on the other hand, continued to visit the man while everyone else stayed away. Maggie tried not to look back on that painful memory for too long because she wanted to believe that her sister was in a weakened state at that time. She knew that any ill feelings toward her sister would be a direct affect from the strong influences of Uncle Doug and April. She was more thankful that Kelsey was spared from the clutches of that monster.

It was well past midnight. Maggie noticed headlights dance around the bedroom walls from the driveway, which could only mean that Chase was home. She knew that Maddie was going to be up for a while longer, but probably not as long as Maggie.

Chapter 8

Her mind raced all night long. She was too wound up with thoughts of that man. She always repressed such memories, but now the emotion of anger settled on the nostalgic horizon of her childhood. She reminisced her past with such contempt. How could any parent be so careless? She thought about how the ugliness of that one man touched her whole family. The women of the family fell prey to that beast while the men later felt helpless to spare them of such pain and torment from not knowing what was happening right before their eyes.

Maggie remembered how Aunt Paula's health worsened and her demise was inevitable. She had so many prescription drugs to take that she could not possibly keep them all straight. She soon became bedridden because her ankles were swollen so bad that her feet became crippled from inconsistent range of motion. Her whole body shook violently from her disease. She eventually got to the point where she was no longer capable of speaking anymore. She was totally helpless and at the mercy of her monstrous husband.

At the ripe old age of seventy-five, Uncle Doug had been dating a younger woman. She would parade into the house at all hours of the day and night because Doug gave her a key. Her name was Candy, who was a divorced mother of two children. One child happened to be a little girl around the age of nine while the other child, a boy, lived with his father. They would drink and celebrate little occasions over Aunt Paula's hospital bed, which was tucked away in the living room. Paula would watch them cavort in her house without being able to say a single word.

April and Maggie stopped by one afternoon and noticed the front door was unlocked, which was clearly something out of the ordinary from their past safety rituals. Paula had been abandoned for hours with soiled sheets. While April went to get a bucket of warm water and a bar of soap to clean her elderly aunt, Maggie noticed a portrait of Candy staring Aunt Paula in the face. Paula tried to point at the atrocity. It didn't take a genius to see that she was disgusted and annoyed.

"What's this?" asked Maggie to her aunt as if she could speak. "Are you using this to scare away the rats?" Maggie turned the picture face down, which was sitting on the TV at the foot of Aunt Paula's bed. Aunt Paula forced a smile, but her eyes told such a sad story. This woman, who was once very strong and independent, was now a frail, broken-down old lady.

She held her hand out for Maggie to clasp. She gently took her aunt by the hand and Paula squeezed it surprisingly tight. She had such desperation in her eyes as if she had something to say to Maggie. Aunt Paula pulled Maggie close to her face and then began to cry. When April returned to the room, she noticed that Maggie had upset Aunt Paula.

"Go outside and wait for me! You've done enough here today."

Maggie kissed her aunt on her forehead and said, "I love you, Aunt Paula." The elderly woman was not letting go of her hand. April marched over and pried apart their hands. Maggie went outside, as ordered, while checking her hand for bruising. It looked as if her aunt had something important to say, but was unable to say it. Maggie felt in her heart that her aunt was begging for her to carry her out of that house forever, which she could relate with that feeling all too well.

April bathed her aunt and changed the bedding. She noticed that Aunt Paula's anus was all black and blue. She demanded to know what happened, but Aunt Paula could not speak. Because of the advanced stages of Parkinson's disease, she could not even hold a pencil to write a message. Any form of communication was now over for her. All she could do was squeeze a hand, when offered, and cry.

They left their aunt alone because April was irritated with Doug. She never called the authorities for her aunt or had her removed out of that abusive environment. All that April said in the car was, "I'm going to *kill* that man!" Maggie never said a word. She felt bad for the woman who was once strong enough to protect her from that demented man when she was little. Maggie thought with a heavy heart, *Who's going to protect Aunt Paula? This isn't fair!*

She was removed from the home one month later due to a rapid decline in her health. While Aunt Paula was in the hospital, the doctors couldn't figure out how she had certain medications in her system. Checking with her physician, he proved which medications he had prescribed for his patient. The remaining medications could not be accounted for. She was in the hospital for two weeks before she died. Uncle Doug never went to visit her. Maggie felt that her aunt was finally safe from that monster once and for all.

Two days before she passed away, April was sure to speak with her aunt about Uncle Doug's lewd acts with her girls. Knowing that Aunt Paula couldn't speak, April really let the old woman have it.

"How could you allow that man to touch my daughters while they were in your care? I trusted you to keep them safe! You *both* ruined my life because of it!" Aunt Paula began to cry, while looking desperate to speak. April continued to grill her, but ended her conversation by saying, "When it is my time to leave this earth, I want *you* to come and get me." That was the last thing April said to her Aunt Paula, her childhood hero.

April talked about that conversation to her girls for years, priding herself on how she defended her, then adult, daughters. Michael and his girls were disgusted by her actions. Only a coward or a person with no human compassion would browbeat someone who could not defend him or herself. April's actions were brutal towards her dying aunt, which made the very act unforgivable in their eyes.

At the funeral, Doug brought his fiancée, Candy, who was sporting her new diamond engagement ring. He buried his wife in a skirt and blouse that belonged to Candy. The family commented on never seeing their beloved aunt in a skirt. She was also buried wearing pink lipstick, which was the one specification she made clear years earlier that she did not want. Paula believed that pink was for a young prissy girl, not for someone like herself. She always wore red lipstick, which highlighted her bold personality.

Doug had no plans for a luncheon after the funeral, but April wouldn't hear of that. She cornered the man and made him pay for the whole family's lunch at a restaurant around the corner. Luckily, for the grieving widower, it was a buffet style restaurant. It was plain to see the discomfort he and Candy shared dining amongst Paula's family. April enjoyed every minute of watching the couple squirm.

He married the woman two weeks later in Hawaii. He bought her a bigger house, while he kept his vacant. It didn't take long for him to be arrested for touching his young stepdaughter. He went to jail proclaiming his innocence to Paula's family because it was clear that a divorce was in his near future. Their marriage was short-lived and lasted under six months. At age seventy-five, he was a widower, a divorcee, and a convict.

Much to Maggie's surprise, Michael was the one who was in disbelief. She couldn't understand why he wouldn't believe the charges since a similar occurrence happened to her just a handful of years earlier. She began to feel that he was ashamed of her and she couldn't look her father in the eye after that. Michael defended the old man's character and spoke to him over the phone while he was in jail. He told Maggie that Doug was convinced that Candy made up the whole story just to get to his money. Maggie just wanted to crawl into a hole. The whole family defended him, especially April and Ruby.

When Maggie was dating Alec, Maddie was pregnant for Kyle, her second child, and miserable. Maddie was ornery for most of her pregnancy. She rented a house across the street from her parents. She saw that Aunt Cami's car was parked in front of her parents' house. Maddie was bored and had nothing better to do, so she went across the street to investigate. Besides, she had not seen Cami in a long while. Maddie lost contact with her favorite aunt since she became a wife and a mother. Cami made herself less available to Maddie because marriage and motherhood was mostly a disappointment to her, which often made her complain.

She was surprised to discover her Aunt Ginny was visiting from Savannah for the Easter holiday and all her aunts dropped in to surprise April on a Thursday afternoon. It was rare for all four of the sisters to get together at any given time. Their reunions were joyous and their laughter was contagious. Michael was in the kitchen pouring four glasses of white wine while the women chatted in the dining room. The laughter ended when the topic landed on Uncle Doug and his incarceration. They were all in disbelief over the accusations.

"Those charges happen to be true," announced Maddie without so much as batting an eye. Everyone had a look of surprise, including Maggie. She instantly went numb as she witnessed her sister tell her aunts the gruesome details of days gone by between Maggie and that man. Maggie felt her head spinning so fast that she thought she was going to faint. She felt betrayed and stripped naked in front of the whole family. Everyone was stunned by such an outburst.

"Yeah, my mom knew about it, too," she said as if she had nothing to lose.

"April? What the hell is she talking about?" demanded Kathleen.

The room remained silent as Kathleen glared at April. The anger within Kathleen's eyes shot out like burning daggers and burned a hole in the lining of April's stomach. April knew at that point she was at Kathleen's mercy. She knew that Kathleen would see through any lie she could create. Kathleen was not an easy woman to manipulate, unlike Cami and Ginny. Her look was bold and insistent on nothing but the truth. April squirmed in her chair and began to cry. She was forced to explain herself to her sisters.

"I—I uh," she stammered.

Michael stormed out the back door in a huff as if this were the first time he heard the news and couldn't bear it. Maggie's heart sank. She felt her father's anger and figured he would never speak to her again because of the disappointment and embarrassment he endured now that the whole family knew about her dirty secret. Maggie had never felt so small in her life. She stood in the corner of the room stunned and speechless.

"April! You let that monster touch baby Maggie like that?" asked Ginny. She knew more than everyone what that man was capable of. Aunt Cami just stood there in shock and never offered an opinion either way. She knew of this secret and chose not to break a promise to her nieces. Cami chose to stare aimlessly at the wall while the massacre continued with each swing of Maddie's machete.

"He touched my mom, too," added Maddie.

"What?!" said Kathleen with total shock upon her face as she turned to look at April.

"He also touched Grandma Ruby when *she* was a child," said Maddie.

"This isn't happening!" said Kathleen as she massaged her temples. "April! How could you do this to your girls?" April did not respond to that question as she looked away from Kathleen. "So, what I'm learning today is that you have allowed this man access to your girls! My own mother was a victim along with her girls, my sisters? Where was I during all of this? Am I that blind?" she asked with an escalating rage in her voice.

"You were safe with Grandma Katherine during all of this," said a wide-eyed Ginny softly.

"Stop your crying, April! This is ridiculous!" said Kathleen as she threw her hands in the air. "You *actually* delivered your daughters to that man on a silver platter!" she scoffed. "Do you realize that you allowed that man to touch the third generation of girls in this family? This was something that you alone could have prevented! Why did you choose to look the other way? I'm curious, April. What was in it for you?" demanded Kathleen.

"He was an old man. I didn't think he thought of those things anymore. I didn't think he would hurt my girls," cried April.

"Yeah! You didn't think at all, April!" said Kathleen as she glared at her sisters who were avoiding eye contact with their eldest sister. "Did any of you know this was happening?" she demanded. Not one person volunteered to answer that question. Kathleen was in shock. She felt that she could not bear anymore truth. After a long pause, she took a deep breath and hesitantly asked her sisters, "I want to pose a question to all of you. Speaking for these two little girls, where were the big people?"

"What do you mean by that?" asked Ginny.

"Where were their protectors? If their mother couldn't save them, then who would?" said Kathleen.

"Maybe that is a good question for *our* mother to answer," stated April with a sniffle and her best attempt at playing the role of the victim.

Kathleen did her best to calm down by ignoring April's pathetic dramatic performance. Ginny and Cami continued to remain silent. "What on earth does Michael think of all this crap?" asked Kathleen in a more temperate tone.

"Oh, he doesn't know and I intend to keep it that way," said April defensively without a single tear in her eye. It was as if another personality was recruited to the frontline.

After all those years Maggie had thought her father was ashamed of her. The truth finally came out that April kept this secret from Michael for years. Maggie walked across the street to Maddie's house to phone her new boyfriend, Alec, feeling extremely nauseous. She had been anticipating speaking with Alec at 4 PM all week. Her brother-in-law was the one who handed her the house keys because he felt she needed a quick escape from the craziness. He felt bad for Maggie as he watched her leave the house while the women argued amongst themselves. Not one person noticed that she was gone.

Maggie was so happy to hear Alec's voice on the other end that she wished that she could crawl through the phone lines to be with him forever. Alec could sense that she was upset, but she could never tell him what had just happened. She feared he would never want anything to do with her if he learned of her past—especially being so early in their relationship. She did not want the man she was in love with thinking of her as damaged goods. Alec was now the only person special to her that did not know of such ugliness. She knew she would tell him one day, but not until she was ready to do so.

On Easter Sunday, the family did gather at April's house as planned. Aunt Kathleen was still angry with her sister, but she did her best to keep the peace for the sake of the family. Grandma Ruby was home with a broken femur. She never traveled anywhere unless it was for a doctor's appointment because she suffered from osteoporosis. The disease kept her in fear of injury since she repeatedly broke that same leg, which Denny once was accused of doing from the family during one of his violent tantrums.

Shortly after dinner, the phone rang and Aunt Cami answered it. Grandma Ruby called wanting to wish her girls a Happy Easter. It sounded like she was drunk again. Cami passed the phone around to her sisters. Aunt Kathleen was the one to speak last. She stood in the kitchen waiting patiently for her turn. As the phone was handed to her, she cleared her throat and let her mother have an earful!

"What kind of a mother are you? How could you deliver your children into the hands of a pedophile?" said Kathleen. Her voice became louder and louder. April and Ginny left the kitchen while Cami stayed behind doing damage control. Maggie stood in disbelief while witnessing her aunt speaking to her own mother like she was. Kathleen was furious!

When Kathleen's conversation was finished, she handed the phone to Maggie and said sharply, "Your grandmother wants to speak with you." Maggie was hesitant for a moment, but she stepped up to the plate and said in her most bubbly voice, "Hi, Gram. Happy Easter."

She about dropped the phone when she heard a deep voice say, "Hello, Maggie," from Uncle Doug. Maggie didn't know what to say! She felt as if she were going to be ill.

Kathleen noticed the expression upon Maggie's face and grabbed the phone. She could hear Uncle Doug on the other end calling for Maggie. "That's the last time you will ever speak to this child! You do not deserve to be breathing the very air she breathes. You can drop dead and go straight to hell you dirty son-of-a-bitch!" She slammed the phone on the receiver and walked out of the house.

After Maggie settled down, she realized that Aunt Kathleen was the first and *only* adult who stood between her and that man. She also spoke out against those responsible for such abuse. Three generations fell prey to this predator and not one person stopped it. April acted as if she didn't even care what happened to Maggie, just as long as she kept her mouth shut.

It took Michael two years to speak of it with Maggie. Maggie was married and pregnant, which she happened to be two weeks overdue for Allie when he decided to address the issue. He was in Indianapolis awaiting the birth of his grandchild and treated Maggie to lunch. He had an opportunity to speak freely since the two were dining alone. Maggie never saw that conversation coming. She about choked on her lemonade when he mentioned Uncle Doug's name.

"I wanted to tell you that I was just told about what you went through with that man," he said nervously.

Maggie looked confused because she knew that he heard all that talk when Maddie threw the secret out onto the table in front of April's sisters. She looked him in the eyes and asked, "How could you have just found out about it?" He had heard bits and pieces of the story, but it took until recently for him to speak to her about it. It was then obvious to Maggie that he did not know every detail and he did not want to know either. It was clear to her that he was very uncomfortable by the way he danced around the topic.

"How does that make you feel?" she asked with hesitation.

"I wanted to kill that son-of-a-bitch with my own two hands! Why didn't you tell me?" he asked with great frustration.

"You just answered your own question."

That statement took Michael back. "You were not supposed to protect me, I was supposed to protect you! I feel that I let you down and I apologize to you for being so blind."

"Why do the innocent people apologize when there is nothing they did wrong in the first place? I am not the only victim; you are a victim as well with this ugliness affecting you like it has. There's nothing to apologize for. We didn't do anything, it just happened to us and we live with it. I know that I am a lucky girl. Some children don't walk away from such an ordeal."

Michael lowered his head and nodded. He looked his daughter in the eye and said, "I hear so many sad stories in the news of families whose lives are torn apart in a single second at the hands of a monster like that. I remember hearing of a ten-year-old girl found on the train tracks. Her nude body was discovered behind that park where he used to take you girls. That story bothered me the most because you were about that age when it happened. To my understanding, they never found who did it."

"Oh, my gosh! That scares me more than anything in this world! It's bad enough to lose a child, but having to deal with a violent loss would be worse. I wish our country would stiffen the penalties for committing crimes of abuse on children. It almost makes me nervous to bring my own child into this world."

"Just to let you know, your mother still takes care of *his* affairs. She goes over to Doug's house four times a week. She takes him for doctor appointments and such."

Maggie was stunned to hear about her mother still visiting that man. She was the only one who visited, besides Grandpa Denny. Grandma Ruby insisted that he check in on her brother-in-law since she didn't get outside of the house anymore.

"Is the man ill?" asked Maggie.

"Besides being a psycho, he has cancer of the testicles and the bladder. It looks as if he's facing amputation of the genitals. What have I always told you about God paying attention? Does this not prove my theory?" he said with a grin.

Maggie was finally sleepy. She prayed for her mother's soul and that all would be right with the world. She also asked God to watch over Alec and her children. She looked so forward to being reunited with them. Not that going to her mother's funeral was something to look forward to, but she concentrated on the smiles of her three children while being safe within Alec's arms. She quickly drifted off to sleep.

Chapter 9

Maggie got up early and phoned her office. She wanted to check on the progress of a few leads for two clients. She told Mr. Jones the details for her mother's funeral arrangements. He offered his condolences and the whole office was sorry for her loss. She remained professional on the phone, as expected from Megan Graham, and thanked him sincerely for his sympathy. He reassured her that it was okay for her to take a whole week off for bereavement, but she said that she might be back to work sooner than expected.

She had to call Alec, assuming he would be getting up soon. The phone rang only once and Alec sounded wide-awake on the other end.

"Good morning, sweetheart. How are things in Ohio?"

"The funeral will be held tomorrow at Kingston's Mortuary at 10 AM. The viewing will be all day today. I do not plan on hanging around there all day long," she said, hoping that he would not question what her alternative plans might be.

"I will tell the kids this morning. We will be on the road soon. I worry about you. I need to see you with my own two eyes to know that you are holding up well. I want to be there for you, Maggie."

"Believe me, you are what is getting me through this. I miss you and the kids more than you could possible know. Please be careful driving and know that construction is in Fort Wayne, as usual. I love you, hon. Kiss the kids for me."

Maggie hung up the phone as Maddie walked into the kitchen.

Her hair was completely frizzed out and her eyes resembled two dark slits. She focused on the coffee pot.

"Well, good morning, sunshine!" said Maggie playfully.

After her first sip of the morning, she was able to say a few words, "Are you hung over?"

Maggie laughed and said, "Sorry to disappoint you, but I feel reasonably well this morning."

Maddie looked at her sister with a sneer and said, "Yeah! Me too."

Maddie was rejuvenated after taking her shower. She jumped into her pinstriped pantsuit, which she claimed was her favorite because it made her rump look more appealing. Maggie threw on a waist level navy jacket with a matching skirt above the knee. She complimented her outfit with a white opened V-neck silky blouse.

She accessorized with a white gold herringbone necklace Alec gave her for their tenth wedding anniversary. She rarely took her diamond earrings out because of their sentimental value, which was a gift from Alec after Mark was born. Her tennis bracelet was a little gift for herself when she cashed her first large commission check. Both girls looked similar in appearance, but Maddie is much taller.

"Well, are you ready to investigate this morning?" asked Maddie.

"I'm as ready as I will ever be, partner."

"Good. I hope you won't mind driving today. Chase will meet up with us at the funeral home after work."

Maggie walked out to the car while Maddie was locking up the house. As she started her car, she saw a school bus pick up the neighbor kids. It made her think of when she was in the first grade struggling with reading and the concepts of arithmetic. She was an illiterate child. One late afternoon she was sitting at the dining room table trying to complete a math worksheet.

April looked over her shoulder and yelled, "Wrong! You can just sit here all night long if I care. You don't listen to a single word I say anyhow! It just goes in one ear and right out the other!" She stabbed Maggie in the upper part of each ear with her long fingernail as she said that old cliché. Teardrops fell from the child's eyes, which she hid from April.

As she walked away, Maggie quickly checked her sore ears for blood. Michael came home late that evening and helped his daughter as she sat at the table for hours waiting for him to come home. Lucky for Maggie it was before her bedtime. He could see that she was struggling and he promised to help her with math every night after supper. He did improve her confidence and her grade in math, but reading was a different matter.

Maggie had to see a tutor for reading every Tuesday after school. She would never forget the feeling of struggling, like a drowning victim, in the classroom. That was why she insisted on teaching her own children to read and write before kindergarten. They all knew their basic math skills, they read at a second grade reading level, and they could write each letter of the alphabet in upper and lower case form. They were fast learners with the right encouragement.

Maddie walked out of the house carrying her purse in one hand and a small cooler in the other. Maggie was sure that there was no source of food inside of it other than her liquid lunch—beer. Maggie popped the trunk for her sister. She thought how sad it was that Maddie drank so much.

April drank a lot when she started to work outside the home. She made everyone's lives a living hell. Assuming that Maggie knew how her niece and nephews felt about Maddie's heavy drinking, she figured that was why they don't come home very much anymore. Kelsey and Kyle split the rent of a two-bedroom apartment in Napoleon. Trey stayed with them as often as he could. Chase's boys were about out of the house except for Jordan, who was fifteen. Maddie's children mainly raised themselves, which was an end result of how Maddie struggled with the fears of screwing up their lives like she felt April did hers.

Trey was the child referred to as the odd man out. He was the youngest child who did not seem to fit in with the rest of the bunch. He always felt that he must compete for Maddie's attention, but usually ended up short. Maddie's children grew up in a household that did not kiss boo-boos. It was important for Maddie that her children grew up tough and independent. Trey once made his own soup one afternoon, at the age of seven, by placing a glass mixing bowl on the gas burner. The bowl exploded; glass and boiling water went everywhere. He burned his wrist in the process. The child was accustomed to being alone because adult supervision was minimal.

Trey was unsupervised at the time of the accident, but Kelsey unexpectedly walked in the door just as it happened.

He struggled with staying focused in school and trouble seemed to easily find him. He believed that there was no Heaven or Hell; it was just a figment of one's imagination. He once told Mark that his mother was mutated when she came into the world, but Mark interjected by saying that what he *really* meant to say was that Grandma was the one mutated. They both laughed. Trey had a phase when he dressed in black all year long. He wore black jeans with black long-sleeved cotton shirts, even on the hottest of days. Everyone seemed to think it was a cry for attention.

The child rarely sees his father, who was in and out of jail all the time. When Trey's tantrums would erupt, something was going to be destroyed. He was like that as a toddler, which was assumed to be a genetic trait from his father. Maddie had always had a volatile temper, but Trey acted out like his father with his quirky actions and carried an untrusting nature about him. He had been caught stealing money at home and it was second nature for the child to lie. Maddie tried to reason with him, but that only worked sometimes.

When she finally lost her temper with him, it resulted in them walking out to the barn and the beatings would commence. Kelsey once confessed to Maggie that it was all she could take to hear such abuse. She thought her mother was going to murder Trey. There were times when Maddie didn't know how to reach Trey, but she was convinced that he would grow up to be a criminal if she didn't get a handle on him soon. When she would feel his mood turn dark, she would speak to the child firmly and say, "I want to speak to the good Trey today. The bad Trey is not invited." That was when she broke through to him because it was like a game that only the two of them could share.

When he was in fourth grade, he had a writing assignment that he was supposed to answer questions for Mother's Day. He said, "Mothers are good to hit you and tell you what to do. My mother was made out of mud, dirt, and sunshine." He omitted the rest of the questionnaire and signed it "Satan."

Maggie was so deep in thought that she didn't hear Maddie open the car door. As she plopped down in the front seat, Maggie gasped with surprise.

"Let's hit the road!" said Maddie.

"I was thinking that we might first stop at the library to check out public records. It might be a place to start," suggested Maggie.

"Do you think they might have criminal records there?"

"I figure that we might be able to collect more information about him such as his birth date and date of death. You know, all that fun stuff. Besides, someone over there might be able to point us in the right direction."

It was a beautiful morning. The sun was shining bright and traffic moved along smoothly. Maggie was happy to be able to pull into a parking spot up close to the Lucas County Public Library's main office. An alarming number of homeless people were sleeping on benches while a few were panhandling near the front entrance.

"What does this remind you of, Maggie?"

"It reminds me of my high school years!"

"I can remember a few bums sleeping in our hallways and we had to jump over bodies between classes at the beginning of my freshman year," said Maddie.

"That was a little before my time. We had security patrol the hallways when I went there. I remember seeing the prostitutes line up across the street every morning to donate blood. I even saw a few students in that line, too."

"Ah, nothing like good old inner city people to jump-start your morning!"

"In all fairness, Toledo has really cleaned up over the years. It is really becoming a beautiful city again. They tore down those broken-down old buildings by Uncle Doug's childhood swimming hole and replaced them with elaborate office buildings. They even brought the Toledo Mud Hens baseball team downtown. The new stadium is sweet! That is such a boost for Toledo and it is awesome!" said Maggie.

Inside of the library was like walking into a beautiful museum. They had their own security on patrol along with cameras everywhere. After clearing the metal detectors, the girls went to the information desk. The librarian suggested that they visit the History Records Department on the third floor.

To get to that department they would have to walk in the new section of the building, which had a huge solarium and mature trees beneath its glass ceiling. The exterior of the main building now serves as an elaborate interior wall for the new section. Maggie was impressed. They had two elevators, but they chose to take the stairs. They could see their destination as they advanced up the stairs. Maggie's heart was pounding with an anxious beat. She felt that her steps began to drag and slow down a pace or two.

Maddie didn't notice her sister's hesitation and she swung the doors open wide. They went straight to the information desk. A kind gentleman pulled up Douglas Carr's name from the computer. Maggie wrote down the microfilm information and he pointed them in the direction they needed to view their film.

As they walked through another set of doors, Maggie gasped when she saw a painting hanging in the microfilm room. It was a painting from their childhood! Maddie didn't recognize it at first, but Maggie gave her hints to help jog her memory. It was a painting of the bank their father used to work for years ago. The painting was of the bank's original structure, which was over a hundred years old.

"This painting used to hang in the cafeteria, remember?" said Maggie with excitement.

"Oh, yeah! I remember now, but I remember it being a much larger painting."

"I guess it's because we were much smaller then. I could never forget the many cups of hot chocolate Dad bought us in that lunchroom. It was such a big deal to us."

The girls pulled their film from the drawer of the file cabinet and found a vacant machine. As they viewed the obituaries of the 1998 issues, they finally came across Douglas Carr. Maggie got a shiver when Maddie read the name aloud. It said that he was an only child of Boris and Lizzy Carr and a native to Toronto, Canada. He died on February 17 and mentioned that he was a World War II cook in the United States Navy. He retired in 1988 from Vapor's Pharmacy. The former Paula Carr preceded him in death.

"The *former* Paula Carr! Who writes this stuff?" scoffed Maggie.

"Did you notice that it didn't mention his ex-wife?"

"Why should it? She's the one who sent him to jail. What a way to retire!"

They wrote down the information such as date of birth and death. They double-checked the spelling of his whole name and his birthplace. The girls giggled at the fact that there was no mention of living family members at all. For the last decade of his life, he would cry, "No one ever visits me. No one comes around anymore." It was music to their ears.

Before they left the department, Maggie asked the gentleman at the desk about where she could go to find criminal records. He suggested that they try the Lucas County Sheriff's Department. As long as the person was arrested in Lucas County, his record should be on file. He warned that if he were arrested outside of the county, it might not be a complete record of his criminal history. Not everything is open to the public, even if the person is deceased.

The girls felt that they were on the right track. They especially felt it when they saw that painting they remembered from their childhood as being a positive sign. They were on their way to the sheriff's department, which also happened to be the jail. It was just a few blocks from the library. As they walked to the car, they noticed the sun was starting to hide behind a cloud.

"I have to admit that I am starting to get nervous," said Maggie.

"We don't have to do this, you know. These records will never go away, just like you always wondering what type of person our mother placed her daughters in the care of. Wouldn't you really like to know? You could always drive back here from Indy when you are ready, but that time might not always be available to you. The choice is yours, Maggie."

She did put some thought to that question. As they got into the car, Maggie turned to Maddie and said, "Let's do it!" She pulled away from the curb and hit green lights all the way to the jailhouse.

"I cannot believe that I hit all the green lights! I've never done that before the whole time I've lived here. Well, except for driving down Erie Street."

"Now see, Maggie! Maybe it's another sign that you are doing the right thing," teased Maddie.

She finally found a parking spot and fed the meter. The sky was now overcast and the temperature dropped a couple of degrees. They walked across the street and up the stairs of the jail. There were a lot of deputy sheriff officers walking around the building. Cameras were everywhere and bars were on each window. They had a special entrance for prisoners that read, "Inmate drop-off here."

As they walked through the main entrance, the smell of stale air hit them in the face. Maggie thought it smelled like a heaping mound of dirty laundry, but Maddie took in a deep breath and had a big smile upon her face. Maggie looked at her with surprise because she thought it stunk bad enough to cover her nose, but she did not want to be rude.

"What's with you, Maddie?" she whispered to her sister.

Maddie stood still for a moment as if savoring the fragrance of a beautiful rose. She took in the stale air as her nostrils could not flare any further. She said with her bedroom voice, "Ah, this smell reminds me of Brad."

Brad Billings was an old boyfriend from the neighborhood who got arrested for robbing a Chicken Joint restaurant. He held up the restaurant while an off-duty officer was dining in a booth closest to the door. As Brad pulled out his gun to rob the attendant, the officer put his own gun against Brad's temple and arrested him on the spot. He only served a six-month sentence because the gun was not loaded and he was three months shy of being eighteen.

Maddie never had any luck picking her men back then. He caused a lot of trouble for Maddie and her family. His name would always be a source of friction for years to come. Michael even paid him $500 to finish high school because he thought Brad deserved a second chance at a normal life for making such a stupid juvenile decision. Brad cashed in on their deal and ended up stealing $300 from April's dresser drawer shortly after his graduation. The young man was banned from the family after Michael noticed how the boy could not look him square in the eye. That was how he knew it was Brad, indeed, who stole the money.

The girls went to the information desk, which was enclosed with bulletproof glass. The officer inside controlled the iron-gate and had to deal with people coming through the front doors. He pushed a button to speak, which instantly made Maggie think of *The Wizard of Oz* when Dorothy and her gang arrived at the Emerald City. She giggled as she thought, *Pay no attention to the man behind the curtain!* She thought the officer sounded just as intimidating. The only things missing were the fierce ball of fire and the levitated head.

The girls were instructed to walk on the opposite side of the building to the criminal records department. Maggie was just happy to be able to escape the stench of the jailhouse. They walked around the corner and found their department. The women working there were extremely helpful. They printed up the booking sheet of Douglas Carr and handed it to Maggie. It cost them nothing to obtain.

"Well, the price is definitely right!" said Maddie.

"Thank you, ladies, for your help and have a wonderful day," said Maggie, trying to sound unnerved.

Maggie's heart was about to pound out of her chest. Maddie took the documents from her sister and started going through it. She flipped through the pages without saying a single word. They briskly walked back to the car because the wind had started to pick up. It looked as if it wanted to storm. As they reached the car, it started to sprinkle. The girls closed their doors as Maggie checked her appearance in the mirror. She tried not to seem too anxious to read the report.

"Well? What's the news?" asked Maggie.

"It's not for me to tell you. You'll have to read it on your own."

Maggie was not as eager to read it as she thought. She found herself looking for an excuse not to go through it as best she could. She felt like a child again trying to escape or hide from a stressful situation.

"We better get to the funeral home, but not until we grab *The Toledo Blade* and read Mom's obituary. Let's see what the old gal had to say for herself."

"I'll get it!" said Maddie with enthusiasm.

Maddie ran to a newspaper box on the corner and grabbed a copy. She just made it into the car when the sky opened up and it rained as if a cloud burst. As Maddie was searching through the obits, Maggie found the courage to go through the booking sheet. She reminded herself that he could not hurt her anymore and she had nothing to lose. The only thing she had to fear was the truth.

Much to her horror, recorded in 1988, she read that he was arrested for gross sexual imposition. A week later he was arrested again and charged with twenty-two counts of rape! The man was seventy-five at the time of his arrest. Just twelve years prior to his arrest was when he stopped his advances with young Maggie.

"Oh, here it is," said Maddie as she was folding the newspaper backwards.

"What does it say?" she asked in a monotone voice as she continued to thumb through the booking sheet aimlessly. Maddie read aloud.

April Connolly-Getman went to be with her Lord on May 1. She was a loving wife of forty-three years and mother of four. She was a very dedicated and active member in her church and donated to many local charities. She raised her children and had enough love to spare to teach children the Word of the Lord and to give affection to those less fortunate. She supervised the cafeteria personnel at the juvenile correctional facility for twenty years. She was compassionate, loving, and patient. She was a real asset to all who knew her.

Maggie looked up from her paperwork at Maddie with a look of disbelief. She wondered which personality wrote their mother's obituary. Maggie wished she had personally met *that* April Getman. Maddie hastily folded the newspaper and slammed it on the dashboard.

"What a crock!" stated Maddie.

"Did she mention any names? How about her parents, sisters, or even grandchildren? Did she actually name anyone?"

"Hell no! She only talked about herself. She even tallied up the years of marriage as if her separation from Dad never existed."

"On a more positive note, Mom did love her job," said Maggie with a smile.

"She *loved* to manhandle those behaviorally challenged kids. I believe that she missed her true calling of becoming a prison guard!"

Trying to divert Maddie's hostility, Maggie started the car and asked, "Funeral home?"

"Not before we grab a beer!"

"Where do we find one at 10:15 AM?"

"I know the way. Just drive."

Chapter 10

Maddie directed her sister to the west end of town, which was where the funeral home was located. April chose the funeral home closest to her church so that she would not inconvenience her church family. Maddie knew of a sports bar around the corner. As the girls motored past the funeral home they noticed a few cars in the parking lot, which brought a bit of comfort to the girls to see.

"Wow! People are actually showing up," said Maddie.

"Let's only stop in for one beer. We should be showing support for Kenneth and Kobe."

"Ah! They're big boys. Mommy stopped wiping their noses years ago. No one will miss us, you'll see."

Maggie pulled into the parking lot of the bar and Maddie grabbed Uncle Doug's booking sheet just before she got out of the vehicle. They found an empty table in a more quiet corner of the room. Maddie ordered two draft beers and an order of wings. Maggie looked all around the room and thought it was a very neat and fun place to be. There were seven TVs over the bar and they had shuffleboard, darts, and basketball hoop units scattered about the place. Music was thumping in the background.

"What did you think of Uncle Doug's wrap sheet?" asked Maddie.

"Honestly, I feel ill. How many other young girls did he rape or destroy?"

"I only remember him serving less than a year for his crime."

"I have regret about that because if my case would have been reported years earlier, then his punishment would have been more severe."

"Maybe."

"I believe that he was released due to the decline of his health. I think he had two years of probation or something like that."

The waitress came to the table with their beers. Maddie recognized her from high school. Lynn had to drop out because she had a husband and baby her sophomore year, which eventually led to her facing an annulment her junior year. There were not too many places Maddie could go without running into someone she knew. Chase always teased her about that. They once ran into Aunt Ginny's ex-husband at the Hoover Dam while vacationing out west.

"It's five o'clock somewhere!" Maddie said as they both raised their frosty mugs.

"Cheers!"

Lynn brought the wings to the table with another two beers. She insisted on buying a round for the Getman sisters for the loss of their mother. She was always a sweet girl; she just lacked the sense of good judgment with the men. Her fifth divorce justified that accusation. Of course, Maddie accepted her generosity with open arms. She sent Lynn back to the kitchen for more barbeque sauce and extra napkins.

Maggie noticed the time was eleven o'clock and the funeral home doors opened at ten. She felt pressured to slam her beers in order to be where it was she needed to be in the first place. Maddie was used to being late to any event in her life, but it annoyed Maggie not to be punctual on purpose. She chugged half of her first beer, which she thought went down rather smoothly.

"Here, have a wing and relax!" said Maddie as she tossed a wing onto her plate.

"Maddie, I have something to share with you that I never told a single person. Well, except for Alec. Honest to God, he is so handsome and I miss his strong loving arms around me."

"Was that what you wanted to tell me? Everyone knows you love your man, silly," she said with an eye roll. "Oh, I forgot that draft beer goes straight to your head. You need to take smaller sips, sis."

"When Douglas Carr died, the first person I thought of was Aunt Ginny. I wanted to call her and offer some words of support with hopes that she could bury such painful memories of the past with that monster in his casket. Alec encouraged me to call her in Savannah, which he agreed would be a decent thing for me to do."

Maggie thought long and hard on what she would say before making the long-distance call, but she kept going in circles in her mind. They had never before spoken of their experiences with their uncle. All that Maggie knew was that Aunt Ginny was his little love puppet and no matter what he had done to her was nothing compared to what he had done to Aunt Ginny. Maggie knew it was bad ever since Aunt Cami told them that one evening, years ago, in the car. Because of that conversation, Maggie always carried a tender spot in her heart for her Aunt Ginny.

She found her courage and picked up the phone. Aunt Ginny answered the phone on the first ring. "Jesus loves you," she said. Maggie was convinced that she had the right number. Aunt Ginny was very active in her church. She really dove into it, more than before, since her husband divorced her and the boys moved out of the house. This was the first time Maggie ever phoned her aunt in all her life.

"Hi, Aunt Ginny, it's me, Maggie."

"Well, praise the Lord! How is my sweet one?" she said in a deep southern drawl.

"I'm fine. I was just checking on you. I was hoping that you are doing well after hearing about the death of Uncle Doug. I was hoping that it wasn't stirring up old painful memories."

"I'm just fine down here, darlin'. I've got my Bible in my hand and Jesus in my heart. There is nothing that can hurt me anymore."

"I am so happy to hear that. I was just like you, Aunt Ginny," she blurted. "He couldn't keep his hands off me either. It was bad, but not as bad as it was for you, I'm sure!"

"You know, sweetheart, that old man was crazy."

"You said it!" agreed Maggie.

"I never refused his money. I figured that crazy old man wanted only a moment of fun and I would laugh all the way to the bank!"

"Excuse me?" said Maggie with confusion.

"I love sex. I love the feel of it, I love the taste of it, and I love the smell of it. I couldn't tell you the last time I was touched by a man."

"Huh?"

"Do you remember him saying play with it until you see the whip cream come out of the top?" She rambled on and on deep in her memory. "He asked for sex the very night before my wedding. That old man was crazy and foolish with his money. He only lasted about two minutes and I walked away with a pocket full of cash. I wasn't afraid to take his money. Do you remember him talking about the whip cream?" she snickered.

"Uh, no!" said a shocked and grossed out Maggie.

"He didn't?" said Ginny, sounding surprised.

"No, Aunt Ginny. I never got paid for my services. He tried to take and take from me until I was eleven years old! Imagine a little girl trying to fight off a grown man's sexual advances for years. I was nearly raped by that animal!"

"Oh, I thought you said we were just alike."

"I was obviously mistaken! I misunderstood. I've got to go now. I wish you peace and I hope you find the comfort of God's love." Maggie hung up before Ginny could respond.

Maddie was speechless after hearing her sister's story. She stared at Maggie with such an expression of disbelief. Maggie finished the remaining half of her beer while Maddie still had a stunned look upon her face.

"Oh, my gosh, Maggie! I don't know what to say. I was under the same impression as you all of these years. I believe that everyone was. That shakes me to the very core!"

"I hope that God forgives me for this, but I never found it in my heart to forgive her. I want to blame her more than I want to blame my own mother! Isn't that sad?"

"I don't know *what* to think anymore."

"A few Christmases ago, she wrote me a letter in a Christmas card and told me that I should be a better daughter and visit my mother more often. Can you believe a person like that telling me how to be a better person? I ripped up the letter and burned it in our fireplace."

"In all fairness, maybe Aunt Ginny was an abused child. As she got older, she probably enjoyed the attention and the money, which was something none of those girls got on a regular basis," said Maddie.

"I can see that side of your argument, but it doesn't wash with me. She probably knew exactly what he was doing with me, a very young child, and she seems to still be able to sleep at night. That's where I sit with all of it," said Maggie with great conviction.

Maddie nibbled on the chicken wings while Maggie sipped her second beer. Maddie, hoping to change the subject, showed her sister a trick on how to keep the cocktail napkin from sticking to the bottom of the glass by sprinkling salt on the napkin. Michael showed her that trick years ago. It was a classy trick he learned while socializing with the bigwigs at happy hour.

"Do you remember when Grandma Ruby died?" asked Maddie.

"Yes, that was difficult for me because she was such a great friend to me and the only pen-pal I ever had. When I was feeling down, I could always count on a letter from Gram waiting for me in my mailbox. It was as if we shared a psychic bond."

"Her death was hard on all of us," said Maddie.

Ruby had been diagnosed with a small malignant brain tumor, which the doctors felt metastasized from a different location in her body. They soon discovered she had lung cancer and they attempted to remove her diseased lower lobe, which later resulted in her death two weeks later. The family knew something was wrong when Ruby was in surgery for only ten minutes when the surgeon addressed the family. He opened her up and decided not to remove the lobe after all, which was all the information he offered to the family.

It was a grave medical mistake and the family doctor admitted it to Maggie. She said that Ruby was too vulnerable for such a risky surgery; they should have let her go home and let nature take its course. Ruby was a wonderful woman who never said a bad word about anybody. She knew that people were not perfect and she always accepted them with their imperfections and all. Above all else, she loved her four girls. Bo came to visit her before her surgery for three hours, which Denny allowed them to hold their conversation in private. She told Bo that she knew she wasn't going to make it.

April called Maggie to share the news about Ruby's cancer and upcoming surgery.

"Your grandmother might die, so be prepared to be coming for a funeral," said April with no emotion. Maggie was stunned and speechless. "Are you there? Did you hear what I said? Say something!"

Maggie was shocked by such devastating news that it was impossible to say anything coherent. Being pressed by her mother to respond, all Maggie could do was cry over the phone. April was so cold. She always seemed to take great pleasure of being the bearer of bad news. She would even call when an acquaintance's mother would die, which no one would know who they even were. Maggie took a shower to try to ease her tension and cry in private so not to upset little Allie. She realized after she began to towel off that she forgot to rinse the shampoo out of her hair. She was really shaken up over the news about her grandmother.

"Yeah, you can always count on Mom to say the wrong thing!" said Maddie.

"I remember seeing Gram in ICU after her surgery. I knew it was bad because no one kicked us out for having too many visitors in the room or being in the room longer than fifteen minutes. She had tubes coming out of, what looked like, every orifice and limb. Her machines provided enough light that there was no need to turn on the overhead light. She was a real mess. She couldn't even talk anymore because her respirator hose was jammed down her throat."

"At least I made her laugh when I wore my Fog Horn Leg Horn shirt. She made me turn around to read the back of my shirt, which said: 'It's not a joke son,'" said Maddie.

"I loved that shirt!" laughed Maggie. "When Alec was with me to see Gram, I was the idiot who broke down and cried hysterically in front of her. Nothing like confirming to her that she was going to die! I felt like a total boob. Gram's hands were restrained to her bed rails and she pointed to Alec and then she pointed to me. She wanted very much to speak. Alec promised Grandma that he would take care of me as he escorted me out of her room."

"When you both came down the hallway, you were crying so hard that we all thought she expired before we all had the chance to see her," recalled Maddie.

When Maggie and Alec came down the hallway, the whole family greeted them. Maggie was trying to control her tears, but was having great difficulty. Everyone had a blank expression upon their faces. Aunt Cami was the only one who asked if Ruby had died. Maggie looked into each and every family member's eyes. All of Ruby's daughters, along with Maddie, Kobe, and Denny were all standing tall while staring at her with blank expressions. Maggie felt pressured to say something.

"Okay, I'm going to just say it. Now I know that I'm not the only one who had heard her say that she refused to be hooked up to any machines, right?"

"Yes, she did say that," said Denny as he stepped out from behind Ruby's girls.

"She said that to all of us," said April, turning to look at her sisters.

"Now just wait a minute. Think about what you are all saying! You *want* her to die?" said Kathleen with disbelief of her family's reaction to such an absurd statement.

"They've already killed her, Aunt Kath. I think we need to help her along her way," said Kobe.

The whole family had an open meeting in the middle of the hallway. Kathleen was struggling over the very thought of unhooking Ruby's machines. Denny grabbed a doctor and asked how they could go about legally helping his wife. The man explained that she needed to sign a living will and that she needed to be off her narcotics in order to be of sound mind when she signed it.

They took her off her medication long enough for her to complete the task. After she signed the papers, they put her into a drug-induced coma. They waited one week to pull the plug. All four girls were present, Denny and Michael were there, too. The nurse injected a solution into her IV and Ruby woke up with a confused look upon her face. She soon realized that it was time to say good-bye to her family.

Ruby nodded and scrunched her nose with a smile as if she were reassuring her family that all was good. She stretched her bruised limbs out for her girls to grab a hold of her hands. Kathleen had a hold of her right hand, Cami and Ginny shared the left hand, while April stood at her feet. Poor Denny couldn't take it and he left the room crying. Michael said that was the saddest sight he had ever witnessed in his life. The girls were all taking their turn saying good-bye.

"Thank you for giving me life, Mother. Thank you for being my mom. I will love you forever," said a choked up Kathleen.

"I love you, Mom. Thank you for being my mother, roommate, and my best friend. Thanks for the many memories," said a tearful Cami.

"It's time to walk with Jesus now, Mom. Go into the light," prayed Ginny aloud.

"I give you my permission to leave now, Mom. Everything is okay," said April bravely.

The nurse quietly turned off each machine while the girls cried softly. Ruby crinkled her nose again reminding them that she loved them all and everything was going to be fine. She closed her eyes and looked so peaceful. She looked as if she were taking a nap. Everyone in the room didn't know what to expect and they feared she would struggle for air. There was a sudden hush that fell about the room.

"She's gone," said the nurse softly as she marked the time.

"But the heart monitor is still showing rhythm," said Michael.

"No, she's gone. Her heart is still beating, but she has left her body. It usually takes a minute for the heart to realize its job is done. I've seen this hundreds of times."

Just then the monitor proved to the family that Ruby was indeed gone. She went peacefully and she had her girls by her side. Michael took what he had witnessed straight to his heart. He would never forget his thoughts at that very moment. *Is that all there is? Life can slip away just that easily?*

April never cried at the funeral until one of Aunt Cami's lesbian friends came in from Cleveland. "You came, you really came!" exclaimed April with real tears. Everyone was shocked by her reaction, especially Cami.

"Yeah, what was that?" stated Maddie rather loud as to divert the painful subject of their grandmother's death.

"I think Aunt Cami had a more confused look upon her face than we did," laughed Maggie.

"I remember that Cousin Trent came to the funeral dressed in his police uniform. He looked so sharp. Kyle was a little guy then and Trent kept picking on him. Kyle motioned for Trent to bend over as if he were to tell him a secret. Kyle grabbed him by his clip-on tie and punched him square in the nose!" laughed Maddie.

"I remember when Alec walked out from the back room without Allie. Uncle Doug was sitting in the back room of the funeral home. I freaked out! I asked where Allie was and he said that she was around somewhere. Trent was sitting between you and me at the time. I remember that he stood up and extended his arm for me to grab on to."

"Let's go find your daughter," he said.

Maggie was trembling and Trent kept her steady against him. Allie was in the manager's office with her cousins, Kelsey and Kyle, watching cartoons. The remaining family members were in the back room drinking coffee and smoking cigarettes. Uncle Doug was wedged in a corner. He looked very uncomfortable sitting in a room with his former family.

"Hello, Trent," said Doug nervously.

Trent just stood in the doorway with his feet shoulder width apart and his arms folded tightly across his chest. He pointed at Uncle Doug and said in an authoritative voice, "I've got my eye on you, old man!"

"Trent was my hero then. I will never forget him doing that for me," said Maggie with admiration.

"I still miss Grandma Ruby. She was the only one who understood me," said Maddie with a sigh.

"When I met Alec, she told me to sleep with him to be certain that he was good in the sack!"

"Yuck! Talking sex with your grandmother? On second thought, maybe I should have had that conversation with her, I could have learned something good!" giggled Maddie.

"Grandpa Denny told me that normal people would never purchase a vehicle without test-driving it first. Marriage is the same thing. If the sex is bad then the mileage would be too and we need to all be aware of the lemons out there!"

"I remember when Mom told me to sleep with as many men as possible. She always claimed that Dad was her only one, but I'm not too sure about that. As you know, that was the *only* motherly advice I took!" laughed Maddie as she raised her beer mug.

"Well, I will never forget walking in on Dad having the sex talk with the twins! It is a conversation that I regret witnessing to this very day."

"What could Dad possibly say that was so shocking?" asked Maddie playfully.

"Boys! You're approaching the age of stink-finger…"

"Oh, my God!"

The girls laughed hard and finished their beers. Maggie was digging for some breath mints in her purse before they left the bar. She paid the bill and Maddie left the tip. They walked to the car when Maddie looked at Maggie with a strange expression and said, "I don't want to do this! I don't know if it is possible for me to say good-bye."

Maggie hugged her sister tight as Maddie cried on her shoulder. She sobbed like a baby. There was so much pain and resentment that could never be fully healed. Harsh words and actions over the years that were never resolved, on either side, would continue to haunt the survivors. Just because April was gone from a physical existence didn't mean she was gone from a mental standpoint. This display of emotion was proof of such a theory.

"Every day of my life I suffer from those damned April showers! I feel her ugliness inside of me. I've accepted years ago that she could never love me, but my whole existence bears her thumbprint that keeps me pinned in such a cold dark place. I feel so trapped!" cried Maddie.

"I feel it, too. I try my hardest to overcome those emotions and focus on the things that are more important. I've accepted long ago that ugly things had happened in my past, but I refuse to let that ruin my present and future. I try so hard to raise my children in a way that I wish that I was cared for as a child. Every day has been a struggle for all of us, but we must put our best foot forward and try our best, always. The important thing to remember is to never quit trying for the sake of survival. Remember where we came from and avoid those same pitfalls that ruined Mom."

Maddie dried her eyes and entered the car. She had done a quick fix of her makeup and checked her hair in the vanity mirror. She reapplied her lipstick and said, "Okay, I'm ready to face her now. Let's go to the funeral home. But not until you give your big sister a handful of your breath mints!"

Chapter 11

As they pulled into the parking lot, they saw Kobe standing outside smoking a cigarette. He was wearing a black suit, which was a real change of style from the usual T-shirt and faded blue jean look. As they approached the building, Maggie noticed that he was wearing Michael's old suit. She was impressed with his brand-new look. She thought he actually looked respectable and smart. He wore a navy blue shirt with a black tie that sported thin black and navy stripes. He greeted his sisters with a hug.

"Hey, little brother! I dare say that you are looking mighty fine!" said Maddie.

"I found this in the back of Dad's closet last night. It was either this or my best pair of blue jeans."

"Well, how does she look?" asked Maggie abruptly.

"The Old Gray Mare didn't have much to say," he said with a nervous giggle.

"Kobe! You're going to hell, boy. Just like the rest of us," said Maddie sheepishly.

"I'm sorry for the bad joke. Mom looks the same. It really looks as if she's sleeping. This feels really strange. I cannot believe that my mother is gone. I stood up there for a few seconds, which felt more like an hour. I felt like I couldn't breathe! Something came over me and I just couldn't take it. It's creepy! I've never felt this way before in my life. So, I've been out here ever since. I've smoked a half a pack of cigarettes already."

"Is there anyone inside that we know?" asked Maggie.

"Aunt Cami is in there greeting a lot of their church friends. Kenneth went to grab a burger. I couldn't possibly touch a bite."

The trio remained outside for about fifteen minutes. Procrastination ran thick in their bloodline. Michael always claimed responsibility for that handicap. They were making excuses for not going in to see April. When one conversation ended, another began. Their conversations ranged from speaking about the kids to laughing hysterically at the misfortune of others falling in public. They avoided any topics that related to what awaited them inside the building.

Just as they decided to go inside, Kenneth pulled into the parking lot. He looked like a serious individual ready to get down to business. He was a sales person with a humorous style, yet he retained a professional stature in his little corner of the business world. The girls always said that Kenneth should have been a male model. They have always raved about his fashion sense. He wore a navy pinstriped suit with a black shirt and navy tie interwoven with a black design. He really looked sharp. He never had a hair out of place. He removed his sunglasses while he strutted across the parking lot as if he were on a catwalk.

He and Kobe were complete opposites of one another in their personalities and in their chosen professions. Kobe was a blue-collar cable guy who enjoyed spending time with the lonely housewives. It was uncanny how they both dealt with paying customers on a daily basis, but they were on different ends of the professional spectrum. Kobe possessed a more carefree persona, which was what kept him in trouble with April on a near daily basis. His wife kept him on a short leash for the same reasons. He had always been his own person. He had always strived to be different from his glamorous twin brother.

The girls greeted their brother with a hug. Just as Kenneth embraced Maddie, he looked over at Kobe and belched out loud in his face. The girls were shocked! Maggie quickly checked over her shoulder to make sure no one was around to hear that while Maddie brushed off her shoulder with a look of disgust.

"I thought I smelled dick!" said Kobe.

"Oh, is your boyfriend back in town?" said Kenneth with a grin.

Kenneth and Kobe were identical twins who complimented one another's personalities with wit. When one set up a joke, the other would finish it. They had been like that since they were little boys. When they were two years old, they used to mock the soaps by kissing each other in the throws of passion. They would say in a seductive voice, "Ooh, I love you, I love you." The girls later blackmailed them with those stories when they brought their girlfriends around the house. April thought it was cute.

"Come on, let's go inside," said Kenneth.

Kobe was quick to grab the door so that he could bring up the rear. They could hear Christian music playing softly in the distance. The hallway was decorated with red and gold wallpaper, a large red oval carpet sat atop the hard wood floor, accompanied with cherry wood end tables and red crushed-velvet furniture. The light fixtures were gold and they had candles burning with hopes to brighten the gloomy atmosphere.

Maggie caught a glimpse of the casket in the room on the right. She quickly looked away. She saw a sign above the doorway that read: "April Getman receiving family and friends." They chose to enter the room from the rear. It was obvious to anyone paying attention that the girls were in no hurry to view their mother's body.

Maddie's attention was directed towards the flowers about the room. She started reading cards from each arrangement starting from the back of the room as she slowly worked her way to the front. Maggie refused to look up, fearing that she would catch a glimpse of her dead mother before she was ready. She stared at the sculpted design embedded in the carpeting while Maddie read each card in the floral arrangements aloud. Kenneth and Kobe stayed close to their sisters for moral support.

As they made their way to the front of the room, Maddie read off the larger arrangements by the casket. Maggie's office sent a beautiful arrangement of pink and white carnations. There were also flowers from Alec's department at General Motors, which brought a smile across Maggie's face. Chase's accounting firm sent a large planter while Kenneth's office sent a beautiful statue of an angel resting on a pillar.

Maddie grabbed Maggie by the arm and led her to the casket.

Maggie continued to stare at the floor with intentions of slowly working her way up to April when she was good and ready. The boys stood on opposite sides of the girls. Maddie let out a gasp, which caused Maggie to involuntarily look directly at her mother. She felt instantly numb. So many thoughts raced through her mind. Maggie had never seen her mother look so peaceful in her life. That very thought alone broke her heart.

Maggie noticed her mother looked as if she were ready to go to church wearing her best outfit. She always looked good in pastels. The lavender blazer was a good color on her. It complimented her white dress along with her white hair. After she turned fifty, it was as if her gray hair turned white over night. Maggie could not get over how much her mother looked like Katherine, the grandmother April hated. The girls both broke down and cried. Kenneth and Kobe gently escorted them to the sofa.

"Oh, my God, it's true!" cried Maggie.

"Yes, it's true. I wish it were some kind of prank, but I could never do something that cruel even to my worst enemy," said Kobe.

Kenneth grabbed a box of tissues and offered it to his sisters. They gently dabbed their tears and looked at one another with a feeling of disbelief. April was really gone.

"I cannot get over how much she looks like Grandma Katherine!" said Maggie.

"She not only looked like the woman on the outside, but she projected Katherine's image from within for years," said Maddie.

Aunt Cami walked over to greet her nieces. She had been in the lounge having coffee with the minister from their church. She commented that April picked out her outfit a year ago from a clearance rack at an after Easter sale. She bought it when she and her sisters were having a lady's day out, which only happened on the anniversary of Grandma Ruby's death. Cami saw more people from church walk through the door and she quickly got up to greet them.

"Where are the flowers from us?" asked Maddie.

"She did not want a spray of flowers on her casket," said Kenneth.

"No flowers? Why?" asked Maggie, being a bit stunned.

"Because she said that flowers are not to be wasted on the dead, flowers are for the living. She warned that if we purchased her flowers like that she would come back to haunt me. She believed that it was a waste of money and beauty to decorate a dead person in flowers," said Kenneth.

"Maybe she didn't feel worthy," said Kobe.

"The way I see it, she saved me some money," said Maddie sarcastically as she quickly folder her arms across her chest.

"This is so sad. The top of her casket looks so naked. It looks like she has a family who hates her," said Maggie.

Aunt Cami introduced a few church members to April's children. Everyone's comments were beginning to sound the same. "Oh, I didn't know April had *two* daughters," they would say when introduced to Maggie. The brave souls would say, "I knew about the twins and I've heard plenty about Maddie, but I've never heard about you," when referring to Maggie.

When they weren't making those comments, they were saying things such as, "She really looks good" and "God always calls the sweet ones home before the rest of us." Maddie and Maggie stood in disbelief when they heard people, they never met, say how loving and generous April had been. They believed that she had the disposition of an angel.

"Your mother has some pretty big shoes to fill, girls," said a church elder.

"Excuse us, we need to get some air," said Maddie candidly as she grabbed Maggie by the arm and quickly ushered her outside.

"Can you believe that?" asked Maggie while looking at her sister with disbelief.

"These people do not know her at all!" stated Maddie. "This is really creepy."

"Maybe *we* didn't know her at all. We only knew one side of her. We rarely saw the good-natured side. We always suspected that she had a split personality."

"Could you pop your trunk? I need a drink!"

Maggie handed her sister her car keys and went back into the funeral home. She found a seat in the back of the room and stared at her white-haired mother as the crowd drifted in and out. In death, Maggie could not believe how much April resembled Katherine. The church members knew a side of April that her family did not. Maggie fell deep in thought. She could not help but ponder, *Is this why she kept us away from her church? Does she want those people to believe that we, her family, hate her enough to not spring for flowers?*

It was now obvious that April had not wanted both worlds to mix. When April got baptized in her new church, she refused to invite her family to witness such a special and sacred occasion. April was initially baptized Catholic when she was engaged to Michael, but her new church did not recognize sprinkling as any proper baptism. In order for her to become a new member of the church, she had to conform to their rules. She even had to take a written test. It was her choice not to invite her family. Aunt Cami was there, but she was sworn to secrecy.

Maddie returned and Maggie handed her a couple of breath mints. So many strange faces were coming and going, but Aunt Cami seemed to keep track of them all. Kenneth and Kobe grabbed a chair by the girls.

"I feel out of place here," said Kenneth.

"Yeah, I feel as if we are the visitors here, not family," said Kobe.

"These are the same church people who cashed Mom's one hundred dollar checks every week and never talked with her about it," said Maddie.

"That's because it wasn't her money. It was Dad's money! She took money out of *his* account every week and donated it to the church; Dad was *never* a member!" said Maggie.

"Isn't that more than ten percent of her weekly wages?" asked Kobe.

"Her church isn't going to ask if she knows how to figure percentages," said Maddie.

"I believe that she did that before she was accepted as a member of the church. There was a period of time when she couldn't miss church or she would not even be considered as a member," said Kenneth.

"Since when did they start having a probationary period with God?" asked Maddie.

"Keeping it in proper perspective, those were Mom's words," said Kenneth.

"Poor Dad had to go to the bank because he thought they were stealing money from his accounts. They showed him proof that it was Mom making withdraws," said Maggie.

"The poor guy had just retired then. Every penny needed to be pinched. That's when he changed his accounts and she could never touch them again," said Kobe.

"When Dad confronted her about it, she played dumb. She claimed that she thought it was ten percent of her wages, but he was quick to remind her that she withdrew from *his* accounts!" said Maggie.

"Yep! That's when the line was drawn and another part of their marriage became what's mine is mine," said Maddie.

"She donated over a thousand dollars before Dad caught her," said Kenneth.

"Christ! I'd do anything for a beer right now!" said Kobe out loud, turning a few heads from the front of the room.

Maddie still had Maggie's keys, which she pulled out from her purse, and they walked to the car. Kenneth sat with Maggie. He was searching the crowd for any familiar faces, but he didn't recognize a single one. Maggie looked at her watch and wondered when Alec and her kids would be arriving.

"I cannot get over how much Mom looks like Katherine," said Maggie.

"I vaguely remember her. All I remember is a heavyset, smiley old woman with white hair."

"I saw her on a few occasions. The last time we met is when we saw her smile. We used to see her at Aunt Kathleen's house at Christmas when you and Kobe were babies, but we never knew that she was *our* family, too. She would watch us play with Trent and Ronnie as she sat on the couch, clutching her purse, in silence. She *never* said a word to us. We assumed that she was *their* grandmother, not ours. Mom just told us not to get too loud because that old grandma was grouchy and it was best if we didn't speak to her."

"What time am I thinking of then?"

"It was for a fish fry at their home in Point Place, which was their farewell party. Mom was invited for the first time for a family function with Katherine. Mom couldn't understand why she was invited after all those years."

"Why the change of heart?"

"It just so happened that the Christmas before they moved, I helped Mom write out Christmas cards. I saw Katherine Connolly in the Rolodex and I knew she must be family. I wrote out a card and signed it 'with love' just like everyone else's card. April never knew that I sent it. I never knew she had a grandmother whom she hated."

"I guess that is something you don't share with your young children," said Kenneth.

"I remember Mom drilled us in the car to use our manners and not to speak until we were spoken to. Dad reminded her that we were good kids and that we had never disappointed them before. When we got there, Grandma Katherine had a huge smile upon her face. I later heard Mom comment, in the car, that she never knew her grandmother had teeth!"

"That would have felt like an episode of The Twilight Zone!" said Kenneth with a smile.

"She took Mom by the hand and gave her a tour of the house. She even framed all four of our school pictures, the ones I sent in her card, in a fancy frame on her wall. She wanted to make sure Mom saw it. She was so happy to have us there, but Mom never saw that because she was too consumed with fear."

Kathleen left early so that Katherine and April could catch up without interference. Katherine was sure to have lots of pictures taken to mark the occasion. She and her husband, Herbert, were about to move to Phoenix and settle permanently into their winter home. Bo and Donna were there with her twin boys, who were now old enough to drive. Katherine really enjoyed having the Getman family in her Toledo home for the first *and* last time.

"It sounded like Katherine really tried to reach for a friendship with Mom before she left," said Kenneth.

"That was one way of looking at it. I thought of it as her way of calling a truce. The sickening thing to me was that when Katherine was dying in Arizona, she was calling for Mom on her deathbed. Dad offered to fly her out there, but Mom refused. Aunt Ginny flew in from Savannah to see Katherine before she died. It was sad because Katherine kept calling her April and told her how glad she was that she came to see her."

"That is sad."

"One summer, when I visited Grandpa Bo, Donna told me that Katherine confided in her on her deathbed."

Maggie reflected on her story to her brother. As she spoke about Katherine, she was discovering memories that she did not realize that she had stored in that file cabinet in her head.

"Do you think April would come?" asked Katherine hopefully.

"I'm not sure if she would do that or not. She's got her four young children to care for," said Donna.

"I wasn't very nice to her, was I?"

"No, you weren't. You've been hard on her since she was a small child."

"Do you think she would ever forgive me?"

"I don't know. That would be up to April."

Katherine asked Donna to take a few gifts back to Ohio for April. Donna honored her mother-in-law's request. Katherine died of breast cancer and she was cremated with no funeral service. Cami could not be in Arizona because she was unable to take a leave of absence from work. April's reasons for not going were strictly by choice. As promised, Bo and Donna delivered the gifts to April on their way home from the airport.

"These are gifts from your Grandma Katherine," said Bo as he handed April two copper skillets.

Her gifts also included two slender iron cats, which were to be hung on the wall. She sent two turquoise bracelets that would fit nicely on the wrists of two young girls. She also received two jeweled ashtrays to complete the package. April was disappointed that there was no note of acceptance or apology that would have been tangible for her to hold dear to her heart from her wicked grandmother. Donna pulled two final gifts from the box, which were two copper teakettles.

"These are the words your grandmother asked me to say to you," said Donna as she carefully placed the teakettles in front of April. "Here are two tea pots, which represent the conversations we will never have. One pot will be mine while the other will be yours. One day we will have our friendship, but it will be in another place and another time," said Donna to an expressionless April, who offered no comment either way.

"Did Mom see her grandmother in a different light after that?" asked Kenneth.

"Mom chose to let those words bounce right off of her heart. She acted as if she ignored what Grandma Donna said to her. She hung the pans and cats on the wall and she displayed the teakettles in her china cabinet. I had once expressed an interest in a bracelet when I was a child. As you could probably guess, Mom insisted that those bracelets were hers, not ours! I believe she hid them from me because I never saw those bracelets again."

"Wow! For years she had carried anger and resentment toward that woman. It sounded like Katherine tried to apologize, but Mom was just too stubborn to allow her to ever say the words."

"What's that old saying about anger can consume you if you don't let it go? For years, after Mom's drinking days, I believed the mean person that was alcohol induced then, in fact, became a monster in her sobriety. The beast was still alive and grew meaner with each passing year!"

"I only wonder if Katherine was as bad as Mom says she was."

"I've always wondered, too," said Maggie.

"Life is too short for such ugliness. Look how much time was wasted!"

"Speaking of ugliness, Uncle Ed, Grandpa Bo's brother, was accused of being Mom's real father throughout her whole childhood!"

"What are you talking about?"

"Because Mom was the only child with green eyes, she was accused of being a bastard child. No one wanted to take a moment to realize that Grandma Ruby also had green eyes. It was just too much fun teasing and tormenting the child about Uncle Ed's having green eyes must mean that he is not her uncle, but her father!"

"That cannot not be possible, can it?" asked Kenneth.

"Well, from what I've heard, Grandma Ruby and Kate, Uncle Ed's wife, were best friends. They did *everything* together. The two girls would swap boyfriends all the time, which included the two Connolly brothers, Bo and Ed. This went on until Grandma Ruby got pregnant and was forced to marry Grandpa Bo. Come to find out, Kate was pregnant for Joe, which is why she and Ed got married too. Aunt Kate was a lot of fun. She was a Go-Go dancer in her day and now she lives in Chicago. Grandma Ruby could never say that woman's name without giggling."

"It sounds like a major soap opera to me!"

"Mom once told me that when she was really little, when Grandpa Bo was at work, she and Grandma Ruby hid behind a chair because Uncle Ed came to the door. I guess Grandma covered Mom's mouth to keep her silent. Mom couldn't understand what that was about because everybody loved Uncle Ed."

"He was the fire marshal, right?"

"Yes. I understand that when he died, he was also cremated like his parents. However, Ed's second wife refused to allow any Connolly family members to attend his funeral because she was a mean and selfish woman. She turned her back on Ed's family."

"I have always believed that a funeral is a celebration of that person's life," said Kenneth.

"Just before Uncle Ed died, Mom asked him why Grandma Katherine hated her so much. He responded by saying that she hated everyone!"

Maddie and Kobe were mingling on the floor. Kenneth had to answer his cell phone while Maggie went to the lounge to check out the refreshments. She saw cookies and pastries with tiny matching plates and napkins for the visitors. She thought the coffee smelled good and fairly fresh. As she made her way into the lounge, she passed by a gentleman who grabbed her by the arm.

"Oh, excuse me," she said nervously. "Oh, my gosh, Dad!" she cried.

"Hey there, baby doll!" he said as he tightly embraced his daughter.

"I didn't recognize you!" she said with excitement. "Look at you! You are so tan and I've *never* seen you with facial hair. You look great! It's so good to see you!" she said as she leaned in for another hug.

Michael was sporting the fashion of a younger man's wardrobe. He was always thin and his physique remained fit. He got rid of his eyeglasses, which surprised Maggie that he braved the optical surgery. He was dressed causally, but he looked respectable. This was a far cry from what he used to look like in his stuffy three-piece suits during the days of his employment at the bank.

"How are you holding up?" he asked with concern. Before she could answer, he asked, "Where are my Hoosier grandkids? Where's that son-in-law of mine?" he asked as an obvious distraction of not wanting to hear the truth to the first question he asked.

"Where have you been?" asked Maggie with a smile.

"I was in California when I got the call from Ken. I've been touring the country, jumping train to train. I've never seen the Pacific Ocean, so I thought it would be a perfect opportunity since I'd been in Vegas a few weeks. After I heard about your mother, I grabbed the first plane back to Ohio."

"Does anyone know you're here?"

"I've been helping Ken with the arrangements and I treated him and Kobe to breakfast this morning," he said as Maggie's smile faded.

"They never told me you were here!" she said, sounding annoyed.

"I asked them not to say anything because I wanted to surprise you."

"Does Maddie know you're here?"

"Yes. I phoned her when I got into Toledo. She told me that you were staying with her for the night and she had things to discuss with you. It sounded important and I didn't want to interfere."

Michael poured Maggie a cup of coffee. They walked outside so they could speak in private. Michael asked Maggie what a sales person of the year drives these days. Maggie pointed to her Cadillac unenthusiastically. He smiled and puffed out his chest with pride and said, "That's my girl."

Over the years, Maggie paid close attention to Michael's work ethic and his communication skills with people. She also saw how he used his political resources to get a job done without losing his temper. Michael remained calm during any given situation. He warned that politics are in everything and it was important to learn how to become a player in order to survive the cut-throat tactics in the business world.

On most occasions, he had won battles by using the corporation's own methods against itself. When he had over twenty-nine years invested in the bank, he lost his job to downsizing when the bank franchise was sold. There might have been the idea of age discrimination involved, but that could not be proven in a court of law. They threatened to revoke his full pension privileges because he did not serve thirty years.

When he threatened them with his exposure of asbestos he had encountered in their bank over the years, which he backed it up with video documentation, office memos, and a letter from his lawyer, he got his full pension. He'd always advise Maggie, "Use what you've got available. You've *got* to have faith in a system in order for a system to work for you."

Michael and Maggie walked over to his truck. He had been storing it at Maddie's house while he had been riding the rails. He had a box sitting on his front seat.

"What's in the box?" asked Maggie.

"I believe they are flowers for your mother."

"What are they doing in your truck? Why aren't they inside with Mom?"

"I wanted your permission first."

Maggie was confused by what he meant by that statement. Michael removed the lid and pulled out a small blanket. Maggie was preoccupied with the idea of seeing a beautiful bouquet of flowers that she didn't notice what was removed from the box. Being baffled that the box was empty, she found herself peeking deep inside, thinking that the flowers must be squished on the bottom. Throughout her childhood, she strived to remain optimistic at all costs, which undoubtedly followed her into adulthood. Michael cleared his throat to get Maggie's attention. She looked up at him and gasped when she saw what it was that he was holding in his hands.

"Mom's quilt!" she exclaimed. "Where did you find it?"

"I thought it was *our* quilt," he said playfully.

"Oh, I'm terribly sorry about that," she said with a smirk. "It's the anniversary quilt I made for *both* of you a few years ago. I thought it was gone. Where did you find it?"

"She kept it in a box in the back of her closet. I pulled it out last night when I was at the house with the boys. I've *always* known where she's kept it."

"What are you planning to do with it?"

"I wanted to ask you if we, as a family, could place this memory quilt across her casket where a spray of flowers would traditionally be."

Maggie was stunned by the question. She stared at the three-by-three quilt with pictures of important events that complemented their forty-year marriage. Their wedding picture was the large block in the center of the quilt. There were eight pictures that surrounded it; pictures of their parents' weddings, there were two pictures of a favorite grandmother and grandfather, April's graduation picture, Michael's military photo, a rare snapshot of the six of them, and all seventeen grandchildren that had been taken one Christmas Eve.

The colors of the quilt represented their wedding, yellow and green, on a white background and it was trimmed with a rich yellow rose border. Each child and grandchild's name and birth date was linking each photo on the quilt. Maggie also added two ex-stepchildren of Maddie's, who no longer make contact with the family, but they completed the available space between each block perfectly. The center of the quilt beneath the wedding photo read "Michael and April (Connolly) Getman, married on June 20, 1964."

Before Maggie could answer, Maddie and the twins came out to the truck. Maggie instantly knew that they were all in cahoots on their private conversation. Maddie looked at Maggie with a perplexed expression and said, "Well? What's it going to be?" Kobe had his hands buried in his pockets and suggested that by viewing the quilt, then the old people might realize who was family without Aunt Cami having to repeat herself over and over again.

Maggie put her hand on her father's back and said, "Let's do it!" They all proceeded into the funeral home with the quilt tucked under Michael's arm. Kenneth held the door while Kobe proudly led the way. They made their way through the crowded funeral home as Kobe announced, "Coming through!" Michael laid the quilt over the lower lid of April's casket tenderly, as if he were tucking her in for the night.

All eyes were on Michael as he stared at his wife with tears in his eyes. He silently knelt beside her casket for a brief moment. He had a lump in his throat about the size of Texas. For the first time since they all have been inside the funeral home, as a family, they felt like they belonged there and all of the spectators now where aware of it. The five of them have always drawn their strengths from unity in the past. Today was no different.

As Michael stood at April's casket, he embraced his children as each of them cried with him. Everyone in the room watched the family in silence. These strangers had no idea that the tears that were shed were not for the loss of April's life, but for the loss of life years ago. Each member of the family carried suppressed pain throughout the years from that woman. There was so much time wasted being angry. Now it was too late to undo any harm from the past. No more opportunities of making happier memories to help ease the burden of the old.

Maddie pulled out Maggie's keys again and invited them all out to the parking lot. Michael said that he brought a cooler, too, for just such an occasion. Maddie tossed Maggie her keys; she and Kobe followed him out to his truck. Kenneth saw a colleague from work walk into the room. Maggie looked at her watch wondering where her family was and hoping that they were safe. She found herself watching for them to walk through the door every few minutes.

Just as she looked away from her watch, her cell phone rang. It was Alec. He said that they were motoring along and that they were going to stop and eat in Fort Wayne. They decided to drive up to the toll-road, just north of Angola, Indiana, to cut over to Toledo instead of traveling Highway 24, but they still had to deal with the construction in Fort Wayne. He had no idea when they would be arriving.

Maggie suggested that her family meet her at her parents' house and they could drive over to the funeral home together as a family. They would be, at the very least, another few hours yet and Maggie thought she might grab a nap while she waited for them. Even though she looked forward to seeing them, she told them to take their time and drive safely.

Alec said that the kids were doing well, but Allie cried a bit. She was one of the two granddaughters who April chose as favorites. Maddie's daughter, Kelsey, was the other favorite. Their conversation was short so that he could concentrate on the traffic.

Maggie recalled one summer when her family was vacationing at a cabin, on Crooked Lake, in Angola, Indiana. Being an hour and a half away from Toledo, Allie wanted to visit her grandparents. They stopped in to visit Kenneth because his daughter was born. Maggie warned Allie not to ask to spend the night with Grandma April. She didn't want to go into too much detail on reasons why since Allie was close with her grandmother.

They had been vacationing at the lake and Michael came to visit often. He would bring some of his grandchildren along to play with their Indiana cousins. It was a much shorter commute for the family traveling to and from Ohio coming from Angola rather than Indianapolis. April visited once, which was for Mark's birthday party, only because she was pressured to go by the rest of the family.

April pouted the whole time there and remained icy towards everyone present. She did not want a tour of the cabin or the grounds when she came and she definitely did not want to check out the lake with her grandchildren. She tried to use her Sunday commitment as a reason not to attend, but Michael waited for her to get home from church so that she would have no excuses. She was irritated that he had outfoxed her with his patience and persistence. He was not going to take "no" for an answer.

When they stopped in to see Kenneth and his family, April was quietly sitting on the couch while nearly the whole Getman family was stuffed into his little house. April's attitude read cloudy with definite rain showers in her forecast. They could see that her horns on top of her head were beginning to stand tall. Allie, being eleven at the time, asked her grandfather if she could spend the night. She figured that her mother didn't say *not* to ask him; she just knew not to ask her grandma.

"Uh, Grandma? Would you mind if Allie stayed overnight?" pleaded Michael. "I will gladly drive her home in the morning right after breakfast," said Michael nervously as he was wringing his hands.

"*I* don't think so! *I'm* not babysitting tonight! *I'm* not sure what *my* plans are for the evening! Besides, *I* have church tomorrow!" she snapped.

"I said that I would take her home, since I don't belong to your church. I'm not committed like you are," he interjected.

"*I* have better things to do with *my* time than sit in a car for an hour and a half just to see them!" she snapped.

Michael was scrunched into a corner as April continued to go off on her little rampage with her finger in his face. Everyone's eyes were huge! Allie looked at her mother with tears in her eyes and an expression of confusion as to what had just happened. She, being too young and naive, did not know how to read into her grandmother's moods and identify the signs of when April was a ticking time bomb. Maggie sprang from the couch abruptly.

"That's it! It's time to go!"

"Allie can stay with us for the night, Maggie," said Brenda, Kenneth's wife at the time. "Really, she's no problem and we would love to have her. Would you mind if we kept her tonight?"

"No way! We need to go back to Indiana and we need to go right now!"

Maggie looked over at Michael and then at Allie. They both shared a look of panic and desperation. Michael's hands were tightly locked together and his knuckles were white from the stress. Alec tugged on Maggie's shorts to get her attention. Maggie glared down at her husband while he remained seated on the couch. He gave a modest nod of acceptance to the request while his back was towards April, who was still yelling.

Maggie looked over at her father and pitied the man she so deeply respected as her mother had reduced him down to a small, helpless child begging for approval. April was still going on about not having time for anyone but herself. She only saw her Indiana family on the average of three times a year. Maggie then looked back over at Allie and saw that a few tears had fallen. That made Maggie even more furious!

"Don't you dare shed another tear! This is *not* worth a broken heart, Allie," said Maggie with a stern tone.

"I'm sorry, Mom. I'm *really* sorry," mouthed a stunned Allie, trying not to make her grandmother even angrier by showing such weakness.

Maggie hesitated for a moment before making a decision to the overnight request. She gazed around the room with such disbelief that April massacred, not only Allie, but everyone present in the room who witnessed such a tirade.

"I will allow you to stay with your Aunt Brenda and Uncle Kenneth. But only for tonight! I do not want you going to your grandmother's house at all." Michael and Allie sighed with relief, even though Maggie was going against her better judgment.

They hastily grabbed their things and said their good-byes so not to get anyone else in trouble with April. No one could look Maggie in the eye, but she knew their expressions said plenty. Allie walked her family to the car while April and Michael remained inside the house. Maggie held Allie in her arms and whispered in her ear, "This was worse than any punishment you had ever received in your life, don't you think?" Allie remained speechless and shaken as she dried her tears.

"Mom, I had no idea," said Allie.

"She treats everyone like this and today it just happened to be your turn. Miss Allie, you are *not* exempt from Grandma's wrath! I hope you learned that I tell you things with hopes to protect you for your own good. Today, you had a crash course in what happens when you go against your mother. I've known your grandmother longer than you and I could see that she had her fangs ready to shred someone to pieces as soon as we walked through the door."

"I'm sorry that I disappointed you today, Mom," said Allie.

"You could *never* be a disappointment in my eyes. Besides, someone inside that house already fits that description," she said with a harsh tone.

"I just wanted to stay in Toledo because I wanted to spend time with my grandparents and cousins. I didn't mean to make Grandma so angry."

"That's just your grandmother at her worst. She loves us all in her own strange way. I have to believe in that because I've been telling myself that for years. One thing I know for sure is that I love you, Allie, and I will never trade you for the world."

"I love you too, Mom," said Allie as she hugged her mother tight.

"Now what I need for you to do is put this behind you and have a wonderful time with your Uncle Kenneth. Besides, for my peace of mind, take my cell phone. Call me at the cottage or call your dad's cell number. You call me if you need to. I don't care if it is in the middle of the night! You know that I'll be here in a flash!"

"I don't know that I can put this behind me, at least not for a long, long time," said a wide-eyed Allie.

"Something ugly happened here today that you did not deserve. The way I see it, you were Grandma's choice of sacrifice in order to torture your grandfather and me at the same time."

"Did you notice how she cleared the room? I mean *everyone* walked outside during her tantrum. Well, except for my grandparents and Aunt Brenda," giggled Allie.

"Yeah, but your grandfather remained wedged in his corner trying to keep the heat off of you. He had done that for years, Allie."

"My grandpa rocks!" said Allie with a smile.

"Your Aunt Maddie claims that Grandpa doesn't have a butt because Grandma chewed it off years ago," laughed Maggie; trying to disguise the fact that her heart was bleeding over such a sad statement.

Even though Maggie was nervous about leaving her daughter in the lion's den, she did feel better that her daughter walked with lighter steps and she had a smile upon her face after their little chat. Maggie found comfort in the fact that even with April's best attempts to destroy the family; her ugliness could never break the strong bonds that had been in place for generations. However, Maggie worried most about the repercussions that awaited Michael over the next few days from April.

After they left the house, Michael contacted Maggie on Alec's cell phone. "I'm just doing damage control. Are you okay? I'm really sorry for your mother's little outburst."

"No apologies, Dad. One day she will have to take responsibility for her actions. Why are *we* the ones who always apologize for her tantrums?"

"Well, I feel at fault because I provoked her and Allie got caught in the crossfire."

"How did you provoke her? Was it because of you expressing your granddaughter's desire to spend time with her grandparents? Or was it clear to her that that request was something you wanted too?"

"Well, I wanted to thank you for allowing Allie to stay with her Uncle Ken. That really took the wind out of The Old Gray Mare's sails. I'll have her home some time after breakfast."

"No, Dad, I will be there after Mom leaves for church."

"Okay."

"You can do me a favor though. Don't let Mom ruin your night. I refuse for her to ruin the rest of mine," stated Maggie boldly.

"She can't touch my evening because my night was made when you allowed Allie to stay! You missed the expression on your mother's face! I love you guys and drive safely back to Crooked Lake. I've got to run! Your mother is coming!"

Maggie just shuddered at that memory. She remembered driving back to Toledo in the morning to collect her daughter and how she avoided Ontario Street at all costs. She wanted to treat Michael to breakfast before heading back to Indiana, but she did not want to risk April answering the phone if she were running late for church. That was a bad episode of only one of the personalities that they swore April had of five.

Even without knowing Katherine like April did, that was the one personality the family labeled as Katherine. They were not professionals to diagnose such a mental disorder, but they were continuously learning their boundaries over the years and watching for such warning signs for the sake of survival. April's episodes were vicious, whether being provoked or not. She also went through periods of being quiet and withdrawn. That was when Maggie worried most about her mother and somewhat pitied her. As time went on, April wanted nothing other than to be left alone.

Maggie sighed as she looked at her watch again. She decided that it would be a good time to drive to the north end to relax a bit at the house. She put Maddie's cooler in her dad's truck and said good-bye to her family. They were going to stay behind and greet the people coming through the door. There were family members, co-workers, and a few young people April knew from the detention facility. The grandchildren would be arriving after school, too, or when their mothers get out of work. Kyle and Kelsey had to work until six and Chase would be bringing Trey and his son, Jordan, shortly.

As Maggie walked to her car, she saw one of Maddie's ex-husbands, Trey's father, walking across the parking lot. When he and Maddie were newlyweds, he had a motorcycle accident. He sustained an injury to his leg and suffered a mild head concussion. He was lucky to survive not wearing a helmet. He was between paychecks and only had enough change in his pocket to make one phone call. He was a bit disoriented and thought that he could phone April to ask for help. He assumed that his mother-in-law would help him, if not as a family member, then maybe as a neighbor—he and Maddie lived across the street. He was just thankful that he could remember her phone number.

"April, this is Braxton. I had an accident and I need your help. I really messed up my leg and my head is throbbing. My bike is totaled! I am on the corner of Glendale and Reynolds Road. Do you think you could give me a ride home?"

"Oh," she said unsympathetically, "that's too bad. Call someone else because I'm waiting for the clothes to come out of my dryer," April said coldly and hung up the phone.

A Good Samaritan took him home. Braxton was then able to phone Maddie at work. She raced home and took him to the hospital right away. Despite the head concussion and fifteen stitches in his shin, Braxton learned to forgive April's cruelty. However, Maddie was not so forgiving. She grew even more distant from her mother that afternoon. The whole family was disgusted by April's actions. They knew that on a normal day he was not the sharpest tool in the shed, but no human deserved to be treated like that. The Getman family knew all too well that April would make an excuse to avoid helping anyone unless there were something in it for her. Most of her excuses were related to what was on the television at the time because she was a firm believer in exploring her options.

On the way to the house, Maggie drove past the intersection where her boyfriend, Bryce, was killed in a car accident her sophomore year of high school. It was one week before Bryce's senior prom. He and Maggie were making plans for their long-awaited prom night and he laid money down on his tuxedo the day before the tragedy. Maggie was devastated by the news of his accident. She was horrified at the reality of him sending his passenger, a former girlfriend of his, to an early grave right along with him. Of course, this was the same girl whom Bryce constantly complained about and regretted dating a few short months prior to their courtship.

His friends later told Maggie that Bryce had never broke up with the girl. In fact, he bragged to his friends how he was so smooth with the ladies. Maggie's heart sank when she realized the *she* was the other woman! She felt like the most ignorant female on the face of the earth. She also learned that he had a few other girls on the hook. It was some sadistic contest between him and his friends to collect as many girls as possible. Bryce was nothing but a player and Maggie got burned by being so young and naive. She was the last to learn the truth about Bryce, even though they had been an item for six months.

Two weeks before the accident, Bryce told Maggie that she was the girl he wanted to marry. He purchased her a baseball jacket to match the one he proudly wore. He had her name sewn on the front of the navy blue jacket and Toledo was proudly displayed in large block letters on the back. He told her that was all he could afford for an engagement ring at the time. He promised to get her a diamond ring as soon as he could afford one. Maggie was moved to tears. During their courtship, he gave her reasons to question his integrity, yet her heart swallowed everything that Bryce had said and done to her. She didn't know much, but she did know that she loved him with all her heart and soul.

So many emotions raced through her mind at that time. She recalled seeing him stretched out before her in the funeral home, thinking that he was the man she would have died for. He was her world. She was emotionally scared for life by his death and betrayal. The accident was caused by him running a stoplight at a high rate of speed. Bryce was ejected from the vehicle through the windshield and his body continued to roll through the intersection. His date had to be rescued from the car with the Jaws of Life. He was dead on arrival and she died of massive head injuries three hours later. The other driver was not injured because Bryce hit the vehicle that the man was towing.

Already having a low self-esteem, Maggie feared to endure more pain and heartache in future relationships. She worried that she would never be able to trust anyone, much less give her heart to another man. She believed that people who knew her looked at her with pity, which made her fall deeper into her depression. It took two years for Maggie to even consider dating again. Alec was the one and only person she trusted to fall in love with after that nightmare. Alec was the complete opposite of Bryce by honoring such values as love, trust, and honesty. Maggie knew in her heart that Alec would never cheat on her.

Thoughts of Bryce directed her memory to her sweet sixteen birthday party because he was there to celebrate with her. April was drunk and she stayed up all night long. Maggie could hear her playing the I Want a New Drug song, by Hewie Lewis and the News, over and over again on the record player. Maggie would cringe when she would listen to her mother scratch the record before the song would finish and then play it again. It was about six in the morning when April staggered upstairs to Maggie's room. April kicked the door open, which sent it slamming into the foot of Maggie's bed. This unnecessary behavior was no real surprise to Maggie.

"How was Bryce?" she said with a drunken slur.

"What?" asked Maggie, acting as if she was surprised by being awakened suddenly.

"I said, *how* was Bryce!" she shouted as she nearly fell backwards.

"He was *much* better than I *ever* dreamed!" growled Maggie with sarcasm and disgust.

"Oh, I was just asking," she said as if she approved of the loss of her daughter's virginity and staggered downstairs.

Bryce was her first love, but nothing sexual happened to her on her birthday. No one knew the intimate details of her love life, but she did enjoy keeping them guessing. One evening, when April was drunk, she allowed her girls to drive to the east side to a party. She instructed for Maddie to keep an eye on Maggie as if she were loose with the guys. Maggie thought it was a twisted distortion of the truth since she was forever labeled as the nun of the family by Aunt Cami and Maddie, which always left Maggie feeling that walking within the lines of good morals was something to be ashamed of in the eyes of her family.

No matter how Maggie tried to shake her saintly image, she was forever branded with the painful label. She always felt as if she were the bud of every joke by the way Aunt Cami and Maddie would giggle amongst one another when Maggie would walk past. Maddie and Cami shared the same views in life and they enjoyed tormenting people around them due to shear boredom. When Aunt Cami became a grandmother was when she discovered religion, which was when Maddie lost her partner in crime. Nonetheless, Maddie was always Aunt Cami's favorite and Maggie was well aware of her place.

The young girls ended up playing a drinking game, quarters, at a friend's house while his parents were gone for the weekend. It was Maggie's first time playing, which was guaranteed that she was going to get drunk. Maggie was apprehensive about drinking, but she felt pressured to play along in fear of giving the impression of being a goody-goody. Maddie wandered off with Eric, her former boyfriend she continued to see on occasions during the Brad Billings era. Eric and Bryce were best friends, which was how he and Maggie first met.

Just moments before they received the phone call to the party, Kenneth was standing on a toddler spinning toy while twisting from side to side. The toy was old, loud, and ready to be junked. The more irritated Maggie grew by its grinding noise, the more Kenneth twisted his weight on the thing making it just that much louder in spite of his sister. She asked her brother to stop being annoying, but he just looked at her and grinned with each twist.

"Mom, will you *please* tell Kenneth to stop? He is so annoying!"

"Maggie! Shut up and leave Kenneth alone! *You're* the one who's being annoying," snapped April.

Maggie became irritated because she missed a name mentioned, of someone she thought she knew, on the local news. April's eyes were becoming slits because she had been drinking all day. The grin on her brother's face was more than Maggie could bear. She could not tolerate the noise and aggravation any longer. She sprang from the couch just as April threw her head back with the bottom of her beer can tipped high into the air. Maggie drew her arm back as if she were tossing a Frisbee to the moon. She let her arm fly back with great force and hit Kenneth square in the chest with a hollow thud.

Much to Maggie's surprise, he flew backwards with his feet about five feet in the air as Maggie panicked and dove onto the couch, looking like a superhero, flying through the air. Kenneth fell to the floor with a loud crash just as Maggie landed on the couch. Maggie had a look of innocence upon her face as if nothing happened.

Just as April finished the beer, she rested the empty can on her lap and said with a slur, "Be careful, Kenneth, those things are dangerous. Watch so you don't hurt yourself."

"Yeah, Kenneth, don't hurt yourself!" said Maggie, feeling all smug that she got away with hitting the favorite child. Kenneth just had a look of surprise, but never attempted to tattle on his sister. April never saw Maggie get up during that last swig of beer. Maggie secretly prided herself on that for years.

Maggie then reflected on when Bryce came to meet the family for the first time. April openly announced, "Maggie's still a virgin!" as if the information would guarantee her daughter to bag a boyfriend. Maggie felt paralyzed with humiliation. She honestly felt as if she could not move. Bryce just smiled at a blushing Maggie. Being the gentleman that he was, he shared that story with his male friends, who later called her Brandy in reference to the alcoholic beverage, cherry brandy.

Maggie had warned Alec of experiencing an embarrassing moment like her virgin story before he drove from Indianapolis to meet her family for the first time. Just as expected, Alec shook Michael's hand and April said, "Maggie's only had sex once." Maggie was in shock while Michael had an ill expression upon his face. Maggie, once again, felt as if she were on the auctioning block. Alec just winked at a mortified Maggie and said, "Well, as far as what *you* know!" Maggie instantly fell in love with the man as Michael quickly turned his head trying to hide a smile from April.

Chapter 12

Before Maggie knew it, she was pulling into a parking spot in front of April's house. There it sat all empty inside with the exception for Tandy the cat. Maggie turned off her engine and sat in her car staring at the house for a moment. She saw a little girl riding her bicycle on the sidewalk, which triggered a memory of when she was seven years old and the fight she and Maddie had one spring afternoon.

Maddie's godparents bought her a bike for her tenth birthday. It was rare for her to share her things, especially her blue bike with a sissy bar and its sparkly blue banana seat. In Maggie's mind, her sister had it all. She always admired Maddie's gregarious personality, her exciting friends, and especially her possessions. These were the things a younger sister would do that would unintentionally irritate her older sister to no end. She always admired Maddie and wanted to be just like her.

April insisted that the girls take turns on the bike that afternoon since Maggie didn't have a bike of her own. She was stressed and to be bothered by noise from the children was the last thing she needed. April was in one of her cleaning frenzies while Michael was home nursing a bad back. He had been camped out on the couch for weeks.

Michael had been helping a coworker move a filing cabinet up the stairs when he slipped and fell. The cabinet went down the stairs with him. He crushed two discs in his lower back that needed to be removed. The girls did not understand that when Michael was home, he was not getting a paycheck. April later confessed to her daughters that they once had to use food stamps to help them through that difficult financial crunch.

"It's my turn, Maddie! You went to the alley and back twice now. We're supposed to ride only once. That's the rules!"

"It's *my* bike and *I* make the rules!" snapped Maddie. "I will let you ride it to the alley twice when *I* say it's your turn. It's still my turn, so back off!" she yelled as she sped past Maggie.

Maggie waited patiently as she sat on the hood of their black 1963 Chevy Impala. She watched her sister enjoying the freedom of riding her own bike up and down Ontario Street. She would even stop and get off the bike just to annoy Maggie. Finally, April came to the door as Maddie was heading back to the house. Maggie jumped off the car in a flash and Maddie knew by her sister's actions that April had been coming out of the house.

"Here, Maggie, it's your turn," said Maddie cheerfully as she rode up to her sister.

"Okay, Maddie. I get to ride five times to the alley just like you did, right?"

"That's right! What's fair is fair," she said with pride as she helped Maggie get on the bike.

April went back inside the house while Maggie was heading down to the alley for her first of five trips. She was excited and wished that she had godparents as generous as her big sister's. She was coming back to the house and getting ready to turn around for her second trip when Maddie started throwing stones at her.

"Stop it!" shouted Maggie.

"Get off my bike!" she demanded.

Maggie tried to race away from her sister, but Maddie chased after her and was quickly gaining on her. Maddie caught up to her and grabbed the bar on the back of the seat. She tried to make Maggie fall off the bike. Maggie started to cry and scream for her sister to stop, but Maddie kept jerking the back of the bike as Maggie lost control and nearly fell. She guided Maggie toward the street and threatened to push her into it if she didn't get off her bike. The front tire of the bike rolled off the curb and slowly plopped into the street.

"I'm telling Mom that *you* pushed me into the street!" announced a stunned Maggie.

"See if I care! That's what you get for not getting off my bike when I told you to. This is my bike and you can keep your big cootie-butt off of it!"

Before Maggie could tattle on her bully sister, April came flying off the front porch with her bridgework showing and all. Maddie froze in her tracks as her mother stomped towards her in a huff. April hooked Maddie by her arm with her claws and dragged her into the house. The child's arm was lifted high above her head. Maddie was walking on her toes into the house as April escorted her to her destination, which was sure to be the kitchen.

Maggie instantly lost interest in riding the bike. She picked the bike up from the curb and slowly walked it beside the house. She knew that her sister was in big trouble, but she didn't know it was going to result in a dozen beatings with Maddie screaming so loud that people would be coming out of their houses to investigate. Maggie was terrified for her sister and herself. She wanted to run away as she heard her sister beg and plead for April to stop, but she kept hitting the child harder and harder.

Michael jumped up from the couch and slammed the front door so hard that he nearly broke the window. Michael rescued Maddie as soon as his incredibly painful and injured back would allow him to move. He grabbed April's arm as it swung back. He then removed the paddle from her hand, broke the wooden weapon over his knee, and threw it on the counter. April was either surprised by his disarming her or she was so consumed by rage that she forgot that he was home. Michael allowed Maddie to quickly race passed him to get to her room.

"Maggie! Get your ass in here right now!" yelled Michael through the front door a moment later. His anger and profanity dramatically intensified her level of fear.

He took his daughter by the arm and hastily escorted her into the kitchen where she could see the kitchen stool in the middle of the room. She couldn't miss the view of the broken wooden paddle on the counter. Maggie was trembling with fear. Michael pushed her into the kitchen and said, "Here! If you're going to beat Maddie, then you need to do the same to this one!" Maggie leaned over the stool expecting to get hers while her parents argued over her. Maggie was crushed when she heard her father say that, but she was too young to understand that he was daring April to beat another child in his presence.

April sent Maggie to her room for the rest of the afternoon, which the child felt was more of a punishment since she was forced to look at her fuming sister. Maggie might not have been physically beaten like her sister, but her heart felt smashed into a million pieces by her father's comment. To this very day, Maddie never missed an opportunity to bring up that incident and blame Maggie for being a crybaby. That event would forever continue to be a sore topic between the two girls.

Maggie dug out her house key as she approached the steps. Tandy greeted her at the door. She was a little orange tabby cat with a loud purr that could be heard through the door. Maggie was not much of a cat lover, but everyone loved Tandy. She had such a loving personality. Maggie turned on a light because the houses within the city are four feet apart on either side, which made it dark inside the house no matter what time of day. April had a wall filled with pictures of her four children and many grandchildren. Her house looked as if a proud grandmother lived there.

In reality, whenever the family would gather, April could not handle a crowd of people in her house—the more bodies in her house, the darker her mood became towards her guests. She acted as if she had no control because there were just too many people to dominate. April would sit at the edge of her chair as if she were a hawk perched on a ledge, just waiting for the perfect opportunity to swoop in for the kill. She would constantly reprimand her young grandkids, pick on her own children for their lack of parental skills, or belittle Michael for the whole family to see.

Everyone in the family adored Michael and April knew it. That was why she would attack him the most so that she could punish the whole family at the same time. It was very hard on the grandchildren to witness and it became the family tradition that his kids never could stomach. There were moments when April would be in one of her quiet moods and Michael would antagonize her for entertainment purposes. She would react as predicted because she could never turn down an opportunity to verbally spar with the man. His actions appeared to be impulsive, as if years of resentment took over his subconscious, which forced him to lash out at her. Sometimes his children thought he was either bored or suicidal when he did that.

Maggie walked to the dining room to put her purse on the table. She paused for a moment as she saw the scarred paneling that was created by Maddie when she threw a pair of scissors at her during an argument. Maddie also had an episode where she was so mad that she threw a kitchen chair across the room and broke the Formica on Michael's new countertop he made when he remodeled the dining room. It was lucky for Maddie that she missed the sheet of glass where April displayed her garage sale china. Her temper was also responsible for the broken silverware drawer that she slammed shut after discovering that her favorite cup was dirty.

Maddie only acted out like that when their parents weren't home. Most of their fistfights would erupt then, too. Maggie always had bruises on her arms and legs, but Maddie would always claim that Maggie would beat her up from swinging wildly with her eyes shut, which always made Maddie laugh hard enough to fuel Maggie's anger. Their fights were often. Maggie once went after Maddie after discovering her sister put her toothbrush in the toilet. Of course, she didn't realize this until after she brushed her teeth.

One dark evening, Maddie had initiated a game of catch with her sister in their bedroom with a rolled up pair of socks. Unbeknownst to Maggie, Maddie thought it would be funny to put their tiny Mighty Mouse alarm clock inside the sock. She proceeded to whip the wind-up clock across the room at her unsuspecting sister, which made a loud "ding" that echoed in the dark. Maggie's forehead cracked the face of the clock. Maggie knew that she couldn't tattle on her sister because she would also be in trouble for the horseplay on a school night. Maddie laughed herself to sleep as Maggie lay there rubbing the throbbing goose-egg on her forehead; plotting her revenge.

Maggie got even with her one night when Maddie thought it would be fun to guess who was who by feeling faces in the dark. Kenneth and Kobe took turns having her guess their identities when Maggie came into the bedroom. She got so excited that she moved the boys to the side and quietly took her position for Maddie to guess who she was. Maggie bared her butt in her sister's face. It took a moment for Maddie to figure out what was happening. Maddie was furious when she realized that her sister pulled a fast one on her. She reacted by punching her hard on her butt cheek with a loud thwack. They never played that game again. However, Maggie was happy and felt that it was well worth the bruise.

Even though the two girls fought within the home, Maggie would defend her sister if she was wronged by an outsider. Maggie was once in a fight when she was in first grade because of Maddie. She and Maddie were walking home from school and a bully from fourth grade threw an ice ball at a bunch of girls. The girls stood in the middle of the sidewalk in a huddle. They had been giggling nervously because they were too afraid to confront him. Maddie was excluded from the group of classmates, which finally resulted in her getting hit in the leg. Maggie was furious at what she had just witnessed. Not one girl in the crowd offered to help Maddie as she cried out in pain.

Maggie promptly called the boy a booger eater, which sent him dashing across the street after her. Maggie screamed as he chased her around the group of spineless girls. Maddie was the only person standing off to the side cheering for Maggie as the girls were rooting for the bully. Maggie turned around and beat him repeatedly in the head with her tin Mickey Mouse lunch box. He ran away screaming like a girl. The tough guy, who once smoked cigarettes and used excessive profanity, lost his reign as being a bully on that day.

"Hey, kid! You dented my lunch box!" yelled Maggie as the boy ran off crying.

"Thanks, Maggie. But you *do* know that I have to tell on you. I hope that you won't get grounded for too long for fighting," said Maddie anxiously with a mischievous grin.

Maggie was nervous having to face her father, but she was thrilled to not answer to her mother. Much to Maddie's dismay, all that Michael said to Maggie was that fighting should be avoided at all costs. The young child knew she was off the hook as she witnessed a smile that crept across her father's face as he inspected the damaged lunch box. He had told Maddie that she should be thankful for a little sister willing to defend her like Maggie had. Maddie tried to give him suggestions for punishments, but he just walked away from the girls and never discussed the incident again.

As the years moved on, Maggie reached her junior high years. She suffered from culture shock because Riverside School no longer went up to the eighth grade. The city bussed kids from the surrounding north end school districts to a junior high on Manhattan Boulevard. She was uneasy about being thrown in the middle of a bizarre bunch of wild inner-city kids. Ethnic fights happened nearly every day on the bus and she was surrounded by lots of kids who smoked and cursed, which was more of a hostile and intimidating environment from what she was accustomed to at Riverside. Some kids spoke of drug usage, sex, and being actively involved in criminal activities.

Her junior high was a far cry from her elementary years and it soon earned a reputation for being extremely rough. Security guards soon replaced the hall monitors. Maggie's school bus was once driven straight to the juvenile detention center downtown when a spaced-out substitute driver got nervous. He warned the students to remain in their seats while he ran inside for the police. The whole bus evacuated with the exception for Maggie, her friend Krista, and about five other students. They knew that they hadn't done anything wrong and they could only hope that they would not be arrested for being innocent.

Five police cars came screeching their tires next to the bus with their lights and sirens announcing their presence. The students were terrified! Krista was standing in front of her seat, but her legs gave out beneath her from fear. She plopped down in her seat while Maggie stood up. The bus driver ran back to the bus screaming how he wanted the students to be arrested. The police sergeant looked puzzled. His eyes scanned the bus with a look of confusion. He made eye contact with Maggie.

"Young lady, tell me what happened here today," he said with an utmost authoritative voice.

"We were on our way home from school and this driver missed our first stop. A few of us shouted that he missed our stop, but he ignored us. The other kids laughed at us when it happened. But when he missed the second stop, all the kids started yelling for him to stop. The driver continued to ignore us. Everyone started to pound on the ceiling of the bus to get his attention. The next thing we knew, we were taken downtown and he told us we were all going to jail!" said Maggie nervously.

"Is this true, sir?"

"Yes it is! I want them arrested for rioting!" said the irate driver.

"If you had intentionally driven past *my* stop, I would have done whatever it took to get your attention, too!"

"But they were loud and obnoxious," said the driver.

"Young lady," asked the officer, "how many students were on this bus when you pulled up to this curb?"

"Officer, this bus was filled with kids. Most of us sit three to a seat."

The officer motioned for the squad cars to leave while he remained on the bus making sure that the students were calm. Two girls had been crying towards the rear of the bus. The sergeant walked to the back of the bus and closed the emergency door. He told the girls that they had done the right thing by not running away from something they had not done wrong in the first place.

The sergeant turned to speak to the driver, who was anxiously waiting to see the remaining children escorted to the building in handcuffs, and said in a stern voice, "Mister! You are going to drive each student home today and you will deliver them to their front doors!"

"Yeah, but they..."

"You better hope that their parents don't press charges on you for kidnapping! I will be calling the department of transportation and reporting your name. You better hope that *all* the children from your bus make it home safely because *you* are responsible for them. Now, get this bus out of here and take these kids home! I will be seeing that you do just that!"

The bus driver had to ask where to drop kids off and he delivered them without further incident. The police officer followed the bus as promised. Rumor had it that the substitute driver was just a mechanic. They were running short of drivers that afternoon. He was ordered to drive the route, which was something he protested. It was just a form of rebellion against an establishment he no longer wanted to be a part of. There was never a dull moment at that school.

Within the school were teachers who were very strict. One in particular enjoyed intimidating his students by walking up and down the rows while sporting a large wooden paddle. He once paddled a child named Rickie Johnson because Maggie hummed a tune in class. The teacher, thinking it was Rickie, warned him not to do it again because the boy couldn't carry a tune to save his life. Maggie forgot the warning five minutes later and poor Rickie was paddled. This man strived to hit at least one student a day.

When the school had its open house, this particular teacher's room was filled wall to wall with angry parents. Michael was one of them because of a math test Maggie failed. She had all the right answers, but he insisted that she worked the problems out wrong. The teacher stood at his podium trying to look bright and sophisticated, but his intimidation tactics were not working on the parents. Maggie was quick to notice that the wooden weapon was out of sight for parent night. On the first day of seventh grade, this man announced to his class that he wanted them to know that he cared for them just as much as he did a turd on the lawn.

Maggie had homework every day after school. She never had time to play with her friends because her first priority was to clean the house and have dinner ready before April got home. She made sure her brothers had their after-school snacks and homework finished. She also did the dishes after dinner, which gave her enough time to finish her homework before she had to go to bed and start her day over again. This was not too long after Maggie stopped going over to the eastside for the weekends to clean for Aunt Paula. The child had a huge portion of adult problems forced upon her emotional plate.

She nearly had a nervous breakdown toward the beginning of that school year because she could not stop crying one morning on the way to the bus stop. She could not explain what was wrong and she began to hyperventilate. Krista walked her back home regardless of the risk of her missing the bus. April allowed her to stay home because she figured it was just hormones working. She never asked what was wrong because she thought it was cute that her little girl was premenstrual.

Maggie's mind thumbed through the pages of her memory as her eyes wandered about the house. Memories surfaced from every corner of every room. The house still had the strong essence of April's presence. Maggie felt as if her mother would walk around the corner any minute. It was such a strange feeling to realize that she was gone forever. Her once thunderous footsteps were now forever silenced. Maggie felt a blanket of sadness consume her at the thought of something so final. She wished that she would have had one more moment to say something nice to her mother, but sadly that moment had passed without warning.

Maggie searched into the depths of her mind of when things got out of control with her mother. She recalled that it was when Kenneth and Kobe were in first grade was when April decided to work outside of the home. She got a job from a neighbor who was an auto parts manager. April took a minimum wage job as an auto parts delivery person. Maddie was a teenager and she ran wild, desperately clinging on to her remaining childhood years. Maggie was almost eleven when her mother became absent in the home, which was the time frame in Maggie's life that marked the end of her childhood.

April began drinking shortly after she started her new career. It didn't take long before her drinking became a problem. It seemed to the family that she couldn't function without her beer. She was always in a bad mood when she came home from work. No one could understand why because she would be smiling in her vehicle, but it would quickly disappear as she walked towards the house. She would scold the girls for not cleaning the house or having dinner ready when she got home. There was *always* something for her to complain about. Judging by April's actions, Maddie figured that her mother was happiest anywhere but home.

Michael would try to shield his daughters from her criticisms, but she would then turn her anger on him. "You're not the only one working outside of the home! You can clean this dump just as easily as they can," April would often say to Michael. She would then snap at her girls, "Now you'll know the hell I went through all these years! This is *my* time now!" They heard that statement for years, which reaffirmed their suspicions of her resigning as a wife and a mother. In April's mind, her domestic titles were viewed as time served.

Every evening after work, without fail, Michael would have an ice cold beer waiting for his hardworking wife. He would do anything to keep her happy. It got to the point where he would plead with his girls to do the dishes long before their mother got home just to keep her content. Michael once got on his knees and begged them not to fight so that April would not have a reason to be in a foul mood when she got home. Their arguments about the dishes usually ended with Michael finishing the task for them while he feverishly raced against the clock. Michael soon became a nervous husband; therefore, he had nervous children to follow his lead.

Maggie felt overwhelmed and trapped with the grueling demands of April's domestic check-off list because she knew that she was in this alone. Maddie was not around long enough to be tied down with silly things like chores. She felt that she was beyond such nonsense. Maggie had dinner on the table every night when her parents got home from work, she did the laundry, she cleaned the house, and she even had to watch over her brothers. It was expected of her.

Michael tried to ease the burden of cooking by purchasing meat and gravy dinners for the oven. All that Maggie had to do was peal five pounds of potatoes every day and make sure she timed the directions of the entrees with finishing at the same time the potatoes would be done. Sometimes Michael would phone from the office to remind Maggie of when she should start preparing the meals. April felt that was too easy for her daughter, so she demanded a fresh salad prepared for every meal. Michael had done dishes on Maddie's nights just to avoid more tension in the house.

Kobe began to suffer with his grades and he complained of health problems until April threatened to take him to the hospital for painful shots. The first grader was instantly cured. April missed his cues of what really ailed him, which was nothing other than a little boy who missed his mother. He ended up struggling with school all the way throughout his academic career. It was later suspected that he might have had a learning disability.

Kenneth got by fine with his grades in school. When he was in third grade, Maggie played a joke on him. She confronted him in his bedroom as if she had incriminating evidence on him and said, "I know what happened today in school. Don't you think you ought to tell me in your own words what really happened?" she asked with a raised eyebrow. "If you don't, I'll be forced to tell Mom," she said with a deceitful sigh.

"I didn't do nothing wrong," he said with painful look of guilt.

Maggie caught the look of panic and rather enjoyed watching him squirm. She folded her arms across her chest and asked, "Are you *sure* about that?"

"Well," he said with hesitation, "I never thought I'd get caught! I mean it was an accident!" he stammered.

"How did it go down?" she asked as if she were interrogating him. "Let's say we start from the top."

"Lucy Lawson told Mrs. Getty that I had a dirty magazine. It wasn't dirty! It had cartoons that just so happened to be naked. Everyone knows that cartoons are for kids!" he said as his bottom lip quivered.

"Ha! I was just joking!" she exclaimed as she pointed a finger in his face. Kenneth was stunned! "I never knew that anything happened in school today," she laughed.

He never forgave her for that little incident. He was a fast learner and he was *never* that gullible again throughout his life. Maggie never snitched on her brother because she felt that he was punished enough through her enjoyment. Kenneth had always been cautious after that, which has made him a much wiser person.

The twins were a handful growing. They knew Maggie was just a kid herself and they pushed the envelope with her on a daily basis. April finally told Maggie that she could discipline the boys when they needed it. That included spankings and groundings. Maggie made a checklist and if they got more than five check marks in one afternoon, then they would be punished. April rarely heard about their poor behavior because they had it worked out before she got home. No matter how angry her brothers would make her, Maggie could never put her brothers through April's wrath.

The mothers in the neighborhood thought of Maggie as the perfect child. They assumed that she just jumped right in with the housework to help her mother at home with no arguments. Little did they know that her duties were expected of her. No one outside of the household knew what exactly went on inside that house. Once again, another well kept family secret.

The neighbors' perception of life in the Getman house was far from the truth. Maggie once got scolded for not moving the couch away from the wall and vacuuming the floor beneath it. April also insisted on polishing the woodwork that was not visible. Mops were forbidden in their house because April claimed that mops are useless because they do nothing but move the dirt around the floor. April insisted that there were no easy methods to cleaning the house. A house could only be cleaned by the good old fashion theory of working one's fingers to the bone. Maggie became exhausted, physically and emotionally, trying to clean the house to meet her mother's expectations. She later learned that there was never any pleasing that woman.

April would march through the door and give her infamous surprise white glove inspections. These inspections usually occurred when the girls had a special event planned with friends. April enjoyed holding that kind of leverage over her girls. Maddie had many plans dashed by the hand of her mother. Sometimes April said "no" just to say it. She rather enjoyed the look of disappointment on Maddie's face the most. Maddie learned to hide her excitement and joy of any upcoming events to lessen her mother's power over her. It didn't take long for the child to quit trying to win her mother's approval all together. Maddie simply didn't care anymore.

The deeper April fell into the bottle, the more rebellious Maddie grew. April and Maddie began to really despise one another with each passing day. Their relationship affected the whole family. Maddie started to cut class when she dated Eric Walters. He was a kid who didn't have a father and his mother worked the streets. He was a good-looking kid, despite his weak eye that would go astray when he was nervous or tired. This guy enjoyed getting his dog high by sharing his drugs. Eric was known for his short temper. He tried to dominate Maddie, which eventually ended their relationship. She knew that he cheated on her several times in the past, but she later enjoyed being his mistress rather than his girlfriend.

Maddie would constantly come home with hickies on her neck just to irritate April. "Why don't you just have him urinate on you to show ownership and dominance," April would say to her about the love bites. He was a poor houseguest and never seemed to know when to leave. He would stay at the house until late in the evening. April would never leave them alone for a moment. They always cuddled beneath a blanket, even during the hot summer months. They both left an impression that they were up to no good. Maddie later confessed to Maggie that her theory was true.

One evening in particular, Maddie went to bed early, which was out of character for her. When April was getting ready for bed, she heard a noise, which came from Maddie's bedroom downstairs. She crept downstairs and tip-toed to Maddie's room. She threw open the bedroom door accompanied with a quick flick of the light switch.

There stood Eric, looking like a deer in the headlights, stark naked, while Maddie said nothing and cowered under her covers. April threw that kid out onto the porch scared and naked. She launched his clothes out the front door before she slammed it shut. He never came back to the house again, but Maddie continued to sneak around to see him.

Later that summer, April was really drunk and was obsessed with spying on Maddie just to prove that her daughter was up to no good. April drove to Eric's house, searching for Maddie, and invited herself into the house without knocking. She walked into every room of the house accusing Eric's mother of harboring her underage daughter. April just missed Maddie moments before because, as luck would have it, she got a ride back home. April was threatened to have the police called on her if she didn't leave their house at once.

"I'll leave alright! This place is a pigsty! Did you fire the maid or did she quit?" she said with a slur.

"Get out of my house, you drunken bitch!" shouted Eric's mother as she pushed April out the front door.

Maddie happened to contract mononucleosis shortly after that little episode, which April was quick to accuse Eric of infecting her daughter. She called his mother and implied that Eric needed to get a blood test to prove that he was the carrier for mono. She accused him of being an unclean individual and his germy mouth infected her daughter. Much to April's surprise, he tested negative. The boy's mother took advantage of a perfect opportunity to tell April that *her* daughter must have received it from another boy.

Their relationship soon ended when he beat her up in the alley. He accused her of sleeping around on him when she had an extracurricular activity with her class after school. After he hit her, he tried to apologize by throwing his fist through a window of an abandoned house. As she walked away from him, he pulled out his knife and cut his wrists to where he left scratches, not gashes. Maddie was horrified. This was something larger than she was capable of fixing. She was in way over her head.

When Eric was in his thirties, he attempted suicide in front of his mother by shooting himself in the head with a gun. He survived it and continued to live with his mother. He hung around harden criminals like Tim Peters, Aunt Cami's former roommate. Eric represented what could happen when one, not only lived in the north end, but became the north end. He was a good-looking man that had always been unpredictable with his volatile temper.

Maddie's chip on her shoulder grew out of control and she carried an attitude of hatred towards her whole family. She would rather be anywhere else but at home, which appeared to be a Connolly women's trait. She started to hang with the drug dealers down the street. She lied all the time and would pick fights with Maggie for entertainment purposes. When she was fifteen, Michael bought her a pack of cigarettes and said, "Here, I know that you smoke anyhow." Maddie claimed that she smoked because she was talked in to it at home. Maddie continued to defend her innocence on not doing drugs, during that time frame of her life, well into her adulthood. However, with her wild mood swings during that period made the family think differently.

April attempted to ground Maddie constantly. April accused her of doing things just to snag an excuse to inflict misery upon her daughter. April's favorite word to Maddie was always "No!" Maddie would finally walk out of the house daring April to try to stop her. Arguments between the two were a nightly event. The screaming matches between mother and daughter took its toll on the family. The family fell to pieces and not one person knew what to do. Michael was always between April and Maddie's arguments while Maggie tried to shield her brothers from the ugliness.

Michael chased after Maddie one evening, around midnight, after he sided with April during one of many arguments. He was at his wits' end and he was tired of the constant bickering in the house. April always accused him of sticking up for Maddie, despite who was right or wrong. He would hear the same complaint from Maddie about April. He always felt as if it were a game of tug of war, in which he was the rope and it was a constant no win situation. Tensions were always high in that house.

Maddie kept a minimal distance of two house lengths away from him. He begged her to stop, but the closer he got to her, the greater the distance she created between them. Finally, a motorcycle stopped on the corner and offered her a ride. She straddled the bike and turned to see that her dad wasn't there. She was a bit alarmed by Michael's absence, but she continued to escape with the stranger. Michael stepped out from behind a tree as he watched the red glow of the biker's taillight fade into the night. He worried himself sick about the safety of his daughter. He often wondered when the heartache would end. He walked home alone feeling helpless and defeated.

April became consumed with her drinking and it only fueled her negative feelings toward Maddie. She told Maggie that she could not legally touch Maddie in a way she fanaticized about, but she suggested that Maggie could do it for the sake of the family. Maggie knew it was crazy, but her mother sounded so desperate. "If we can get Maddie straightened out, then our family will go back to the way we used to be. Think about it, Maggie, *you* could be our only hope."

Maggie was in the eighth grade then and took her mother's suggestion to heart. It sounded tempting for things to go back to normal. Maggie figured that she could take on her sister with no problems because April suggested that the good guy always wins. After listening to her mother, it *was* obvious to everyone that Maddie was a bad seed. Maggie started to get her mind set on having a confrontation with her sister that morning before school.

Like clockwork, Maggie just got in the bathroom to get ready for school and Maddie started beating on the door. Maggie warned her to go away and leave her alone, but Maddie turned the light switch off, which was located on the outside of the bathroom door. Maggie got dressed in the dark. She sat on the side of the tub for five minutes only to infuriate her sister. Maddie tried to walk into the bathroom, but the deadbolt wouldn't allow her to do so.

After about twenty minutes in a dark bathroom, Maggie decided to let her sister in to get ready for school. As Maggie walked past her, Maddie gave a shove with her shoulder, sending Maggie into the wall. Maggie stood there for a brief moment being stunned and then reacted by pushing her back as hard as she could. Maddie took a swing at her sister and the fight was on. They continued with the punching all the way down the stairs. They'd been in fights before, but they only hit on the arms and legs.

Maddie pushed Maggie into the kitchen table to where she fell backwards and skid the furniture across the room. Maggie got up and started swinging wildly at her sister. Maddie put her new class ring to the test and punched her sister in the eye so hard that it sent her airborne. She flew into April's owl lamp and nearly broke it along with the end table Maggie landed on. Maggie grabbed her face with a scream while Maddie tried to shake the pain from her aching hand.

Michael and April ran downstairs to break up the fight, but it was plain to see that it was now over. April ran for Maddie and pinned her up against the wall. Michael grabbed April to free his daughter. Maggie could not help feeling betrayed that her mother showed no concern for her being injured. She was stunned watching how her parents fought over her sister. Maddie was heading for the door as Michael threw his car keys to her so she could make a quick get-away from April.

"Go to school and we'll talk about this later!" he said.

"Hey! Thanks, Dad!" she said with a grin as she ran out of the house.

The argument between Michael and April was just about as short and severe as the girls' fight. Maggie got no sympathy from either of her parents. After Maddie left the house, Maggie became invisible. April was furious that Michael didn't punish Maddie. After listening to their argument, it suddenly occurred to Maggie that her mother put her up to this fistfight only to see if Michael would punish his precious Maddie. It was obvious that Michael failed the test. Maggie felt betrayed by both of her parents that morning. She even felt disappointed with herself for being so gullible. She was used as a pawn in her mother's pathetic game of parenting.

As her parents' argument continued, Maggie had to walk to the bus stop with her throbbing black eye. Maggie was embarrassed, especially when the assistant principle of her junior high had questioned her when she got to school on who did that to her. It was obvious that he was ruling out child abuse from home. He sent her to the nurse's office for some ice. Maggie's friends confirmed her story when they were called down to the office throughout the day. It was all in a days work for the public schools to investigate any suspicious activity involving a child.

Later that afternoon, Maddie confronted Maggie about their little morning scuffle. Maggie initially thought she was going to apologize or call some sort of truce, but she was being naive and overly optimistic, which was a large part of her nature that usually left her disappointed many times in her life. Maddie's intentions were bad. In fact, she wanted to continue where she left off earlier that morning.

"Did you enjoy the special ingredient I added to your breakfast this morning? It really packs a *punch*, doesn't it?" said Maddie smugly.

"Don't you worry, I'd be willing to go again," Maggie said as her sister laughed. "It might not be today or even tomorrow, but I promise you that you'll get yours. And when you do, you will know it," she promised.

"In your dreams!" Maddie responded sharply.

"Be patient, big sis. I promise you that you will get yours! I may not even have to result to violence. I am much smarter than you and I have more patience. Just remember this conversation and know that I am watching you. You have been warned and you better watch your step."

"Whatever! That's an awful big threat coming from a little girl who got her ass kicked this morning!" she said as she flipped Maggie's math book off the table. Maggie chose to ignore her sister as she continued to walk away from her.

Nearly one year later, almost to the very day, Maddie's senior year was coming to an end. Her friends from school approached Maggie at her locker to have a conversation about Maddie. Maggie was frightened at first because Maddie told her that her friends wanted to beat her up and shove her in a locker. Maggie was never sure if that were true because they always said hello to her in the hallway between classes.

"Maddie hasn't been to class in two weeks! We are getting tired of her getting away with it. Especially when *we* have to be here every day like she should be."

"What do you mean she isn't here? She drove us to school today."

"We're tired of her bragging about spending time with Brad and not getting caught. Sometimes his dad picks her up while she leaves your dad's car in the parking lot to throw off any suspicions. She gets dropped off just before school lets out for the day."

"Are you serious?"

"We thought your mother might like to know about it!"

Maggie went home that afternoon and was surprised to see April home for the day because she was ill. Maddie never drove Maggie home after school because she always had more important things to do. Maggie had to rely on the Tarta bus for transportation. She didn't mind it much because she was with her friends. The kids in her school called the public buses, "The Iron Pimp!" That afternoon, it was just Maggie and April home alone having a little chat.

"I saw Maddie's friends at school today. They're a nice group of girls."

"Maddie has friends?" she said sarcastically.

"They told me to give you a message," which held April's attention.

"What would any of Maddie's friends have to say to me?"

"Oh, something like Maddie has been skipping school the past two weeks."

"What?! I'm going to kill her! Grab the phonebook and get the school on the line!" demanded April.

Being a Friday afternoon, Maggie wasn't sure if anyone would still be in the office. After the phone rang about seven times, someone finally answered. It happened to be Mrs. Dupont, Maddie's school counselor. April grabbed the phone and told the woman what she just learned about her daughter.

She put April on hold while she pulled Maddie's file from the drawer. She came back and said that there was a stack of written excuses dating back to her freshman year. She said that Michael Getman signed most of them while the rest were signed by April. She did notice a discrepancy in handwriting. There were three notes signed by April that were different from the other twenty or so. All that April said after she hung up was, "I'm going to kill her!"

It was a long weekend in the Getman household since the truancy was discovered on a Friday afternoon. April phoned Michael at the office and he came home immediately. He walked to Brad's house from the bus stop to retrieve his car and daughter. He had given up his vehicle so Maddie could drive to school. He thought he could trust her. Maddie never said a word in her defense because she knew that she had made her only ally furious.

April was infuriated with Maddie. Michael sat quietly while his wife grilled her for hours. Maddie pleaded the fifth and kept her mouth shut, which made April even angrier. She was being stripped of privileges starting with not seeing Brad, and then came the loss of her car privileges, and finally, she had dishes for a month. Maggie was shaking in her shoes but refused to let Maddie see her sweat. Maggie had learned to master the poker face.

On Monday morning, during third hour, Maggie was in gym class. She and Krista snuck into the hallway to catch a glimpse of the counselor's office across the courtyard.

They could see that April was sitting on the edge of her chair while Maddie remained slouched in hers with her legs sprawled about. Maggie never saw Michael so upset and serious in her whole life.

"Oh, my gosh, Maggie! I will say a prayer for you. Maddie is going to kill you!" said Krista.

"I know. I have to live in the same house! What have I done?" said Maggie being wide-eyed and nervous.

"Wow, this is big."

"Yeah, now I wish I didn't leave that note in the cover of her book."

"You left a note? What did it say?"

"Pow! I gotcha!"

During the meeting, Maddie was threatened with being brought up on charges of forgery. There were only three excuses from April and two from Michael that were legitimate. She was also threatened to repeat her senior year due to truancy. April was all for sending her daughter to the juvenile detention facility, but Michael refused to send her down that road. Family counseling was strongly recommended, but April refused that path. Maddie only had to serve detention for the remainder of the school year, which was only about six weeks, and her senior prom privileges had been revoked.

Maddie never said a word about her getting caught to Maggie. She chose to ignore it altogether. Arguments still occurred on a near daily basis between the girls, but it was life as usual during that time period. The twins still adored their big sister, but she never gave them a second glance. She broke their hearts regularly, which really irritated Maggie. Maggie spent more time with the boys than her sister did, but she knew that she could never be looked up to as much as Maddie. After all, Maggie had once looked up to her sister, too.

Maddie's behavior was out of control. She once came home from school with a friend to discover that Maggie was wearing a lavender blouse of Maddie's that she had outgrown.

"Take it off!" she warned. Maggie started to go upstairs to her bedroom to change her shirt, but Maddie couldn't wait that long. Maddie lunged at her fleeing sister.

"I'm going, I'm going!" she said as she attempted to run upstairs while Maddie was on her heels.

"You don't have the tits to wear such a shirt!" she said as she grabbed the back of the blouse and ripped it right off Maggie's back.

She was embarrassed as she tried to cover herself in front of company. Maddie's friend, Penny, was not impressed by Maddie's display of bullying. Penny was the friend who, later that summer, slept with Maddie's hooligan boyfriend, Brad. She was also the same friend who was cruising up and down the streets with Maddie, jamming to the radio while listening to their favorite songs from Journey on a beautiful sunny day. Penny drove a huge pea-green Buick that they referred to as the boat.

They had their hair and makeup perfected only moments before they left the house. The teens did not have a care in the world as they smoked their cigarettes while trying to look cool. April was washing her car in the front of the house as the girls motored down Ontario Street. April watched them coming down the street and crouched between the parked cars like a stalker. Out of nowhere, she lunged at them with the hose just as they drove by and fired the nozzle as if it were a gun. They screamed as Penny nearly hit a parked car.

"You stupid bitch!" screamed Penny.

The word bitch was a fighting word for April. That was the one word she could never tolerate. On that particular day she chose to ignore it. Maggie witnessed the event and couldn't believe her mother's actions. April had a direct hit. Penny's window was rolled all the way down when April jumped into the street with the nozzle of the hose, which was only about two feet from Penny's face. Maddie just happened to lean around Penny to see what was happening when she, too, was blasted in the face. Maggie couldn't help laughing out loud at her mother's juvenile behavior.

That was the same summer Maddie discovered her new boyfriend, Brad Billings, the young man who robbed the Chicken Joint. He was a drummer in a country and western band with his family. Their family was not very reputable. His father was a con artist from Kentucky and Brad had a brother in jail for grand theft auto, which Penny corresponded with regularly.

Maggie knew he was bad news before she even met him, but Maddie was head over heals in love with him. Brad was smooth with the ladies, all of them! He sang songs to women and wrote them poetry. He always knew what to say during any given situation. Maggie tried to warn her sister about him being a bad seed, but what did a child know about love? Maddie was convinced that he was the best thing in her life. It was destined to be another rough summer with Maddie.

Chapter 13

Maggie opened the refrigerator to see what looked good to eat before she had to be back at the funeral home. She hoped that Alec and the kids dined somewhere nice. Maggie really wasn't hungry, but it was as if she was scanning the chilled shelves for suggestions out of habit. She saw a meat tray, which she did not have to worry about it being too old because Kobe said that the neighbors had been bringing food to the house.

She saw April's chocolate covered nuts on the top shelf. Sweets were her mother's downfall. April was approximately eighty pounds overweight and she had to have her daily chocolate fix. Maggie turned around and looked at the snack drawer with a chuckle. She already knew what was inside of it without having to look. Her mother had a sweet tooth just like Grandpa Bo. April loved her chocolate covered nuts while Bo's favorite snack was Oreo cookies with butter and peanut butter. Nothing looked good to eat, so she closed the refrigerator door with a sigh.

Thinking about Grandpa Bo's living until he was eighty-five was amazing. He was a man who had expensive toys. He invested in fast cars and Harley Davidson motorcycles, which he has crashed a number of bikes in his prime. He always had the best of everything. It appeared that he had all he needed in life to be happy. It even seemed to his family that he was contented with being secluded from his four daughters. He was always a prideful man, but his Alzheimer's disease took its toll in the end.

Kathleen lived the closest to her father and she looked after the elderly couple. But when Bo's life was nearing its end, it was sad to learn that Donna could not handle visiting him in the nursing home. Kathleen felt that her father did not notice her absence much, but in the end, he would ask to see Ruby. Donna told Kathleen that she could not handle seeing him in such a frail and weak state. She said that she was humiliated for his being reduced to a small man. This was a state of mind that Kathleen had trouble understanding. She felt that Donna had abandoned her father when he needed her the most. His girls were at his side when he died while his stepson, Thad, had been busy sorting through possessions he might inherit at home.

It was assumed that Donna was the one responsible for not relaying phone messages and letters to Bo over the years from his family, but no one could know that for sure. There had been speculation that Donna convinced Bo throughout the years that his girls wanted nothing from him but his money and possessions. After hearing it time after time, he started to believe her. He trusted no one and he locked all his valuables in various safes around the house. He kept his special key ring in his front pocket for safekeeping. His disease made him paranoid enough to bury his most prized possessions in his yard.

"Your grandfather is not an easy man to live with," Donna would tell Maggie on rare family get-togethers. "In fact, you have no idea about living life with the real Bo Connolly at all. There are days where he's downright unbearable!" she would say with a look of desperation on her face.

After Bo's death, it was learned that his Alzheimer's disease was getting dangerous for Donna to be alone with the man. Kathleen would report to the family that he might repeat the same story in about a five minute time span while Donna would say that Bo would hit her when no one was around. She said that he demanded sex in the middle of the night after he accused her of cheating on him. Donna told the family that she had to constantly remind him that she was *not* Ruby! He apologized to his girls for not being a better father and he asked Cami to tell Donna that he was sorry for deserting her. That confirmed to Cami that her father understood that he was dying. Cami and Ginny began to question Donna's accusations about their father.

Here sat an example of two people who lived with the consequences of an adulterous mistake years ago and continued to deal with it every day of their marriage. Donna's twins, Thaddeus and Theodore, always called him Uncle Bo and his ex-wife Aunt Ruby. These fraternal twins were treated differently from their stepfather. Bo was harshest with Thad, who later became a raging alcoholic. When that child was young, there wasn't anything he could do right in the eyes of his Uncle Bo. It was always sad to see a family suffer the way they had from making bad choices from days gone by.

A few years prior to Bo's death, Maggie drove from Indianapolis to visit her grandfather in Providence Hospital, which is located in Sandusky, Ohio. She got stuck in a rainstorm in Fort Wayne and was forced to pull to the side of the expressway. Her windshield wipers quit working in the middle of a downpour.

Her car shook violently as a semi-truck, pulling double trailers, rumbled past her. The truck appeared to be about a foot away from her car. She wondered if her car was sticking out into the lane, so she opened the passenger door to judge how much of the shoulder she could see. Much to her surprise, she saw a drop-off about one hundred feet down. She only had a remaining six inches or so of the shoulder before she would have found out the hard way.

She was at the halfway point of her trip and decided to motor on to see her grandfather. He had a heart condition and she feared she might not ever see him again. She had a nagging urge to tell her grandfather something from the heart. She feared this would be her only opportunity to tell him. The rain slowed down and she latched on to the taillights of a tanker truck all the way to her exit in Ohio.

She picked up April on the way to the hospital, which was something Maggie felt pressured to do. She wanted to thank her grandfather in person for being the *only* member in her family to ever offer her support with college. She felt that she could not openly say it in front of her mother. Besides, she felt it was a private matter that was just between the two of them. She ended up writing a thank-you note, which Maggie told April was just the standard get-well-soon card.

As they entered his room, Maggie stifled a giggle when she saw him sitting on the edge of his bed with his boxers hanging out the back of his opened hospital gown. He was always a big tough guy, which he still carried the same look despite his hospital attire. Maggie was relieved to see that he actually looked healthy. He was hospitalized because he had a racing heart that was having difficulty getting regulated. They discovered it when he went to his doctor for a bladder infection. Donna was sitting next to his bed. They were both surprised to see April and Maggie.

Maggie gave her grandparents a hug and she slid the card behind the water pitcher on her grandfather's nightstand. Bo saw that she tried to hide it, but he grabbed it as she turned away.

"What's this?" he asked with a lighthearted tone.

"Oh, it's nothing. It is just the same old boring get-well-soon card," she said with a red glowing face.

"Okay, I guess I will just have to read this later," he said with a smile. He knew something was in there, but he respected her feelings enough to open it in private.

The women in the room stood against the wall making small talk and commenting about the rain. Maggie told her grandfather about her windshield wipers and he teased her about driving a GM vehicle. She half expected that because he was retired from Ford. He and Alec used to go back and forth with the teasing at family functions. Aunt Kathleen's husband, Sam, worked for Chrysler and he, too, got in on the action.

"I have something to say to you, Maggie," Bo said out of the blue with a serious tone to his voice. April and Donna stopped talking to hear what he had to say.

"Yeah, Gramps?" she said, hoping that she wasn't in trouble.

There was silence in the room as he paused a moment, which felt like an eternity to Maggie. He looked his granddaughter in the eye and took a deep breath. An uneasy feeling came over her. Maggie searched her mind to find some sort of hint as to what it was she might have done wrong. She always loved and respected her grandfather, but to make him angry was something she never wanted to do. Maggie's heart started to pound so hard that she could almost hear it out loud.

"If I would have known what *that* son-of-a-bitch from the eastside had been doing to you over the years, I would have killed him with my own two hands," he belted out without batting an eye.

Maggie tried real hard not to drop her jaw to the floor. She really concentrated on maintaining her poker face. She was shocked by the conversation and how it came out of the blue. She had felt stripped naked in front of her grandfather. She wanted to scream, *Oh, my God, he knows! They all know!* Maggie had a lump in her throat that forbid her to speak. Her whole body felt numb. Bo never took his eyes off of her.

"When I found out about it, which was recently, I nearly came unglued. It was lucky for that bastard that he died before I got a hold of him!"

She knew then that Aunt Kathleen told him everything. She lived closest to him and Uncle Doug was his former brother-in-law. He sat on his bed as they all witnessed his face getting red. Donna tried to warn him not to get angry because his heart was being monitored around the clock. He never looked at anyone else in the room but Maggie. It was as if their conversation was for no one else to hear but the two of them.

"The very thought of any mother putting her children in the care of a monster like that ought to be shot! I mean that literally! What type of behavior is expected of individuals who openly ran around with gangsters? I would really like to know the answer to that question," he said as he glared at April.

He finally looked away to the floor as April nervously shifted from foot to foot. April remained silent as she gazed out the window. Maggie had to concentrate on her breathing because she felt as if she were holding her breath the whole time. She was feeling a bit lightheaded. Bo picked up his card and placed it under his pillow. The nurse came in the room to check his blood pressure. She made sure he was comfortable before she left the room. His eyes again met Maggie's. He knew she was uncomfortable with the topic at hand. He knew he had to comfort his granddaughter somehow.

"There is one thing I need for you to know," he said tenderly. "Where ever you go in this world or whatever you may do, I want you to remember what I'm about to tell you. If ever you feel a sudden surge of heat come over you, just know that it's me sending you a big hug reminding you that I love you very much. I always have and I always will. There is nothing or no one that could possibly destroy that."

April's and Donna's jaws dropped simultaneously. Maggie stood against the wall with tears in her eyes. As she walked over to him, she felt as if she were floating, as she gave him a hug. He held her tightly in his arms and whispered that he appreciated her coming and he would read her card later. He kissed her on the cheek and reminded her to never forget what he said and that he meant every word of it.

When April and Maggie left the hospital, April never said a word. That was a turning point in their relationship for the worse. Maggie felt bad for her mother because she knew those were words she has always longed to hear from her father and she now knew that she never would. Donna was just as surprised by Bo's rare display of affection. He had always been a gruff kind of a person. Warm and fuzzy was not part of his character.

Maggie's reminiscing made her feel as if she had taken a mental nap for hours. She turned the radio on to help liven up the house. Music was always the wonder drug for her when she was feeling blue. As she was drawing a glass of water from the tap, she heard a song that reminded her of the days when April was drinking heavily. In the beginning, April was a funny drunk, then she advanced to a frisky drunk, and finally the monster that the Getman family has known for years was born.

Pat Benatar's song Hit Me with Your Best Shot took her mind back to her Uncle Thad's farewell party. He had to serve ten days in jail for drunk driving in the morning and on the eleventh day he was heading to the Navy. There were a lot of guests and booze circulating in the hall. Music was playing all night long. Donna's ex-husband and his wife came for a short while. He and Donna had some words after the alcohol was flowing, which was why he and his fourth wife left abruptly.

As the night progressed, a man in his twenties was following Maggie around for the majority of the evening. She was only thirteen at the time. His eyes were bloodshot and he looked very creepy to Maggie. She tried to remain calm and not panic, but this man would not leave her alone. She sat at a table by the door where Maddie and her date were sitting. This man invited himself to the table. Maggie panicked when Maddie and her friend went to the dance floor.

"Hi! My name is Greg. What's yours?" he said as he straddled a folding chair and leaned into her face.

"That's nice," said a distracted Maggie with her best attempts to get her sister's attention from the dance floor.

"Don't you have a name? How can I invite you outside to my Porsche if I don't know your name?"

"I'm not interested in sports cars. I'm a truck kind of gal."

"Well, baby, I've got whatever you desire," he said in a drunken, sleazy voice.

Maggie excused herself because she felt like she was about to vomit. As she turned away from the table, he grabbed her by the arm and tried to force her out of the building. She tried to break free from him, but he was much stronger than her. As she was passing through the doorjamb, she quickly grabbed a hold of it with all her might and stomped down hard on his foot with her heel. He let out a yell and she ran for the restroom, which was located on the opposite side of the hall.

After hiding out for about twenty minutes, she peeked out the door to make sure he had moved on and not in sight. She was relieved to see the man was gone. She decided to sit with her parents for protection in case the sleaze ball should appear again. April was sitting at the table chugging her beer. Maggie kept looking over her shoulder fearing that creep would find her. She was just about to tell April what had happened when her mother sprang from her chair and hollered a few tables over, "Greg! Here she is! Come on over here and meet my daughter."

Maggie was in shock! The grease ball maneuvered around bodies and slithered over to their table. He had a beer in one hand while he extended the other to shake Maggie's hand. Maggie never moved.

"Don't be rude, Maggie!" said April as she nudged her daughter in the ribs with her elbow.

"Yeah, don't be rude, Maggie," he said with a smirk.

"Maggie, I would like for you to meet Gregory. Isn't he cute?" said April as she rubbed his grimy back.

Greg looked as if he had more than just alcohol in his system. He had a fixed grin upon his face while his eyes looked sleepy. He wore a black silky shirt with black jeans. He sported a gold necklace that looked as if it were leaving a green mark around his neck. His long dark hair looked as if it had not been washed in a month. The red glow on his face made his acne look like a string of Christmas lights. Maggie was horrified by her mother's indiscretion.

Not one person noticed how this man was pouring his perverted charm all over the young girl. Maddie and her date were feuding because Thad had been paying too much attention to her. In all honesty, he did have a crush on his step-niece and it was obvious to Maddie's date that the feeling was mutual. Michael had been mingling about the hall while Bo and Donna were trying to salvage their night after the little tiff with Donna's ex-husband.

"Yeah, isn't my daughter pretty? She's also available!" said April as if Maggie were for sale.

"I've been trying to tell your daughter how beautiful she is, but she keeps hiding from me."

"Maggie! Don't be rude! I've taught you better than that. Where are your manners?"

"I can see where she gets her good looks from," he said to a beaming April.

"Let me tell you where we live so that you may come pay us a visit anytime you like. Do you know how to get to the Toledo Sports Arena? If so, we live across the river in north Toledo. The first street you would take is—"

"Mom, stop it! Don't! He's a stranger!" cried Maggie.

Michael heard Maggie as he was walking back to the table with two fresh beers. Maggie saw that April changed her tune and refrained from using her bedroom voice in front of Michael. Maggie got up from the table and ran to the restroom.

She had gone inside her little hideout and saw that Donna was crying. Uncle Ted's girlfriend, Kari, was in there too. Maggie didn't know whom she could trust to tell about that creep who kept chasing after her. Maggie was desperate and felt that she had nothing to lose.

"Why does Ted have to be so damn jealous?" said Kari as she and Donna were standing in front of the mirror.

"Why do men in general have to be such assholes?" scoffed Donna.

"Excuse me for changing the subject, but do either of you know that man who is standing by the bathroom door? He won't leave me alone!" said Maggie nervously.

Kari, being surprised by such a statement from a soft-spoken child, peeked out the door and saw Greg standing close by, leaning against the wall. Maggie said that he had been hitting on her earlier that evening and that she used the restroom as her hideout.

"Me, too!" said Kari. "He's the reason for our argument!" She told Maggie to stay with Donna and she was going to get rid of that clown once and for all. She left the bathroom and Donna dried her tears. Donna took Maggie by the hand as they walked out to the party together.

A large crowd of people gathered in the center of the dance floor. The lights were all turned up and the music stopped playing. Standing in the very center was Uncle Ted and Greg. Ted had a hold of him by his cheap black shirt. The whole crowd was cheering as if there were going to be a lynching.

"Who are you?"

"I—I am Greg. Don't you remember me?" he said with a nervous giggle.

"I don't know who the hell you are! Does anyone here know this grease ball?" he asked as he shouted over his shoulder to the crowd.

"I don't know who the scrote is, brother," said Thad with amusement.

"I was invited. C'mon on, guys, you know who I am. I'm Greg. Remember me? I'm Greg," he said anxiously.

"I understand that you have been harassing my woman tonight," said Ted as he pointed to Kari.

Greg's eyes shifted to Kari and said, "I've never seen her before, man. I don't know what you're talkin' about! You've got me mixed up with someone else, dude."

"And this little girl here is off limits to everyone! She's my niece and she's only thirteen years old! Now that deserves an ass kicking in itself, don't you think?"

The expression upon Greg's face as he looked at Maggie confirmed his guilt. The whole crowd cheered and Greg looked like a scared rabbit. He kept pleading that he didn't know that Maggie was a child as the crowd repeatedly chanted, "Take him outside." Ted never had to lay a finger on him because he was so scared that he ran himself into a light post when he tried to escape. The crowd cheered the whole two seconds they were outside.

Maggie shuttered at that memory because April was insistent that Maggie be coupled with a total stranger like that. She was only a thirteen-year-old child. She had never experienced her first kiss and her mother was throwing her hide to the wolves. Greg was a walk-in from the street. After he had been thrown out, there were three other unidentified people who left the party rather abruptly.

Greg had been so desperate to get Maggie out to the parking lot, and she always knew that if he had succeeded, she might not have gotten away from him. She'd always respected her Uncle Ted for coming to her rescue like he had. No one had ever done that for her. For the first time in her life, she felt protected and safe after such an ordeal. It was too bad for Maggie that her own mother couldn't see that Greg was a bad man with bad intentions. It sadly occurred to the child that her mother didn't care for her safety—again.

Maggie was about to turn on the TV when Michael, Maddie, and the twins came through the front door. "Wilma! I'm home and I'm hungry!" shouted Kobe with his best attempt at his Fred Flintstone impersonation. Maggie was happy to have them home because she really didn't want to be alone. She already knew that a nap was out of the question because of her being too wound up.

Tandy greeted each one of them with an ankle cuddle as they passed through the living room. Michael was her favorite because he was the one who rescued her from starvation when she was just a kitten. She was small, helpless, and abandoned while trying to survive living in the alley. He found her in a garbage can licking a taffy wrapper. He picked her up and felt nothing but fur and bones beneath her. He took her into the house and told April that he found her a baby that needed a home.

April wanted nothing to do with a pet. She was sitting in front of her television when Michael placed the kitten in her lap. She balled up in April's lap and began to purr as April pet the little thing's head. Michael could see that April was softening up on the idea of keeping the little girl. He tried to explain how he found her licking a wrapper in the trash can and he jumbled up the words taffy and candy, which was how they named her Tandy. That was twelve ago and she had never left the house.

Maddie pulled out the trays of food from the refrigerator and placed them on the table, from which Kenneth moved an old television that had sat on it for years. The grandchildren watched their videotapes on that table, but it became a permanent fixture and it offered no room to dine at the table as a family. When April did get company, mostly Kenneth's and Kobe's girls, she liked them watching their videos out there while she sat in the other room watching hers.

It was rare when the family would gather at the table since April's drinking days. When Maggie was about finished with high school, she began to protest on cooking all the time. That was when Michael came up with the idea of "Fetch and Get!" Basically, it was every man for him or her self!

"I remember Mom would wait until after we all ate to walk out to the kitchen to make herself a nine course meal!" said Kenneth.

"I would laugh when I'd see her come into the living room with a steak, a baked potato, and a salad that looked as if she needed two bowls just to safely contain it. She also arranged her food on her tray as if she were being served in a fancy restaurant," said Maggie.

"I noticed that her meals were extravagant after we all ate a bowl of cereal for supper. She also indulged in her sweets after she had been drinking, which was all the time!" said Michael.

"Heaven forbid asking for just a morsel because she would be prepared to fire off the word no in a blink of an eye," said Maddie.

"I remember that, too. I hated the way she chewed her food because she had an expression upon her face as if she were having sex," said Kobe as he tried to imitate her.

Everyone broke out into laughter! Constant joking and laughing was a way this family could relieve pressures that bubbled within them. There were not many times when they would share their stories, but it appeared that everyone received April's showers in one form or another that deserved some tender loving care. The Getman family viewed this form of relief as the typical comedic bandage. Even though they could laugh, they could also disguise their pain at the same time. They were all great actors to anyone outside of the family.

"Speaking of food, when I was in first grade, Mom never got up in the mornings to help me pack my lunch. I barely got myself dressed and out the door on time much less wasting time to pack a lunch. My teeth and hair saw a brush on rare occasions," said Maggie.

"I know. We have documentation of portraits from kindergarten through fifth grade. I love you, Maggie, but it was a bit embarrassing to have to explain at the office why my daughter's hair was sticking up all over her head," said Michael playfully.

"It was photogenic proof of the absence of your mother," said Maddie.

"Anyhow, I went to the lunchroom on most days to get a free meal ticket so that I could eat that day. I learned that little trick when I was in third grade. On *many* school days, I would tell the lunch lady that I forgot my lunch. On other days I had nothing to eat. I would only do that when I was starving. Sometimes my classmates would give me something they didn't want to eat. Mom told me that starvation was my punishment for being lazy and not packing my lunch in the first place. For years, I got away without paying a single dime for my lunches. I felt like such a con artist!" giggled Maggie.

"I knew what you were doing. I got the bills in the mail once a month. Your mother never knew about it because I knew that my little girl did what she had to do for survival. I paid the bill and never said a word to your mother," said Michael to a stunned Maggie.

"We always got our lunches with no problems. Mom paid the lunch bill every other Monday," said Kenneth.

"I guess she didn't want the hassle of packing our lunches," said Kobe.

"I remember asking for some change once and she would say that she had none to spare. Two minutes later she would be sending the twins off to school with an envelope of cash for their lunches," said Maggie.

"That's how the coin jar became incorporated into the family budget. If you needed it, then it was there. I never had a problem with either of you kids abusing that privilege."

"I'm surprised that Mom didn't end that little deal," said Maddie.

"She tried, but I simply told her that it was *my* money for *my* children! I had to fight fire with fire."

"I can see that your ammo was the word *my*," said Maddie.

"That's right. She knew that you children were my strength, which was why she tried to block the idea of the money jar. I told her that I knew exactly how much change I put in there a week and that I would be asking each of you how much you took. She believed me because that jar still exists today."

"Yeah, all thirty-nine cents of it," laughed Kenneth.

"See, I kept my end of the bargain," scoffed Michael as he pointed to the large dusty goblet sitting on the shelf.

Maggie's mind wandered off and she jumped with a start when everyone shouted her name. She didn't realize that she drifted away like she had. She did not get much sleep the night before and there were so many memories rushing back that completely consumed her.

"Where were you just now?" asked Maddie.

"I was thinking of the time when I asked Mom and Dad for an allowance."

"By the sound of your tone, I am guessing you never got one?" said Kobe.

"That's right. Mom told me that I didn't do enough around the house that deserved an allowance."

"Are you kidding me?" said Kenneth with disbelief.

"Sadly, that's no joke. Your mother and I had arguments about it, but she wouldn't hear of it," said Michael.

"She thought only spoiled children got allowances. She told me that I should be thankful for her letting me live in her house rent-free. She told me when I was in high school that I could start buying groceries, especially the ones that I eat. My main diet at home was milk and cereal," said Maggie.

"Why did I never hear of that before now?" asked Michael.

"I knew that it would do no good. Why should I cause more tension between you and Mom? She even made me pay for my own doctor's bills with my Christmas or birthday money. She stopped buying me clothes for school in seventh grade."

"Maybe that's because you never made a fuss about it," said Kenneth.

"That's why you got a lot of Jenny's hand-me-down clothes. Her mother knew about you not having anything for school. Jenny once told me that her mother bought you some underclothes one year and lied about it not fitting Jenny so not to embarrass you," said Maddie.

"Why did I not know of this?" demanded Michael.

"Dad, you had to take care of your own skin during those days. Mom was always looking for an excuse to sink her teeth into you. We all knew we had our part and it was to try to take each day as it came," said Maddie.

"I try not to be bitter because in my heart I've always known that she was mentally ill," said Maggie.

"I believe that her actions were strictly by choice!" said Kobe.

"The verdict is still out on that one," said Michael.

"I would have to say that she treated us the way she did out of habit. With each passing year she got worse and worse. Everyone was too afraid to put her in her place!" said Kenneth.

"Yeah, and that was what gave her power over us," said Maddie.

"Are you saying that we *asked* to be treated like crap?" asked Kobe.

"I'm just saying that maybe we all might be somewhat responsible for the way Mom treated us. I mean, are we really innocent victims?" said Maddie.

The room was silent for a few moments mulling over what Maddie had just said. It was a harsh statement, but there might have been some truth to it. Not very many people stood up to April. Whenever Michael had been pushed to his breaking point by April, she would straighten up like a scolded school girl after he lost his temper. Sometimes she acted as if she depended on that kind of discipline to survive. April was a mystery to her family and no one would ever know why she acted the way she had.

"Mom was different. There's no denying that," said Kenneth.

"I'll never forget the time when Dad needed to have both feet operated on at the brand-new out-patient facility at Riverside hospital," said Maggie. "Mom refused to take the time off from her auto delivery job to show support for Dad. My heart went out to Dad because I knew that he was nervous," she said as she teased her father by patting him on the knee. "The poor guy only had me to offer him encouragement. The nurses even asked me to show proof of a valid driver's license because I looked too young to drive."

"The nurses in back were giving me the silent treatment because they thought you were my honey!" said Michael with a laugh. The room broke up in laughter as Maggie looked stunned. "That must have been the *real* reason that they asked to see your driver's license to help kill the curiosity. Just before they wheeled me into the operating room is when they were all as good as gold to me after realizing that you were really my daughter."

"How come you never told me that story, Dad?" asked Maggie.

"Because it was embarrassing!"

"No offense, Dad, but it is a sick world out there and anything goes anymore," said Kenneth.

"Surgery cannot be preformed if the patient doesn't have transportation arranged at the time of the appointment," said Maddie.

Michael's mind drifted off into his own little world as his children noticed the sad expression upon his face.

"Dad? Are you okay?" asked Kenneth.

"Oh! I'm alright," he said as if someone nudged him hard to get his attention.

"You looked as if you were a million miles away from us. Where did you go?" asked Maddie.

"I was thinking about the letter Maggie sent to April years ago. The letter was potent. I was so proud of Maggie for venting her feelings to April about the past. I'll never forget that. For about two months, I had the woman I married back in my life due to the powerful punch the letter delivered, which was right between your mother's eyes!"

"Oh yeah, *the* letter," said Maggie with a grimace.

Chapter 14

The letter came about when April refused to call Missy on her first birthday. Even though the child was too young to care either way, Maggie was fuming. Days after the little girl's birthday, April confessed to Maggie, over the phone, that she didn't call on Missy's birthday because she was too angry to speak to anyone. She claimed that her neighbor's dog made her mad and it ruined her whole blasted day.

Maggie was insulted by such a stupid excuse. Not so much in the dog story, but expecting Maggie to accept that as being a good enough reason for her purposely avoiding her granddaughter on her special day. Miles may keep them apart, but there were no excuses when phone lines were readily available. Maggie was offended and hurt.

Because of April, Maggie was one person who could not tolerate excuses period. She, herself, went to great extent to not offer them because Maggie wasn't too egotistic to admit when she made a mistake. Maggie believed that a simple apology would be acceptable in any situation and by claiming responsibility for human error was noble. There should never be the word "but" in an apology due to it being a way of denying responsibility and it cheapens the sincerity, if it were there in the first place. April felt that a person was weak to apologize, referring more so to herself. April never apologized for anything in her adult life. Although, April would insist on an apology if she felt that she were entitled to one.

After April received her letter, she was beside herself. Maggie called her father and siblings ahead of time to warn them all about her sending it. She knew that April would have reacted in some fashion, but her actions were always unpredictable. She received it on a Friday and Michael called Maggie to tell her that it had arrived. He also phoned Maggie early Saturday morning to say that April got up a 5AM, which was something she never did.

"Where are you going?" asked Michael.

"I've got some things to do," said April quietly.

"What's in your hand?"

"I got a letter from Maggie."

"Oh, that's nice. What did she have to say?" he asked enthusiastically.

"She had a few things to get off her chest, that's all," she said sadly.

Michael told Maggie that after their brief morning conversation, April left the house and did not return until nearly midnight. He was worried about April. He said that she acted withdrawn that morning and it was a coincidence that he caught her before she left the house. She was very humble, which was out of character, and he worried that she might do something desperate like commit suicide right after killing that child molester across the river.

No one ever knew where it was that she went that day, but she did confront Maddie about the letter on Sunday morning. April had time to digest the contents of the letter and was ready for a battle. Maddie was anticipating her visit. She had many things to say to April and she was more than ready for a confrontation. Now that the harsh realities of the letter called their mother out, it was no time to cower. April was inebriated while she faced Maddie the following day, which, once again, made Maddie regret living across the street from the woman.

"What do you know of this letter?" she demanded with a slur as she held up the crumpled envelope.

"What are you talking about? What letter?" said Maddie nervously, trying to size up the situation.

"Your sister is too much of a coward to say these words to my face! She had to send them to me in a letter. Can you believe that crap?" she said with the envelope clutched tightly in her fist.

Maddie took a deep breath and decided to be straightforward with the woman. She chose not to shy away from such an opportunity and said, "Frankly, Mother, I applaud her courage because she was able to say her feelings, even if it is on paper, without you intimidating her. Maggie has always been the quiet one in the family. Personally, I believe that she should be the most rebellious one of us who earned her time to be loud and obnoxious!"

April rolled her eyes and plopped down hard at Maddie's kitchen table. Her hair was messy, her eyes looked angry and bloodshot, and her mascara was smeared looking as if she had been crying. To Maddie, she looked as if her mother had not slept all weekend. "I gave you kids the best years of my life!" barked April.

"Well, if that was your best, it just wasn't good enough!" shouted Maddie.

"Give me an example! I bet you can't come up with one off the top of your head," said April with a smirk. "Show me what you've got, mouth!"

"Uncle Doug!" stated Maddie without hesitation.

Much to Maddie's surprise, April had a stunned look upon her face. April looked away from her daughter and stared at the floor. Maddie stood in the kitchen staring at April with her hands planted firmly on her hips. Maddie leaned closer to her mother as she anxiously awaited her mother's reply. April ran her fingers through her gray hair and shrugged her shoulders. Maddie grew more agitated with the woman with each passing second.

"How do you mean? I don't know what you're talking about," said April while doing her best to avoid eye contact.

"What I mean is what kind of a mother would place her daughters in the hands of a pedophile? You sent Maggie over there as if she were payment for your house! What do you have to say for yourself? Answer me, damn it!" There was a long pause as April did her best to act surprised by Maddie's candid statement.

"I thought he was harmless," she cried aloud without shedding a single tear.

"Cut the crap, Mother! Why did you send us over there?"

"Because..."

"Because why, Mother?"

"Because he used to do that to me too, that's why!"

"We've heard this before and it still doesn't make any sense to me now!"

"No one stopped him from touching me. You have no idea what that was like," she said as she buried her face into her hands sobbing.

"So you gave that burden to Maggie to carry for the rest of her life." April continued to carry on with the theatrics. Maddie walked towards her sink to look out the kitchen window to check on her young children. She saw Kelsey and Kyle playing happily on their swing set. Maddie wanted to weep at the thought of how young and innocent they were. "Do you realize that Maggie isn't sure if that man stole her virginity or not?" she said with a lump in her throat. "Her first sexual experience was nothing like anyone else's first experience at all. This is a question she will carry for the rest of her life that will *never* be answered." Maddie turned to look at April and said, "So, tell me, Mother, what was it that Maggie did to deserve such a punishment?"

April became enraged because she felt cornered. "Hey! Listen to me, Toots!" she said while pointing her finger at Maddie. "It's not *my* fault that she never told me that it was happening! How was I to know that there was trouble if she chose to remain silent about it?" snapped April.

"I'll tell you why, Mother. She was just a child!" yelled Maddie as she pounded her fist down hard onto the table close to April. Maddie was now nose to nose with the woman. "You were supposed to be her mother! Her protector! You *intentionally* delivered her into the hands of that monster when you *knew* about his behavior! How could you? What did you expect to happen? We were *both* just children!"

"I told you before that I thought he was an old man and that he was harmless. I honestly had no idea," she cried.

"And you continued to send Maggie over there *after* we told you about it. She felt as if she were contracted out!"

"You don't understand," cried April.

"You're right about that! I *don't* understand. I don't understand why Maggie even talks to you at all! I can't even believe that she allows her children to call you Grandma. I don't understand how she can be so damn forgiving to you when you don't even deserve it."

"I don't have to listen to this dribble!" said April as she stood from the table.

"You know something, Mother? Most parents want the best for their children. But in your case, you wanted your daughters to be punished like you were."

"Your childhoods don't even measure up to mine. You kids are all spoiled!" snarled April.

"I don't get it, Mom. Did you think Maggie wouldn't remember anything? If so, that's where you made a grave mistake. You know that Maggie is the one in our family that God blessed with a photogenic memory. I just don't understand why Maggie kept quiet either. Maybe it was because she was protecting you," said Maddie as April bolted from the house.

April called Maggie the following evening. Maggie had been sick all weekend long because of her nerves. Alec reassured her that nothing could get worse from here and not to be afraid to speak with her mother on the phone. When April phoned, Maggie hardly recognized her voice because it sounded too deep and sober to belong to her mother.

April's voice was dull and monotone while Maggie remained calm, but numb. After April addressed the letter, she began to sob on the phone. Maggie remained unaffected by her mother's crying because she had worried so much over the weekend that her endorphins had long since been activated, which left her feeling physically and emotionally numb. Each time Maggie tried to speak, her mother would sob a bit louder.

April began to settle down after Maggie, as predicted, tried to comfort her mother. She said things like "regardless of your mistakes, you are still my mother" and "if you choose to seek help, we will all stand by your side because that is what a family does." After they exchanged a few "I love yous," April's voice started to sound normal and strong. Before their conversation ended, she sounded as if she never shed a single tear, which Maggie was betting that she had not. Her mother was the ultimate drama queen.

The letter addressed many hurt feelings that had occurred throughout the years. It took Maggie less than an hour to type up seven pages. There were years of pain and suppression that finally had an opportunity to be heard. It was mostly about Uncle Doug, but other issues had been addressed, as well. Maggie felt that the time had come for someone to speak for the whole family and she took that responsibility upon herself to do just that. Maggie began the letter by addressing the most recent hurts created by that woman.

When Maggie was pregnant for Allie, she was visiting in Toledo because she had to throw a bridal shower for a friend. Alec drove her to Fort Wayne where Michael met them to pick her up to drive her to Toledo. Alec phoned Maggie as soon as he got home, which was part of their agreement. Michael handed the phone to Maggie with a serious look on his face. She was quick to pick up on the tension and immediately asked Alec what was wrong.

"Did you do something silly like arrange for your car to meet you in Toledo?"

"Stop joking around, Alec. What are you talking about?"

"When I got back to the apartment, your car was gone."

"What do you mean gone?"

"Well, the police just left here and they made a report."

"What! Oh, my God! Are you serious?"

"Yes, babe, your car was stolen."

Alec and Maggie were having a serious financial strain when they were first married. The doctor Maggie had worked for gave her bad financial advice that she took. He suggested that she reduce her car insurance to PLPD with no comprehensive. He insisted that since her 1982 Pontiac Grand Prix was paid off, it would save her a ton of money. Unfortunately for them, the policy meant no reimbursement for loss and no coverage for damages inflicted to the stolen vehicle.

April had been secretly visiting Uncle Doug that afternoon, which was a near daily commitment shortly after his release from prison. He was on probation for an extended period due to his early release on account of his declining health. The whole family later believed that April was doing it for an inheritance or something desperate like that. It was obvious to everyone that pride was not an issue with the woman. April believed that she was his sole beneficiary.

When April came home, she found Maggie crying in the back yard. April staggered from the garage with a sneer. When Maggie told her mother about her car being stolen, April laughed so hard in her face that Maggie nearly vomited from the stench of beer on her mother's breath. April stumbled from laughing so hard. Maggie was heartbroken by her mother's lack of compassion. She also couldn't believe that her mother drove a vehicle in her drunken condition.

Maggie walked away from her mother so that she could compose herself in private.

Later that evening, when Maggie was finally calmed down, she sat at the dining room table wrapping frivolous prizes for the bridal shower she was hosting. April plopped down at the table while opening another beer. The conversation landed on Uncle Doug, which Maggie thought April was finally curious enough to know just how far he got with her daughter. Maggie assumed that was why she was so intoxicated because of struggling with her conscience. April had given that impression on rare occasions and Maggie thought maybe she would let her mother off the hook. It was a long day and Maggie just didn't care anymore.

"Don't worry, Mom," said Maggie openly, "Uncle Doug never made penetration, as far as I could tell. He was more of a butt man," she said without giving it another thought.

"Shut your face! Shut your filthy face before I shut it for you!" warned April as she sprang from her chair and lunged towards Maggie with a fist waving in her face.

Maggie sat there in fear. She honestly thought her mother would have knocked her right out of her chair. Maggie was seven months pregnant, yet she felt more like a five-year-old child again. Maggie thought, *Mom had never cared in the past about my early introduction to sex by a trusted uncle. Why did I say such a thing? I must be delirious! Honestly! What would make me think that my mother was concerned about it now?* April showed no compassion for Maggie's hardships. Maggie was now without her paid-off vehicle, Alec was currently unemployed, and they had a baby on the way. April was rather enjoying her daughter's hard times.

As luck would have it, the car was found two weeks later, which was only ten miles from their apartment. Maggie couldn't afford to fill the gas tank before she went to Toledo, which meant the car was sitting on empty. Growing up in a rough neighborhood, she knew to have a locking gas cap accompanied with the good habit of keeping the car doors locked. For once in her life something worked out in her favor. She was ecstatic to have her car back, but she had to deal with starting her car with her screwdriver because of the cracked steering column. She could not afford a car alarm, but it took her last dollar to invest in an anti-theft device for locking the steering wheel in place.

Michael congratulated her on getting her car back while April refused to offer a kind word.

The letter also addressed Maggie's hurt feelings of when she was overdue for Allie. April had made a statement to Maggie, in front of Maddie, that she and Michael would not be seeing the baby until Maggie discontinued breast-feeding. April was drunk at the time, but Maggie's heart was broken just the same. Maggie just sat there and remained expressionless. That was her only defense against her mother so that April could not celebrate the direct hit upon Maggie's heart.

"Wow, Maggie. You're going to breast-feed? I knew that you would be a good mother!" said Maddie in her sister's defense.

"It's not so much that I want to, but it's too much of a financial crunch to buy formula *and* disposable diapers. Financially speaking, if I had to choose between the two, I refuse to use cloth diapers! Besides, they claim breast-feeding is healthier for the baby."

Allie was three weeks old when Michael dragged April to Indianapolis to meet their new granddaughter. April was emotional and she cried real tears when she held the baby girl. One picture was taken where April was holding Allie and she had such a loving expression on her face as if Allie had her instant approval of being a favorite grandchild. It looked as if April opened her heart and tucked Allie deep inside of it. Maggie was touched to see such a tender side of her mother that, to her knowledge, no one had ever before witnessed.

Maggie's letter mentioned all the things she never experienced with her mother like Maddie had. Maggie never spent a day shopping with her mother for a new bra, a prom dress, or even a wedding gown. She had to depend on the hand-me-downs from Maddie and her friend, Jenny. The prom dress she wore was her classmate's bridesmaid dress, which had visible stains all over it. She never had a graduation party, which Maddie had two. Maddie had parties for eighth grade and high school graduation while Maggie had nothing. Maggie felt her accomplishments of graduating in the top ten percent of her class and being a member of the National Honor Society was worthless and unimportant.

When Maggie was about to marry Alec, she returned a beautiful white strapless prom dress that she was going to wear as a wedding gown so that she could pay for the reception hall. Maggie's wedding was bland. Her decorations were scarce, unlike Maddie's first wedding. April re-mortgaged her house to pay for Maddie's wedding expenses, and she was divorced before the final payment was made. April vowed to *never* do that again. Maggie wore April's twenty-five-year-old wedding gown instead, which was itchy and a few sizes too large. It made April happy and Michael was speechless when he saw her in the dress. Even though April was honored, Maggie just went with what she could afford.

Maggie, embarrassed to mention her feelings about Christmas in the Getman household on how Maddie, despite all the trouble she's caused the family during her teen years, always got the nicer gifts while Kenneth and Kobe always got things that were top-of-the-line. When the twins were younger, they got all the latest toys on the market. Between the three of them, they all got school jackets or leather coats, while Maggie got the usual socks and underwear. It was always typical of Maggie to never complain. She always did her best to act surprised with each new pair of socks she opened out of respect for her parents.

One Christmas in 1983, she asked for a Cabbage Patch Doll that came with adoption papers, a new concept at the time, which created a huge demand on the market. Maggie's friend, Krista, had a mother who worked for a department store and she was able to hide two dolls in the layaway department. Maggie could not believe that her mother found a way to deliver her *only* request for Christmas. Her heart was overjoyed! However, Maggie lost interest instantly with her keepsake when she read, "Love Aunt Paula and Uncle Doug," on the label.

Maggie's earliest complaint in the letter was when Michael decided to travel to Iowa for the Manovich family reunion. This was Grandma Getman's side of the family. Since she had recently passed away, Michael wanted to attend at least one reunion in Iowa in his mother's honor. April was quick to refuse taking the vacation when she saw how badly her family wanted to go. Michael mentioned that maybe on the way back home they would stop at Crooked Lake at Aunt Gabby's cabin for a few nights. This was the same cabin, some years later, where Maggie met Alec when his family was renting the cottage next door.

"Come on, Mom, please come with us," pleaded Kobe.

"Nope!"

"Please, please, please with sugar on top," said Kenneth.

"I've got better things to do with my time," she said with a scowl.

"Why won't you come? It will be an adventure," said Michael.

"I *can't* go, that's why! Someone's got to take responsibility around here! Not everything is fun and games. My fish is about to have babies and I need to be here so they won't be eaten by the other fish!"

"I'll buy you another guppy at the store if that would make you happy," scoffed Michael.

The family left without her, which took April by surprise. Michael allowed Maddie to navigate directions from the map while Maggie looked for the road signs. They drove through Chicago for the first time in their lives. The twins occupied themselves by playing the alphabet game. They all had a good time. Maddie was excited to have the opportunity to drive in another state with her learner's permit for about a twenty minute stretch. Kobe worried about his mother being stuck at home, but Michael was quick to tell him that she *chose* to be there alone.

Aunt Gabby was laughing out loud about April's reason for not coming to the reunion. She took it upon herself to announce to the other family members about April not coming to Iowa because she was home nursing a hangnail! Gabby was good for scrambling the truth just for a laugh at someone else's expense. She always exaggerated stories about her siblings and their families to direct the spotlight away from her own troubled family life. The girls were surprised to see all of their cousins from Toledo. They were happy to see familiar faces for being so far away from home. They had a great time without April.

After the reunion, Aunt Gabby was delighted to know that Michael and his children would be staying the remainder of the week at her cabin on Crooked Lake. She had one rule at the lake for her nieces; they were not to lift one finger around the cabin. Aunt Gabby insisted that they relax and enjoy themselves because *they* were on vacation! Even though they were having a great time, Maddie kept getting an uneasy feeling about home. She was getting anxious about heading back to the north end because she felt that bad news was on the horizon. After much persistence, Maddie convinced Michael into leaving early.

Maddie could not wait to get home. She kept asking Michael to drive faster. She was so anxious to get home, but she didn't understand why. The kids cheered as they crossed the Ohio state line. They even applauded when they drove into Lucas County. They celebrated when they saw the sign welcoming them to Toledo. Maddie saw the skyline of the city and wished they were there already. She could not wait to see Ontario Street, which would take her home. The car was barely in park when Maddie jumped onto the curb. Maggie and the twins were close behind her.

"Yep," said April as she threw her hands up in the air with disappointment, "*my* vacation just ended!" as each child filed through the front door.

April was entertaining her drinking buddies from across the street. She had a twelve-pack of beer on the floor next to her. It appeared that she had not yet opened the box, which irritated her. She never got up to greet her family who had been gone nearly a week. The neighbor lady told Maddie that the group of friends that Maddie hangs with got into a car accident and one of them was killed instantly. The accident happened the night before, which is when Maddie's gnawing feelings of trouble intensified. She said that funeral arrangements were still being made. Maddie ran out the front door to check on her surviving friends. She nearly knocked Michael over as she sprinted down the street.

Michael was the last person through the door because he was carrying luggage that was stuffed with clean clothes. They went to the laundry mat before coming home so that April would not accuse them of bringing their dirty laundry home just for her to clean. The family became accustomed to outthinking April to lessen the odds of her constant complaining. Michael was diligent on having his children think outside of the box with any given situation. Outsmarting April was their daily lesson.

Michael did hear April's remark to the kids from the front porch. By the expression upon his face as he entered his house, the neighbors were quick to feel the tension and quickly exited through the front door. For years, all five of them never forgot April's crude comment. It was heartless and cold, especially knowing that there was a death of a child in the neighborhood, the same age as Maddie, from an auto accident. They all felt in some twisted way that she wished the same fate for her own family. She did nothing to console Maddie for the loss of a friend. April showed no remorse for her outrageous, but sober, statement to her family on that night.

April drank heavily for years. She was once found on an elderly widower's porch engaged in a compromising position one evening. Michael marched across the street and dragged her by the arm after the neighbors, April's drinking buddies, called him for an education about his wife's extracurricular activities.

"Aw, leave her alone, Michael. She's just having fun," said Wally.

"Shut up, old man!" warned Michael.

"If you could be more of a husband to her, she wouldn't need to be looking for comfort elsewhere!"

"Listen up, Weirdo Wally! If you don't shut your mouth, I'll knock your dentures down your throat!"

April laid low after that drunken episode. She never mentioned that evening to anyone. When referring to that man, Michael called him "Weirdo" ever since that evening. April's drinking was out of control. She and Michael fought every weekend, guaranteed, because alcohol was always the source of the problem. They would watch Brad Billings' band play at the bar on the weekends. April caused a scene when she stroked the lead singer's beard in front of his jealous wife. Michael and Maddie were humiliated as the two women openly argued. That was an embarrassment to everyone sitting at the table.

In Maggie's letter to April, she mentioned one evening in particular when a huge fight erupted downstairs. It was 3 AM when Maggie and the twins had been awakened by their parents' screaming match in the kitchen. Maggie would routinely walk into the twins' room and turn on their radio with the hopes of drowning out the yelling from downstairs. Maggie was surprised to meet Kenneth at his bedroom door. She told him to go back to bed and turn on their radio. She promised him that everything was going to be all right.

She could hear Michael daring April to take a swing at him. She could hear pots and pans crashing on the kitchen floor while April shouted obscenities. She could sense such rage within her mother that she feared that April would one day kill Michael. Many nights she feared it because she knew April was capable of doing it to all of them. She finally heard the back door slam, which she knew it was her father heading out to the garage, which was his sanctuary away from that crazy woman. The garage was as far as his marital leash would allow him to roam.

Maggie could hear April stomping up the stairs. She cowered beneath her covers praying that her mother would just go to bed to sleep it off. April kicked Maggie's bedroom door wide open and sent it crashing against the wall. She grabbed her daughter by the arm and tried to pull her out of bed.

"Get up!" she demanded. "I said get up!"

"What—what's wrong?" said Maggie, trying to sound sleepy and confused. She swung her legs hard off the edge of the bed and nearly knocked April to the floor. A small sense of victory entered Maggie's mind. April dug her nails into Maggie's arm even deeper. She dragged the child downstairs and into the kitchen. Maggie's adrenaline was pumping heavily into her bloodstream and she refused to be hit in any way that evening by that woman. In her mind she was preparing to fight her mother at all costs.

"Look at this kitchen! Look at it!"

"What's wrong with it?" she asked as her eyes were trying to adjust to the light.

"Does it look clean to you?"

Maggie learned not to answer her rhetoric questions from previous years. She had cleaned the cupboards, scrubbed the floor by hand as her mother demanded, washed dishes, dried them, and put them away. She even removed the clutter from the refrigerator door earlier that evening. She went the extra mile because she wanted to attend the sleepover at Krista's house the following weekend. Maggie knew that she needed to build positive points to improve her chances of attending the party.

Maggie scanned the room while still trying to adjust her eyes to the light. She saw a few pots and pans on the floor, just as she assumed. April grabbed Maggie by the chin and repeated her question. Maggie pulled away from her mother sharply, which her own actions surprised even herself. Maggie found herself thinking of an escape route if her mother would start hitting her. She found herself sizing up her mother, which she had never done before. April was really drunk and Maggie felt she might have a fighting chance with her. Maggie was a teenager then and was strong enough to defend herself.

"Do you call this clean?" she asked as she rolled the refrigerator away from the wall.

She scooped up umpteen years worth of dirt and threw it in Maggie's face. She then walked over to the toaster. She turned it upside down and shook the crumbs all over the clean countertops. She was yelling the whole time she was trashing the kitchen. Maggie turned away and went back to bed. She was surprised that April didn't charge after her to continue her nonsense. Maggie went to sleep with her baseball bat by her side just in case of a surprise attack from her mother during the night. She always listened to make sure that the twins weren't being harassed by their bully mother. Maggie knew they were young and needed protecting. She knew that she would defend them to the death.

Maggie's letter to her mother was effective for a short while. Michael sent Maggie a dozen of yellow long-stemmed roses with a note that read: "Thanks to you I have my wife back! I love you and thank you for your courage. Lots of love always, Dad." April did confess to Maggie that she needed help. Maggie felt that was better than any apology she could ever expect from her mother! On the other hand, she wanted nothing more than to get her mother the help she so desperately needed. She knew it would be difficult for her to make sure that her mother stayed faithful and consistent with her therapy because of their long-distance relationship. Maggie had to trust that her father and siblings would have to be more committed in helping her.

"When I die, I want to be buried with this letter you sent me," said April at the end of her phone conversation with Maggie.

Maggie could never understand what she meant by that statement. Michael enjoyed April's new outlook on life, but the idea of getting her psychiatric help was soon swept under the carpet. For reasons only Michael could understand, finding a therapist for his wife wasn't as important anymore. April slipped back into her vicious mode and eventually turned the letter around on Maggie. She accused Maggie of turning the family against her.

In April's mind, Maddie was forever accused of corrupting Michael while Maggie poisoned the minds of her brothers against their own mother. April became colder than ever. In fact, that is when she became impervious to any form of affection. She held no more love in her heart for no one but herself. She was now a woman scorned by the hands of her own family. Maggie felt shame and resentment with herself for putting her mother and family at great risk.

Chapter 15

Aunt Cami phoned the house and declined the offer for a bite to eat because she made last-minute dinner plans with a friend. Michael invited her earlier, at which time he reminded her that his house was just as much hers because she was still family. Michael was the only man she had ever truly admired in her life. Cami was always close with April, but she knew how to jump like the rest of them when her sister was in one of her moods. Some of April's behavior resulted in a feeling of all the joy in the atmosphere being bled dry.

Cami knew that her sister was not well and she had heard the Getman family speak about a possible mental illness. At first, she felt that April's family was too harsh and that they had been forming allies against her sister. Cami held a high respect for April because when her two children were little she took them in when she could. This was how Cami was able to see her children without too much shame after she abandoned them and her husband. She never forgot such generosity and kindness from April. But as Cami spent more time with April, she, too, could see that her quirky nature was undeniably getting worse.

April enjoyed her sister's companionship. At times it seemed that Cami was April's only trusted friend. April believed that her family was sneaking around behind her back to visit or chat with one another while she remained out of the loop. She claimed that every time the phone would ring, it was for Michael and not her. She accused him of scaring the children off and having them hate her. Cami saw an opportunity to tell her sister that God would *never* turn

His back on her and He would love her despite all the sins she had committed. April went to church with Cami and was soon deep in her religion.

"Do you remember Mom using excuses on why she could not participate in any family functions because of church?" asked Kobe.

"Yeah, it was all the time!" said Michael.

"Oh, I can't make it because I have church on Sunday," said Kobe snidely while mocking April.

"Yeah, she's been known to say that on a Monday!" laughed Maddie.

"I remember your mother being upset with Kobe for saying Jesus in her presence, which infuriated her so much that she marched outside and removed her Ten Commandments sign from the front yard," said Michael.

"I demand respect in *my* house!" she said as she yanked the sign out of the ground. Michael witnessed this with great concern for her actions. He could understand her being upset for Kobe using the Lord's name in vain, but with her uprooting the sign made absolutely no sense to him whatsoever. If nothing else, reading the sign might have been an education for their adult son. "There, that will show him!" she growled at Michael as she stormed past him to put her sign in the garage.

"Did you learn anything that day, Kobe?" asked Kenneth with a grin on his face.

"What Ten Commandments sign? I only counted five!" he said innocently.

"That's because the other five were on the back of the sign, dummy!" said Michael.

"Really?" said Kobe with surprise.

Everyone laughed and teased Kobe as they cleared the table. Kenneth was proud of his twin for even taking notice that there were five Commandments on one side of the sign in the first place. He also knew that it never occurred to his brother to look on the other side of the sign for the remaining Commandments. That was a perfect summary of Kobe's personality, which they all loved him regardless.

Michael looked as if he were happy to be back home. He enjoyed his kids being around him. He especially lit up when the grandkids came around, which was what he lived for. Michael stayed on his "vacations" months at a time, just for sanity reasons. The kids felt recharged when they were all together, too. They knew that it was safe to unplug from the stresses of the world and just be themselves. No matter what pains in life they would endure, there was always laughter when they were united.

Sadly for Michael, April drove him out of their bedroom some time in the eighties. She justified her actions by claiming that he snored too loud and that his toenails were like claws. Michael moved into Maggie's old room when April started to turn the air conditioner on during the winter along with the ceiling fan being on the highest setting. On some winter mornings, she would open her bedroom window. She always complained about being too hot while Michael nearly froze to death no matter what the season. There were a few occasions when he would go outside just to warm himself.

The older he was getting, the less he could tolerate the cold. April would hit his hand when she would catch him turning up the thermostat in his own house. She was not playing around when she would strike him. She hit him once in the car when Maggie was visiting. April had hip-hop blaring on the radio, which was obvious to Maggie that it was for nothing other than attention. Michael tried to turn the volume down a notch to hear Maggie from the back seat. April smacked his hand so hard that her nails drew blood.

"Don't you touch *my* radio!" she growled.

"I was straining to hear Maggie from the back seat. I realized that we were having a shouting match instead of a civilized conversation. I thought our having to scream over the music was ridiculous!"

"Bring your paw over here again, Grandpa, and see what happens! This is *my* car and you don't touch *my* stuff!"

One Christmas, Maggie made her father a patriotic quilt for his twin bed. She knew that she had to make something special for April too, so she made a Christmas lap quilt that she could put on the back of her rocking chair for the holidays. Maggie figured that would be ideal for her mother since she complains about being hot all the time. Much to Michael's misfortune, Maggie was wrong with her theory.

"How on earth can I snuggle up in this dinky blanket? Why did *I* get the small one? Your quilt looks better than mine," said April in a childlike voice to Michael.

Michael never put his quilt on his bed because he heard April complain to him for six months. He placed it on the daybed in the spare bedroom. He finally confessed to Maggie that April *still* nagged him about his quilt in June. Maggie apologized for the friction she created between her parents. She never intended for there to be any hurt feelings.

"Mom is always complaining of being too hot. Why would I make her a quilt that she would not use? They are time-consuming and expensive, not to mention that she has a king size bed!"

"I know. I tried to explain to her about her constant complaining of being too hot, but I guess it's about principle, not common sense," said Michael.

Maggie tried to redeem herself and she decided to make a memory quilt for her parents' fortieth wedding anniversary. April cried when she saw her favorite grandmother's picture on it. Everyone was stunned by her reaction. Michael and the twins never saw her shed a real tear in their lives. Kobe, the amateur photographer, was quick to shove his disposable camera in her face to capture the historical moment.

"This is nice, but I still can't keep myself warm in a blanket like this," she said through her tears.

"It's not a blanket to cuddle, it's one to display," said Michael in awe.

One month before the following Christmas, Maggie drove to Toledo to have her mother choose a pattern for a king size quilt as a gift. Maggie intended on treating her mother to lunch after choosing her fabrics at the store. April wanted nothing to do with that. She randomly chose a pattern, which was the most challenging one out of the book. Maggie had to write down the colors her mother wanted on a notepad instead, which she could have done over the phone. She felt it was a wasted ten-hour round trip.

Maggie and Alec chose the fabrics together one afternoon in Indianapolis. She worked on her mother's quilt day and night. She was also making other projects for Alec's family, not to mention the three homemade denim beanbag chairs for her own kids. Maggie's health was not good. She was diagnosed with bronchitis a week before Christmas. She made the drive to Toledo to hand-deliver

April's gifts. She made seven throw pillows out of the scrap materials from her quilt that were of various colors and sizes.

When April opened the boxes, her quilt was so expected that she showed no enthusiasm. She showed more interest in the projects that required the least amount of work, the pillows. April tried to stuff her things back into the boxes, but Maggie wouldn't allow it. She marched upstairs to put the quilt on the king size bed. Even though Maggie was being treated for her illness, it finally went into pneumonia on New Year's Eve.

Maggie's holidays were ruined. She was in bed for two weeks. She never got a single thank-you note or phone call from her mother. April did send a musical dancing bee through the mail for a laugh, which she took great pleasure in telling everyone that she was such a wonderful mother for doing so. Maggie would have rather had words of encouragement over the phone from her mother, whom once had pneumonia, too. Michael called every other day to check on Maggie's progress.

"Aren't you going to call Maggie and offer any motherly advice during her recovery process?" asked Michael.

"No," said April coldly.

"Why not?"

"Because *your* little chat sessions cover the both of us."

"I just thought it would be nice because now that you two share something in common; I figured that you could sympathize with her a little or something. Who knows? Maybe your maternal instincts would finally kick into gear," he said sarcastically.

"*My* pneumonia was different! *I* was in the hospital and I nearly died!"

"You were hospitalized because you got ill back in the seventies. They try to avoid hospitalization these days at all costs because of insurance companies! People *still* die from pneumonia!"

"Well," said April as she turned away from Michael, "that's not my problem now is it!" she snapped.

Maggie did recover from her pneumonia, but around Valentine's Day she was again diagnosed with bronchitis. April told her that it must be something Maggie was doing wrong. Maggie had been volunteering an hour out of her busy schedule for the holiday parties in Mark's and Missy's classrooms. She tried real hard not to become paranoid about visiting public places like April did worrying about catching an illness.

Since Maddie contracted mono, decades ago, April never drank from a public water fountain ever again. Anytime she got a cold or the flu, it was blamed on one of the grandchildren or her kids from work because all children were loaded with germs. Things cannot happen just because; she was always quick to point the finger of blame on someone.

Michael wanted to grab a beer before heading back to the funeral home. He pulled out five beers from the fridge and handed them out to each of his kids, whether they wanted one or not. "I would like to propose a toast," he said. They all raised their bottles in the air. Michael had a look on his face as if he were about to say something very heavy. There was a long pause as the kids all looked at one another with wonder.

"This toast is for my family. Keeping things in perspective, without April, you all would not be here today. And without you, I would not be living. Each of you represents the rhythm of my heart that gives me a reason to dance. And each of your children is the very blood in my veins, which gives this old man life. I thank God for giving an old fool such a wonderful family. I am truly blessed. I guess what I am trying to say is that I love you and I salute you all for your courage and bravery throughout the years. We've all had our battles with April and we are still standing. Here's to survival!"

"To survival!" they said collectively.

They all took a swig of their beers. Maddie and Kobe were competing to see who could finish theirs first while the others remained in their little circle and just stared. It was no surprise to any of them that their childish contest ended in a tie. Maddie tried to stifle a belch, which she claimed burned the inside of her nose. Her eyes were instantly watery. Kobe belched so loud and long that it seemed to rattle the windows. He looked at Maddie and said, "I win," with such pride and confidence.

"Nice speech, Dad," said Maggie, trying to change the subject.

"Thanks. It came from the heart."

"Speaking of survival, do you remember when Mom became paranoid with the neighborhood?" asked Maggie.

"Yeah, that's when I got my new job after I was fired from the bank. There would be nights I would not be home because of the demands of the profession as a traveling salesman."

"What triggered such paranoia?" asked Maddie.

"Maybe she saw something on TV, which was highly probable. Maybe she watched a movie about silver bullets or something," scoffed Kobe.

"I don't know what happened, but since I was going to be gone overnight, she insisted that I install a deadbolt lock on the inside of her bedroom door."

"Isn't that when she bought her 357-Magnimum?" asked Kenneth.

"Yes, she did. She got her permit and learned how to shoot it."

"Dad, we thought she was going to kill you with it when she bought it," said Maddie.

"We weren't the only ones in the family who thought of that. Aunt Gabby phoned me one night and asked me if I knew that Mom purchased a handgun. She told me that she was afraid that Mom would finally succeed in killing you," said Maggie as she looked at Michael. "She felt it would be a perfect setup since Mom wasn't used to being alone and your wacky schedule would have secured her alibi."

"Yeah, that thought ran through my mind, too. That's why I told her that she had to warn the perpetrator that she had a gun before she fired off a round. Just for safety precautions, for the first month, I crawled through the hallway on my belly before going into my bedroom!" laughed Michael.

"Let me get this straight, who was the paranoid one?" asked Kenneth.

Everyone laughed at the thought of Michael sneaking into his own bedroom at night while April slept in her own room, safely locked in at night, with her gun tucked beneath her pillow. The neighborhood had always been a rough area. The first time Maggie witnessed April show fear with the neighborhood was when she had a visit from her rebel cousin, Danny Connolly.

Danny was Uncle Ed's youngest boy. He was known as the wild child, the complete opposite from his older brother, Joe. Maddie and Maggie were really young when he and his family came to visit from Arizona. He settled out west when Katherine and Herbert moved out there. It was good to see him settled down with a nice young lady and their baby girl was precious. He was a proud Vietnam veteran, who had a crash course in appreciating life, liberty, and the well-being of all mankind. Being a family man was his newfound passion. April had not seen him for nearly five years.

It was a hot summer day and April suggested that they continue their visit on the front porch. Danny was disappointed that Michael was at work, but he was kept busy with the million questions from ten-year-old Maddie, who thought he was the most handsome man she had ever seen. Life was as usual in the neighborhood with rock and roll music blaring down the street, kids riding their bikes, and Dave, the neighbor, was washing his car across the street.

All was well until the neighborhood punks, who Michael labeled as the North End Gang, polluted the atmosphere by their presence. There were about six hooligan teenage boys strutting down Ontario Street carrying ball bats and chains. They looked to be around the ages of seventeen and eighteen. It was obvious that they were looking for trouble. Danny watched them from April's porch as they scattered the neatly stacked lumber, which was sitting against a neighbor's house across the street, about the yard. The owner was not home at the time, but Dave put down his hose and yelled for them to stop.

Even though it was not Dave's property being threatened, most neighbors watched out for one another. The leader of the gang started to yell and curse at the Good Samaritan, trying his best to intimidate the man by his perverse profanity and tough-guy image. Little did the ruffians know that Dave was a fighter himself and he was not about to back down from a bunch of punk kids. They did stop scattering the lumber because they found the fight they were looking for. They surrounded Dave and Danny could no longer sit still. Danny sprang from the porch to assist the innocent man across the street. Just as Danny approached the middle of the street, April grabbed him desperately by his arm.

"Let it go, Danny. This is none of our business; just let it go!" pleaded April.

"What the hell are you talking about, April?!" yelled Danny as he turned on a heel with a wild look in his eyes. Danny's wife was surprised that he did not hit April out of reflex by her interference.

She grew up with the idea that if a man was going to fight, it was dangerous and unwise to stop him. Especially since he was a Vietnam combat veteran and his mind was set to fight.

"Please, don't do anything. Please."

"That man needs my help, April! Don't tell me that it is none of my business. These punks do not represent what it was that I was fighting for over there, April! This behavior is *not* what I was defending. It kills me to see people in our country afraid to walk down their own street! This is wrong, April! So is telling me that this is none of my business!" he said as he yanked his arm from her grasp.

"They'll burn down my house tonight, Danny," she said in a desperate voice as she grabbed his arm with both hands.

He looked over at the girls and then at his wife. He was angry with April for saying that. He turned to look at Dave, but the confrontation ended when the hoodlums saw that Danny was on his way over to help. Not one punch was thrown. They heard something about him being in Nam and quickly lost interest in any fight that afternoon.

April was relieved, but Danny was angry at such a passive and paranoid attitude from his cousin. Maggie never forgot his heroic attempt to help a total stranger that day. She remembered him announcing, "It's time to bust some ass!" after he quickly assessed the situation. Twenty years later, Danny's life ended, sadly by his own hand, when his wife wanted to end their marriage.

The neighborhood had always held the reputation for being rough. The most unforgettable experience for the Getmans was the fall of 1976, when an elderly widow woman was raped by one of the gang members. She resided two houses down from the Getman house. Three men broke into the house and each had a job to do. One man stole money and jewelry, the other looked for the prescription drugs, while the other raped the eighty-year-old woman. After they left her house, she got dressed and wandered to the Getman residence at 2 AM asking for help. She remained calm throughout the whole ordeal.

"Dorothy! What's the matter?" asked Michael as he opened the door wider to welcome her into the house.

"Oh, I'm sorry it's late, Michael, but I need to use your phone," she said with her hair a mess, her coat was buttoned wrong, and her glasses were cockeyed.

"What's wrong with your phone?" asked April, thinking the old woman was suddenly senile.

"They ripped it out of the wall while they were robbing me," she said calmly.

"I'll call the police!" said Michael while April was looking Dorothy over.

"Oh yeah, tell them that I was raped, too," the elderly woman added just as Michael's call was answered.

Michael nearly dropped the phone while April became hysterical. Maddie and Maggie learned that night what the term rape meant. Dorothy never cried and she cooperated with the police to the fullest. The police asked April to tell Dorothy that they would need a sample of pubic hair for their crime lab. Dorothy, being all too eager to help catch the criminals, was happy to oblige the officer's request as she promptly reached under her dress and ripped out a handful of pubic hair in front of the officer. The man was stunned by what he witnessed and he nearly fainted when she asked with an opened hand, "Is this enough?"

The Getman house was a mini-precinct in the early morning hours. The girls were allowed to stay up to help serve coffee and cookies to the officers. Ontario Street was lined with police cars. Many officers walked in and out of the house freely, which made the Getman girls feel important. April had transported Dorothy to the hospital while Michael and the girls did their duty by helping the police officers find the bad guy. They witnessed the sergeant call for the police dog, which the girls could hardly wait to see.

Unfortunately for the dog, the officer got him out of the vehicle from the driver's side rather than the passenger side, which got the dog hit by an oncoming car. He returned to his job an hour later after seeing the veterinarian. He sustained bruising to his hind leg, but that did not stop the dog's spectacular performance of completing his task. The rapist was sniffed out by the dog across the street, which was where the perpetrator lived. The judge threw the book at the rapist, who later died in prison from a fatal stab wound from another inmate.

In all the years the Getman family resided in that neighborhood, they have seen drive-by shootings, numerous street fights, and drug related episodes of many kinds. There was one episode where a drunk driver demolished nearly a dozen vehicles parked on the street with his three-ton truck. Neighbors attacked the man and hogtied him until the police got there. The fire department was the first to arrive at the scene and the chief strongly suggested for the neighbors to untie the man before the police came because they could have been arrested for such brutal and barbaric tactics. Maggie's earliest memory was when the whole neighborhood was held hostage when a crazy man had a box of dynamite and nitroglycerin that he was willing to ignite if the police did not meet his demands. They had also seen their share of vandalism and heartbreak.

One year, a young woman was stabbed to death by her best friend's strung-out brother. He was on some narcotic when he stabbed his sister nearly to death. The friend tried to stop him, but he turned the knife on her. The sister survived the stabbing, but her friend did not. That tragedy affected the whole neighborhood. There were no words of comfort to offer her grieving family. The young man sobered up in jail when he realized that he killed the woman of his dreams and paralyzed his sister for life.

Maggie once drove Michael's car to a friend's house on a Saturday, but it broke down before she left the neighborhood. The sixteen-year-old got three blocks away when the car died. Michael only bought his vehicles from the repossessed car lot at the bank. He didn't believe in having a nice vehicle because it was an invitation for someone to come steal or destroy it. She was able to coast the car to the curb, which happened to be in front of Maddie's friend's house. Maggie used their phone to call April.

"So! Why did you bother calling me? There's nothing I can do about it," she said.

"I just wanted to tell you to be expecting me home because I'm walking and I should be there in five minutes."

"Maggie! You are so paranoid, I swear!" she said as she hung up the phone.

Maggie thanked the family for allowing her to use their phone. They tried to have her wait at their house until April would come for her, but Maggie knew that would never happen. They assured her that the car was fine parked in front of their house on Huron Street and to phone them as soon as she got home. It was a ritual in that neighborhood with most families, especially those with girls. Being in broad daylight, she thought she had nothing to fear.

As Maggie briskly walked down Buckeye Street, she noticed two men, she had never seen in the neighborhood before, walking together across the street heading in the opposite direction. She tried to ignore them, but the hair on the back of her neck began to stand up. She was almost to Ontario Street when she noticed that the men separated. They were now walking in the same direction as Maggie. They walked about twenty to thirty feet apart from one another, to where Maggie would be in the middle if she were on their side of the street. They both crossed the street at the same time. Maggie's heart raced as she picked up her pace.

She knew that the main thing for any situation was to never panic. As soon as the man behind her jumped onto the curb, she ran into the corner store, which used to be the neighborhood candy store. The two men followed her inside the store. She stood at the counter making small talk with the cashier, who she knew. The men went to the farthest corner of the store and were whispering amongst themselves while pointing at Maggie. She did her best not to show fear and acted as if nothing were wrong.

After realizing that they were still in the corner of the store, she suddenly raced out of that store and she never looked back. She could see her house in the distance. She saw the neighborhood ruffians sitting on their porch. Maddie hung out with them on occasions, which was how Maggie learned their names. They saw that she was running with a look of terror on her face. Dillon cautiously walked off the porch to investigate.

"Hi, Dillon, what's up?" asked Maggie winded, but trying to remain calm. She stopped for a moment to catch her breath.

"Hey, what's going on?" he said as he approached her. He looked into her eyes and then he looked past her shoulder. He stared down the street for what seemed an eternity.

Maggie nervously chatted with the group as she nonchalantly looked over her shoulder. She did not see those men anywhere in sight. She was instantly relieved. The gang was surprised that Maggie took a minute to talk with them. "Well, I've got to go, but you guys have a good one!" she said as she jogged home. She would never forget being so thankful that they were outside on that afternoon. Their faces were angelic to Maggie that day and they were always decent with her ever since. To her knowledge, they never knew how indebted she was to them for just being there.

When Maddie was married to her first husband, their first house was on Michigan Street, which was behind her parents' house. They moved into that house just before Maddie filed divorce papers on the man. It was the morning of the first snow of the season and Maddie had to warm her car before her drive to work at 6 AM. Her car was parked in the alley. She got into her car and started the engine. She never noticed that her dome light never came on.

She reached between the bucket seats to feel the back seat, which had become a habit with her over the years. She felt something warm in her backseat. Maddie let out a gasp and the man sat up, which she could see his silhouette in the rearview mirror. He grabbed her by the neck as she reached for the handle on her door. They struggled for a moment, which felt like an eternity. He tried to pull her into the back seat, but she was able to elbow him in the face.

She opened the door and ran to the front of the car, where she fell to the ground. The man was climbing out of the car and all Maddie could do was scream as loud as she could. The man didn't know what to do. He hesitated for a moment and then locked the car door and slammed it shut.

With her keys in the ignition and both doors locked, he escaped down the alley while Maddie ran to her house. Her husband ran into the yard completely naked looking to kill the guy who attempted to assault his wife. Maddie always suspected it was her neighbor because he had a starring problem when it came to her. Her husband talked with the suspect that evening and noticed that he could not make eye contact. Before he walked away, it was plain to see that he was hiding a black eye.

The police complimented Maddie for her quick thinking and knowing the best thing was to get out of that car. They commended her on making noise, which was her best weapon. The police discovered that her dome light had been completely cut out by a sharp object. They are guessing that it was a knife that he had.

Because it was such a cold morning and the perpetrator was warm to the touch, it was possible that he was a neighbor. However, evidence was lacking to launch any further investigation.

"I would have maimed that man for life if he would have tried that crap with me," said April boldly.

"I would have liked to see you try, Mom," said Maddie.

"I'm just saying that there is no way any male is gonna try that crap with me! I wouldn't just run away like a sissy," she said.

"All due respect, ma'am, your daughter did exactly what she was supposed to do. She did enough to get away. Because she didn't play superhero, she is alive and in one piece," said the officer.

"I'm just saying, *I'd* like to see some punk try that with *me*!"

The neighborhood was always lively and no one was exempt. Michael once had an alarm system for his garage, but he kept it in the box for two months before getting around to installing it. He was reminded one morning when he awoke to find his garage door open and beer cans scattered around the back yard. He went outside to investigate and saw that they raided the freezer, which was stocked with half of a cow. They took the liberty of drinking his twelve-pack, which Michael normally drank warm when in the garage. They did save him one, which was more of an insult to him than anything else.

After Michael was finished licking his wounds, he decided to dust off his alarm system and install it that afternoon. It had a loud piercing buzz sound that was activated when the door would open and the string would turn on the light. He had it looking like an obstacle course with tiny nails behind the door supporting the string that was tied around the light switch and the doorknob. The light switch was the alarm system. He claimed he got that idea when he was a kid trying to pull his tooth.

Since the girls both shared a room in the back of the house at that time, they were given strict instructions to *never* look out the window if they heard the alarm. He told them that if the crook had a gun, he could shoot the witnesses. The girls took his warning to heart and were the first ones to the window when it sounded the following week. Nothing was stolen, but the back gate was removed off its hinges as if someone forgot that it was there, as they plowed through it making their escape.

"I think it was our lunch lady's son, Dad," said Maggie, doing her best trying to give a full description.

"It is not a good idea to accuse someone without proof. We'll just have to see who will be limping in the neighborhood tomorrow," he said after he scolded his girls for looking out the window.

As luck would have it, it was exactly who Maggie said it was. He was in trouble with the law in the past and he chummed with a bad crowd. His mother told him that he had to join the military or he had to get out of her house. He ended up making a career out of the Marines and was forever thankful to his mother for giving him the necessary push in the right direction. His former buddies made a career of being in and out of prison; the ones who lived past the age of twenty-five while the others died of their addictions.

Just like the change in seasons, the neighborhood also had its changes. Michael would try to sell the idea to his girls, "See, this is better than watching it on TV." The girls would just roll their eyes. Maggie hated for her kids to be in the front yard without adult supervision when visiting Toledo. April once walked Mark and Missy to the corner store when a police chase was just announced over Michael's police scanner. They could hear the sirens in the distance.

"They sound close!" said Michael with great excitement in his voice.

"Be advised that the suspect is heading down Ontario Street heading north," said the dispatcher.

"Oh, my God! Here they come!" said Maggie as they could hear the chase quickly approaching.

Standing at the corner of Ontario and Galena Streets was April clutching her two grandchildren as they waited to cross the street. The blue car sped past them with a police car from Northwood County on his tail. The Toledo Police attempted to cut him off on Galena, but because of the high speed of the chase and three pedestrians standing on the corner, they had to abort the attempt at that intersection.

Maggie and Michael could barely breathe! April told the kids that it was no big deal as they continued their trip to the store. The car, which was stolen, later hit a vacant house a few blocks over and the young man escaped on foot. Mark and Missy didn't react to such excitement, but Maggie felt as if she lost ten years off her life that afternoon with worry. The very image of her white-haired mother clutching on to her two small children would forever be etched in Maggie's memory.

"Now see, wasn't that better than anything you've ever seen on TV?" said Michael with a nervous smile upon his face.

"Dad!" she said as she put her hand up. "I don't want to hear it!" said Maggie as her heart began to find its normal rhythm.

That neighborhood was not filled with bad people. There were families who lived there for years. Many families have formed bonds with their neighbors over the years and watch out for one another. Michael started a Crime Stoppers group in the neighborhood and he got a better response from it than he anticipated. He knew many people and he was not afraid to say hello to those he didn't know.

His favorite story about those who did not know him was that they always thought he was a detective because he wore business suits and a pager, which was not common in those days. Every morning, the same group of people standing on the drug corner would wave at him on his way to work. Some of them even called him "Mr. Getman, sir." He would be cordial and he never corrected them with their beliefs of his law enforcement status. He swore that was why his home had never been vandalized or burglarized after all those years they resided there. Despite the theft of his steaks and beer in the garage, he did lose a few gallons of gasoline in the seventies and a car battery or two in the early eighties. Yet, he still professed his love for that neighborhood.

Chapter 16

Michael was enjoying the conversations of days gone by with his children. Once the stories began, it was as if no one wanted them to end. Maybe it was another form of procrastination, but no one seemed to mind. Maddie always labeled their gab sessions as therapy. Michael swore that if he did not have his children to vent with, he would explode. Maggie always worried about getting carried away to the point of having a "Mom bashing" session. They all loved April, but they could never understand her.

"It feels strange to speak freely in this house without April sneaking up on us, making us feel as if we did something wrong," said Michael.

"How many phone calls did we have that were interrupted by her? She would always tell Dad to stop wasting our time with his boring stories or she would tell him to wrap up his conversation with his daughters because he was wasting money on the phone call," said Maddie.

"I remember when we all got on the same cellular plan and it cost nothing for either of us to call person-to-person. Mom grew suspicious that every conversation would pertain to her and that we were all talking about her behind her back," said Maggie.

"Paranoia would be the word you are looking for to describe April. She would eavesdrop on my conversations with you girls and she would tell me not to tell the whole world about our business. I have never seen any mother so jealous of her own kids in all my life!"

"Mom answered Dad's cell phone one day as if she caught a mistress setting up a rendezvous with a married man. It irritated me because she knew it was me that was calling! She could see my name on the caller ID, yet she spoke to me as if I were a stranger who just got caught with my hand in the cookie jar," said Maggie.

"What was Mom doing with your phone, Dad?" asked Kenneth.

"If I was without my phone, it must have been on the charger. She never told me that you called."

"That was Mom's way about her. She didn't tell you about a lot of things," said Maddie.

"It was a form of dominance she held over you," said Kenneth.

"More like control, that is," said Kobe.

"Mom had us all marching around here for years," said Maggie quietly.

"That's why Dad has no butt! Mom chewed it off years ago!" giggled Maddie.

They have all accepted years ago that the day could not begin until they knew what April's mood was going to be. They have all learned to jump around certain landmines she would set. April was quick to annihilate her family's spirit with an unsuspecting blow by them unintentionally triggering a spiteful personality in one form or another. Heartache and disappointment were no strangers in that house; April's house.

"I wish I had a dollar for every time Mom would announce that this was *her* house. I know that I would be a billionaire by now for sure!" scoffed Kobe.

"The words us, our, and we were nonexistent from Mom's vocabulary. Her favorite words were me, mine, and myself!" said Maggie.

"I swear that she had five different personalities," said Michael.

"I bet I can name two of them," said Maggie with certainty.

"I know all of you met them from one time or another, but enlighten me, Maggie. Tell me the ones you know," said Michael as he challenged his daughter.

"Okay, Dad. I'll accept your challenge. I hear a whiny childlike voice when she wants something. Sometimes she sounds like that when she doesn't get her way. I call that one little April Ann. The other one I'm familiar with, the one who uses me, mine and myself, is Katherine. Sometimes she comes out of nowhere."

"Katherine was the more dominant of the two. April Ann was provoked when the young grandkids were around and there was a confrontation or showdown over toys," said Kenneth.

"We cannot forget April, the woman I fell in love with and married. She did have her good days, but they were rare. I labeled one of them as Lucy, from the Peanuts gang. She could get my hopes up for something and at the last minute she would retract her offer. It was like the football that Lucy would yank away from Charlie Brown just before he would kick it. I always fell for it, knowing in the back of my mind that she would do that. The other personality was called The Basher. That was the one where all the joy in the universe was sucked out by her dark force."

"So you say there are five personalities?" asked Maddie.

"Yeah, don't you agree?"

"So, there's April, Katherine, Lucy, April Ann, and The Basher. I've met them all and I think that each one was a total bitch!" stated Maddie harshly.

Michael had tolerated April's abuse for years. At first, he thought it was a small price to pay in order to protect his children. He later carried on with the same sacrifices for his grandchildren. All four of his children asked him on numerous occasions why he put up with her like he did. He would just smile and say that old habits were hard to break. Maggie suspected that her father did something wrong in his life that he felt guilty for and her mother's constant abuse was his punishment. She knew that whatever was behind her father's reasoning, the punishment could not possibly fit the crime.

One Sunday morning, when April was at church, Michael phoned Maggie to vent some frustration. He told her that April was in one of her moods and they got into a screaming match in the back yard on Saturday. April, once again, reminded him that he was nothing more than a guest in *her* house. They argued only because Michael didn't feel like being passive anymore. He realized that his children were adults and child-support, no longer an issue, convinced him that he had nothing to lose. He decided that when April would push him in the future, he was ready to push back.

He reminded her that he remodeled and paid for everything in the house. That makes the house his, too. She was quick to remind him that Aunt Paula sold *her* that house, not him! He pointed out that when she refinanced the house for Maddie's first wedding, his name was on the re-mortgage contract. As their argument escalated in the back yard, April grew more irate with the man. Michael had just finished mowing the lawn moments before the argument while April rinsed the grass-clippings from the sidewalk.

"You never finish any project around here that you start!" she snapped.

"That's because every time I start something, you have to stand in my way criticizing my work *before* it gets done. I can handle your bitching to a point, but when you constantly tell me that this house is not my home is when I quit! Why should I fix something for you if I am not a part of it?"

"What are you talking about? You're talking crazy!"

"You looked me in the eye two weeks ago and told me that this is your f-ing house and..."

April, standing only three feet from Michael, proceeded to squirt him in the chest with the high power jet stream from the nozzle of the hose. He was crouched down cleaning the bottom side of the mower when she hit him in the chest. He was surprised by the sudden sting of cold water, cold water was one of his biggest pet peeves, and he lost his balance and fell to the ground onto his back. He was stunned by her actions and he never saw that coming. He felt as if he had just been sucker-punched by his wife. April stepped forward and continued to spray him in the center of the chest for a few seconds longer.

"There! That ought to cool you off," she said with a sneer. "*I* am a Christian and *I* do not use the 'F' word in *my* house!"

Michael restrained himself as best as he could after that incident. He watched April walk into her house without giving him a second glance. He remained silent with her for about two weeks after their argument. She thought it was funny enough to call Maggie in Indianapolis to share her excitement. April did not know that Michael already told her the news, but Maggie had to act as if it were the first time she heard the story. This was something she learned from her childhood when dealing with her feuding parents. She always did her best to remain neutral.

"Yeah, I sprayed him with the icy cold water right in the chest. I knew that would get his attention and cool him off. You know how your father is with cold water," she boasted.

"Oh, my gosh, Mom! I cannot believe you did that to him. Why? What did he do to deserve that?"

"You mean other than breathing?" laughed April. "He claimed that I said that this is my f-ing house. Can you believe that? I am a Christian woman and *we* Christians do not speak like that!"

"You told me that you said that to Dad months ago. Remember? It was when you tried to stop him from smoking on *your* property. You accused him of smoking too close to the front door. You were angry that he refused to stop smoking and he continued to smoke on the porch. Don't you remember? Maybe you weren't a Christian woman quite then," said Maggie, surprising even herself with such a statement.

April never initiated a long-distance conversation with Maggie after that comment. The family knew that April was growing meaner by the hour. They worried about such an aggressive move against their father. Alcohol was not a factor then because she had been sober for years. April acted out of hatred towards Michael and made no apologies for doing such. Everyone had a breaking point, including Michael, which the family feared that he might one day snap. The neighbors witnessed the ongoing tension between the couple and openly talked about it. Some made jokes to Michael about April.

"Hey, Michael, I thought about you when I watched the Channel 11 News last night," said Tanner Beason, the neighbor kid who grew up with the twins.

"Really? Why was that?" asked Michael with an upbeat tone.

"There was an eighty-year-old man who was in the hospital for mysterious bruises and lacerations on his body. The man was in a wheelchair and his injuries did not look as if he fell. The hospital personnel were puzzled. When they asked his wife if she did it, she admitted to it because she said that he got on her nerves! They didn't take her too seriously because she looked like a sweet, loving grandmother. When he was healed enough to go back home, she did it to him again! It was so funny because they were fighting over the

TV remote," laughed Tanner hysterically. "I instantly thought of you!"

That was when Michael realized that his situation wasn't funny anymore. He always hid his pain with humor. He would be the first person to laugh at himself just to bring a smile to someone else. He treated strangers the same way. Everyone in the neighborhood liked Michael. One woman down the street asked Michael if there was a Mrs. Getman. He was stunned by such a question, but he quickly realized that April lived her life like a hermit. She spoke to no one and wanted nothing to do with the outside world.

April's routine consisted of her getting ready for work in the morning, motoring off to work until 4 PM, walking through the door without a single word to her husband until she'd had her afternoon nap in her rocking chair, she would eat dinner that Michael cooked, had another nap, wake up in time for the evening news and a bowl of ice cream, and finally go off to bed. She never liked to do anything but sleep. She claimed that the kids were especially wild at work and that she needed a few minutes of quiet time for herself, but Michael grew tired of her excuses for her unhealthy lifestyle.

Michael warned his family for years that he was about to act out his fantasy of jumping a train and traveling the country. April always laughed at his hopes and dreams. The kids learned that was his code for leaving and never coming back. The grandkids thought he was dying, but he got them all straightened out on that matter. Michael had two bags packed in his truck for the day he was brave enough to walk out the front door.

That day came at a moment's notice when Michael walked in on April's rare telephone conversation with Maddie. April told Maddie that Michael would fall into the premature ejaculation category, which in her mind justifies the absence of sexual relations over the last twenty years. She continued with regretting that Michael was the only partner she had intercourse with and that she had nothing to compare, unlike Maddie. Michael did what he normally did, which was to ignore her harsh comments and walk away from her.

He went upstairs to grab a quick shower because he knew that was the last straw. He knew that tonight was the night. He took one last look around his room before he got dressed. He went downstairs to find April watching TV, which was her only means to having a life.

The TV was more important to her than her own family. She refused phone calls from family members in the past because of the television. The idiot box was a form of company that she accepted because she could manipulate it with a click of a button.

"I believe we've all caught Mom during those moments," said Kobe.

"I remember when I was home visiting and I shared a scary experience with Mom that a coworker had experienced with his two-year-old daughter. Little Michaela swallowed three quarters, which they had no idea until an X-ray revealed the reason for her difficulty breathing. Mom was watching a commercial on TV and she was annoyed for me talking through it. She snapped that she did not know Michaela and that story meant nothing to her!" said Kenneth.

"Well then, I guess no one was exempt," stated Maddie, being a bit stunned by Kenneth's harsh treatment by April. After all, he was the good son.

She turned away calls from her own mother and Aunt Paula by whispering, "Tell her that I'm not here," as she watched a program that was in syndication. She later treated her daughters with a similar attitude, who would call long-distance, but she would ignore them or tell them to wait until a breaking point in the dialog. She made it obvious that she did not want to speak with them because of her preoccupation with the boob tube. It was clear to the girls that she was simply uninterested in what they had to say.

Michael sat in his chair, which was on the opposite side of April's. He looked refreshed on the outside, but he felt numb and wounded on the inside. He tapped his fingers on the end table that separated their chairs. He stared at the old owl lamp contemplating what it was that he was going to say to her. He always felt guilty about leaving her in the past because he felt as if he were dumping a lame dog in the country to fend for herself. He had so much to say, but he did not know where to start. He figured simplicity was the better approach to address his farewell. Beneath the surface, he could feel the familiar feeling of him about to lose his nerve.

"Who was on the phone?"

"I was speaking to Maddie."

"How is she? Is everything alright?" he asked while trying his best to sound concerned.

"I was just telling her that you've been a good boy and that I haven't had to hose you down lately in the back yard," she said with a sneer. He just stared at her in silence as she turned to watch the television.

After a long pause, Michael said, "Do you remember what I said to you on our wedding day? It requires some thought, so take your time."

"How on earth am I supposed to recall something *you* said four decades ago?" she barked without looking away from the TV.

"I said that I promise to make the living if you promise to make the living worthwhile."

"I remember that now. That was the corniest line I ever heard," she scoffed.

"Well," he said as he slowly stood up, "I kept *my* end of the bargain," and walked towards the front door.

"Where are you going?" she asked with a look of surprise.

As his hand was on the doorknob, he turned to face his wife. He took a deep breath and smiled as he said, "I'm going *out* for a pack of cigarettes!"

Michael fantasized about using that line for years. He should have left under more intense situations, but on that particular day he had a low-tolerance for her abuse. He traveled as much as possible and when he was in town, he stayed with Maddie knowing that was one place April would stay away from. On rare occasions he would send April a post card that would read: "This looks better in person. The television cannot capture the total essence of such beauty." Michael had rediscovered life while April's stayed the same.

April continued to live her life acting as if she had no part in Michael's absence. She went to church and still refused luncheons with the members because she claimed that she had to race home and fix lunch for Michael. She did not like being around people, so she thought lying would be her best defense. It was in her nature. No one outside of the family knew Michael was gone, much less her ever fixing him lunch after church.

Aunt Cami accidentally told Maddie about April's little fib one Sunday afternoon, which made Maddie furious for such a blatant lie, especially in God's house! April never fixed lunch for her husband because she refused to be an inferior female to the dominant male species. She only acted as if she were a caring wife when she was surrounded by strangers who did not know the real side of her. Everything was an act with April. She was the leading lady in her mind's nonstop production of April's Little World.

"Do you remember the Christmas Eve we spent at Grandpa Getman's house when Mom got really drunk?" asked Maddie.

"I remember her doing a header in Uncle Irvie's shrubs," laughed Kobe.

"She was so wasted!" said a wide-eyed Kenneth.

"I remember her being in the living room using the f-word while all the men in the family were in the basement playing poker," said Maggie.

"I was so embarrassed when the younger kids ran downstairs to tattle on the profanity being said in your grandpa's house," said Michael.

Grandpa Getman stood at the bottom of the stairs while Michael dealt the next hand. The three youngsters stood by their grandfather as he yelled upstairs. "Who's using bad language up there?" he yelled. There was some giggling coming from upstairs as the whole group of kids collectively shouted, "It's Aunt April, Grandpa." Aunt Gabby cackled out loud as she witnessed her brother about slide under the poker table from embarrassment.

Grandpa Getman had a look of surprise upon his face, too. He took a deep breath and yelled, "April, stop it! Don't make me have to come up there!" In the distance, they all heard a small voice say, "Okay." Her nieces and nephews sold her out. She slammed a few more beers and Michael poured her into the car. When they made it home, April decided to challenge him to a fight. She attempted to throw a package at him, but she lost her footing and fell backwards into a snow bank.

"I remember that being our worst Christmas ever," said Maggie.

"I remember two kittens running all over her Christmas morning as she was sprawled out on the dining room floor," said Maddie with a giggle.

"Yeah, the spike of her shoe got caught in the floor vent, which sent her crashing to the floor. She was too drunk to realize that she could have removed her shoe to free herself, but under the circumstances, I was disgusted and I left her there," said Michael.

"The vent is bent today, marking the occasion," laughed Maddie.

When April was drinking, she could not stop at one beer. Michael loved his beer and it did not matter if it was warm or cold. He drank a lot too, but he wouldn't allow himself to get blitzed as often as his wife. He once offered her one hundred dollars if she could quit drinking for one week. He quit drinking during that time frame to show support for his wife. She accepted his wager and remained sober for seven days to the very minute.

She walked down to the corner grocery store and purchased a twelve-pack. April sat at the table and watched intently for the clock to strike noon. The whole family stood in the dining room watching her with great disappointment. Her fingers were ready to rip open the seams of the box. Michael offered to pay her one thousand dollars to go a full month.

She glared at him and said, "Get out of my face!" The minute hand reached the twelve and she ripped the box open and downed four beers in the matter of minutes. Michael just shook his head in disappointment and threw the prize money on the table and walked away. She bragged about Michael being a sore loser. She enjoyed arguments of males being the weaker gender in the world when she was drunk. Michael would never give her a nibble when she was fishing for that kind of argument.

"I hated when she would talk about dealing with *her* men at work. She acted as if she owned them," said Maggie.

"I hated when she hung all over Jack! That was so embarrassing to me because that was my best friend's father," said Maddie.

"Just imagine how she treated him at work," suggested Michael.

Jack Johnstone was not only Jenny's dad, but also a neighboring friend of the family, and he was the boss at the automotive parts company. He was the only person in the neighborhood that Michael claimed as a friend. They enjoyed conversations about NASCAR, politics in the business world, and beer.

Their families would gather every weekend for a cookout in the back yard. April's drinking increased and so did her obvious attraction for her boss. Mrs. Johnstone was beginning to get annoyed by April's drunken advances toward her husband. She and Jack had numerous arguments over April. Finally, they stopped coming to visit altogether.

"She was so in to her Women's Rights that she announced how she was never a weak female and that she loaded her own car parts into her delivery truck without help from any male," said Michael.

"She was like that with us, too. Anytime I would confide in Mom about any problem with my marriage, she would be quick to call me a pushover. She would tell me that I was a weak female and she would never just lay down for any male to walk all over her like I do," said Maddie.

"Yeah, I could never share any conversations about struggles or concerns with my kids because she would say that now I know what hell *she* went through and how Dad always sided with Maddie," said Maggie.

"It always irritated me that no matter how big of a problem we had to deal with, she always found a way to belittle us about never addressing it properly," said Maddie.

April had to put herself in the center of any situation. She was not capable of sympathizing with anyone unless she could manipulate the conversation to revolve around her. She took great pleasure in her children's suffering because it was as if she could kick them down lower than they originally felt by her insults and calloused feelings about motherhood. She made them feel as if their feelings were unimportant because she survived her trials and tribulations on her own. She was a self-proclaimed mother-of-the-year.

"When I was pregnant for Allie, she saw the picture of me posing on my stolen car after it was towed back to our apartment building from the impound lot. I was stunned that she claimed that *she* took that picture. She was in Toledo then and Alec took it for me, not her. She became insistent that she took that picture."

"I took that picture, remember?" April would say in her most convincing voice to Maggie.

"She's done that on numerous occasions," said Michael.

"I think she's done it more to Maggie than she has to the rest of us," said Maddie.

"That's because she expected Maggie to agree with her," said Kobe.

"I could tell her a funny story about my kids and she would claim that she was there when it happened. It could have taken place that day, but Mom would swear that she was present when it happened. It became very alarming to us all," said Kenneth.

After April stopped drinking, the family noticed that she could not drink enough water. She also started to speak about being included in her family's stories when it was apparent that she was not around them. Michael figured that she was just filling in the voids of her drunken memory. The mean personality that surfaced when she was drunk soon became a permanent member of the family during her sobriety, which horrified the family.

"I was so proud of her when she quit drinking. She also quit smoking at the same time. I applauded her tremendous accomplishments often. But then she learned to knock me down with her newfound sharp-tongued remarks," said Michael.

"I did *not* do this for you! I did this for *myself*!" April would snap.

Michael tried to quit drinking and smoking too, but he felt that he needed some sort of vice in order to survive living with her. For many years Michael wished for death to free him from his wedding vows to that woman. He even had their tombstone placed on their cemetery plots in order to keep him bound to her. When April had a bad day, Michael's would be worse. She would ridicule his drinking and smoking on a daily basis.

"Get out of my face! You smell like a brewery and an ash tray," Michael would hear April say repeatedly.

Michael had to leave many public establishments because of April's refusal of being around cigarette smoke. They went to the cinema one evening and April refused to walk inside the building because patrons were smoking outside the door. She would throw her hands across her face and pretend to gasp for breath. Michael was always embarrassed by her absurd actions in public and he was heavily disappointed knowing that the Lucy personality showed herself as they walked back to the car. Michael learned not to get his hopes up on anything. Not seeing a movie that night was the least of his discontent.

Since April quit smoking, Michael moved out to the front porch to smoke. He took the initiative to smoke outdoors out of respect for his nonsmoking wife. She smoked in front of her children since they were infants, which she claims she never did such a thing. There was a picture that surfaced of April smoking while she was pregnant for Maddie, but it quickly disappeared.

The twins took turns going to the hospital when they were toddlers for severe respiratory infections, which the doctor repeatedly asked April not to smoke around the children. She refused to believe then that her smoking would cause health problems to her twins. Now she was quick to chastise any smoker and accuse them of child abuse for smoking around their children.

April always used Michael's smoking as an excuse for not allowing him to kiss her on the lips. However, she would occasionally complain to Maggie about Michael only kissing her on the top of her head, which eventually ended altogether.

"I remember the time when Maggie scrubbed the walls of the living room one afternoon to remove the smoke stains off the white paneling," said Michael.

"I did that when I was in eighth grade. I took it upon myself to clean the walls and dust all the picture frames and figurines on the shelves. I tried to finish before you and Mom got home from work, but I did not count on having to change the bucket as often as I did, which slowed me down."

"Your mother and I walked in the door at the same time. Do you remember what she said?"

"Yeah. She was furious with me for trashing the house."

"Look at this dump! What have *you* done? Where's our dinner? I don't have time for this crap!" April growled.

"I'll never forget the expression of hurt on your face when she said that. You were standing on the top of the ladder wiping down the farthest corner of the wall when she said that. You started to climb down the ladder to clean up the picture frames off the floor. I was never so disgusted with her at that point in time. I was very touched that you took on such a monstrous project by yourself."

"I remember you taking off your suit jacket and rolling up your sleeves to help me. You told Maddie to order pizza, which was a huge treat for us back then. We could not get over how white the walls actually were! There was so much tar that covered the walls over the years, which made it look like a dark yellowish-brown. We were both amazed!"

"No one had ever done that project again. Shortly after that is when I started smoking outside. After April quit smoking, no one was allowed to smoke inside that house again. Besides that, years later I covered up those two windows to make room for more pictures to display on our grandchildren wall," said Michael with pride.

"Speaking of the grandkids, we had better be getting back to the funeral home because that is where we are all meeting," said Kobe.

"Yeah, Chase should be there in about twenty minutes with Trey and Jordan. He said that he has something for my cooler," Maddie said with a smile.

"Brenda is dropping off the girls after dinner. I want to be sure that I won't miss them coming in. This is their first funeral," said Kenneth.

"I'm going to stay here until my family arrives. They should be here shortly," said Maggie.

"Okay, we'll see you there. Drive safely and call me on my cell phone if you need anything," said Michael.

They all headed out the front door to their vehicles. Maggie went to lock the front door behind them. Michael came back into the house before she had the opportunity to turn the lock. He smiled at her and announced that nature calls as he ran upstairs. It was always a family joke that if anyone had to poop, they used the upstairs bathroom. Maggie preferred that particular bathroom because there was a lock on the door and a window to open. Privacy was a true privilege in that house.

She remembered when Alec first came to Toledo to meet Maggie's parents. He used the downstairs bathroom and then returned to the living room. He was nervous getting acquainted with his girlfriend's family. He believed that first impressions were important. Kenneth and Kobe came in the house to meet him. Kobe ran upstairs to use the bathroom while Kenneth walked into the one downstairs. Maggie laughed out loud over the memory.

"Who pooped downstairs?" demanded Kenneth as he ran out of the bathroom with his shirt over his nose.

"Why? Is the plumbing backed up?" asked Michael.

"No! But it smells like shit!"

"Uh, sorry, man. I used the bathroom when I got here," said Alec with embarrassment.

"Dude! No one poops downstairs, it's the rule!"

"Sorry, I did not know that," said Alec.

"Well, now you know."

Kobe came running down stairs and caught a whiff of the aroma coming from the little bathroom at the bottom of the stairway. He stopped dead in his tracks.

"Who took a dump in here?" he said.

"We've already been through that," said Kenneth.

Maggie wanted to crawl under a rock after the interrogation of her new boyfriend. Michael and April never reprimanded the twins because they treated everyone like that. Alec was no exception to the rules. That very evening, Alec and Maggie were laying on the couch watching TV. Kobe told Alec to quickly look over at him. When he did, Kobe had his rear end about two inches from Alec's face and proudly broke wind! Maggie jumped up to hit her brother, but Kobe was too fast. Kobe grinned and quoted Eddie Murphy by saying, "It's the fart game, everybody plays!"

The next morning, Maggie made Alec a nice home-cooked breakfast. Alec kept a close eye on Kobe, who was sitting in Michael's chair in the living room. April was sitting in her rocking chair watching TV. Alec leaned over to Maggie and whispered, "It's payback time!"

He proceeded to approach Kobe and lunged at him with his hip high in the air. Poor unsuspecting Kobe tried to get out of the chair, but it was too late. Alec landed on Kobe, nearly knocking over the owl lamp, and returned fire on his lap. Kobe laughed while April and Maggie shared an expression of shock and disbelief on their faces. It was then clear to Alec that he was accepted into the family with open arms. Alec and the twins became smut buddies shortly after that. Today Alec accepts them as the best brothers he never had.

When Michael came back downstairs he approached Maggie with an envelope in his hand.

"What's that?" she asked.

"You're not going to believe this, but I found this last night under the doily of the owl lamp," he said as he handed it to her.

Maggie took the envelope from her father and studied it with great curiosity. She read everything visible on it. By the looks of its yellowish appearance, it was obvious to her that it was old. She read that it was addressed to Mr. and Mrs. Michael Getman and family.

She noticed the postmark read September 9, 1974, from Phoenix, Arizona. She looked up at Michael as her heart about beat right out of her chest. She looked at the return address that read, "Katherine Connolly."

"What's this about?"

"I thought you might be interested in reading it. I didn't tell the others because you were the one who always expressed an interest in Katherine."

"I always wondered if she was as mean as Mom claimed she was," said Maggie, still staring at the envelope.

"Now you can read the letter and judge for yourself."

"Is it right for me to read her personal mail?"

"Did you see who it was addressed to? You have just as much right to read that letter as April. It was addressed to all of us. I never saw this letter a day in my life! I never got a chance to get to know Katherine out of respect for your mother."

"This letter says 1974. I was only six years old then. What does it say?"

"Since you are here alone, read it and tell me later what you make of it. I need to get out of here before Maddie raids my cooler in the back of my truck!"

Michael left the house as Maggie sat in the rocking chair in disbelief. She slowly removed the letter from the envelope. She read the letter three times. Maggie felt as if she were in a time warp. She read the letter with tears in her eyes over such compassion from a grandmother to her granddaughter. Maggie became more confused by the stories of the past with each word she carefully read:

Dearest April and family,

Thank you so much for the nice letter. It is always good to hear from family back home. I am so glad to hear that the babies are out of the hospital and doing much better. I did not know they were ill until your mother wrote and told me. Did you watch Evel Knievel? We witnessed it live! I just worry about the thousands of kids out there killing themselves by imitating such stunts. Your grandfather's lemon tree has its first lemon. We are so excited about that. Arizona is beautiful out here and I would love to have all of you visit Herbert and me. Arizona's beauty would not be whole without you visiting us here.

We send you all lots of love and good luck,
Grandma Katherine

So many thoughts raced through her mind. She had to go outside to clear her head. She wondered why April never spoke of her correspondence with her grandmother. Maggie knew all too well that this was something that was impossible to slip one's mind. She was beginning to feel anger that her mother destroyed any possibility of a relationship with her great-grandmother. Her mother's secret delivered a sense of betrayal. Maggie and her family knew nothing about the woman other than what April told them. She felt her stomach bunch up in knots.

As she was getting her thoughts together, the neighbor widow woman, Mrs. Dooley, came over to offer her condolences. When the Getman family first moved into the neighborhood, the girls were told by Aunt Cami that the old woman's name was Mrs. Locks. Rumors circulated that she was a very wealthy woman. She was a little on the exocentric side. It was said that every weekday she would ride the Tarta bus downtown to the Toledo Savings and Loan just to visit her money.

As the girls grew older, they realized that was just a label given to the elder because she would lock her house up tight every night without fail. She would even check her windows at night with a flashlight from the inside and outside of the house. She never changed her nightly routine. She was known to be frugal and it was well-known that she turned her plumbing off to save money. She would urinate in Mason Jars and pour it on her bushes every night at 10 PM while wearing only her moth-eaten under-slip. The stench of urine was her attempt at keeping burglars away. She would stand on her front porch for a few minutes thinking no one could see her in her half-naked appearance.

She lived her life similar to Mrs. Havisham, a character from Charles Dickens' novel *Great Expectations*. She was married once and her husband, heavily involved in politics, never came back home from the office. She was a newlywed then and set the table for a romantic dinner. It was said that the table was still set today just as it was the night of his disappearance, waiting for the love of her life to return. She never dined at that table again. He was presumed dead after seven years. She was quite a catch in her day and was once crowned Miss Toledo when she was a teenager. She never remarried.

She was wearing a bright pink dress, charming in its day, which was tattered and torn. She wore a brown mink Stoll and a hat to match. Her hair was thin and unkempt. Her teeth were as yellow as an ear of corn, which gave her breath a horrific and offensive odor. She was wearing a pair of black galoshes, like she always did, just so she would not be caught off guard by an unsuspected rainstorm. This was the same woman who paid the neighbor kids a nickel to trim her stinky and dying bushes.

"Hello, Mrs. Dooley, it's so nice to see you. You are looking lovely, as usual," Maggie said with a smile.

"Are you Maggie or Maddie? I can never keep you girls straight!" she said in an elevated voice. She spoke loud because her hearing was poor and she was oblivious to shouting at those conversing with her.

"I'm Maggie. Maddie is the one with better legs," she joked.

"I'm sorry about your mother. It is a real shame. She was just a child herself."

Maggie just smiled thinking that all centenarians must say the same thing. She was a walking history book of the north end. She used to work for a lawyer on Galena Street during the depression. She told the Getman girls that the north end was once considered the upscale part of town. Riverside Park, which was now called the Jamie Farr Park, was once like a country club. Getting past the smell of her breath, she was very interesting to listen to.

They made small talk while Maggie saw a familiar glow of an orange Avalanche truck turning the corner from Buckeye to Ontario Street. She got excited and announced, "Oh! I see the Great Pumpkin!" She always called the truck that referring to Charles Shultz's Halloween special called *It's The Great Pumpkin Charlie Brown!* Alec always laughed when she said it. She told Mrs. Dooley that she had to go because her family was just pulling up to the curb.

Alec pulled in behind Maggie's car. She saw her three kids waving to her as Alec parked the truck. She missed them more than she realized. She felt tears of joy welling up in her eyes. They greeted their mother with hugs that nearly knocked her to the ground. Alec stood there watching the excitement of his kids as he removed his sunglasses. Mrs. Dooley was watching from a distance. Maggie worried that she might be confused and thought she was witnessing a mugging on the street.

"Do you think they missed their mom?" asked Alec with admiration.

"Nowhere near as much as what I missed all of you," she said.

The kids grabbed their overnight bags from the back of the truck and marched into the house. Missy was the first one in the house to raid Grandma's chocolate covered peanuts in the refrigerator. Allie and Mark were close behind her. Alec and Maggie remained outside on the sidewalk for a quiet moment. He leaned down to hug his wife around her waist. He lifted her up into his arms as if she were a child. He had not done that since they were dating.

"I missed you so much, baby," he said tenderly. "I worried about you just as much."

"You would not believe the past twenty-four hours I've had. I swear this is a bad dream that I cannot wake up from."

The couple sat on the porch while Alec gave Maggie the emotional status of the kids. Mark and Missy seemed to be fine, but Allie was still having periods of crying spells. For the most part, he assured Maggie that they worried about her more than anything else. Mark wanted to give his mother all of his allowance if it would make her feel better. Missy drew a booklet of pictures for her mother, which was a perfect analogy of the little girl's feelings. She always expressed herself with her artwork. Allie wanted to be in Toledo as soon as she heard the news. She was angry that Maggie left without her.

"Allie did not want you to be alone. She complained the whole ride here that this was the longest ride of her life!"

"Yeah, I can sympathize. Fort Wayne construction can make anyone feel that way," she joked.

"She is going to miss her grandmother, but she is more concerned about you."

"We've always shared a special bond. Remember when she was little and could pick up on our thoughts?"

"Yes! It scared the stuffin' out of me!" said Alec.

"I remember once, when she was having a nightmare, our dreams merged together and I saved her on the playground from millions of snakes," said Maggie.

"She claimed that you *did* save her in that dream. She told me that she was having a nightmare and you appeared out of nowhere to save her. She said that she was playing on the playground and snakes came slithering up to her. She said that you grabbed her and you carried her up a very tall slide. You slept in that morning and you told me the same dream before you had an opportunity to speak with Allie! That freaked me out a bit, Maggie."

"I've always said that Allie was an extension of myself. The poor girl is just like her mother!"

"Yes, and Missy is loaded with your orneriness while Mark has your sense of humor! Some days I feel outnumbered!"

"Oh, honey, without you they would not be here. Mark looks just like you and for the record, they are all just as gullible as you," she said with a mischievous grin.

"Okay now, I'll except that because that brought a smile to your beautiful face."

"How many times do I have to tell you that you are the sunshine to my cloudy day?" she said in her most convincing voice.

Mark came outside to announce that Grandma was out of her chocolate covered nuts. Missy soon followed and said that it was time to leave because of the same reasons. Maggie just sighed and leaned into Alec.

"Can I just stay right here in your arms forever?" she asked.

"This spot is reserved for no one but you," he said as he kissed her on the forehead.

"When do we have to be there?" asked Allie from the screen door.

"We'll leave whenever you're ready. There's no hurry. You are welcomed to stay here for a while and stretch your legs before we head over there," said Maggie.

"If we don't go now, I don't know that I'll ever be ready," said Allie.

Maggie was quick to pick up on her daughter's tone. She looked at Alec as if he could understand what it was that she was about to do. He kept Missy and Mark outside while Maggie went in the house to speak with Allie. Maggie took Allie by the hand and walked her to the kitchen. Maggie thought, *Whenever I went to the kitchen with my mother, it always resulted in her digging her claws into my arm and blistering my butt.* She looked in her daughter's eyes with such compassion that it made them both breakdown and cry. They held one another for support as they appreciated the comfort of a shoulder in return.

"How are you holding up, Ms. President?" she asked as she wiped away her daughter's tears.

"Obviously I'm not doing very well, Mom," she said with a half-hearted smile. "The very thought of the importance of yesterday's election means nothing to me today knowing that my mother's heart is broken."

"Oh, Al, it's not a sin to be happy over such a spectacular achievement despite any bad news you may receive. Please don't let Grandma's passing ruin it for you. It was just her time to go. Remember what Grandpa Getman always said about everyone being born with a book. Each page represents a day, which is filled by the life we live. Everyone has a story to tell when they get to Heaven. Some stories are long; some are short, some are happy, while others are sad. Some things we have no control over. That is what life is about. Just like birth marks the beginning of life while death marks its end."

"Mom, I never got to tell her that I made class president."

"Trust me on this, I believe that she knows."

"How can you be so sure?"

"I have no tangible proof to offer you, but I have that female intuition that tells me so. Who knows, maybe she is in Heaven holding my future grandbabies right now while sharing family secrets."

"I really loved Grandma and I am going to miss her, Mom."

"Me, too."

"My heart is broken more over the stories you have with her. They are not as nice as mine."

"Allie, don't you go worrying about things out of your control. This is all recorded in my book of life. I've accepted long ago that bad things had happened to me, but I put them in God's hands and prayed that I wouldn't carry hatred in my heart towards anyone; especially my own mother. You know something, Allie, He listened to me. I've always felt sorry for my mother more so than hating her."

"I have seen many times in the past her being mean to you when you didn't deserve it. She would make you sound like a terrible mother when you were not around her, but not as bad as she talked about Aunt Maddie!"

"If someone is physically challenged, do we hate him or her for it?"

"No! Of course not," said Allie.

"We need to also ask ourselves that same question if someone is mentally challenged. Most people in our family believe that your grandmother was just mean, but I have that nagging thought that maybe she was ill. Live your life with minimal regret, Allie, and you will be rewarded in ways that cannot be measured by money. You, your brother, and your sister are living proof of that. You are all priceless to me."

"Don't forget about Dad!" said Allie with a snicker as a smile lit up her face.

"I could *never* forget your dad. I have countless blessings every day of my life. I've learned that if we carry hatred and negativity within our hearts, we become blinded to life's little treasures. It is so important that you know to never let anger consume you because it makes you ugly on the inside, which becomes visible by your actions on the outside."

Allie hugged Maggie and said, "I love you so much, Mom," and then raided the snack drawer. She found more chocolate in there and grabbed a glass of milk. She brushed her teeth and touched up her makeup in the downstairs bathroom. She yelled out to her family, who was still sitting on the front porch, that it was time to leave. Maggie felt better after having her little chat with Allie. She watched her daughter with admiration and thought that she was truly a promising young lady. Allie's graduating class would not be sorry for electing her as their senior class president.

Chapter 17

The funeral home was busy and Maggie noticed more familiar faces. Her children's initial viewing of their grandmother went just as she expected. Allie cried while Mark and Missy remained wide-eyed and silent. Michael invited his grandkids into the lounge to find a sugary treat. Allie wiped away her tears and asked with a sniffle, "Is there any chocolate?"

Michael gave a sheepish grin and said, "Have I ever let you down before?" She asked no more questions and went off with her grandfather with no hesitation.

Aunt Kathleen came with her granddaughters from Put-in-Bay; a small island on Lake Erie. She assured Maggie that Trent and Ronnie would be there for the funeral in the morning. Aunt Cami was on her way back from the airport picking up Aunt Ginny. April's stepbrothers, Thad and Teddy, were there with Donna. She never got her driver's license and now that Bo was gone, she had to rely on her boys to chauffeur her around for shopping and doctor appointments. There were a few neighbors who stopped by to pay their respects along with some coworkers associated with the Getman family.

"Isn't it refreshing to see so many people come?" whispered Alec.

"You sound surprised," teased Maggie.

"You know what I mean by that," he said nervously.

"Relax, hon. I was only joking."

"I know it's that stupid nervous tension that your dad always talks about."

"What ever do you mean?" she said sheepishly.

"Your high-stressed emotional energy makes me nervous!"

"If you are referring to my jokes, I will take that as a compliment."

Kobe was tending to his family while Maddie was still waiting for Chase and the boys to appear. Kelsey and Kyle were mingling about the room greeting family members they had not seen in years. That was the advantage of being the eldest grandchildren; they had been around longer to remember faces farther down the family tree. Kenneth saw Brenda bring his little girls into the room from the rear entrance. Kobe's girls were quick to point out that their young cousins had arrived and ran merrily to greet them.

"So, ding dong the wicked old bitch is really dead, huh?" said Brenda as Kenneth approached her.

"Brenda, this really isn't the time or place for your charm," said Kenneth.

"Well, I'd love to stay, but I have a date," she said as she flipped her hair over her shoulder to reveal the love bites on her neck.

"Don't you want to approach visiting the casket with our daughters as a family since this is their first time in a place like this?"

"Nah, I think you can handle it. I really have to be going now. Oh, by the way, did you hear that I took fourth place in an amateur strip-contest?" she said with excitement.

"Wow! Was that out of four contestants? I didn't know that there was a dog show in town," said Kobe as he stepped between the couple during their conversation.

"Whatever, Kobe!" she said as she rolled her eyes.

She tossed the girls' overnight bag to Kenneth and left the funeral home without saying a single word of sympathy to any of her former in-laws. She was always the main character in her little world, which didn't leave room for anyone else. She wanted a divorce because she said that she lost the person she really was, which Kenneth figured she found the real Brenda swinging naked from a poll in a strip club. Kenneth was slightly embarrassed by her actions and disrespect, but the family was more relieved just to see her leave the building.

Kobe's wife looked less than pleased to be there, too. She was sitting on a chair with her arms tightly folded across her chest. She had her legs crossed at the knee while kicking her foot high in the air as if her leg were a pump. She was sporting the notorious scowl upon her face. Maddie witnessed Kobe walk past his wife as she kicked him hard in the shin. He was quick to sit beside his loving wife while waiting for the throbbing pain to subside. Maddie swooped in wanting to scratch her eyes out, but Maggie stepped in between them while facing Maddie.

"Haze—" Maggie gave her sister a major motherly look of disapproval. Maddie caught her sister's drift when their eyes met and said, "I mean, what's up Angie? I'm glad you made it."

"Hello, Maddie," she said with little enthusiasm.

Kobe was rubbing his shin with his other leg, trying to conceal his attempts to alleviate the pain. Maggie nearly had heart failure with Maddie's near disaster of calling Angie "Hazel" to her face. Witch Hazel was a name that Maddie had labeled the woman since the day she and Kobe said, "I do." Angie was the mother of six children and had recently lost forty pounds or better. With each ten pounds she lost, she rewarded herself with a new body piercing or tattoo. She had the temper of a ten-foot-tall man within her petit frame. Maggie thought Angie looked as if she had a bad day at school. She was studying to become an electrolysis technician.

Michael came to greet the rest of his grandkids and Angie. He gave her a hug and said, "You are looking *really* good." She just smiled and stuck her chest out with pride. Maggie knew he was about to push her over the edge just by the way he was studying the three rings dangling from her eyebrow. "What on earth have you been doing? Did you fall in a tackle box?" said Michael as everyone, but Kobe, giggled.

"If you really want to see something good, look at these!" Kobe said as he raised his shirt to expose his pierced nipples. He was desperate to find an immediate distraction from his wife to keep her from losing her temper.

The expression on Michael's face was priceless. Angie even laughed out loud when Kobe did that. For the first time in years, Michael was speechless. Kobe smiled and said, "These were a gift from Angie. Don't you like 'em? You should see the gift I got for her!" Kenneth laughed out loud when he remembered when Kobe got his ear pierced at sixteen and Michael threatened to make him wear a dress because of it. Michael was never one who was open to change.

"Uh, excuse me, I—I need to talk with your mother!" said Michael as he made a quick beeline toward the casket.

Everyone remained in a small huddle laughing at Michael. Kobe broke the tension by his unexpected display of his latest fashion in body jewelry. The mood was much lighter, including Angie's mood, which made Kobe a hero in the eyes of his family for the hour. Angie became cordial and she even leaned into her husband throughout the evening as he introduced her to family members she never met. She was happy to see that her parents came to pay their respects to the Getman family, too.

Michael was stunned to see a face from the banking days enter the room. George Thomas came in to see his old boss. He was quick to shake his hand and look Michael straight in the eye, which was something he struggled to do in the past. George looked a bit heavier around the midsection and his hair was much thinner on top. He appeared to be sober, which was a side of him Michael never saw. George's eyes were clear and he did not have problems standing in one spot without stumbling.

Michael once told his family that George only carried two things in his briefcase, which were bottles of whiskey and mouthwash. There were only a few occasions when he would come home with Michael, which happened to be for their famous cookouts with the neighbors. Maggie once walked in on George telling his wife on the phone that his boss *made* him go to his house and that he was having a lousy time. Maggie was too young to understand that George was lying to his wife. He always left the house late when he came because he was having too much fun drinking up the boss man's beer.

"Michael! How the hell are you?" said George with an extended hand.

"George, it's really nice of you to come!" said Michael as he reciprocated a firm handshake.

"I read about April in the paper. I'm sorry for your loss. I had no idea that she was sick!"

"Hey, these things happen. I've always told my kids to keep their bags packed because we just never know when we will be called home. You know what I mean?"

"Isn't that the truth!"

The two gentlemen stepped outside for a cigarette. They were catching up a bit, filling one another in on what they had been doing since the Toledo Savings and Loan days. George ended up making manager at a local food chain while Michael made his living as a salesman for nearly fifteen years. Michael got his employment opportunity from a former contact at the bank. George was a bit jealous because he did not have a prized reputation like Michael's, but everyone had his or her own path to walk in life.

"Do you miss the bank at all?" asked George.

"I miss the people, not the ulcers."

"Do you see anyone around anymore?"

"I still keep my accounts with the building we worked in, even though the name of the bank keeps changing. I see some tellers from our old team and they call me by name when I walk in the door. They all tell me the same story on how they think it was terrible for the bank that I lost my job and that it was unfair. I just smile and tell them that being canned was the best thing that ever happened to me. They don't believe me, but I swear that job was going to kill me if I didn't get out soon. I've always believed that they did me a favor by showing me the door," said Michael.

"Wow. I never got that treatment. You were *always* the favorite!" scoffed George.

"What do you mean?"

"I had two security guards meet me at my desk and told me that I had twenty minutes to clean out my desk. They collected my keys and escorted me to the front door!"

"Really?"

"Yeah! At least you were walked down by the river to get your bad news from your boss. Weren't you allowed to finish out the work week?"

"Do you really want me to answer that?" said Michael with a smile.

"Spoiled brat."

"Hey, I really fired myself because my boss was crying too hard to actually say the words."

Michael changed the subject by asking about George's wife and family. His wife was about to retire from the hospital and his youngest boy got a football scholarship at the University of Toledo. His eldest son was a military man with a wife and two kids. Michael could not believe that his family was all grown up when he still remembered them as babies. He could recall when his wife graduated from nursing school at St. Vincent's School of Nursing, much less thinking of her retirement already.

"Wow! Where does the time go?" asked Michael.

"You know, Michael, I missed most of it."

"Are you talking about the long hours you put in at the bank?"

"No. I was always inside of a bottle. I missed the highlights of my life because of alcohol. My kids are grown and I can only depend on their stories of the past because I cannot remember much. It's like I have a *huge* void in my life when it comes to my boys growing up."

"I know alcoholism is a sickness. It affects everyone, not just the person drinking."

"How did you become such an expert on alcoholics?" asked George sarcastically.

"I was married to one."

"April?"

"I called myself one for years, but then I realized there was such a difference between the two of us. I quit for six months, even though I thought about a beer every waking day of my life, but I was able to resist the temptation. April, on the other hand, became a monster in her sobriety. There had been times when we thought she would sneak a drink, but we later realized it was just her personality. She turned into a cold, dark person."

"Wow! I had no idea."

"Well, these are things that we are not supposed to openly talk about."

"I went into rehab because my wife threatened to leave me. I've been clean and sober ever since. I still think about having a drink on a daily basis, too, but they teach you to be strong and resist at all costs. It sounds to me that April needed counseling to help her fully beat it. Being a recovering alcoholic involves much more than just stopping the flow of alcohol, you know."

"It's hard for me to think of it as a disease because I've always viewed it as a choice."

"They are not sure if alcoholism is genetic or if it just happens, but nonetheless it is a horrible disease and the innocent bystanders develop hatred and mistrust towards those individuals. They don't realize that the alcoholic loses much more than the other people involved. Alcoholism robs them of their self-worth and they eventually end up hating themselves. Alcohol is a depressant, my friend, which feeds self-destruction and increases suicidal tendencies."

"How do you mean? You lost me," said Michael.

"Families of alcoholics have their own support groups learning how to deal with bad memories from the alcoholic monsters they encountered on a daily basis. How could you manage going through life knowing you were the one who inflicted such pain and misery on your family? I am still having a hard time forgiving myself for the pain and disappoint I caused my own family. That's the thing about becoming sober, we have to face the damage we created and accept full responsibility—that's the easy part. Finding forgiveness within one's self is the hardest to achieve."

"That's the difference between you and April. She would be quick to blame her drinking on me, the kids, or even her change of life! She had my kids believing that menopause took nearly thirty years! She showed no remorse for her actions because she had to blame someone other than herself. My wife was the number one person in her life. No one came before her. She was never capable of accepting blame or responsibility and she was definitely not capable of hating herself!"

"See what I mean?" said George with sincerity. "Do you hear the pain and anger coming from memories from years ago? This is all like the ripple effect. Alcoholism, like any life-altering disease, touches everyone associated with that individual. Those closest to that person receive the most damage, while others further away are less affected. Nonetheless, it still touches them in some way."

"I remember the grand opening for one of the branches downtown. April was so drunk that she could hardly walk. She threw herself at the president of the bank! I thought I was fired on the spot!"

Michael recalled April saying, "Hello, Bud," in a seductive voice as she nearly tackled the little man with her best attempt at an affectionate hug. After the realization that she made a mistake, which slowly occurred to her, she nonchalantly said, "Oh, *you're* not Bud!"

She giggled as she nearly fell to the ground as the man darted away from her with disgust. Little did the man of such prestige know that April confused him with a security guard.

"My favorite memory of your wife was when our bank sponsored the Memorial Day celebration on the waterfront and we had access to golf carts to maneuver through the crowd for various errands. April was toasted! She was driving full speed through the crowd of pedestrians," laughed George.

"Yeah! I remember a huddle of people diving onto the grass screaming and the woman in the red dress, standing in the center of the crowd, was the Mayor of Toledo! The poor woman was abandoned while looking like a deer in the headlights."

"So, the cheese really does stand alone," giggled George.

"It was a damn good thing she dove to her right, because if she would have gone left, she would have done a header into the Maumee River! I could just imagine the headlines that would read Mayor struck down by drunken woman while husband gets canned!"

"Ah, the good old days!" laughed George out loud.

"It was great seeing you again. Thanks so much for stopping by, George," said Michael as he shook his friend's hand.

"Yeah, me too. I hate to have to leave so early, but I promised to take my wife out for dinner and a movie tonight."

"Sounds like fun. You two kids have fun. Tell Renee that I send my regards."

George started to walk across the parking lot as Michael's smile slowly disappeared from his face. Just as George opened his door, Michael waved at his friend and yelled with sincerity, "Take care of her, George. Hold on to her tight." Michael was not sure if George heard him or not because Cami pulled into the parking spot next to George. He pulled away as Cami and Ginny were getting out of their vehicle.

Michael walked across the parking lot to greet his two sisters-in-law. Ginny looked exhausted and on the verge of becoming emotional. Michael offered to escort Ginny into the funeral home when she seemed strong enough to proceed. He tried to keep conversation light, but she looked too intent on getting her viewing of

April over with as soon as possible. Cami went into the building to use the restroom.

"Michael, I cannot believe that she's gone. She's only three short years older than me," said Ginny in her deepest southern drawl.

"When we enter this world is the same as when we exit, we have no say in the matter."

"I haven't seen her in a long time. I feel that I should have kept in touch with her better, Michael. I am carrying such guilt and heartache," she said as she started rummaging around in her purse.

"You shouldn't feel guilty, Ginny. How many times did April pick up the phone and call you? How many letters did she write you? Do you see where I'm going with this? Any relationship requires both parties to make an equal effort. Your sister was simply not interested in any relationship with anyone. She wanted to be left alone."

"No offense, Michael, but I believe that she needed more support from me, her sister. Now that she's gone, I feel that I let her down," she said as she blew her nose on an ancient tissue she discovered in her purse.

"Ginny, she's had many opportunities to make her life better. I've offered to get her help ten years into our marriage. She's given up on everyone around her, which has left us all wondering what the hell we did wrong to deserve such a punishment. She treated us all as if she hated us!"

"Maybe it's not *all* her fault," she said as she was still wiping her nose. She stared into the distance and said, "Michael, did ya know that Grandma Katherine was diagnosed with a mental disorder?"

"That's news to me! What was it exactly?"

"I can't remember the name, but she was medicated for it before she died."

"Why am I hearing about this now? These things can be genetic, you know! The secrets in this family represent the noose that is choking the very life out of me!"

Ginny stood there and searched her purse for another tissue. Michael wanted to scream some obscenities to the world, but he choked them down because God blessed him with a very large gullet for such occasions. Swallowing feelings had been a family tradition since the beginning of time. Michael had done it for years along with all four of his kids. Towards the end of his marriage, he became furious with how afraid his family had become of their own mother. He pondered the example he set for his children and grandchildren. He felt solely responsible for them choking on such repressed feelings.

Obviously being preoccupied with the contents of her purse, Ginny asked, "Would ya happen to have any breath mints on ya? Oh, never mind. I've got one here from the last baby shower I attended." She blew the lint off the small pink candy and threw it in her mouth. "That baby is now in preschool! Time sure does fly."

"Ginny, you've *got* to remember the name of that illness! Pardon the pun, but this is going to drive me nuts!" exclaimed Michael.

"For the life of me, I cannot remember, Michael. Whatever it was she had, I believe that I have it, Cami has it, and April was *loaded* with it."

"Have you been diagnosed?"

"Lord have mercy, no way! I'm afraid that they would have me committed," she said with a sigh. She threw her used tissues into her purse and said, "I feel better now." She stuck her arm out like a chicken wing and said, "I'm now ready to go inside." Michael was forced to escort his southern belle, wannabe, sister-in-law into the funeral home as if she was a personal guest at the cotton farmer's formal ball at the plantation.

Maggie was chatting with Aunt Cami in the hallway. She really looks good with her gray hair. Cami had always been a beautiful person. Since she found religion, she had torn down the walls of her old life and she continues to work hard at constructing a stronger foundation for her new life. She remains close with both of her kids and her grandchildren. When she gave her life to Jesus, ten years ago, she ended her lesbian lifestyle immediately with no regrets or hesitations. She remained friends with her lover, who had never fully recovered from the breakup. Cami was unaware that her family saw that she had longed for the companionship of her female lover, but she fully denied it.

"Aunt Cami, do you miss living in the north end?" said Maggie.

"No. Because I see that neighborhood on the news nearly every night! It's as if I never left," she smiled.

"I have a personal question to ask you about the house on Ontario Street."

"Ask away! I have nothing to hide."

"When you and Grandma Ruby lived there, how did it come about us getting the house?"

"Uncle Doug owned the house and told us one day to get out. He said that he sold it to your parents. He was nice enough to give us one week to move."

"How could he do that? Were you behind in rent?"

"We *never* missed a rent payment. We both feared getting evicted, especially from a family member. Just for safekeeping, we agreed to pay rent one week in advance."

"I once heard my mother say that you and Grandma Ruby were evicted because of being behind in rent." Cami looked stunned by Maggie's statement. Maggie was quick to say, "But then again, maybe I misunderstood what I heard." The question that raced through Maggie's mind was: *Why would Mom lie?*

Cami had an expression of hurt surface upon her face. She sighed slowly and said, "Maggie, I don't want to get into it anymore tonight. It's done and over with and I prayed for God to erase the hurt feelings from my heart. I'll talk to you later because I see someone from the church."

As Cami walked away from Maggie, a woman was quick to approach her. She looked familiar to Maggie, but she could not quite place her. The woman was quick to introduce herself and her husband. They were a professional looking couple who possessed such an essence of poise and power. Maggie was pleased to learn that the Jensen couple used to roller skate with her mother and aunts long ago. Maggie remembered playing with their children at the skating rink when she was a small child. She was impressed to learn that they were the owners of Jensen and Associates, a well-known law firm.

Al and Sondra offered their condolences. Maggie was quick to thank them with a heartfelt hug. For whatever reasons possessed her, Maggie whispered into Sondra's ear, "Mom lived her life as *she* saw fit." Maggie was stunned by her sudden lack of tact and was afraid to pull away from her mother's oldest acquaintance with fear of offending this woman of class. She could feel the familiar rush of heat race across her face, which glowed red with shame. Sondra patted her back sympathetically and slowly pulled away from Maggie, which she was surprised to see that Sondra was smiling with the utmost compassion and understanding.

"Maggie, you need to understand that your mother was odd because of how she was raised."

"How do you mean? Mom was the most peculiar sibling in her family."

"Honey, it's not just your mom. The girls are different because they were never truly taught right from wrong. Well, except for Kathleen, of course. The others' socially challenged ways were so obvious that it hung from them like a loud, tattered, outdated dress. Please understand that it is not all your mom's fault how she turned out," said Sondra.

Al looked at his wife with great hesitation. Her gaze caught his own for a moment. "Sondra," he said sweetly, "please, this is not the time or the place to speak of such negativity."

She put her hand on Maggie's back and calmly stated, "It's okay, Al. Relax." His eyes darted nervously toward Maggie. Sondra cleared her throat and smiled. She looked at Maggie and said, "Come. Let's talk in the antechamber, shall we?"

They found privacy in the quiet little room. Sondra explained that she knew all four girls well when they were teenagers. She said that Kathleen was the most normal one because she spent most of her childhood with Katherine and Herbert. She always felt sorry for the other three girls. She also knew that it was no secret that Katherine hated April. She admitted to knowing about April's sudden outbursts of rage. She suggested that April must have suffered from bipolar or something closely related to it. She said that all the kids at the rink knew to stay away from April during one of her unprovoked episodes they referred to as tantrums.

"I always had a soft spot in my heart for your Aunt Cami," said Al.

"Actually, we both do," admitted Sondra.

"All those girls strived to please Bo," said Al as he glanced at his wife.

"Maggie, your mother and her sisters had no guidance in their lives. They were being raised by children that thought of life as a party. I have always liked Bo and Ruby, but their party life came first," said Sondra.

"I know that my Grandma Ruby was an alcoholic and Grandpa Bo had an affair," said Maggie.

Al offered his story of why he pitied Cami the most. He told of when Cami was just twelve years old and she had won the regional title for speed skating in her division. Al and Sondra were dating then. Sondra, then a skating coach, had a few students competing for various events that afternoon. It was sad that no one in Cami's family was in attendance. Cami rode home with the couple and Al could remember how she was hugging her trophy, which stood about as tall as she did.

"I watched that little girl through the rearview mirror and wanted to cry. This was a huge event in that child's life and no one was there to share it with her," said Al sadly.

"Yeah, we only talked about it amongst ourselves. Cami does not know how we feel about that because we tried to protect her dignity. However, when we drove her home, the house was locked up and dark. It just added to the pathetic situation at hand," said Sondra.

"My Aunt Cami was locked out of the house?" asked Maggie with surprise.

"All of them had experienced being locked out many times. I had your Aunts Ginny and Cami stay with me the most," said Sondra.

"My mother locked Maddie and me out of the house when we were little, too."

"That's because she didn't know any better. That behavior was not out of the ordinary to your mother," said Sondra with a sympathetic smile.

"I don't mean any disrespect, but what I know about your grandparents is that your grandmother drank heavily and your grandfather enjoyed using his size to intimidate and bully people," said Al.

"I've heard stories about how he enjoyed a good fight," said Maggie.

"Maggie, all that we're saying to you is please examine the evidence of her background and allow room for sympathy for your mother. Yes, she had problems, but she loved you kids more than what she ever received from either parent. Those girls had to muddle through life under those conditions. They truly had nothing," said Sondra tenderly.

"If nothing else, it made them all independent," said Al. "I remember Cami pulling into my dad's garage wanting to change the plugs in her Vette. I was too busy to help her because I was pulling an engine from another car, but I told her what tools to grab to get the job done. I told her to get started without me and I'd help her when I get a minute. My look of surprise matched hers when I heard the roar of the Corvette after she finished the job," said Al with delight.

"I'll tell you something sad, you know that your grandfather had an affair with Donna, right?" asked Sondra.

"Of course," said Maggie.

"It was like a regular soap opera with that family at the rink. It was said that Bo stole his best friend's family. Donna's twins were very young then, but she left Thad, Sr. for Bo. The rumor at the rink was that one twin belonged to Thad while the other was Bo's son. Thad, Jr. is believed to belong to your grandfather."

"What? How can that be possible?" asked Maggie with surprise.

"It is possible for fraternal twins to be conceived a week or two apart," she said. "It was a perfect opportunity for another man to father her child."

"That is some story," said Maggie as she thought how sad it was how her grandfather treated Thad harshly when he was growing up. It was obvious how he always favored the other twin, Ted.

"Keep in mind that they are just rumors, Maggie," said Al.

After hearing such a grotesque story about her grandfather's sex life, Maggie felt comfortable enough to share the news about the pedophile in the family, which was of no surprise to the couple.

"These things can happen when neglect is involved," said Sondra in a rehearsed tone. "Well, sweetie, it was great seeing you again. The last time I saw you is when you were just a small child. Here's my card. Call us the next time you're in town," said Sondra with a smile.

Maggie gave the couple a hug and gave them both her business card. Sondra smiled when she saw that Maggie was the sales person of the year. She admitted that Maggie must favor Michael in the business department. Maggie smiled when Sondra said that they all grew up together. She even knew Michael's family. It appeared to

Maggie that Sondra knew everything about everyone from that generation.

Al let out a chuckle and said, "Your dad is quite the character! I can tell you stories about that man," he said as his face lit up. "However, we'll have to save that for another time."

"I'll hold you to that," smiled Maggie.

After the couple left, Maggie stood in the corner still digesting their conversation. She couldn't help but feel overwhelmed by Sondra's calloused statement about Uncle Doug's pedophile acts as if being readily acceptable due to a long history of neglect in the family. Maggie couldn't help but feel like a statistic. Alec came over to Maggie because he could see that she looked distant. He brought her some water, which was the only beverage allowed outside of the lounge. He handed her the cup as he put his arm around her. She looked into his eyes and her lip started to quiver. He gently escorted her outside as Chase and the boys were coming in.

"Hi, Aunt Maggie, where's Mark?" asked Trey with excitement.

"He's in there somewhere, buddy. Just don't get too rowdy inside. I know it's difficult when you two boys get together. By the way, Grandpa has chocolate," she said without giving it a second thought that chocolate makes that child hyper.

"Thanks a lot, Maggie," scoffed Chase.

Chase shook Alec's hand as he entered the door. Maddie was happy to see her boys. Jordan and Trey searched for their cousins and the chocolate. People have been coming and going all evening. April had a great deal of people that the family was unaware of that she knew. It was a great comfort for the Getman family to know that April was cared for and respected, if not by her family, then by strangers. Maggie took Alec by the hand and led him to the parking lot.

"What's going on?" he asked.

"I am about to have a meltdown."

"This place and this situation can do that to anyone."

Maggie had recently absorbed so much information, whether she asked for it or not, and was about to explode. Everything felt as if it had no order. Maggie felt lightheaded as if she were spiraling out of control. She felt detached from her body as if everything taking place around her was just a dream. She almost felt drunk. She wasn't sure if it was stress or fatigue that was getting the best of her. She had the sudden urge to steal a few private moments alone with her husband to address the documented truth awaiting her in the glove box. She had no idea how to deliver such an atrocity to her husband, but she knew it was important for him to know what she had uncovered earlier that day.

"I wanted to show you something while we have a quiet moment."

"It sounds serious. What is it, Maggie?"

Maggie opened the passenger door and reached into the Caddie's glove box. She had a lump in her throat as she pulled out Uncle Doug's wrap sheet. She held it to her chest, as she looked her husband in the eyes. She was struggling with herself on whether she should show it to him or not. She held the door and asked him to have a seat. He looked at her with confusion for a moment and then he honored her request. She closed his door and walked around the car to enter from the driver's side, still clutching her papers in her hands. As her door slammed shut, she made eye contact with Alec.

"What's this about?" he asked nervously.

"I have something to tell you, but I almost feel ashamed to say it."

"I am your husband, Maggie. You know that you can tell me anything. You're safe with me. There's nothing that you could say or do that will change my love and respect for you."

"I feel as if I am standing on a high-dive for the first time. I am on the board, but as I look down, the water looks much more intimidating. So, here I go. I am going to just jump in and say it!"

"Good! I thought you were going to procrastinate for another five minutes or so," he joked, trying to lessen the tension the only way he knew how.

"Last night Maddie shared something overwhelming with me. Do you remember the question I asked you one night in bed?"

"Ooh, it sounds interesting so far," he grinned.

"No!" she said as she playfully slapped his leg. "It was a thought that popped into my head about if I had one opportunity to ask a renowned psychic one question, what would it be?"

"Yes, I remember that you would have wasted an opportunity like that on that stupid uncle of yours."

"Well, I asked Maddie the same question in an e-mail. She has it saved on her hard-drive."

"And?"

"She went to see a famous psychic in town who claims that Maddie was raped by a man who might have used drugs, women in the family knew about the abuse but chose not to do anything about it, and that Maddie still sees this person in her dreams, which is because he is no longer living. Maddie was freaked because it was as if the psychic read my e-mail word-for-word. She felt the psychic was no longer reading her, but she was reading me!"

"Maggie, those psychics are used for entertainment purposes only. You should know better than falling for that. Come on, where is my old sensible Maggie?"

"Don't treat me like a child, Alec," she said with an irritated tone as she handed him the papers.

"What's this?"

"After hearing the recording of that psychic, it prompted us to do some investigating this morning. We picked this up at the sheriff's department."

"You went to the jail? Are you crazy?"

"Just read and tell me what you think."

There was a moment of silence as Alec thumbed through the pages. His eyes were becoming wider and wider with each page he ripped through. He got to the last page and carefully folded the papers and handed them back to Maggie. Without a single word, he leaned over the seat and embraced his wife. He buried his face on her shoulder for a long time.

"I am so sorry, baby," he whispered in her ear.

Maggie was touched by his reaction. She didn't know what she could possibly say or do to cushion such devastating news. All that came out of her mouth was, "Yeah. That was quite a bombshell to us this morning, too."

After a few moments of silence, Alec sat up tall as a look of rage crept across his face. "Twenty-two counts of rape. Rape!" he shouted as he punched the dashboard. "He got away with that behavior until the age of seventy-five!"

"Alec, please calm down."

"That dirty son-of-a-bitch!" he said as his voice cracked. "He was much younger when he had his hands on you."

"I'm fine, Alec. Really, I'm okay with it all," she said, trying to comfort her husband.

"I see so much of you in our daughters. I would kill *anyone* who would hurt them like that. I want to dig up that bastard and kill him again!" he shouted as he stared out his window. He took a deep breath trying to collect his composure and said, "Out of respect for you, I won't tell you what I think of your mother," he said angrily as he looked away from his wife.

"Are you okay?" she said as she desperately tried to hold his hand and look him in the eye. She felt that she made a huge mistake by sharing such news with him. Maggie thought it would have been nothing for her to keep this a secret. In fact, that's what she had been trained for her whole life—secrets.

"I believe that sexual abuse to a child should result in castration and the death penalty! Your mother should have received some sort of jail time for her crime, too! Honestly, I cannot believe that you came from that woman," he said sarcastically.

"I'm fine with it now. I've accepted it a long time ago. Really, Alec, calm down."

"How can you ask me to calm down? What makes you think that you are fine when you are still dealing with it, Maggie? You've got certain issues that you need to overcome."

"What issues are you talking about?" she asked with a crisp tone.

"I can see a difference in you sometimes when we're intimate. That monster ruined lots of things for us, Maggie. I hope that he is burning in hell!" He looked away from his wife and there was a long pause. This was a conversation that the couple had never before held.

"I'm sorry, Alec. I'll try to do better," promised Maggie as she began to cry.

"I am not fishing for an apology from you! I am angry at *those* people you call family!"

"I don't know what to say. I had no control over what happened in my childhood. I'd hope that you can be sympathetic to that," she said.

"My heart breaks for all the things that were ruined for you, Maggie. I cannot touch or hold you in a way I want because of that man. If I try, the kill-switch for the mood is activated with you. You are so self-conscious with your physical image that it tears me up inside that you see yourself as a disgrace. Above all else, it kills me to watch you cower in the middle of the night hoping that I won't touch you."

"I was unaware that you knew about the middle of the night thing."

"I can hear you hold your breath, as if you'd become invisible, when I come near you."

Maggie could hardly speak. She could not believe that her husband knew so much about her deep-rooted feelings. It broke her heart to see such pain in his eyes. He reached over and held her hand. He feared that he might have revealed too much to her at such a fragile moment.

"I'm sorry, Alec. It has nothing to do with you. I never wanted to tell you about my nighttime phobias because I knew it would hurt you. I admit that there are times when I wake up in the middle of the night not knowing what man is next to me. I find myself on the far edge of the bed shivering with fear that you are going to touch me. Maybe I had a nightmare that I couldn't remember that might create such a reaction."

"I would never hurt you, Maggie. I wish I could prove that to you."

"Alec, it's not you. When that happens to me I am consumed by such fear and an overwhelming feeling of distrust and insecurity. When I come to my senses and realize that it's my husband lying next to me, I feel nothing but shame wash over me."

"You can fool the rest of the world that you are unaffected by abuse from your childhood, but I am your husband and I love you more than anything in this world. My heart breaks when I think of you in the hands of that monster. It's bad enough that he did the crimes, but your mother knew what he was capable of and she still shipped you over there. That monster may have done things to you that I would thank God that you don't remember! But it is obvious to me that the horrors inflicted upon you still linger somewhere in that precious mind of yours."

"I can't speak for my mother, but what I can tell you is that I am just as hurt and confused by the whole mess, too. However, I cannot change the past. I just look forward to making happier memories. I struggle more than you could possibly know. I try not to visit the past for too long because I always fear being trapped in that painful part of my memory."

"I remember being told that Doug was arrested for molesting his stepdaughter. Your mother never said anything about rape. Why? What was she hiding?" said Alec.

"I think she was protecting him for some reason. We all believe that she was hoping for a large summed inheritance, but she never got one. I guess the joke was on her!" snickered Maggie.

"This is going to sound harsh, but I am going to share a thought that I had for years about your mother. She never purchased new clothes for you because she figured that you weren't going to be around for too long."

"What are you talking about, Alec?"

"Think about it. She squeezed you out from the herd. Maybe she and Doug lost their nerve on what was really supposed to happen to you. Why else would she spend the least money on you and be so lax about your safety?"

"No. I don't believe that. I figured that was because I never complained outwardly to my mother like my sister had. The old saying about the squeakiest wheel gets the grease is true. They don't come any squeakier than Maddie!" laughed Maggie.

"That is definitely a proven fact!" smiled Alec.

"Do you feel better now?"

"How can I possibly feel better thinking about that animal having his way with my wife? It kills me inside for such torturous memories you carry around with you. And for what you don't know about what he did exactly, you can only speculate and wonder. You did not deserve the mother that you got, Maggie, that's for sure."

"Alec, welcome to my crazy world. I've been living with this secret my whole life. The people who do know are the ones that Maddie told. You are the only one I could confide in years ago. I do thank you for not telling our children because I don't want them to hate their grandmother. Especially, now that she is gone."

"The day will come when you will be ready to tell them, Maggie. I know that when you do, it will be in your own unique way. I promise not to stand in your way, but I will be beside you when that time comes. Until then, I promise to keep this little secret with you. I love you, Megan Graham. There is nothing, and I mean *nothing* that could make me love you any less," he said as he cradled her face in his hands.

Maggie leaned in to kiss her loving and handsome man. Her heart felt as if it opened wide and swallowed him whole. They shared a passionate kiss, which seemed like years since they had such a moment. He then took her by the hand and tenderly kissed the back of it. She leaned against his shoulder with a smile. She rubbed his arm, which felt as if he were flexing. It was obvious that he was still very tense from their conversation. She reached for the glove box again and pulled out the newspaper.

"Do you want a laugh?" she asked.

"I could always use one of those," he smiled.

She proceeded to read him April's obituary. He chuckled through the whole article. He laughed as if Maggie were doing standup comedy. He always laughed the hardest at her jokes, which she claimed was why she married him. She even threw a few ad-lib lines into it for a deeper laugh.

"April loved her nuts covered in chocolate, just ask her men," she added.

"All right, now! You are stretching the truth a bit too much. You are going to make me pee my pants if you don't quit! We better get inside so we can check on the kids."

As they were getting out of the car, they saw a huddle of people around Michael's truck. They saw Chase, Maddie, Kobe, Angie, Aunt Gabby, and other people drinking beer. Much to Maggie's surprise, she saw a few more coolers loaded in the back of her father's truck. There were about five different brands of beer circulating, which made it look like quite the party. It resembled a typical Getman family reunion, with the exception of it taking place in a funeral home parking lot.

Maddie approached her sister and offered her a beer. Maggie refused as she and Alec were about to enter the building.

"Maggie, I've got to tell you something I heard tonight," said Maddie as she approached the couple.

"What's up?" she asked as she kept Alec anchored at her side.

"Aunt Ginny told Dad that Grandma Katherine was crazy."

"Is your Aunt Ginny really a credible source?" asked Alec, trying to protect his wife from any unnecessary scandal.

"That is a good question, Alec," said Maddie with a slur.

"Is that what you wanted to tell me?" asked Maggie. "We need to go inside to check on our kids."

"That's not all. I bumped into Mom's cousin, Joe, tonight and we had quite the conversation."

"Who is Joe?"

"He is Uncle Ed and Aunt Kate's eldest son. Danny, his kid brother, lived with his mother after the divorce while Joe lived with his father. Because of the marital circumstances and a five-year age difference, the boys were never really close."

"Who is Uncle Ed again?" asked Alec.

"He is Grandpa Bo's brother," said Maggie.

"Yeah, there is quite a spicy rumor about my Grandma Ruby being a swinger between Bo and Ed when she was a youngster," stated Maddie.

"Oh, yeah! I remember the family soap opera now. I just forgot the names of certain characters," said Alec.

"Where is he?" asked Maggie.

"He and his wife had to leave. They stopped in to pay their respects and had other obligations," said Maddie.

"I remember Joe. We've only met him once or twice when we were just kids. I've never really heard Mom talk about him much, but then again she didn't speak too much about her past in general," said Maggie.

"I mentioned to him that we heard that Grandma Katherine had a mental illness. I asked him what he knew about it since he did reside with the woman for a short while."

"He did? I didn't know that," exclaimed Maggie.

"He stayed one summer when Kathleen was there. He said that Grandma never had an illness because she knew just when to be nice, which was *only* when she wanted to be!" said Maddie.

"That kind of behavior sounds familiar," scoffed Alec.

"He also told me that Katherine was so mean that when Herbert was dying in the hospital, the doctor wanted to try some new experimental treatments on him to help prolong his life. Aunt Kate was in the room at the time and she told Uncle Ed about what she witnessed between his parents."

"I thought Ed and Kate were divorced years ago?"

"Yes, they got divorced around the same time Grandma Ruby and Grandpa Bo did. Ed and Kate remained civil toward one another because of their sons."

"I always respect couples who could put aside their differences for the kids," said Alec.

Maddie continued to build up the story to her sister about the last days on Earth for their great-grandfather, Herbert. The Arizona sunshine was peeking through the curtain of Herbert's room while Katherine marched her short rounded frame around the foot of his bed. The sunshine reflected off her white hair that was nearly blinding to everyone in the room. She clutched her purse tightly within her grasp as she leaned over the bed with her face close to his. If she had been a normal person, someone would have been under the impression that she was going to kiss him. She just stared at the man as a ghostly silence fell about the room. A $95,000 bill that was run up in two days time had ruffled her feathers.

"Do ya wanna live, Herbert?! Well, do ya?" she shouted in his face as if he were a deaf man.

"Yes," he said in a frail voice. "Yes, I want to live," said the frightened elderly gentleman with tears in his eyes.

"Good!" said Katherine as she walked away from her husband. She marched up to the cardiologist and said, "Pull the plug, Doc!" Everyone in the room was speechless. "You con artists are doing nothing other than extracting money from my pocketbook! You are robbing me blind!" she screamed. "You cannot fool *this* old lady!" she said as she left the room in a huff.

"Holy shit!" said Alec.

"Oh, my gosh, that poor man. What happened?" asked Maggie.

"Cousin Joe said that Herbert passed away two weeks later. He said that Katherine was furious about such a large hospital bill that she refused to pay any extra expenses for a funeral. Herbert was cremated," said Maddie with a hint of sympathy.

Maddie always held a special place in her heart for Grandpa Herbert from when she first met him, which was at the fish fry. Maddie hit her head on a low entryway to their basement so hard that she nearly knocked herself out. He carried her up the stairs in his arms. April was embarrassed for such a ruckus in front of her grandparents. She was too preoccupied with being on edge around Katherine to know any better. Herbert took an instant liking to the child; he got to dote over at least one of April's children without being punished. Maddie always held a respect for the man for exhibiting such tenderness and compassion. That was a one and only visit, but Maddie never forgot it.

"Was there a memorial service or anything?" asked Maggie.

"According to Joe, they only scattered his ashes at a sun dial in a cemetery," said Mattie.

"It sounded like a private type of service to me. Maybe that is what Katherine felt was best to do at the time," said Maggie.

"No. It was cheap and disrespectful!" stated Maddie candidly.

"How do you mean?"

"Joe told me that his father, Uncle Ed, drove to the cemetery the next day to witness Herbert's ashes being sucked up in the lawn bag of the ground keeper's mower only to be discarded with the weeds and grass clippings."

"Oh, my gosh!" exclaimed Maggie.

"He said Ed placed Katherine in a home shortly after Grandpa's death. It nearly killed her to have her son sell all of her possessions, but he had to do that to pay off hospital expenses."

"Did she miss her husband at all?" asked Alec.

"Joe told me that she missed ordering him around to clean her house or to fetch her things. After Herbert's first heart attack, she made him scrub the kitchen floor the day he came home from the hospital. He finally told her that he was tired and he went to bed instead."

"Was there anything positive Joe could have said about Katherine?" asked Maggie.

"I don't know about positive, but he did say that Katherine died more frightened than her husband. In the end, Katherine was like a small frightened child, which was a complete opposite of the tyrant facade that she once portrayed," said Maddie.

"Wow," said Maggie with a sigh, "that is so sad."

"How do you mean?" asked Alec, being surprised by his wife's lack of emotion.

"I was hoping to have a logical excuse for Mom's behavior in life, but this story brings us back to square one."

"I'm sorry, Maggie. Insanity might not be in our bloodline after all! Maybe we are just mean," giggled Maddie as she opened another beer and walked back to the private tailgate party in the parking lot.

Maggie turned to Alec and said, "It's sad how Grandma Katherine was so weak and small in the end, which might have been the real person who she had hidden behind her gruff exterior her whole life. I will always wonder what type of hell that woman endured in her childhood. I guess we will never know."

"You have a big heart, Maggie. I suppose that is what I love best about you."

"I do remember one story my Grandpa Bo once told me about his mother."

"I could only guess what he said," scoffed Alec.

"He told me that Herbert announced that he was going out for a haircut and did not come back home for two weeks. When he came home, for whatever reasons, he found Katherine waiting for him with a pair of scissors. It was said that the man never saw a barber again."

"What would have possessed him to go back to that woman?" asked Alec.

"That will always be a mystery. But I do remember my Grandpa Bo telling me one week before he died that his mother used to feed the homeless people at the depot. He said that Katherine could never stand to see people starve. He was so desperate for me to know the compassionate side of his mother," said Maggie tenderly.

Alec and Maggie continued to walk into the funeral home while absorbing the stories about Katherine. He held the door for his wife. As she began to enter the building, she looked at her husband for a moment as she stood in the doorway.

"What is it, Maggie?"

"I cannot wait for this day to be over!"

"I'll drink to that!" he said with excitement.

"Listen to you!" she said with surprise. "You sound like you've spent five minutes with my family," scoffed Maggie.

Chapter 18

Alec and Maggie found their children sitting with their cousins in the rear of the funeral home. Kelsey and Allie were consoling one another while the others were there for moral support. Missy was quick to inform her parents that Kelsey made Allie cry. Alec took Missy by the hand and asked the other kids if they wanted to grab a soda in the lounge. He had six takers on his offer while the older kids stayed behind. Mark was the youngest of the group, which was a brand-new concept for him being included in the "big kid" bunch.

"Are you girls all right?" asked Maggie tenderly.

"Yeah, Aunt Mag, we're fine," said Kelsey, wiping away her tears.

"We were just telling stories about Grandma," said Allie with a sniffle.

"Your grandmother was quite the character. I have *lots* of stories stored up here," she said as she pointed to her head, "about your grandmother. In fact, I have enough to fit *any* category!"

Kenneth wandered over to the group since his daughters were with their Uncle Alec and the other sugared-up munchkins. He was trying to squeeze in twenty minutes of adult conversation for the remainder of the evening. Maddie and Chase came inside and joined the group with Michael bringing up the rear. Angie went to the lounge to give her girls the ten-minute warning about having to go home. Kobe grabbed a chair while Angie proceeded to be the killjoy in the eyes of her young children. Michael was mingling with what was left of the crowd.

"My mom was about to tell us some stories about Grandma," announced Mark.

"I think we all have a few stories," mumbled Maddie.

Maggie searched her memory to find a light and upbeat story about their grandmother. She tried to find one that was age appropriate and fun. She looked at Maddie, as if she would offer any input, but Maggie soon realized that she was on her own with the story telling. Maddie looked as if she were ready for bed, not that her left eye closes when she's had too much to drink was a telltale sign. Maddie tried her best to muffle her yawns.

"Okay now, I have a story that you will *not* believe to be true about your grandmother," said Maggie with excitement.

"It better be true because you told us it's not polite to tell a fib, Mother," warned Mark.

"Okay, if I tell a story then everyone else has to tell one, too."

"That would take all blasted night!" said Trey.

"Don't worry little brother. Aunt Maggie isn't *that* long-winded," said Kyle as he folded his arms across his chest.

"Thanks, buddy, I think," she said with a wink.

Maggie told the story about when April and Michael were visiting in Indianapolis and went shopping. They all made an afternoon of taking in the sites of the city, dining at a small family restaurant, and browsing at the Circle Center Mall. They were hoping to visit the Indianapolis Zoo, but the weather did not look too promising for such a trip that afternoon. Besides, April was starting to lose interest in shopping. The family could easily recognize the signs when she becomes ornery or distant.

"Your grandmother and I were at the checkout counter at a thrift shop while your grandfather had been outside smoking a cigarette. Alec, Mark, and Allie were keeping him company as they stood by the front doors. Your grandma was in front of me in line and she was not making conversation with me at all. I could almost see her horns start to peak."

"Yet another family trait," sneered Maddie.

"Anyhow, we were at the only checkout lane and there were about six customers behind me. As soon as the clerk rang your grandmother up, she grabbed her receipt out of that poor man's hand; she snatched her bags and bolted for the doors without looking back. She never said a single word!"

"Oh, my God! I know what happened! She polluted the air, didn't she?" laughed Kelsey.

"It still remains unclear because I swore that she filled her drawers! The smell was so strong that I could visualize being stuck behind an uncapped stink-wagon that was overflowing! It was as if I were standing in the middle of a farmer's freshly fertilized field."

"I've witnessed that once and I prayed that there would never be a twice!" laughed Kobe.

"I was so embarrassed, but I put on my best poker face and acted as if I didn't know that woman. I looked that clerk in the eye with an Academy Award-winning act of repulsion. 'The *audacity* of some people' was all I could muster to say."

"You said it, lady!" said the clerk as he sprayed the area with air freshener.

"I paid my bill by trying to hold my breath while that poor man pulled his T-shirt over his nose."

Maggie took a quick look behind her as she saw people holding their noses. She even witnessed one gentleman turn away from the checkout and walk towards the other end of the store saying that he had a weak stomach and he could wait until the line died down. Meanwhile, April was halfway to the car while Michael was trying to catch up to her in the parking lot. When Maggie confronted her mother, she was quick to deny it.

"The rule in our house is he who smelt it, dealt it," said Jordan.

"Trust me on this, we all smelt it and if we all dealt it, we would have destroyed the ozone layer!"

"I would rule in that case that she who denied it, supplied it!" said Kyle with a grin.

"I hate the smell of air freshener," said Kobe.

"Believe me when I say that can smelled better than Mother's! I consider that clerk's behavior as heroic that day. It was almost as if he had been trained for a terrorist attack," said Maggie.

"I always laugh at the scent of the air freshener labeled country fresh. When I think of that scent, I prepare myself for smelling cow manure in a can. I mean, what's up with that?" said Kenneth.

"That's just you being a city boy, Uncle Ken," said Jordan.

The kids were feeling better after Maggie's story. Kids always laughed at such bodily functions, especially if it came from someone like their grandmother. Even though she was not very cordial to her company, unlike her sons, she seldom expelled gas in their presence. She was a stickler about manners and she demanded respect; even though people around her would not receive the same in return.

The family often reminded themselves as they would attempt to assess her behaviors, on a near daily basis, the Getman phrase, "It's just Mom. Don't try to understand her, just love her." It was another way for them trying to find comfort and acceptance with her erratic mood swings.

"I remember when Grandma came to visit us in our new home when I was about three. She came in and picked me up off the floor and then dropped me on my face!" remembered Mark.

"What? On purpose?" asked Trey.

"That was when Mark was settling down from having a little tantrum. I was glad that he was on the tail-end of it before his grandparents showed up. I remember that like it was yesterday," said Maggie.

"What happened?" asked Jordon.

"I can't remember what Mark's tantrum was over, but that behavior is expected with any three-year-old child. He had just stopped crying and was in his cool-down mode when Grandma walked through the door. She was annoyed that Mark didn't jump for joy when she made her entrance. I could see that challenged her spirit by the look on her face. I told her to leave him alone because he was in his recovery stage and we respect his space while he gets himself together. She proceeded to straddle over Mark and pick him up by his little hips. He was hovering about a foot off the floor. He remained stiff as a board, but he never said a word. She got angry and purposely dropped him to the floor."

"That's how we handle unruly children in *my* cafeteria!" said April as she walked away from the child.

"Yeah! She dropped me on my face while my mom told me not to bleed on the new carpeting!"

"Wow! Such love, Aunt Maggie," said Kelsey.

"Wasn't that the age when he was experiencing those horrific nosebleeds?" asked Kenneth.

"I think I was a little older when those came around. I saw Dr. Val for a few years because of my nose problem," said Mark.

"I was stunned by what I had just witnessed. I actually panicked on the inside, but I didn't know how to react on the outside. I had just witness my own mother intentionally hurt my son, for which I initially wanted to pin her to the wall! No one but the three of us had been involved. My heart was broken into a million pieces. It delivered such a harsh impact on my heart that I can still recall what you were wearing when she did that to you," said Maggie while looking at her son.

"Grandpa wasn't even through the front door yet!" announced Mark.

"I do feel bad as a mother because I did let you down, Mark. However, I tried to keep her from going crazier by not provoking her. I honestly did not know what to do. I will tell you that all that kept coming to my mind was ending that scuffle with violence, but I didn't want to do more damage by having you witness me and your grandmother involved in a fistfight."

"I can appreciate your mother's actions, Mark. It isn't wise to approach a crazy person when she is in one of her moods," said Kenneth.

"When isn't she in a mood?" said Kobe.

"Well, I've been there before," said Maddie.

"Oh, boy, here we go!" said Chase.

"After my first divorce, Mom offered to watch Kelsey and Kyle for me so I could go to work. It was a day that I had an opportunity to work overtime in the factory, which I really needed the money. Mom took the kids to a fast food restaurant for lunch, which I appreciated the gesture. However, I didn't know that my four-year-old son was injured until I got home late that evening."

"Grandma had me by the hand and she was walking too fast for me, which made me run along side of her just to keep up. I tripped over a crack in the sidewalk and flew headfirst into the corner of the brick doorway. Blood was everywhere!" said Kyle.

"I remember this story. Your grandmother refused help from the manager," said Maggie.

"Yes. She made me sit in that restaurant and eat my lunch as she packed my head with napkins."

"When I got home from work, I about had a heart attack!" said Maddie with resentment. "My little guy's shirt had been blood-soaked and he had a large patch of dried blood in his blonde hair. I picked my sleeping child up from the couch and saw the gash in his head. I demanded that your grandmother tell me what had happened!"

"He fell today at lunchtime. That's what he gets for running!" April said sharply.

"Why didn't you call me at work?"

"I didn't want to interrupt you while you made your cash. I know how much that means to you. Besides, this was no big deal."

Maddie now scooped both of her sleeping children into her arms and raced them to the car. She drove her son to the hospital for stitches and an x-ray to rule out a possible head concussion. The hospital cleaned the wound and told Maddie that it was too late for stitches, which would have been about two or three. They advised for her to watch him for vomiting and excessive drowsiness. They also told her to follow up with the restaurant in the morning because they were usually good about paying for medical expenses.

"Did you talk with the restaurant, Aunt Maddie?" asked Allie.

"I went to speak with the manager the next day, who just so happened to be on duty the day before. He told me that he insisted on calling an ambulance for Kyle and that they would pay his medical bills. He was very concerned for his safety, but Grandma refused to have him make a fuss. He even tried to give Kyle a free lunch, but she refused his charity! She went so far as to sign a waver that the family would not sue over the incident. The manager told me that he was alarmed when Grandma told Kyle to stop crying like a baby and eat the lunch that she paid good money for."

"I don't know about all of you, but I believe that she had a problem with the boys in the family," said Chase.

"No, that's not true," said Kenneth. "I believe that she had a problem with a certain age group. Kobe and I have girls, which she possessed a low tolerance of patience with them. We've even seen her treat Missy the same way she did our girls. I believe she was more accepting to those ten years and older. I don't think that it had *anything* to do with their sexes."

"Maybe the younger ones pull out that April Ann personality," said Maddie.

"I feel funny talking about this here, but when Trina was staying with her grandmother, she told me that Mom bullied her at the breakfast table," said Kenneth.

"Trina could find a spot to eat at that table? Oh yeah, the TV is small," said Kobe sarcastically.

"It was a time when Dad was in town and he took her to the store so that she could pick out her favorite cereal. She chose something chocolaty, of course. Trina packed her cereal box in her bag and looked forward to eating it at her Grandma's house in the morning."

"Good morning, Trina," said April as she kissed her granddaughter on the head.

"Good morning, Grandma. I'm eating my cereal that Grandpa bought for me," she proudly stated.

"Well, you need some fruit to help balance out all that sugar," she said as she set a small bowl of fruit on the table for the little girl. April reached into the cereal box to nibble on a few pieces of cereal.

Trina's eyes grew wide and it was obvious that the child looked offended. "Grandma, that's *my* cereal, not yours. Grandpa bought that just for me," said the five-year-old matter-of-factly.

"Trina, this is *my* house and everything inside of it is *mine*," said April, while pointing her finger in the child's face. She then pointed to the cereal box and said, "That cereal is *mine* because *my* husband, which constitutes it being *my* money, paid for it! This bowl of fruit *I* brought to you is *mine* too! I *chose* to share it with you this morning, but now I've changed my mind!" she said as she walked away from the child while eating her bowl of fruit.

"Wasn't it funny how she used Dad to her convenience?" said Kobe.

"Mom ignored the painful truth that she and Dad were separated," said Maggie.

"Yeah, he was staying with us during that time frame," said Chase.

"I knew better than having my kids stay with The Old Gray Mare. My girls can't do anything right in that woman's eyes. They got in trouble for running in the house, which would really be a brisk walk in reality. They even got in trouble for running *outside* from that woman, too. But she did allow them to do cartwheels inside of her house. I could never figure that one out, but I heard on numerous occasions that my little girls knew that it was *safe* to do cartwheels in her house because they had the room to move," said Kobe.

"That's because you live in a pigsty, according to Mother," said Kenneth.

"Well, I have to admit that our little home is not tidy because we have eight bodies squeezed inside of it, but nonetheless, it's home to all of us. We cannot afford to move from our three-bedroom single story home. The rent is cheap, since Angie's grandmother willed it to her. I can't argue about having no house payments," said Kobe.

"I remember a time, before Dad left, when he invited your girls over for a little cousins' get-together," said Kenneth to Kobe. "Mom was furious! She felt that she was being forced to baby-sit again, which was her usual feeling towards the younger company."

"Dad tried to explain that he wanted to see his granddaughters and he invited them to the house. When Angie and I walked through the front door, Mom announced that we must have *had* to drop our girls off at the house because our housecleaning must not have happened *again* today," said Kobe with some hurt in his voice.

"You might not have noticed, but Dad about crawled under his chair when he heard that statement," said Kenneth.

"Yeah, why do you think we didn't come over very often? We live in town, but we could not stand the constant criticism," said Kobe.

"Even though we lived five hours away, we still got caught up in the middle of the ugliness. When Mom used to call us, it was always the same story hearing how wonderful of a mother she was and how she was a hands-on mom, unlike Maddie. She would always run down Dad and talk about her wanting to beat the daylights out of him. She always carried such a tone of anger and hatred in her voice," said Maggie.

"If you think you were exempt from her wrath, you were sorely mistaken," said Maddie.

"I have learned that if someone is going to talk badly about another person behind their back, then that very person is saying the same thing about me behind my back. One day I snapped and decided to not be a part of that ugliness in Mom's life. I used to think that it was good for people to vent, but I always felt as if I was just as guilty as if I said those words myself. I told her one day that we are a family and that we needed to act like one. If there was a bad thing said about one of us, then it would affect us all. I told her it was like poisoning the well," said Maggie.

"You said that to our mother figure?" asked Maddie with surprise.

"No offense, Maggie, but we are shocked that you had it in you to stand up to her," said Kobe.

"I never yelled at her nor was I being disrespectful. I was just having a bad day and I really didn't want to hear it. I would always carry a cloud of negative funk around with me after her venting sessions. I would feel guilty about partaking in those conversations and I felt as if I carried layers of crud on my whole body. Alec could tell when I spoke with my mother before I could even tell him."

Michael walked over to the group and said, "Hey, may I join your little hen party?"

"Yeah, Grandpa. We were just telling stories," said Mark.

Michael grabbed a chair next to his youngest grandsons, Mark and Trey. The group was silent until Michael got settled. Kobe was eager to offer a painful memory.

"Mom once told me that Kenneth and I was a by-product of rape," said Kobe.

"What?" they all said collectively. That was also a surprise to Kenneth, who was now sitting on the edge of his chair.

"Mom claimed that when Dad went bowling on Wednesday nights, he would come home drunk and climb all over her. She said that she felt as if she were being raped," he said as his eyes drifted to Michael.

"I remember Mom telling me about those post-bowling evenings and using the word rape rather freely," said Maggie.

"That was when sex was no more. She claimed that I was violating her body, so I just quit sex altogether," said Michael calmly. His eyes then stared at the floor with a combination of hurt and embarrassment by having such a private conversation with his kids.

"Ouch!" stated Maddie and Chase at the same time. At that moment the grandkids decided to make their own conversation amongst themselves.

"Yeah, isn't it funny that April accused me of rape while she had no problems sending my two daughters to the home of a pedophile. Nothing makes any sense," said Michael.

"Amen to that," said Maggie.

"How come I've never heard that story about us being conceived by an act of rape?" asked Kenneth in an agitated voice.

"Well, Kenneth, that's how our mother talked with me. You know how she strived to make you look like the good son," said Kobe with regret as soon as he said it.

"That is something that I had no control over!" said Kenneth as he slapped his knee. The grandkids, not knowing what the adult conversation was about, all jumped by his outburst. Kenneth looked at the group apologetically and said in a low voice, "Really, it wasn't my fault."

"I know that, brother," said Kobe as he patted his twin's back. "Just like I know that it wasn't your fault when Mom got angry with me and threw your plastic toy gun at my head. Do you remember that?"

After searching his memory, Kenneth painfully said, "Yes, I do remember that."

"She hit you in the head with a toy gun?" asked Maddie with surprise.

"Yes," said Kobe, while rubbing the side of his head, "she just missed my temple."

"How old were you then?" asked Maddie with an agitated tone.

"I believe I was five at the time because it happened after lunch on a school day. Kenneth and I attended morning kindergarten."

"Why would she do that?" asked Maggie with tears in her eyes as she painfully learned that she didn't protect her little brothers as well as she had hoped.

"Because she accused me of tripping Kenneth," he said as he looked at his brother. Kenneth was silent, but he slowly nodded to confirm Kobe's story to be true. "We had been playing on the stairs when Kenneth tripped on the top step and fell into the bedroom door with a loud thud. The Old Gray Mare flew out of the bathroom with her bridgework showing and all. I knew my goose was cooked. She never asked what happened; she just *assumed* that I tripped Kenneth. That was when she grabbed his gun off the floor and whipped it at me."

"Yes, that's true. I was running after Kobe up the stairs and I tripped on my own. I dropped my orange plastic gun on the floor while I barreled into the bedroom door. I wasn't hurt, but the noise was horrific!" said Kenneth.

"She hit me hard on the side of the head, but I refused to let her see me cry. I was amazed that the thwack of the toy gun ricocheting from my skull didn't hurt me nearly as much as the idea of my mother intending such pain and anger towards me."

"Why haven't I heard of this story before now?" asked Michael with a look of bewilderment.

"Dad, there were many things that you did not know about," said Kenneth.

Alec came from the lounge with the kids, who were running down the rows of chairs. Angie had her group rounded up and Kobe jumped up to greet them. They all said good night and loaded up in their van. Alec joined the family for some wind-down conversation. Kathleen, Cami, and Ginny were saying good night to the family. They were all staying overnight with Aunt Cami. They were looking forward to catching up for the evening. Kathleen's granddaughters were even excited about the girly party. Michael excused himself and walked his sisters-in-law to their cars.

"We were just telling stories, Dad," said Allie as Alec was about to be seated.

"What's the topic?" he asked.

"I was just getting ready to tell about the time when Grandma watched us when you and Mom went to Las Vegas," said Allie.

"I remember that. I called your grandmother to ask if she would be interested in sitting with you kids for three nights and four days so that I could surprise your Mom with a honeymoon that we never had. I remember there being a long pause on the phone and she said what she always says…"

"I don't know what my plans are going to be then!" they all said in unison.

"That was just her way of saying no," said Maddie.

"That statement really cranked me off and she knew it. She agreed to do it, which I was glad that she had. We really enjoyed ourselves."

"Well, I constantly had to call home to check on the kids, but other than that we had a good time! Go on, Allie, and tell them your story," said Maggie.

"I remember after Mom and Dad left for the airport, Grandma let me ride my bike to Preston Wheelie's house."

"For the record, he was the child who was extremely hyper and he had been exposed to adult knowledge in the X-rated category," said Maggie.

"Allie knew that we did not approve of her being down there. Right, Allie?" said Alec.

Trying her best to ignore her dad's comment, she continued, "Preston was one grade above me and, being an only child, he didn't have very many friends. I thought he was hilarious! He was the one child that other parents banned their children from playing with him. I figured that what Mom and Dad didn't know wouldn't hurt them."

"Tell them what happened," insisted Alec, while being impatient for his daughter to get to the point.

"Well, we were playing in their garage and Preston kept trying to kiss me. I told him to quit, but he wouldn't stop. I rode my bike back home crying and I told Grandma what had happened. Grandma was waiting for Preston to come to the door to confront the little horn-dog. He had no idea what he was about to receive when he rang the doorbell."

"So, you're the little punk who kisses girls who tell you to stop! Just who do you think you are, young man? Alec and Maggie aren't here right now, so now you have to deal with *me*!" said April with fury. Preston stood on the doorstep trembling with fear. April leaned into the boy's face and said, "I live in Toledo and I will not have any problems driving down here to tend to you if you ever touch my granddaughter again! *We* have ways of dealing with people like you where I come from. I'm also a gun owner. I want you to remember that the next time you try to kiss Allie. I know where you live. When a girl says no, she means no! Do you understand me?" she said as her icy stare nearly paralyzed the terrified fourth grade boy.

"I laughed because Preston ran from the house screaming as if Grandma beat him nearly to death! He never bothered me or played with me again," laughed Allie.

Alec leaned over to Maggie and whispered, "Don't you wish you had that same woman speak for you at that age to your uncle?" Maggie just shook her head at the very thought of that memory.

Maggie recalled Mark saying that April spanked him because he did not put his toys away fast enough. She knew something was wrong by Mark's actions when they returned. The little guy confessed after his grandmother left the house. Maggie was horrified at the very thought! Maggie did confront April about it, which April swore that she would do it again if she had to do so. Alec and Maggie never went on a trip without the kids after that.

"Your mother was insanely jealous of both of you girls for being the mother she could never be," said Michael.

"I know. Every time I would confide in her about a phase one of my kids would be in, she would be quick to say that she would love to see that child try that crap with her! I don't know what I was thinking or why I would ever expose that side of us to her. I knew she would say that every time. I guess I was a glutton for punishment," said Maggie.

"Maggie, that's just your nature. I've told you a million times that you were just being hopeful that somewhere in time your mother would act like a compassionate mother to you. I'm just sorry that you never saw that side of her as often as you craved," said Alec.

"She was jealous of the vacations you kids would endure. She would be green with envy," said Michael.

"How many times would she turn down your vacation proposals?" demanded Maddie.

"They're countless," remembers Kenneth.

"I would have to ask her where she would like to go. She would seem half interested, but she would never give me an answer. I would take it to the next level and offer a neat place that I would like to explore. If she could detect the excitement in my voice, she would smash that idea to pieces," said Michael.

"Didn't Mom win an all-expense paid vacation for two to California?" asked Kenneth.

"She told me that her name was drawn at her union meeting. She made them draw another name because she was too afraid to fly. That was news to me. It would have been nice to be able to get away. I had never before seen the Pacific Ocean and she threw away that opportunity for us both to view it together. Besides, I told her that she's earned those tickets because her union dues paid for them over the years. You all know how I feel about the union!"

"Oh, don't get started, Dad! We know that you are a company man 'til the end, but you're among mixed company," warned Maddie.

"If you and Mom would do anything together, it would be done locally. Right, Dad?" said Maggie, trying to keep him on topic.

"I remember she got two tickets for the Jamie Farr Golf Classics, which were given to her from a coworker." Jamie Farr was the local celebrity from the hit TV series M*A*S*H. His character was Klinger, the man who wore dresses with hopes of getting discharged from the Korean War. He, too, once lived in the north end of Toledo." Michael paused for a second. He then continued, "I was so excited about going and I couldn't wait to get there. Our first stop was to pick up a trampoline that her former coworker was giving away, which happened to be across the street from the tournament. It was good that we could kill two birds with one stone. Much to my surprise, April gave the woman our two tickets in exchange for the trampoline!"

"Here, Betsy, these are the two tickets that I promised you. We don't feel like standing around in this heat. Besides, we have better things to be doing today," said April as she glared at Michael with a look that dared him to say something.

"What was better than going to the golf classics?" asked Alec.

"We went home, where she wanted to be. I swear she did that to me on purpose. I was so disappointed! That was the Lucy personality I've mentioned before."

"Wow. I still admire your love for the game after I took you and Kobe to see the seniors play in Indy years ago," said Alec.

"Hell, yeah! I'm not going to let a little thing like me getting fourteen stitches in the forehead from a stray golf ball ruin my love for the game," giggled Michael.

"I remember when you got hit! You were sitting in my folding chair. I was standing behind you. I thought the ball hit the chair by the ping sound it made!" laughed Alec.

"Yeah. You, being the tender and caring son-in-law that you are, leaned down and thanked me for blocking your family jewels with my head! Since Allie was two weeks overdue, I thought I would scare Maggie enough to put her into labor."

"And it worked!" exclaimed Maggie. "Allie was born twelve hours later. The three of us were in the hospital at the same time. The nurses on the maternity floor were talking about some man, crowding the ninth hole at the tournament, got knocked unconscious. The rumors were really flying in that hospital! I had nurses from different floors come in to ask me the full story about my dad! They claimed that they didn't want to embarrass you anymore than what you already were," said Maggie, trying not to laugh.

Everyone broke out into laughter! Allie had pictures in her baby book of her grandfather's head before and after his stitches. He even gave her the bloody golf ball and his hospital band as a souvenir. The golfer felt awful about striking a spectator, so he autographed a golf ball and hand-delivered it to Michael in the hospital. Michael teased the golfer and told him he feared that he would have to play through from his forehead. Humility was no stranger to Michael and he accepted it with open arms.

"What did Mom say when you called her back home to tell her about it?" asked Maddie.

"She was angry that I interrupted her television program. She didn't care."

"Wow! I only thought that Grandma was getting icy towards the end, but I guess I was wrong," said Kyle.

"Grandma got nasty with me when I was about done with high school," said Kelsey. "She got to the point where she would judge me and criticize anything I would say or do. Since I got my job, I could afford my own cell phone. I would call Grandpa more often because it was cheaper. Besides, he's much better company!" giggled Kelsey.

"Tell them about your high school graduation," said Maddie.

"First of all, during my senior year I was inducted into the National Honor Society, which I thought was a big deal. Since Mom and Chase were on vacation, I invited Grandma and Grandpa to attend my honors banquet. Grandma refused to come because I asked Grandpa first, which was only because he was the one who answered the phone. On graduation day, she didn't stick around after the ceremony for pictures because she decided to sit in the car instead. She had a bug up her rear and I refused to let her ruin my special day! So much for me being a favorite granddaughter."

"I remember a time when I was at the house and your grandmother answered the phone. She immediately handed the phone over to me after she heard your voice. I'll never forget what you said about your grandmother. It was something I swore I would have never heard you say," said Michael.

"I said that she was a bitch! That woman did *not* want to talk to me at all!" said Kelsey.

"I have to confess, moments before you called, I told your Grandma that you call me all the time when I'm out and about. I thought I was just making conversation, but I guess I ruffled her feathers."

"Everyone had experienced disappointments with Grandma," said Chase.

"You don't even have to be family to experience her wrath," said Maddie.

"I remember one afternoon when Mom was hung over. I kept bouncing the basketball on the sidewalk as hard as I could just to annoy her. Mom swore that if I didn't stop, she was going to pop the ball," said Kenneth.

"*You*, the good son, challenged mother?" asked Maddie.

"I couldn't resist. Believe it or not, I was tired and ashamed to have my mother drunk all the time. Johnny was with me and he witnessed Mom puncture the ball repeatedly with a pair of scissors."

"Oh, my gosh, Uncle Ken! What did you do?" asked Kyle.

"I laughed because Johnny initially began to cry, but then he got angry and held out his hand demanding that Mom pay him ten dollars to replace *his* basketball," laughed Kenneth.

"Did she pay him?" asked Chase.

"Johnny had ten bucks in his hand before the ball was totally deflated."

Everyone laughed about that story. They could only imagine the look of surprise on April's face. Kenneth's story triggered memories about how April treated other kids in the neighborhood.

"I could never forget the first time I heard Mom tell trick-or-treaters that she only gives candy to the little kids, not to any teens. I about died when I heard her say that! I remember the arguments that would escalate between her and the teenagers!" said Maggie.

"I'm surprised that her house was never vandalized," said Alec.

"She's the reason why I get nervous when Allie walks up to the doors on Halloween night with her high school friends. I really find myself on edge expecting to come across a person like my mother!"

"Kids today grow up way too fast anyway. I say that it is good that these kids are grasping on to their childhoods as long as they can," said Michael.

"I'm surprised that she never had a big scuffle with the kids at work," said Maddie.

"Yeah, because they are quick with their tempers to begin with!" said Chase.

"Your mother was perfect for that job!" interjected Michael. "She felt superior and very much in charge of those kids. She would tell me how she would strip them of their good behavior points in the cafeteria if they pissed her off. I told her that positive encouragement was always the key for reaching a positive goal, but she would bully them instead. I warned her to be careful. She did get into a physical scuffle on a few occasions, but she lived for that," said Michael.

"I remember when she was out sick for a week and those troubled kids took the initiative to make her get-well-soon cards. When she returned to work, they had the cards neatly stacked on a table in the cafeteria fastened with a shoestring. I was touched by the gesture when she told me about it. I asked her if she was going to bake them some cookies as a reward for such kindness, but she said no because that would be rewarding bad behavior," said Maggie.

"How is that rewarding bad behavior?" asked Maddie.

"She said that when she walked into the lunchroom, she saw candy wrappers on the floor next to the trash can. She also said that they were not behaving properly for the substitute aide from the previous week."

"That would be your mother; focusing on the negative," said Michael.

"I told Mom that she should celebrate the moment, not let the past ruin the present. But she did not agree with that statement and she said that is why kids are screwed up today, which she stood firm on not rewarding the bad behavior in her absence."

"She would be the expert on that topic!" said Maddie.

"Do you remember that one boy who would come to the house to visit? He was sweet and polite. I even gave him a ride home once during a summer's afternoon downpour. He told me that Mrs. Getman was his favorite person while in lockup, even though the rest of the kids thought she was a real bitch," laughed Maggie. "He was in high school then and he missed her constant disciplinary reinforcements in the lunchroom from when he was in juvenile detention," said Maggie.

Michael added, "That child came around for about a year. His growth hormones were activated and he went from a little boy to a grown man overnight! Your mother started to fear him. He would bring his little sister with him when he would visit. They would ride their bikes from the projects. I was working in sales at the time and was gone a lot. That was when I started to notice the paranoia settle in with her."

"I remember her telling me that she saw him and his sister knocking on the front door, but she hid behind the curtain and hoped that he would just go away. She even turned the TV off before he got off his bike. She claimed that he helped himself to a juice box and a beer from Dad's cooler on the porch. There was no ice in there, but he didn't mind. He handed his sister the juice while he quickly downed the beer. When she saw him a week later, she told him that the neighbors told her what he did. She told him that he was never welcomed back to her house again," said Maggie.

"I do not know if that is a true story or not, but she was glad when he stopped coming around. I think for the first time she really got scared and didn't know what to do," said Michael. "Of course, that was just before the purchase of her gun."

"What was the most embarrassing thing Grandma had ever done to you, Mom?" asked Kyle to Maddie.

"She was really drunk one afternoon and she was partying with the neighbors across the street. She marched home and into my bedroom to find my bras in my dresser. She continued to walk back across the street with them and she burned them on the sidewalk! Do you have any idea how that made me feel? She had no reason to do what she did. I remember the neighbors laughing at me for weeks over that," said Maddie.

"I was furious at what she had done to you! But I did guilt her into compensating you for the bras. I'm just sorry that I couldn't do anything to retract the humiliation she caused you," said Michael.

"If she would have compensated me for each hurt she had inflicted in my life instead, I would be a flippin' millionaire!" she stated sarcastically.

Chase stood up and stretched a bit. He asked Maddie if she was ready to go home. Everyone followed his cue because it was nearly 9 PM. Allie went to get Missy and Kenneth's girls, who had been in and out of the lounge all evening. Michael went up to the casket alone. Missy looked over at him and asked, "What's Grandpa doing, Mommy?"

Maggie was touched by the vision and she knelt down to her daughter and whispered in her ear, "Grandpa is just saying good night to Grandma, sweetheart."

Maggie scooped Missy up into her arms. She felt as if she needed to hide behind her daughter the tears that were welling in her eyes. The realization of tomorrow being the very last time she would ever see or touch her mother again was more than she was ready to accept. She understood that her mother would always be with her in spirit, but that little voice in her head whispered, "The mental scars are constant reminders that she *was* in fact there. She may not have been the perfect mother, but she was my mother. Don't try to understand her, just love her."

The family waited for Michael in the parking lot as a way of giving him some privacy. They all said good night after their father returned. Michael acted slightly embarrassed when he realized that he was alone, but he did seem to appreciate the quiet moment with April. Mark and Missy insisted on driving back to the house with their grandfather while the rest of the Graham family followed.

Michael had plenty of questions and conversation for his trip back home from his young grandchildren while the Graham's car was silent. Everyone had drifted deep in thought as if they had floated into their own corners of the universe. Maggie's body felt light and exhausted as her mind raced into a million different directions. She was staring at her father's taillights as if they put her into a trance.

She had different emotions run at the same time. A few of them even felt as if they had collided. She had feelings of grief and anger that was the most dominant, but the feelings of elation was the one that made her nervous. She thought for a moment that she was thinking irrationally, but she experienced similar emotions when

Bryce died. She experienced the grieving process alone because no one in her family knew how to console her. She really thought she was going crazy at that low period in her life.

She called that grieving period "the emotional roller coaster" because each twist and turn was unpredictable. One moment she would be happy and the next she would be in tears, sobbing like a baby. When she thought of her mother, a small part of her was happy that her suffering was finished and that she was in a happier place. Maggie could only hope and believe that God would show mercy on her mother's soul.

Before Maggie could realize it, Alec was pulling up to the house. She looked around in disbelief that they were there all ready. She was really glad that she didn't drive because she was daydreaming from the moment they left the parking lot until the moment they arrived at the house. That really alarmed her. Allie even mentioned that it was a quick ride back to the house.

Mark was running up to the porch with Grandpa's keys to unlock the front door while Missy was bragging, "Ha-ha! We beat you!" Tandy was lying in the window watching them come in to the house. Maggie suggested that her family grab something to eat before going to bed. She warned for them not to eat anything too heavy so they would not get nightmares. Before too long she sent them upstairs to get ready for bed.

"Dad, where are we going to bunk down for the night?" asked Maggie.

"Mark can sleep in my room and the girls can sleep your old bedroom in the back."

"Okay. Alec and I will sleep downstairs."

"No you're not. You two are sleeping in your mother's room and I will sleep in Maddie's old room down here."

"Really, Dad, that is *not* necessary," she said anxiously.

"I wouldn't have it any other way. You need a good night's rest. I'm sure Alec will agree with me on that subject," said Michael as he looked at his son-in-law.

"I don't care where we sleep, but I agree that Miss Maggie needs her sleep," said Alec in an authoritative voice.

Maggie shot her husband an ornery look, which he could almost feel a burning sensation in the pit of his stomach as he tried to ignore her unpleasant expression. Alec meant well, but he was prone to miss many of his wife's cues, which almost always got him into trouble.

"I'll go check on the kids!" Alec blurted out of desperation as he ran upstairs.

Chapter 19

Alec grabbed a quick shower before going to bed. Maggie had tucked her children in for the night with a big hug and a kiss on the cheek. They were all exhausted. They had always insisted on using a nightlight in that house. As a child, Maggie was also afraid of the upstairs at nighttime and tonight was no exception. Michael always appreciated honesty, especially when it came to the children expressing their feelings so openly. In fact, he had fears of his own. He would never allow the grandchildren to sleep downstairs alone because of his fear of a drive-by shooting or some thief breaking and entering inside the house.

Maggie chatted with Michael before turning in for the night. He grabbed himself a beer and contemplated smoking a cigarette inside his house for the first time in years.

"Dad, I'd be shocked if there are any ashtrays lying around the house."

"It would be pointless anyway for me to be defiant now with your mother gone and all; it just wouldn't be any fun! Besides, I have to get caught up on the neighborhood gossip," he said as he walked toward the front door.

"I can certainly appreciate that. Would you mind if I joined you?" asked Maggie.

"Since when did you start smoking?"

"I don't smoke, Dad. I meant to ask if I could join you spying on the neighbors. You know, like the good old days!" she said with a smile.

"Maggie, you don't ever need an invitation. This is your home, too. You may be a Hoosier now, but you have our Buckeye blood running through your veins, no matter how far you move away from us."

"Oh, Dad, you're so patriotic."

"I really missed Toledo when I was traveling. I missed this neighborhood just as much as I missed my family. I know that sounds crazy, but I love this old neighborhood. I guess that's who I am. I've become a sentimental old fart."

"I'm sorry that I don't share your loyalty to the neighborhood. Maybe it is different for men than what it is for women."

"What do you mean?"

"I got tired of being scared all the time. I still carry my inner-city training with me to this very day. In public, I always look over my shoulder and I do my best to avoid eye contact with strangers. The one little quirk of mine that I cannot seem to stop doing is when I'm in a bank or a gas station, I find myself planning an exit in case of a sudden need of an emergency escape."

"Ah, you worry too much! You always did."

"It's awful, Dad. I get exhausted being on edge all the time. Well, I have to admit that I've become a bit more relaxed with age."

"Like I've said a million times before, the stuff you kids witnessed in this neighborhood was better than watching it on TV. I love the action and excitement. This city makes me feel so alive!"

They both sat on the front porch watching the neighborhood starting to come to life. Many families were sitting on their porches enjoying the fresh evening air. The springtime air welcomed all walks of life to the outdoors, which also guaranteed the action. The neighborhood had many new faces, but it was always good to see the old. Ontario Street used to be a two-way street, but in more recent years it became one-way. Maggie found it amusing to watching people still driving the wrong way up the street, which the neighbors would shout, "Wrong way, stupid!" Depending on the time of day or scorching temperatures, they might shout obscenities instead.

Earlier that day, Maggie noticed many trees on the street had been numbered by the city, which only meant that they were scheduled for demolition. Michael said there are only two trees on the block that happen to be maple trees, but the rest are ash trees that are infected by the Emerald Ash Borer disease. Those trees were planted to replace damaged trees from the Palm Sunday tornado in 1965.

There were nearly fifty tornadoes touch down in the Great Lakes region resulting in approximately 300 deaths. The Point Place area took the greatest damage in Toledo, which was located in the north end and bordered Michigan. There were nearly twenty deaths in that area with just under two hundred people injured. April was pregnant for Maddie when that happened, but they resided in Perrysburg at the time. Michael remembered Ruby mentioning that she saw it and said that it looked like a killer monster on the ground.

Maggie enjoyed the familiar smells of the neighborhood, which gave her the sense of a warm and welcoming feeling back home. After Michael finished his cigarette, they decided to go back inside for the night. As Maggie walked through the front door, she could not help take notice of all the pictures April had hung on the wall over the years. On the left side of the wall she had displayed pictures of when she was a child playing with her sisters while on the opposite end of the wall hung a few pictures of Michael and his siblings. The children and grandchildren were displayed in chronological order, which filled in the enormous space in the middle of the wall.

"Isn't it sad that Mom refused to have a family picture taken?"

Michael just shook his head and said, "There are many things that are sad. I believe that was just her way of removing herself from our lives."

"I could never understand it. She refused to have a picture taken with us when we were little. As I grew older I thought she was just too ashamed of us to want to have a family portrait."

"I don't have the answer to that mystery. Maybe it was just one of many annoyances in her life that she could dominate."

"But then again, maybe she was ashamed of her own image," said Maggie.

April did have snapshots taken of her holding her grandkids when they were little, but that was because she could hide behind them. No one knew for sure if the reasons were because of her insecurities or just a power trip. Maddie thought it was just a way of bringing attention to herself. April ruined so many pictures by holding her hand in front of her face. Michael enjoyed sneaking around a crowd to snap April's picture unexpectedly, which ultimately involved many snapshots of her eating mostly junk food. He was always up for a good challenge.

Maggie laughed when she saw the caricature of Maddie, the twins, and herself displayed on the other wall. It was made when they went to Cedar Point one year. The girls had families of their own while the twins were still in high school. They had it framed and gave it to April for her birthday. For it being a cartoon drawing of her four children, she claimed that it was the nicest picture of all of them that she had ever seen. They knew that a compliment lingered in there somewhere, but they were happy that she enjoyed it all the same.

"Do you remember when I got a sketching done of my kids?" asked Maggie as she turned away from the cartoon smiles.

"Of course I do. If my mind serves me correctly, you have it displayed above your mantel."

One year, Maggie saved her Christmas money from her parents for six months. She saved her fifty dollars for something really special. It was rare for her not to spend it on a bill or the kids. Maggie had always wanted a professional sketching of her children; the closest she came to a professional was when a street artist approached her in Tarpon Springs, Florida. He sketched the kids for twenty-five dollars. She purchased a nice frame for twenty dollars, which came with matting. She was so pleased with it that she sent her parents a thank you note for purchasing the Christmas gift she always wanted.

"Do you remember how Mom reacted to the sketching when she first saw it?" asked Maggie.

"Yeah, she said that it wasn't as nice as hers. I stated that her sketching was just a cartoon while yours was an actual look-alike drawing of your children. I couldn't believe that she said that out loud!"

"I guess she thought of it as a contest or something. You know Mom."

"No, she was just jealous. You got that sketching in Florida that one year Alec surprised you and the kids with a spur-of-the-moment vacation. She never would have done something like that."

"Well, I still think of her saying those words every time I look at that sketching. That very artwork is my constant reminder to be the best wife and mother I could possibly be. I have learned years ago to keep a stiff upper lip."

"That's due to me constantly hounding you about being too damned thinned-skinned!" laughed Michael.

Maggie just rolled her eyes after that comment. When she was young, she was a naïve girl who wanted to play an innocent game of Monopoly with her father. She never knew that he was a bloodsucking vampire when he played that game. He massacred the poor child! When she was left with one dollar, he did a victory dance that made her cry. She vowed to never play that silly board game with him ever again. Maggie hated playing games with the man after that incident. She about had a nervous breakdown when he taught her to play Euchre.

Before Michael left April, he found an old photo he took of all his hotels on the Monopoly board, which he was sure to send to Maggie with a note attached: "Thinking of you! Love, Dad." Memories of that one afternoon stuck in Maggie's crawl for years. Michael had labeled his daughter as being thinned-skinned from that day on. She still cannot look at a Monopoly game without getting a shiver. Maggie figured that her tears made her father feel a bit guilty, which always brought a smile to her face.

"Well, on that note, I'm going to bed. Good night, Dad, I love you," she said as she hugged him tight.

"Good night, baby doll. Please try to get a good night's sleep," he said sincerely.

"You do the same, Dad. Now don't be staying up too late or I'll have to ground you!" she teased.

"I'm going to watch the local news so that I can catch up on what I've missed in the city. I'll be going to bed shortly after that," he promised.

Maggie went upstairs to get ready for bed. Alec had just walked out of the bathroom as he met his wife on the stairway. He nearly dropped his towel when Maggie whistled at him. He looked surprised because he did not expect anyone to be standing in the hallway as he crept to the bedroom wearing a skimpy towel. He quickly kissed her on the cheek as he tiptoed toward the bedroom at the end of the hall. Maggie couldn't resist as she grabbed his towel from him, which sent him running naked into the bedroom.

She giggled as she heard her husband yell from behind the closed door, "I'm going to get you for that, Megan Graham!"

"Thanks, baby. I really needed that," she said with a smile.

"Really. Is that sales person of the year behavior?" he asked as he spoke through a small crack of the door.

She thought about that question and carefully answered, "Yes. Only if she is human *and* her husband is hot!"

"Nice answer," he said as he closed the door with a playful smile. "I'm still gonna get you for that!"

Maggie walked into the bathroom to get ready for bed. She thought she looked so pale as she assessed the damages of the day while viewing her reflection in the mirror. Her makeup looked as if it had retreated hours ago. She pulled her hair into a ponytail so she could wash her face. She shuttered as she noticed just how much she was looking like April. Maddie shared her sister's feelings on that subject, but unfortunately for Maddie, she felt April lingering beneath the surface the most.

Maggie drifted deep into thought while standing at the sink. Maddie once confided in her that she experienced panic attacks to the point of cowering in the corner of her bathroom in fear. She felt as if the Grim Reaper himself had touched her on the shoulder. She worried about the safety of her whole family to where it drove her to the brink of insanity.

Maddie told Maggie that she purposely motored through life with blinders on so she would not have to worry as much. She always feared harsh repercussions by telling her kids "no" and she went broke paying for expensive vacations for her family every year, which was an extreme opposite of April. Maddie was aware of her heavy drinking, but alcohol was something that she depended on for inner-peace and comfort. Even though April was an alcoholic and Michael a heavy drinker, Maddie proudly blamed her drinking on the genes from her German-Irish heritage.

Maggie realized that she gets overwhelmed herself, but it was more with the housework. She never assigned various duties, with the exception of cleaning their own bedrooms, to any of her kids. She wondered why she got moody and overwhelmed when she had a whole house to clean by herself. She, like Maddie, became angry during and after the chore of cleaning the house to where the kids tried to make themselves scarce due to the heavy tension in the air.

Trying to avoid the same pitfalls as her mother had caused its own set of problems for Maggie. She had overcompensated her nurturing by trying to protect her children from becoming slaves within their own home, but she had soon realized that her children needed to learn how to survive in the world because they would not be living at home forever. She was also a parent who was afraid to spank her children, especially in public. She soon found herself battling ghosts from her past colliding with the demands of modern society. Spankings were quickly becoming an unacceptable form of punishment.

Alec once videotaped their eighteen-month-old daughter's tantrum that resulted in her beating and throwing herself headfirst into a protruding corner of a wall. Maggie swore that in the days of the Puritans, they would have deemed that child as being possessed. Alec feared that Missy was autistic. Maggie called the doctor right away. Missy was the child who the pediatrician insisted on using the "spanking spoon" because she experienced screaming, eardrum splitting, tantrums that would last at least a half hour long. Most of her tantrums would end by putting her in a tub of water, clothes and all, to calm her. Alec and Maggie were always on edge—especially in public.

Maggie remembered Missy running around the examination room while the pediatrician came in to counsel Maggie. He let his nurse view the videotape in another room. Maggie was near tears while the doctor was quick to put the blame on the parents.

"A spanking spoon? We never used a *weapon* with our other two children," Maggie said matter-of-factly to the pediatrician.

"Missy is obviously *not* a time-out kind of child. If you don't get a handle on her now, you are looking at a teen pregnancy, runaway, criminal, or even a suicide. You are not beating her! Spankings are not meant to break her spirit, but it should be thought of as a tool to break a bad habit," he said while pointing sternly at Missy.

Missy had stopped running around the room at that very moment and rested her little elbows on Maggie's lap. The doctor looked down at the small child as there was a pause in their conversation. Much to

Maggie's total horror, Missy looked up at the man with an ornery scowl upon her face. She pointed at him with a stern finger and growled, "You, you *weave* my butt awone!" Maggie's eyes nearly bulged from their sockets as the doctor glared at Maggie with anger and said, "Use it!" The nurse returned to the room with a look of surprise as she handed the tape back to Maggie.

"Was it *that* bad?" asked the doctor smugly.

"It was the worst tantrum I had ever witnessed," said the nurse.

"The prescription is in your utensil drawer at home. I strongly recommend that you use it! Each time she steps out of line, she bought one swat on the bottom."

Maggie left the office in tears. She was so confused on what to do. She did not trust the doctor's advice. She did try the spanking regiment first thing in the morning, but she did not feel good about it. She used a wooden spoon ten times in a fifteen minute time span before 8 AM. The doctor's office called at 8:20 AM to check on progress. They were delighted that Maggie followed through with the doctor's advice. It totally broke Maggie's heart. She truly felt torn between two worlds and didn't know what was best for her daughter. *How can I possibly be a good mother by spanking?* Maggie constantly thought.

Remembering beatings she and Maddie received from April, she could see how easy it would be for a parent to lose control on a child. Deep down inside of Maggie's conscience she feared turning into her mother. She did not want to risk putting her children through that kind of experience. She threw the wooden spoon in the kitchen drawer and cried. She even prayed for God to give her a sign on what was the right thing for her to be doing. She felt so helpless that she could not reach her toddler while there were cases in the news of parents being arrested for child abuse because of spanking their children.

Three days later, a little girl from their neighborhood died from a blow to the head as an end result of temper tantrum. She hit the back of her head on the marble tile in the bathroom while protesting bath time. The child fell backwards after resisting her mother's grasp. Attending the toddler's funeral was the hardest thing Maggie had ever witnessed. Her heart ached for the youngster's family. It was a tragic accident that affected so many people. Maggie prayed especially hard for the child's mother to one day find peace and to not dwell on what she could have done differently to prevent such a tragedy.

Missy was reintroduced to the spanking spoon after that child's funeral and this time it worked! Maggie found the importance of consistency. They used the spanking spoon faithfully for two weeks, which was enough to pull little Missy in line with the rest of the family. When she acted out, she would retrieve the wooden spoon on her own with tears in her eyes. That was when Maggie and Alec stopped using it. They realized that they finally reached their child. The spoon was still hung in the kitchen as a reminder of those days. Missy remained strong-willed, but she was no longer out of control.

Maggie realized that she was daydreaming again when the water in the sink nearly overflowed. She washed up and brushed her teeth. As she was putting her things away, she realized that she and Maddie had been struggling with the same issues. When it came to motherhood, they both tried to correct situations of their own childhoods without realizing that they were both overcorrecting the problems. It was okay to ask for help around the house and it was definitely okay to say "no" to the children once in a while.

Maggie checked on her kids before she headed to her mother's chambers. They were all fast asleep. She snuck in to kiss them on their foreheads and whisper, "I love you and sweet dreams," softly in their ears. She flicked the hallway light on and off as a way of saying good night to her father downstairs. It was a silly family tradition that Michael initiated when they moved into that house. He was quick to respond, "Good night."

As soon as she opened the bedroom door, the nauseating scent of her mother's perfume hit her in the face. Her stomach was beginning to turn. She nearly had a heart attack when she saw Alec lying on her mother's quilt wearing nothing but a smile.

"What on earth are you doing?!" she said frantically.

"I'm just waiting for my woman," he said in his most sexy voice.

"Not in my mother's bed, mister! Are you crazy?"

"Sorry, honey. You can't blame a man for trying," he said with a smile.

"I love you, baby, but you're going to open yourself up for nightmares sleeping naked in *my* mother's bed. Please, at least put on some drawers!" she said as she threw a pair of boxers at him. Maggie had to collect herself. She was thankful that no one else had walked into the room.

As he was stepping into his skivvies, he looked up at her with a smile and said, "Gotcha!"

She openly shivered at the very thought of having sex in her mother's bed. Alec giggled at her reaction. He never had to witness April's drunken sexual advances like Maddie's boyfriends had. The only problem Maggie had encountered with her mother was after Bryce died. His family took Maggie out for dinner one evening and they returned late. April met them in the street because there were no parking places in front of the house. She claimed that their daughter called looking for them. As Bryce's mother exited the car to use the phone, April was quick to jump in and insisted for the man to drive away.

Bryce's father drove April down the darkened city street while Maggie stood on the curb in shock. They had been gone for about ten minutes. They parked near Galena Street while Bryce's mother found them both in a compromising position. Maggie only assumed that they were kissing. April sprang from the vehicle and put herself straight to bed. April reeked of guilt while Maggie suffered with humiliation. Maggie rarely spoke with her deceased boyfriend's parents after that incident. April would squirm at the mere mention of the family's name. Maggie did confide in her father a few months after the occurrence, but Michael chose not to confront his wife of such accusations.

Maddie once told Maggie that she walked in the house and caught April watching her and Bryce kissing in the back yard. April had been drinking as she watched through the open window at her youngest daughter's intimate moments with her boyfriend. April appeared unnerved by her being caught spying and she invited Maddie to watch with her.

"Mom! What on earth are you doing?" insisted Maddie.

"Shhh! I'm watching your sister. Watch how he kisses her. He is so tender and gentle. She is so lucky to have a man who knows what he's doing."

"I'm not staying around to watch this because it's sick! She deserves her privacy, Mother. She will be devastated if she finds out what you have been doing. She'll never trust you again."

Maggie about gagged when Maddie told her that April appeared to be turned on by what she saw. Maggie remembered April warning her to watch how she conducted herself in public with Bryce because people might get the wrong idea about her reputation being too loose. This was why Maggie chose to visit with her boyfriend in the back yard in the first place. She wanted the privacy and she certainly did not want to offend anyone by her kissing him. She never dreamed that she was providing entertainment for her own mother.

Alec turned off the light as he snuggled close to his wife. She was so happy to be in his arms again. He kissed her gently and held her tight until she fell asleep. Maggie was so tired that her eyes kept tearing all on their own. Poor Alec thought she was crying herself to sleep, but it was just her eyes' way of rejuvenating themselves from the lack of sleep and other eyestrains throughout the day. Maggie was quick to fall asleep and she fell immediately into a dream.

Maggie could feel the vibration and high speed of the roaring motorcycle she was on as she motored into a blinding white light. She could feel her hair whipping against her face, while stinging her eyes, making it difficult for her to see. She was horrified when she realized that she was not driving the bike. She could feel that she was being restrained by a strong force with her arms compressed tightly at her sides.

She looked down at the instrument panel and could see one arm operating the bike, which was covered in black leather. Maggie instantly thought, *Oh, my God! He's got me! It's the man in black!* as she could see the other arm pressing her body tightly against his while her legs were pinned against the sides of the bike with his large and powerful legs. Maggie felt trapped and helpless. She was at his mercy.

The roar of the motorcycle was deafening and it succeeded in drowning the vicious sounds of her pounding heart. She could see that he was driving onto a bridge. Her surroundings, even though a blur, looked bright white. The louder she would scream, the louder the engine would rev. She could not move. As he was nearing his destination, Maggie could see her husband, children, father, and siblings standing on the side of the bridge cheering her on and shouting, "You can do this, Maggie! You can defeat him!"

As they entered the bridge, Maggie saw that the other half was missing just before the bike careened off the edge, freeing Maggie from that monster. She could feel the weight of the bike fall from beneath her as she could feel the man in black tear away from her, which made her body feel light as a feather. She watched the bike plunge into the water as the man in black quickly followed. She could feel the butterflies in her stomach as if she were on a roller coaster. Not realizing that she was suspended in midair, she screamed as loud as she could with her arms flailing about, yet there was a small sense of peace when she could hear her family still cheering in the distance.

Suddenly, out of nowhere, appeared a woman in white. She came to Maggie looking like an angel.

"Maggie, they cannot help you now. Only you can help yourself," she said calmly.

"How? Who are you?" asked Maggie with a wild expression on her face; still unaware of being suspended in midair.

"You know me, Maggie. I've known you since you were a child. My name is Tosconda. When the time is right, you will remember me and everything will fall into place for you."

She was a beautiful woman with dark hair that was full and wavy down to the middle of her back. Her white gown was long and flowing on her thin, petite frame. She had dark-set eyes and a comforting smile. Maggie did sense a hint of familiarity about the woman, but nothing was coming to mind of how or when she met her. She possessed an essence of love and peace that took her back in time, but she could not remember the exact event of such feelings of her childhood. Maggie quickly dismissed thoughts of her past and she concentrated on the fact that Tosconda was her Angel of Mercy and asked no more questions.

As Tosconda reached her hand out for Maggie to grasp, she slowly faded away and turned into a rope. Maggie seized the rope as her life depended on it. As she was swinging towards safety, she could hear Tosconda say, "Remember me. Say my name so you won't forget me. Say it, Maggie. Tosconda. Tosconda." Maggie was distracted by the sounds of her family celebrating as she could feel the tension on the rope as they pulled her up the cliff beside the broken bridge. She was safely delivered back to them as the dream ended.

"Tosconda. Tosconda. Tosconda," said Maggie as she woke up still saying her name aloud. Before Maggie could open her eyes, she heard another name in the distance, "something Gazarri." She looked over at Alec wondering for a moment where they were. She was still thinking about the name of the angel from her dream. Maggie actually felt for the first time that she had defeated the man in black. Her adrenaline was flowing pretty strong and there was no way possible for her going back to sleep. She needed to write down those names before she forgot them.

When she got out into the hallway, she saw Allie wandering around in her bedroom. Maggie went in to check on her and suddenly realized that Allie was sleepwalking again. Allie always did that when she was stressed. She said that she needed to find a pencil. Maggie gently tucked her back into bed. She thought it was funny for Allie to say that since Maggie was on her way to write down those names. She always swore that she and Allie were telepathic during one another's nightmares. With their strong mother-daughter bond, they were always tuned in with one another's thoughts and emotions.

She found her purse downstairs and entered, in her day planner, the names Tosconda and Gazarri, which she could only assume since the second name sounded muffled in her dream. She checked her address book to be sure that the names were not those of clients. She thought the names Tosconda and Gazarri sounded Italian. She was baffled by the dream, but she was glad to have defeated the man in black. She felt in her heart that he was gone for good! As Maggie put her purse away, she noticed that the front door was open and she could hear Michael's police scanner from the porch.

Maggie was not too surprised to find her father sitting alone on the front porch. She carefully opened the screen door with hopes not to startle him. He did not hear her open the door because he was lost in his thoughts. Even though it was dark, Maggie thought she caught him crying as she approached him.

"Dad, are you okay? It's four o'clock in the morning."
"Yeah! I'm fine. What are you doing up?" he said with surprise.
"I couldn't sleep. How about you?"

"Same reasons," he said as he looked away from her.

Michael invited his daughter to join him on the front porch. She sat beside her father as he lowered the volume on the scanner. He only slept two hours because had too much on his mind and all hope was lost for a peaceful night's rest. He felt that there was no point staying in bed any longer. There was a ghostly silence between the two and Maggie could feel her stomach start to knot up again. She could sense that Michael had a truckload of feelings that he was dying to unload.

"What's on your mind, Dad?"

"Bad choices, Maggie."

"Are you talking about bad choices in shoes or relationships?" she said lightly.

"I'm referring to your mother."

She was shocked by his response, but she tried to keep a poker face with hopes not to make him nervous about venting his feelings with her. He was quick to apologize for his outburst and he told her that he didn't want to make her feel uncomfortable for being so negative, especially at the time of April's death. Maggie was raised with the belief that if someone had something to say, then let them say it. That was Michael's philosophy in life. Maggie knew that he had something to get off his chest and she would be more than happy to help free him of his burden.

"Dad, we are on the same team. There is nothing that you could possibly say to me that would upset me. We both have vented with each other in the past and I hope that Mom's death will not change our relationship in the future."

"I have some things on my mind that might be alarming to you. I'm not sure if I'd be doing the right thing by sharing them with you."

"Try me. I might have some things to share with you that are similar," she said. "What's on your mind?"

"Have you ever wondered what life would be like today if you would have done something different in your past?"

"Sure! Who hasn't?"

"I've often wondered what life would be like today if I made different choices with your mother."

He elaborated on a story that when he and April were engaged, she had been cheating on him. He told Maggie that her friends came to him to ask if he and April had broken up. He confessed to them that he was busy with a few extra jobs that week and he had not talked with her in a couple of days. They told him that they saw her hanging around Dick Mosley and Stan Weinstein. Michael was in disbelief at first, but he got cleaned up and went to check on his fiancée.

"I'll never forget walking into that bar. I saw your mother and Grandma Ruby sitting at the bar with their dates! I walked over and stepped between your mother and Dick Mosley. I slammed my fist down on the bar and said to her, 'It looks like *you're* out whoring around with Mommy tonight!' She never said a word to defend her honor and she turned her back on me. I left the bar in a huff and smoked my tires in the parking lot."

"Wow!" said Maggie with surprise. "Did you break up?"

"As far as I was concerned, it was over. She called me a week later telling me that I blew it all out of proportion. I'm an idiot because I took her back."

"Do you regret it?"

Michael nodded as he continued to say, "A month later I heard the talk about her hanging out with Stan Weinstein. I drove down Miami Street and saw her standing next to him, as if they were about to kiss. Sam took one look at me and jumped into his new car and peeled out of her driveway. I chased him down and ran him off the road. I pulled him out of his car and was about to punch his lights out, but I realized as I pinned him against the car, with my fist drawn back in anger, that I was simply after the wrong person. I'm glad I let him go. Besides, how could I hit a man who wet his pants?"

"Wow! What did Mom do?" asked Maggie with great anticipation.

"She was just sitting on the front porch watching the excitement. I think that's what she was hoping for. I just walked up to her and held my hand out. She never said a word as she placed her engagement ring in the palm of my hand. I drove away calmly and stopped to sit along the Maumee River to do some soul-searching. I threw your mother's ring into the river as I followed right along with it."

"What? How on earth did you find it in that muddy water?"

"I couldn't find it in my heart to let go of the damn thing!" he scoffed.

"What happened between you and Mom after that?"

"I felt that we needed some time away from one another. I didn't speak to her for a month."

"Then why did you take her back?"

"I've been asking myself that same question for the last thirty years of our marriage."

They conversed about other peculiar things that April had done throughout the years. Their conversation eventually landed on when April locked the girls out of the house when they were little. Grandma Getman once informed Michael that April was doing that, but he didn't take his mother seriously. Maggie told him about the neighbor lady, Heidi, letting her use her bathroom because April locked the girls out of the house when they were newcomers to the neighborhood. Michael said that Heidi never told him about it, but the little German woman must have gotten a hold of April instead.

"I could have sworn that you knew about that!" exclaimed Maggie.

"The only time I heard about it was when I thought my mother was causing trouble for April. Your mother told me on numerous occasions that she never felt accepted by my mother. I figured that it was just an in-law thing."

April told the girls over the years that they moved to Toledo because her Getman in-laws had a white dog that kept urinating on the playpen when she would lay Maggie down for a nap beneath the shady tree in the back yard. She told Maggie that Grandpa Getman refused to do anything about it, which was April's sole reason for moving to the city. Maggie realized that story was inconsistent with the whole truth since they moved to Toledo when Maggie was four and a half years old. Maggie just assumed that Grandma Getman knew too much about April, which is what really instigated their move.

"No offense, Dad, but I don't consider this house as home. I have always thought of Grandma and Grandpa Getman's house, in Perrysburg, as my home."

"Why? You've only lived next door to your grandparents for the first four years of your life," he said with curiosity.

"Why? It was home to me because that was the only house that had never locked its doors to us. Our grandparents had always made Maddie and me feel welcomed there. We learned that lesson early in life."

"And that's why, in this day and age, I made damn sure that all who are responsible enough to own a house key, in this household, got one. That also includes the older grandchildren," said Michael sharply.

There was a long pause in conversation. Maggie could see that Michael's face was blotchy and red as his lighter illuminated his face when he lit his cigarette. He always looked like that when he was upset. Sitting in the darkness made it easier for them to speak openly to one another of such painful memories. Maggie felt the anger begin to bubble inside of her, too. She was about to share some thoughts and stories that she had kept buried for years. She felt that it was safe to tell him her secrets, whether it was right or wrong. Michael was easy to talk with because he was a great listener.

"You know what Mom had done to me one night when I was in seventh grade?"

"I could only imagine," he said sarcastically. Maggie could see him tense up as if he were preparing himself for a devastating blow.

"It was about two in the morning and it was apparent that she had been drinking. She woke me up and made me go downstairs with her. She sat me at the dining room table and told me that you were dying."

"What the hell? Why would she say something like that, besides it being her ultimate fantasy?"

"At first I thought she was going to kill you. She lectured me for an hour about how you had prepared her to be alone in life. You had been training her on taking care of herself for years. Being devastated, I asked her if you had cancer. She admitted that she didn't know for sure, but she *did* know that you were definitely going to die one day. I finally had enough of her nonsense and went back to bed. She told me that same story up until you left her. She eventually got Maddie and her kids believing her story!"

"Before I left is when I realized that it was important for me to outlive her."

"Why?"

"Because I refused to give her the satisfaction of watching them close the lid on me."

"I do remember a time when you would speak as if you were going to die, but I figured that you would welcome death before a divorce."

"I've always said that you were a smart girl," he said with a chuckle.

Michael talked about April's spending habits. It would make him furious when she would purchase two hundred dollars worth of groceries every other week when it was just the two of them. She would purchase shoes that she might never wear. If someone at work collected some silly fad, then her collection would have to be twice as big as theirs. On a more positive note, Michael did mention that April was good at sending birthday, graduation, and sympathy cards to family members.

"Speaking of cards, we would always laugh when she would have her invitation in her hand at a shower and insist that the time on *her* invitation read 3:00, not 3:15, and that they were officially late!" laughed Maggie at the very thought of her mother's boldness.

"Let's get this show on the road!" April would say. "It's too bad for those who are late. *My* invitation told me to be here on time, so I'm here and let's get it started!"

"When it comes to Mother's Day cards, Maddie tells me that she finds the cards that say the least to send Mom. She doesn't believe in sending anything that she wouldn't say herself. Isn't that sad?" said Maggie.

"Your mother deserved it. Besides, she never suspected any disrespect. Lots of times she was totally oblivious to reality. The older she got, the more naive she became to what was going on around her. It was as if her brain was numb or something."

"I did get a birthday card from her one year and I thanked her for its heartfelt message. It came with a small plastic card to carry in my purse that read all the reasons why a daughter is special to her mother. When I thanked her, she was unaware of what I was saying because she never read the card when she purchased it! So now I carry a card in my purse of all the things my mother never said to me. I was initially crushed, but now I just laugh about it."

Michael had warned April for years that she was going to die a lonely old woman. He told her that she was the one who chased the family away, which she took as a personal joke. April never wanted to be included in any family affairs and did her best to remain distant. She refused to go on vacations because she remembered the only vacation they went on she was saddled in a laundromat washing cloth diapers the whole time. That statement ruined any future trips with her family. She even refused to visit Maddie when she moved to Tennessee one summer. Michael took his kids down south without her.

"Mom eventually hated getting phone calls from us. She would complain that we would call you on your cell phone, but when we called her, she didn't want to talk to us. If we called the home phone from our cell, she would panic as if we were in the car on our way over for a surprise visit! Her conversation would start out with no enthusiasm in her voice. Her tone would pick up when she realized that we weren't coming over."

"Normally, if I were sitting there, she would pass the phone off to me. It was automatic when Maddie would call and eventually it happened to Kelsey. She was becoming impossible to bear! I was running out of excuses for her poor, insensitive behavior."

One month before Michael left April, he purchased a new grill. He had nursed his old one along for fifteen years, but it finally rusted completely through and the racks bottomed-out. He was so proud of his new purchase and he was looking forward to grilling on it that evening. April made a huge bowl of potato salad, which she would only do for special occasions. Michael got excited that she did that because he assumed that it was okay to invite their kids and grandkids over for dinner. After he assembled the grill he walked down to the store to buy hamburger and buns.

"Why did you buy all that meat?" snapped April as she watched him unload the groceries.

"Well, I thought I would call the kids over for a cookout with our new grill. I assumed that would be alright since you made potato salad. You made enough to feed a small army," he said lightly.

"That grill is for *us*, not them!" she snarled.

Michael shuddered at that memory thinking that she sounded like a wicked old witch. Now that he was retired, he was enjoying being a part of his family again. He hated being separated from his kids while he was a banker, but now he wants to strengthen his relationship with them while getting better acquainted with his grandkids. When April was at work, he would volunteer to watch his younger grandkids during the day just to make enjoyable memories with them. It was unfortunate that the very idea was short-lived.

"I'll never forget when I had Ken and Kobe's girls at the same time. Those little girls had a blast! I got rid of an old TV upstairs and they played school all afternoon in that newfound spot on the floor, which they used as an imaginary teacher's desk. The older girls took turns reading to the younger ones as if they were school teachers. I almost forgot that they were here at all! It warmed my heart to witness them play like they did. They were perfectly content by pretending to be an inspirational adult figure that afternoon. Everyone was happy! What more could I possibly ask for?"

"Don't tell me, the fun and games ended when Mom came home."

"Just before she came home, I called the girls downstairs for some ice cream. They all about knocked me down to get to the freezer. I told them that they didn't act like they wanted ice cream bad enough because they were being too quiet. Trina asked me what I meant by that, and then I introduced them to the old saying of I scream, you scream, we all scream for ice cream! They were excited and yelled so loud that I bet the neighbors could easily hear them. That was *exactly* the reaction I was looking for! Then *she* slithered through the door."

"What's going on in here?! I could hear you all screaming from the garage!" snarled April.

Michael remembered how his granddaughters were looking at him with hurt and confusion in their eyes, wondering why they got in trouble. She gave them all a time-out for screaming in the house by sitting them down in the living room without the TV. She was furious for having the grandchildren in her house without her permission in the first place. Michael's heart was broken after seeing such pain inflicted upon his young granddaughters from that woman. He felt that he was about to explode.

"I am *not* babysitting! No way! Not today, nay-nay, my friend," she said as she flipped the palm of her hand in his face with her head resembling that of a bobble-head doll. She picked up that expression from watching the female comedian, Stephanie Hodges, on cable and she used it to death!

"Who said anything about *you* babysitting?" said Michael. "We were having a party until *you* came home. I thought Grandma April was home, but I see that Katherine showed up instead!" he said bravely as he scooped his granddaughters an extra scoop of ice cream.

April never commented on Michael's remark. She chose to ignore him as she went upstairs to bed for her afternoon nap. The girls remained silent as they sat in the living room. Michael brought their ice cream to them on a large tray. They were so upset that they did not even notice that Grandpa put sprinkles on their ice cream. Michael recalled what was imprinted in his heart forever.

"Jillian looked me straight in the eye with her big, brown doe eyes, which were weighted down with tears, and asked in the sweetest and most concerned voice of any child I have ever heard: 'What's wrong with Grandma?' I just looked at them all and smiled. I said, 'Grandma was just being cranky and that we will not invite her to our ice cream parties ever again!' They all cheered is silence and quickly devoured their ice cream while I turned on the TV," said Michael.

Maggie sat there with tears in her eyes. She knew that was exactly how the little girls would remember their grandmother. They thought of her as being a mean bully, which was the side of her she chose to show them. Maggie always thought of each family member as a doll on a shelf. When April wanted to play with one, she would pick them up, dust them off, and manipulate them at will. When she was finished, she would simply place them back on the shelf and not give them the time of day until she wanted to do so. Maggie shared such thoughts with her father.

"Why do you think I call all the girls in this family baby doll?" said Michael.

"What are the boys? Action figures?" giggled Maggie, trying to make light of the conversation.

"We are nothing but objects to be toyed with in her eyes. However, I see that we are both in agreement with your analogy," said Michael.

Michael walked over to his cooler and grabbed himself a beer. He gave one to Maggie, assuming that she would have a drink with her dad. She was surprised that it was cold. They both opened their beers in unison. Michael gently clinked Maggie's beer can with his and said, "Here's to new beginnings." They both sipped on their beers as they watched a car or two quietly pass by on the street.

"When you spoke earlier about wondering what life would be like now if you had done something different in the past had triggered a memory that I had not thought of in years," said Maggie.

"What would that be?"

"One night, when Mom was drunk, she passed out on the loveseat. She was sweating profusely and she was unresponsive. I told her to wake up and go to bed, but she didn't move. So I slapped her gently across the face. She never moved."

"Just how hard did you hit her?" scoffed Michael.

"Well, I only hit her about five times; each being a bit harder than the one before, of course," she said with a hint of shame. "I did have a moment of remorse, but it quickly passed. I was about sixteen when that happened and I felt strong enough to defend myself if she woke up. I looked over at the telephone and had the urge to call for an ambulance."

Michael's eyes were wide at the very thought of Maggie doing that. He could only imagine his wife waking up in a hospital because of alcohol poisoning. He had a hard time thinking of what the consequences might have been on him and the family if Maggie had acted on her impulse.

"Why didn't you do it?" he asked.

"Because I didn't know where the state would have placed me after my mother came back home," laughed Maggie.

"Yes, she would have killed you!"

"Maybe that's true, but then again maybe she would have received the help she needed back then. If she got help then, maybe we would be telling different stories about Mom today. Maybe she would have become an influential and positive person."

Michael thought about that statement for a moment. He believed that she was too mixed up on the inside to care about becoming someone like that. She had her uses for each family member and called on them when she needed something. He loved April, but she had been so cold to him for so long that it was hard to thaw a freezer-burnt heart. He grabbed another beer while Maggie was still nursing on hers.

"Your mother had it easy, you know."

"I agree. I believe that she was a blessed woman who never knew just how good she had it."

"The very thought of my girls having to raise my boys breaks my heart. She threw those babies at you girls with both hands. When Maddie was out of the picture, you got saddled with everything around here. I thank God that you girls never showed resentment towards the twins or me. That was one of the biggest thorns in my side when I think of my wife."

"Because of my mother, I was never allowed to participate in extracurricular activities. It was amazing that I was allowed to join driver's training after school. Do you realize that my mother quit her minimum wage job one week before I graduated from high school? That was such a slap in the face to me, but I never complained. You know, my whole life revolved around what she wanted to do."

"That's why I gave you money as often as I could as a way of saying thank you."

"I know. It ended when she found out. She said that I didn't do enough around the house to deserve an allowance."

"I could never understand how she found out about that."

"Well, I have to confess. Mom cornered me in the bathroom one night and asked me if you had been giving me money. I told her the truth because I didn't want to be accused of lying. She always intimidated me when it came to her interrogations."

"I kept the gas tank filled when you were driving as a way of expressing my gratitude for all you did for us. Besides, your mother could not control that benefit because it never occurred to her."

"Speaking of driving, she told me that since she had to purchase her first car on her own, then so did I. I thought it was strange that she would say that because I would never ask my parents to buy me a car."

"I don't recall you ever asking for such an expensive purchase. In fact, I don't believe it's in your nature."

"It's not about ownership of a car; it's about her being a liar. After I moved out of the house, she bragged to me that Grandpa Bo bought her first car on the eve of her sixteenth birthday. The older I got, the more I realized that she lied to us on a regular basis."

"I think that she forgot whom she told what. She literally got tangled up in her own web of lies. Speaking of such wickedness, what did you think of that letter from Katherine?" asked Michael.

"Honestly, it was a bit overwhelming. It sounded to me like a grandmother was trying her best to reach for a friendship or establish common grounds with her granddaughter. Mom must have had her reasons to distance herself from the woman, but we never had an opportunity to know anything about her."

"I never knew the woman either. When I read the letter, I didn't think that she sounded all that bad. I was shocked to read that she still kept in touch with her former daughter-in-law, your Grandma Ruby."

"I really don't know what to think anymore other than the feeling of Grandma Katherine was in our lives more than we could ever realize."

"Do you mean personality wise?"

"Yeah, she lived within our mother!"

"It sickens me that she kept you from your great-grandmother, but she had no problems sending you to a criminal's house on the weekends!"

"I've spent my adult life wondering if there was an arrangement."

"What arrangement are you talking about?"

"I felt that this house was purchased so cheap because Mom had two daughters to offer as collateral. She knew what that man was and she chose to ignore the dangers."

"That whole scenario makes me want to vomit!" said Michael.

"It's because of something like that is why I have a hard time accepting expensive gifts from anyone other than Alec. I always feel that there is a hidden expectation in the acceptance of such gifts. This is something that drives my mother-in-law crazy about me, but it is something that I have to deal with on a daily basis. It's too complicated to explain to someone who doesn't know everything about me. I'm not totally sure if I understand it myself."

"I can see clearly what you mean by that."

"Did Maddie tell you what we did yesterday before going to the funeral home?"

"No."

"We went to collect Uncle Doug's booking sheet. We read that he was arrested in 1988 for gross sexual imposition and twenty-two counts of rape! Is that not disgusting?"

Michael sat perfectly still as he stared at his daughter. He took a deep breath and said, "That was only the evidence against him when he was caught. How many other things had he been allowed to get away with?"

There was a silence between the two of them. Michael rubbed his knees as if he had something to say, but was afraid to say it. Maggie was quick to pick up on his nervous behavior.

"What is it, Dad?"

"The night we were told the old bastard died, my plan slipped into gear. I never told anyone about this. The following Friday night was opening night for the Toledo Mud Hens. I knew that there was a family of six living next to Doug's house, so I sent them free tickets in the mail along with a bogus note that their family was randomly selected from the phone book to attend opening night at the ball field."

"Why would you do that?" she nervously asked her father.

"I believed that it was time for me to put some old ghosts to rest once and for all. I parked my car around the corner after the neighbors left that Friday evening. It was good that the house only had one immediate neighbor to worry about and they had been taken care of for a few hours. I entered the house from the back door with April's key. It was then that I realized that the locks had been changed. I was forced to enter by breaking the window. I didn't know what I was going to find when I got in there, but I had my flashlight in one hand and a sledgehammer in the other, just in case."

"What happened?"

"The stench of mothballs polluted the air. That was the first time I was inside that house after learning that monster touched my girls. I wanted to vomit!"

"Did you find anything?"

"All that I will tell you is that I found something hidden under a loose floorboard beneath his bed, in the back bedroom, that sent me into frenzy. I took my aggressions out on everything associated with that house. The house looked like Swiss cheese by the time I was finished. There was nothing left. It was dark by the time I walked out of the house. I threw my hammer in my trunk and drove to a nearby phone booth to call the police."

"Oh, my gosh! What did you say?"

"I told them that I was a concerned citizen and I wanted to report, what sounded like, malicious destruction occurring at that address. When they asked for my name, I said it was Douglas Carr."

The city had possession of the estate and they leveled the little green house without any investigation. Since the pedophile's obituary was in the newspaper, the authorities figured that it was a random act of vandalism from juveniles, especially since the dead man's name was used to file the complaint. Michael was careful not to leave any evidence. He left the house in such a condition that it looked as if kids were in there having a good time. He refused to tell Maggie what set him off, but she knew that it was bad and she did not really want to know.

"Oh, my gosh, Dad! How did you feel afterwards?"

"I felt good. I only wished that you could have been with me to take a swing or two."

"No, not really. I think I would have declined the offer."

"Why? I don't understand," said Michael with surprise.

"Because my beef wasn't with that man, Dad. It was with my *mother*," she said with a growl.

"Oh, come on. There has got to be a small part of you that wishes that man was still alive so that you could at least tell him off."

"No, Dad, I don't. I know in my heart that God is taking care of him in the way he deserves. He is no longer my concern. He hasn't been for years," said Maggie as her voice dropped. She looked at her father boldly and said, "After all these years it has occurred to me to finally place the blame for all the nightmares and molestations on her—my very own mother. *She* is the reason why I have issues with my confidence. I struggle daily by trying to prove to the world, and myself, that I am a normal person and that I'm okay!"

"You are okay, Maggie. You're a survivor. You made it, babe. You're strong," said Michael.

"No, I'm *not* okay. I'm nothing but a coward!" she said as the words were choking her. She looked away from her father while trying to hide her tears. "My whole life was one big secret to cover up the unspeakable acts inflicted upon me by my family." Michael was stunned by her words as he remained silent. Maggie found the courage to look at her father and said in a small voice, "I was just a little girl with no superhero to save me. I might have looked okay from the outside, but on the inside I felt dead. No one knew of it because no one cared enough to ask out of fear of exposing the truth."

"The past is just that; it's history. Look at you now! You are a healthy, beautiful woman with a blessed marriage, you are a wonderful mother with three kids who adore you, and you are a very successful businesswoman. These are all prize possessions. You should be proud of yourself, Maggie."

"I chose the real-estate business to help me develop a stronger self-confidence and build up my self-esteem. For the first time in my life, I wanted to be the one in control. I guess I should have gotten into acting because that was what I did on a daily basis and I was good at it. My clients and coworkers have no idea about my past and they treat me like a normal human being because of it. I guess that was all that I have ever wanted out of life was to feel somewhat normal! I just want to feel like a whole person, Dad. I don't expect you to understand because I don't fully understand it myself."

Her confession left Michael speechless. He had never heard such hurt and anger come from his daughter in all her life. It was something that alarmed him in a way to where he wondered just how much damage was actually done to her in the past. He knew it was bad, but Maggie spared him the gruesome details of such events. Her heart felt as if it were about to explode. It reminded her of when she was in labor for her children. When the time came to push, she pushed whether she wanted to or not. The body had a way of riding itself of things when the time was right. Maggie's time had finally arrived.

"My mother hated us," she said as her voice cracked.

"Your mother hated all of us!"

"I had always admired you, Dad. When we were little, you could have left at any time, but you didn't."

"I would never leave my children, my wife maybe, but never my children."

"After all those years of suppressing memories of pain that she had inflicted upon all of us just breaks my heart. The repeated dangers of a little girl fighting off a grown man's sexual advances left a mark on me forever. I have a hard time finding trust with anyone. I have never before told a soul, but I am telling you now. I feel so broken inside no matter how hard I try to motor on with my life. I have never had the courage to express such pain and anger to my mother in person. I once tried in a letter, but it only exploded in my face."

"I don't understand it either, Maggie. I swear to God that I wish you had told me. It kills me that you were afraid to ask me for help. My little girl needed a protector and no one was there for you. I hate your mother for doing that to you; to us."

"My mother was a woman who should have *never* had children. She should have *never* been allowed to conceive us," she said with tears streaming down her cheeks.

Michael had a lump in his throat, but he never took his eyes off of Maggie. She looked away wiping her tears as discreetly as possible. She could feel her body shiver from her nerves also screaming out. Every ounce of her body felt relieved that she said the words she had carried in her heart for years. The day of her mother's burial marked the day when her words of freedom were born. It was definitely a milestone for Maggie. It was too bad that she told them to the wrong person.

"Maggie, I am sorry for your pain. I'm so sorry," he said with tears in his eyes.

After a few moments of silence, Maggie went into the house to bring out a box of tissues. She never said that she wished she were never born, but that might have been the way her father heard it. Maggie believed that maybe she should have been removed from the home because she might have had a better chance of a normal life with strangers. Michael shared in the responsibility for choosing April to be the mother of his children. Maggie understood that she was one of many victims in the family, yet she blamed April for such careless heartaches and pain that could have been prevented.

"I feel that the time has come for me to share a story with you," said Michael.

"Is it a happy story?" she asked, being hopeful as she continued drying her tears.

By the way that Michael was fidgeting around, Maggie could see that it was going to be a difficult story to share. He lit another cigarette and looked out towards the street. Maggie could feel her palms sweat profusely, which was something she also inherited from her father when she got nervous. She conveniently dried her palms on her pajama pants.

"You know that I was in the service before I graduated from high school, right?"

"Yes. Mom said that you were a high school dropout. She said that you were a loner and boundaries of any kind did not fit your style," she scoffed.

"Well, something happened that I am not too proud of. I had just turned eighteen when I made the varsity baseball team. It was the first time I had ever tried out for a sport. I was a damn good ballplayer and my coach was saying that I could have a shot at a promising baseball career if I worked at it."

"I didn't know that you played baseball," she said with a sniffle.

"I was at practice one afternoon and your Aunt Gabby was tagging along with me, as usual. We swore one another to secrecy back then and I'm trusting you not to ever tell a soul!" he warned.

"I won't, Dad. What happened?"

"Well, later that evening, I got in trouble with the law. I was arrested and the judge gave me a choice, which was either jail or the military."

"What on earth happened? There has to be a logical explanation," she insisted.

"Your Aunt Gabby was around ten years old and she was the typical pain in the ass little sister. She had to be *everywhere* I went. She was sitting in the stands watching us practice like she did every day. I saw her talking to an elder from our church. It worried me because I *never* liked that man. I had trouble concentrating on practice because I kept an eye on Gabby. The coach noticed that my head wasn't in the game and he yelled at me to pay attention. After practice, I was surprised to see that she was gone. Normally she would not leave without telling me first."

"Oh, this doesn't sound good."

"This old guy always called me Mike. He would always rub my shoulder when he'd say it. His bony hands gave me the creeps! He enjoyed hanging out with the children, but he acted differently from the other elders in the church. There was just something not quite right with that man."

Michael remembered walking home with his ball bat resting on his shoulder and his ball glove dangling from the end of it. He often thought of himself as a hobo waiting to jump the next train car. As he walked past a secluded section of the park, he noticed Gabby's bike on the ground by an old oak tree. He could hear some wrestling behind the bushes in the distance. As he quietly walked around the bushes, he was shocked by what he saw. Michael reached for Gabby and forced her behind him.

"Oh, hello, Mike. Do you want to play, too?" said Mr. Johnson.

"Michael!" cried Gabby desperately while clinging to her brother.

"Go home, Gabby!" insisted Michael as he pushed his sister towards her bicycle.

Mr. Johnson pulled out a knife from his pocket and attempted to open the blade. Michael swung his bat at the old man and knocked him to the ground. He hit the man until he didn't move anymore. Michael was in shock at the sight of the beaten old man that sent him running home after his sister, both vowing they would never tell what happened. Later that evening, the police came to the house. They found a ball glove with Michael's name on it lying next to the unconscious man. Michael kept his promise to his sister and never said a word.

"Why didn't you tell? They would have let you off the hook! You were a hero for saving your sister!"

"I promised Gabby that I wouldn't tell. Besides, I lost my temper and that deserved some discipline. I joined the Army and enjoyed every waking day in there. I only regret not making a career of it."

"What happened to the old man? Did he survive?"

"That doesn't really matter now, does it? This was something that I am not proud of, but believe me when I say that he never touched another child ever again."

"It sounds to me that you sent that demon back to hell," she said softly while trying to digest his story.

"Maybe," he said as he looked away from her.

"I'm so sorry, Dad. That's an awful story, but I see you as an absolute hero! You saved your sister from that monster. It could have been so much worse if you hadn't come along when you did. You never told *anyone* about this?"

"Well, I did share this story years ago with Maddie. I used it as ammo when she was having a hard time with her first marriage," boasted Michael. "I told that piece of shit husband of hers that I went to jail once before for defending my family and that I had no problems doing it again! Why do you think he walked out of Kelsey's and

Kyle's lives forever?" he asked with pride. "After the divorce, I warned for him to leave and never return! I was beginning to think that moron did have a brain after all for taking me seriously," he said with a grin.

"Wow. That explains a lot," said Maggie with little enthusiasm. She was baffled by her father's calloused words while trying desperately to understand why he shared such a story with Maddie and not her.

One part of Maggie felt such sorrow for her father and Aunt Gabby while the other half felt betrayed by her father for choosing Maddie over her, again. She could not believe that Maddie kept their little secret for years. She felt left out and hurt by such a situation. Maggie might have found some comfort in her father sharing that story with her years earlier. She felt that her father's story was more of a devastating blow to her where she felt cut deep enough for her soul to bleed. She thought of April's notorious statement, "Maddie has her father wrapped around her little finger!"

Deep down inside, Maggie was glad that she knew not to say anything to her father about Uncle Doug. In her heart, she knew that her father would have gone to prison for the rest of his life over that man. Regardless of her father's past, in his daughter's eyes, he was still sitting tall upon the same pedestal like he always had. Maggie would never have forgiven herself for her father throwing his life away because of her, no matter what the situation.

The whole thing made her sad to think of such tragedies kids suffer with in silence. A silent victim generates power for the perpetrator to continue to act out their desires.

"Did Mom know about that incident?"

"If she did, do you think she would have provoked me like she had all these years?" he said with a nervous laugh.

Maggie pondered the idea of April's lack of empathy towards Michael's tragedy, if she would have known, brought about such rage from deep inside of her.

"Ooh my mother!" she said with a growl as she missed her father's joke.

"Crazy comes in different forms. Your mother had five personalities and four of them were bitches! I told her that to her face once and she was really nice to me for a week!"

"You know something, Dad? I carry issues around with me from that woman on a daily basis. I try my best *not* to be like her, but there are so many similarities that make me wonder if I am a crazy person, too. I have given so much of myself to people in the past as if I were offering a basket of fruit to fill the bellies of starving people. After my basket was empty, I felt that they were after my basket, which left nothing for my family and me. I think I gave so much of myself because that was something my mother would have never done. Isn't that pathetic?"

"You have always had a heart of gold, Maggie. Gold dust flows in your veins. I believe that we get where we are today because of where we have been. It's a miracle to me that you kept your sweet nature and you have not become a bitter person. Life can be brutal, Maggie, and you are a survivor. You are a true inspiration to all of us. The thought of nearly losing you when Bryce died still haunts me to this day. God spared your life that evening because He has a plan for you. I remember you being ill that afternoon and you declined Bryce's offer to go out that evening. It was unfortunate that he had someone else to take in your place, but I am glad that you are still here with us."

Maggie was speechless by her father's heartfelt words. She never had any idea that he ever felt that way. She once suspected that he might have showed his fear of losing her when she asked to use the car after Bryce's funeral to visit his grave. Michael was so afraid to let her leave his sight, but he was too exhausted to drive her to the cemetery. He hugged her so tight to where he hurt her neck. He held her so close that she could feel his tears drip onto her shoulder. She could feel his sorrow within her own heart that she didn't attempted to pull away from him. She never got that response from April.

"Well, the sun is coming up. I suppose we should try to grab a few hours of sleep before we have to be running to the funeral home," said Michael.

"I love you, Dad," she said as she stood. "We are going to be all right. All of us!" promised Maggie as she hugged him tight. She could feel the tension throughout his whole body. He was actually trembling, which made him pull away from her. It was obvious that he could not speak at the moment because of the large lump in his throat. Maggie looked away from her father as she held the door for him.

Michael nodded as he turned off his police scanner. They both went inside the house. The coffeemaker was activated and the aroma of fresh brewed coffee filled the air. Michael used the downstairs bathroom as Maggie went upstairs to bed. Her head was drifting as if it were a float in the Macy's Thanksgiving Day Parade. She felt way beyond her automatic pilot mode and she was about ready to crash.

She snuggled next to Alec as she tried to relax her mind and body. She felt absolutely overwhelmed by her conversation with her father. Her eyes were puffy and her body felt as if she were carried out of a boxing ring. As she closed her eyes, she thought to herself, *Such ugliness contaminates us all, but we have learned to mask it over the years for the sake of survival. Which is worse, the vicious acts of a crime itself or the secrets we bury deep within ourselves that continue to violently torture us throughout our lives?* She said a quick prayer for God to grant her family peace before she passed out.

Chapter 20

Alec and Maggie arrived at the funeral home moments before the ceremony was about to commence. Michael had their kids with him earlier that morning while Maggie grabbed herself a quick shower. She refused to go another minute smelling like her mother. The smell of her mother's perfume was thick and her bed sheets reeked of it. Alec joined her in the shower for the same reason, which was an opportunity he could not refuse either way.

"Thank God we made it on time," she said as they walked into the crowded funeral home.

"Do you think they saved us a seat?" asked Alec as his eyes scanned the room for familiar faces.

As the couple searched the jam-packed room for their children, Allie discreetly greeted her parents and quickly escorted them to their seats along the wall. Maggie noticed that there were no traditional seating arrangements in the front of the room for the immediate family members, who were scattered throughout the funeral home with the other guests. Mark and Missy were sitting next to their grandfather towards the front of the room. There were more of April's church members in attendance than what there were family and friends. Maddie pulled Maggie aside while Alec and Allie were seated.

"What's up?" asked Maggie with curiosity as she looked into her sister's exuberant eyes.

"I was up all night putting together a presentation. I'm sure you will like it. By the way, you look really good this morning. Is it because your husband *rocked* you to sleep last night?" she said with a devilish grin.

"Believe it or not, I actually slept in a little this morning," she said, being half annoyed by her sister's nervous tension. "What prompted you to make this presentation?"

"It's my farewell present to Mother," she said excitedly as she raced back to her seat.

Maggie could only wonder what her sister was up to. Maddie had started a side business of making DVD slide shows of weddings, anniversaries, and retirements. She had been doing real well for herself. She was talented and it was apparent that she put her heart into her work. There had never been a disappointed customer since she started her new found career. Just as Maddie reached her seat, the pastor began walking towards the front of the room. Maggie's stomach began to bunch up into knots as it was time for her mother's funeral to begin.

Maggie had a look of surprise on her face when she realized that she forgot something of importance in the car. "Alec, I'll be right back." By the time she came back inside, they had all just finished saying the Lord's Prayer. Maggie was able to sneak into the crowd without being noticeably out of place. Her timing was perfect since they were all standing for the prayer.

Alec glanced at what his wife was holding in her hand. He could see that it was the booking sheet that she showed him last night. He was initially surprised that she would want to bring that trash into the funeral home, but then he realized that she must have a reason for doing so. Maggie looked at him with a gentle smile and then looked ahead at her mother lying in the casket. She had a clear view of her mother's face from where she was sitting.

The room was filled with the heavy aroma of flowers, which was nauseating to Maggie. As the pastor started the eulogy, Maggie could not help but wonder why her mother refused for her own children to purchase a spray of flowers for her casket. She felt that flowers would have been a beautiful gift, which would have been the last gift they could collectively give to their mother. Maggie saw it as being a nice gesture, not a financial burden. In a small way, Maggie felt cheated. April's church friends must not have received the same memo. Maybe this was April's way of keeping her family at a distance from her church family. Again, nothing made any sense. Maggie did not know what to think anymore and tried to stay focused on the pastor.

"Before we head over to the church for an appropriate service for April, there is a short presentation that her daughter, Madelyn, put together for her mother. I hope you will enjoy it."

A TV was wheeled into the room with a DVD player hooked up to it. The room was silent as the music began to play softly. "Here's to you, April Connolly-Getman, with a lifetime of memories," was displayed on the screen. There were a few baby pictures of April, pictures of her at her senior prom, a picture of her in her wedding dress, a few more pictures of her being drunk, and the rest were pictures of April with her possessions. There was an old picture of her house when they first moved in, pictures of her fad collections over the years, pictures of new vehicles Michael had purchased for her, and even the large collection of shoes she had purchased throughout time. The woman never threw anything away. Maddie was sure to put a picture of the church in the video at the end. "Even though we remain here on Earth, we will miss you," was what the caption at the end of the slide show read. Maddie was sure to put a plug in for her business with an advertisement at the end. Alec giggled while Maggie appeared to be in a state of shock.

Alec chuckled and leaned over to his wife and whispered, "That really summed up your mother in a nutshell!"

Being hurt by his remark, she candidly replied, "What, that no living being was important enough to be included in my mother's life history? There was not *one* person in that video but my mother!" Maggie thought about what she just said and looked at Alec for a moment with a look of astonishment. "I stand corrected. I guess you're right! Maddie did capture the true essence of April Getman."

Maddie's presentation was short, but extremely powerful. Only the Getman family understood the message loud and clear. Not one person, other than April, was shown in the presentation. It represented their mother's priorities and how there was no room in her life for family. The Getmans always knew Maddie's sense of humor as being harsh, such as the video portraying April's possessions saying farewell, not the family.

Even though the majority of the people missed Maddie's sarcasm, the pastor complimented Maddie's performance and asked for the back of the room, and so on, to form a single-file line to say a final farewell to April before heading over to the church. Michael stood at the foot of the casket holding a bushel of yellow roses, which was for each grandchild to place with their grandmother. He had five white roses set aside for his children and himself to send off with April. The gesture was sweet. Michael greeted his family with reverence and a warm smile as he handed each of them a rose. One by one, they all made their way past the casket.

Alec escorted Allie and Maggie to the casket as he motioned for Mark and Missy to join them in line. Allie tenderly kissed her rose and placed it across her grandmother's chest. Mark aimlessly tossed his in while Alec had to pick Missy up so she could choose the right spot for her flower. Allie took her brother and sister outside to wait for their parents.

"Are you okay, Maggie?" whispered Alec.

Maggie stared at her mother as if she were imprinting the very image into her brain of how her mother looked on that day. Alec sounded as if he were speaking into a tin can. He sounded miles away from her. She stood there for a moment just staring, which seemed like an eternity. She looked down at the paper in her hand with hesitation. She took a pen from her purse and wrote on the back of the paper. "Forgiveness is yours. I have always loved you, Mom, and I always will. Love, Maggie," were the words expressed in her final letter to her mother. She folded the report and gently tucked it under her mother's folded hands. She placed her rose by April's shoulder as Alec quietly ushered her out of the room.

"You did the right thing, Maggie," whispered Alec.

"I'm not so sure, but it seemed more appropriate than that stupid letter I sent her years ago."

As the crowd all waited outside for the casket to be placed in the hearse, the funeral director stripped April of her jewelry and handed it to Michael. He stood and watched the man close the lid to her casket. Maggie was watching her father from the hallway. Maddie and Kenneth stood by their father, but Maggie felt that she could not be in that room any longer. Michael held Maddie as she wept while Kenneth carried the memory quilt. The pallbearers entered the room, which were six young men from her church. The family went to their vehicles, which were also scattered throughout the parking lot.

Michael was catching a ride to the church with Kenneth and his girls while Kobe had his group pile into their van. Maddie hugged Maggie before they got to their vehicles. Missy was hanging out of the Caddie's window like a monkey while Mark and Allie fought over which CD they would be listening to in the car. Alec was giving them the same lecture about not fighting and how they needed to be fair with one another by taking turns. That was an early argument because the stale ones usually resulted in threats of being grounded or being forced to listen to Dad's music.

"Oh, my God! Our mother is really gone! Maggie, we don't have a mother for real now," sobbed Maddie.

Maggie just rubbed her sister's back gently and said, "I know, Maddie. I know."

Maddie stood tall and straightened her dress. She dabbed her tears and said with a sniffle, "What did you think of my video?"

"It was fitting. It was a powerful message and it was fitting just the same. You did a great job, Maddie. I loved it," said Maggie.

"I better get to my car because I don't want to see the casket being stuffed into the hearse."

"Me too."

As Maddie walked away, she was approached by Aunt Ginny. She shuffled up to her niece with some tears. Maggie was surprised by the display of affection by the aunt she rarely saw and tried to hurry to her car before Aunt Ginny caught her, too. Aunt Cami was close behind with the man she had been separated from over thirty years, holding hands. Maggie was thrilled to see that her aunt was finally reunited with the person who had never fallen out of love with her. They never got a divorce and they never stopped loving one other. *What a pleasant surprise to see Aunt Cami so happy again*, Maggie thought as she was reaching for her door.

"Hold on, my little sweet one," said Aunt Ginny, shuffling up to Maggie.

"Hello, Aunt Ginny," said Maggie as she turned to greet her aunt with a hug.

"I have something to discuss with you. The last time we spoke on the phone I never had an opportunity to tell you everything."

"What are you talking about?"

"Maggie, I peeked at that wrap sheet you buried with your mother."

Maggie was in shock that someone would be so bold to remove something so private from her dead mother's hands. She felt so violated, which had become the premise of her life in that family.

"I just needed for you to know that before I moved to Savannah, I warned your mother, in front of your Aunt Kathleen, about what Uncle Doug was capable of doing with her little girls. I did try to spare you the pain and suffering I had endured as a child."

"You spoke up?" she said in shock. Her whole body went numb as she stood on the curb trying to imagine anyone trying to save her during her imprisonment in hell.

"Yes, darlin'. They both accused me of being a troublemaker and that I needed to keep my mouth shut! Your mother is the one who accused me of lying. I felt outnumbered. So, I had to turn my back on it and I never mentioned it again."

"So, that was that, right?" snapped Maggie. She tried to collect herself enough to stifle the sarcasm, but she knew it would be difficult. "Well, at least you tried," she said as she viewed her aunt as a woman thinking she deserved a metal for being a hero. "I hope that God rewards you for trying your best to save us, Aunt Ginny," said Maggie sarcastically.

"I know, darlin'. I did the best I could, but no one wanted to listen."

"When did this happen?"

"It was the last Christmas I spent in Ohio. I moved to Savannah in 1975. Well, my sweet, sweet Maggie, I need to catch up with your Aunt Kathleen. We won't be attending the graveyard services because I have a plane to catch, but we will see you at the church. Remember that I love you and Jesus loves you, too!" she said with a deep southern drawl as she gave her niece a quick hug.

"Thanks," was all that she could muster to say.

Maggie was insulted by her aunt's attempt at easing her own conscience by placing blame on others. This woman had done unspeakable acts with Douglas Carr and she knew that he would be forcing the same acts upon her two innocent nieces. Maggie was angry at the very thought of Ginny believing that she was not responsible for what happened to her just because she lived out of state or because no one would listen to her. If Aunt Ginny really cared, then she would have found a way to make people listen. In Maggie's heart she believed that what had been done was done and God had seen it all. At that very moment, she found comfort in the thought of God knowing everything indeed.

Maggie finally made it to her car, which was just a few feet behind her. She could see the pallbearers bringing April down the steps. Allie was weeping softly in the back seat. Maggie assumed her tears were for her grandmother, but it could have been a combination of things since Mark obviously won the argument over the music selection. Missy leaned between her parents from the back seat and studied their expressions intently. The small child then stared at her mother with a look of concern.

"Why aren't you crying, Mommy?"

Maggie took her daughter by the hand and said, "Well, sweetie, I have cried for a very long, long time. I don't think I have anymore tears left to cry because they've all been used up."

"Oh," she said with amazement.

"Buckle up, baby, because we're about ready to go," said Maggie as she reached for her seatbelt.

The caravan began to creep out of the parking lot as the funeral director stood on the curb holding a sign reminding the people to turn on their headlights. Mark enjoyed the fact that the funeral flags were green, which had always been his favorite color. Maggie reached for Alec's hand. He looked over at his wife sympathetically and asked, "Are you okay? What's racing through that mind of yours?" he said as he kissed the back of her hand. "Come clean now because I can see it in your eyes." Maggie just smiled and replied, "You have no idea."

The church was about three miles down the street. Mark thought it was neat to be able to drive through the red traffic lights during his grandmother's parade. Missy could not understand why they had to go to church on a Saturday. Allie explained that their grandmother got a special church service because she was a special member of the church.

"Have you ever been to Grandma's church, Mommy?" asked Missy innocently.

"No, I have not. I think only your grandfather had once or twice."

"Why didn't you go?"

"Well, because your grandmother never invited me."

"That's silly!"

"What's silly?"

"No one needs an invitation to God's house. Right, Daddy?"

"That's right, Missy Jane," said Alec with a smile as he glanced at his wife over his sunglasses.

Maggie just smiled at the logic of her six-year-old child. She could only wish that life could be so easy. "Since when did you become so smart, little girl?" asked Maggie.

"Since the day I was born. I have lots of brains, remember?"

Maggie giggled at that comment and drifted into a memory of when she signed up to sell quilts at April's church bazaar. It cost her $40 to reserve a spot. She was willing to make the five-hour trip with hopes that April would join her at her booth. She did not sound thrilled that Maggie joined the craft sale in the first place, but Maggie suggested this would be a way she could meet some of her mother's church family. April's reply was, "*I* am needed in the kitchen. *I* don't have the time to just sit around talking with you!" Maggie was crushed. She withdrew from the craft show and allowed them to keep the money as not to embarrass April. The church used Maggie's reserved spot and tables she had rented to sell raffle tickets.

Maggie could see the steeple of the red-bricked church standing tall on the corner. The landscaping was nicely manicured, but in another week or two it will be beautiful with all the flowers coming to life. The trees are just about filled in with their new plush green leaves. The smell of the springtime air was breathtaking and it always made Maggie feel so alive. Spring offered so many beautiful things such as the warmth of the sun waking the slumbering flowers, budding trees, and the upbeat tunes of the birds filling the air with their melodies. Maggie always believed that spring represents a time for new beginnings, not endings.

Alec followed the traffic to the parking lot on the east side of the church. Missy could see that her grandmother was already being carried inside the church.

"Hurry, Mommy! Grandma is leaving without us!" shouted Missy.

"Don't you worry, sweetie. They will wait for all of Grandma's guests to arrive before they start the ceremony," promised Maggie.

"Let's run just in case!" said Mark.

All three kids ran across the church lawn, clearly ignoring the *keep off the grass* signs. Maggie giggled at that very sight. She could just imagine her mother yelling at them for running, outside, no less.

"I hope they don't fall," laughed Maggie.

"Yeah, remember when Allie fell on her face when she was little? She put her front teeth through her bottom lip."

"I could not forget that with amnesia! I can still remember the smell of that little girl's blood. She was walking with her hands buried in her pockets when she fell on her face in the church parking lot."

"Wasn't that just before her second birthday?" asked Alec.

"Something like that."

Maggie couldn't get that image out of her mind. She still shuttered at the very thought of that event in Allie's young life. She and Alec caught up with their children and sat in the middle of the church. Missy wanted to sit on Maggie's lap, which she never minded snuggling with her children. She even pulled Mark into her as the three looked huddled together while sitting quietly in their pew. The kids settled in and were anticipating getting the church service started. Maggie reflected on their conversation about Allie's little accident years earlier and fell deep in thought.

"Look at me, Maggie! I can swing with no hands," said little Donnie Johnstone, the boy Maggie had a crush on until puberty. He was also Jenny's little brother.

"Oh yeah? Watch this! I'm pretending that I'm sleeping on this horse while still driving!" said Maggie with excitement.

Maggie and her friend were playing together at Riverside Park one Friday afternoon while April coached Maddie's sixth grade softball team at the ball diamond. Maggie was in third grade and her friend was in the fourth. Kenneth and Kobe tagged along with Maggie, which was the first time she was entrusted to baby-sit them.

They were all playing on the glider swings, in the toddler's area of the playground, which had four horse swings in a row. Maggie rested her chin down on the horse's head and the handle of the glider came back and hit her square in the mouth. She sat straight up with a look of being dazed and confused. She caught a large piece of her front tooth in the palm of her hand.

"Oh, my God, Maggie! What happened?" asked Donnie as he jumped off his swing.

Maggie was looking at what she was holding in her hand and was in disbelief. She looked at her friend with a horrified expression upon her face. She reached up to her mouth with the other hand to check for blood. Donnie was asking her over and over again what had happened. She did not answer him right away.

"Open your mouth, Maggie!" he insisted.

Maggie opened her mouth and asked, "Is it bad? Is there blood?"

"Oh! Maggie, you broke your tooth off!"

"Don't tell my mom! Please don't tell," she begged repeatedly.

Maggie was so frightened that she was going to get into trouble that she threw her tooth on the ground. The child simply panicked. She initially thought she could hide the broken front tooth from her mother for the rest of her life. She knew that April was going to be furious with her. Donnie collected the twins and assured Maggie that April needed to know that she was injured and that she would *not* be in trouble. Donnie and the twins ran ahead to tell April about Maggie's accident.

Maggie slowly made it back to the ball field as April was walking to meet her in the middle of right field. Since Maggie was walking and not crying, she assumed that her daughter was fine.

"What happened?" she snapped.

"I bumped my mouth on the swing," she nervously replied.

"Go sit in the car, Maggie! I do *not* have the time to be checking on you every five minutes! You sit there and I don't want to hear another sound out of you! Do you understand me?"

Maggie did as instructed and took an opportunity to look at her mouth in the mirror. She was shocked by what she saw. The corner of the nerve in her permanent front tooth was exposed! Maggie began to cry. It only hurt when she touched it, exposed it to air, or when she would attempt to eat or drink anything, which felt like an ice cream headache that was magnified a hundred times. She was quick to understand that she had knocked the guts out of her new tooth that was not fully grown in yet. Maggie's new smile was nothing compared to the fear of receiving the beating of her life when April looks at her mouth.

After ball practice, April threw her equipment in the trunk while Maddie and the twins climbed inside the car. Maddie turned to her sister and said, "So, I hear you broke your tooth off at the park." Maggie's eyes were huge with fear that everyone knew about it. She wanted to beat up Donnie for being such a blabbermouth.

"How do you know?"

"Everyone knows! Let me see how bad it is." Maggie smiled at her sister with great hesitation. "Oh, my God! You are so busted and disgusted," teased Maddie.

"Don't tell Mom!" said Maggie in fear as she watched her mother approach the door.

April climbed into the car and drove straight home. She never asked Maggie if pain or blood was involved at the playground incident. They arrived at home and April cracked open an ice-cold beer. The kids were getting things together for making sandwiches for dinner, for which Maggie had no appetite. April insisted that Maggie join her family, but Maggie just stood there with a look of panic on her face because she did not know how to tell her mother that it hurt too bad to talk, much less eat.

"What's wrong with you?" she growled.

"Why don't you take a look at Maggie's mouth, Mom," said Maddie with a sneer.

"Open your mouth," she said as she grabbed Maggie by the chin.

Maggie smiled big for her mother. April was speechless, but her expression upon her face told Maggie a million different things. She stammered for a moment as she tried to find the words to say to Maggie. Her daughter nearly knocked out a permanent tooth. April was furious! This was an upper front tooth that the whole world saw when her daughter smiled. April did not know what to do.

All that she could say was "Look at what you did! How could you be so stupid? You will look like that for the rest of your life!" Maggie was devastated and she thought she would rather have her mother hit her instead of yelling. "It's too bad for you that this is Friday afternoon. The dentist office is closed for the weekend. You'll just have to wait until Monday to see Dr. Apex! You better hope that they have an opening in their schedule for you!"

When Maggie told April that part of the tooth flew into the palm of her hand, she was furious that Maggie threw it to the ground. She loaded the kids back into the car and raced to Riverside Park to search for the broken tooth. Maggie felt embarrassed while April stood there shouting for her to search on her hands and knees to find it. Children from Maggie's school were in the park watching April belittle her. She never found it and she soon began to believe her mother that she would always look like she did on that day. In fact, the child felt that she deserved it.

It was a long weekend for Maggie, but she never complained. Maggie was just happy to not be beaten because of her little accident. April called the dentist office early on Monday morning to schedule an appointment for Maggie. April was surprised that they got her in immediately. Maggie had known Dr. Apex since she was three. The whole Getman family in Perrysburg were patients, too. He was the best dentist around town. He was a very sweet and gentle man, which his younger patients thought of him as a father figure. He looked at Maggie's tooth and gasped.

"Don't worry, Maggie. I think I can save your tooth."

Maggie thought it was bad enough that she nearly knocked it out a few days ago, but the thought of an extraction never entered her mind! The dentist hooked his young patient up to the nitrous oxide unit and left the room. He told Maggie that she was going to float off to space so that he could fix her tooth. A few minutes later, he entered the room to find Maggie laughing hysterically. She told him that she could see fangs growing beneath his curling nose hairs. "Yep! She's ready!" he chuckled as he called for his dental assistant.

After he was finished bonding the inner corner of her front tooth, he told Maggie that she could never eat sticky candy again because it could come off. She knew all too well that would mean pain, lots of pain! He called April into the room to tell her the same dos and don'ts. April entered the room relieved that the tooth was saved. The dentist looked at April with a sense of anger that Maggie had never seen or thought was ever possible for this man to possess.

"April, I have to ask you a question. What is your definition of an emergency?"

"What do you mean?" she asked, being clueless.

"How could you not call this situation an emergency?" he said as he pointed to Maggie.

"She seemed fine to me. Besides, your office was closed for the weekend. What else could I do?" April said as if passing off the blame.

"April! We have an emergency number! This child suffered the whole weekend with her nerve exposed. Would you be able to handle such a torture? At the very least, we could have prescribed her some pain medication to ease her suffering. This breaks my heart, April. No child deserves this. Especially when help was just a phone call away! This is the profession I chose and with it is my obligation to be available to my patients for such emergencies."

"Dr. Apex? Can I live with you at your house?" asked a delirious Maggie.

"I will just have to keep that in mind for next time," said April calmly as it was obvious that she had ignored her daughter's comment.

"April, take this patient of mine home and put her to bed. I don't think she is any condition to be sitting in a classroom today. Don't hesitate to call me if there are *any* problems."

Maggie smiled as she remembered getting that dental work replaced after eleven years. It had discolored badly and she was dating Alec at the time. Dr. Apex was about to retire and he was pleased that it stayed on as long as it had. He was especially thrilled that the tooth never died. He smiled at Maggie and told her that she needed her wisdom teeth removed, which took her a few seconds to comprehend what he said because he did not look as if he just told her shocking news.

"Hey, Dr. Apex, I love you like a father, but can't we just let the wisdom teeth slide?"

"Maggie, you have a beautiful smile, but these third molars of yours are going to grow and push your teeth forward, which will shift your midline. We do not want to stress that front tooth because it's been through enough."

"When can we do it?"

"I usually send my patients to the oral surgeon, which is becoming a common practice these days, but since it's you we are dealing with, I will be happy to do it for you," he said with a reassuring smile.

Maggie got up from the chair and was going to walk to the reception window to make the appointment. He stopped her at the door and told her to sit down. She was so distracted by the fear of having four extractions that she forgot to have her front tooth fixed.

"Sit down, Maggie. After I fix that front tooth, I will take care of that other problem for you today. Next week is when I retire."

"Really, you don't..."

"For you, Maggie, I will make the time," he said with a warm smile.

"What? You've got to be joking!" she said desperately as he was guiding her towards the dental chair. "But I haven't had the proper amount of time to psych myself up for it!" she said nervously.

"Relax, Maggie," he giggled. "If you want to hear something really scary, I will confess to you that when I fixed your tooth the first time I didn't have a clue on what I was doing. I read about another dentist from my dental magazine doing a procedure similar to what I had done for you. I didn't agree with some of the materials that he used, so I altered it to what I thought the job called for. Looking at this date in your records proves that you were my very first one out of hundreds that I have preformed over the years. I am so proud that it lasted eleven years! Let's hope this one lasts twice as long for you!"

Maggie snapped out of her daydream and had not noticed that the ceremony had begun. Mark was telling his mother to stand while the pastor said a prayer. She could not believe that she was so deep in thought. She looked around the church to see who came to say farewell to her mother. She was amazed at all the people. She saw a few people from the neighborhood along with a few faces from the past. There was a cluster of April's coworkers sitting behind Maddie and her family across the aisle.

Her eyes wondered about as she admired the beauty of her mother's church. The windows were full of bright, vibrant colors as the sun shone through its stained glass. She was glad that they did not sit towards the front of the church because there was a little pond with running water, which would be a sure bet to make her children need to use the restroom. Its altar was covered in plush red carpeting and the woodwork within the church was the same color of oak as the large crucifix, which was stationed in the front of the congregation from the floor of the altar to the ceiling. She reminded herself that she needed to pay attention in church.

"We will never forget all that April had done for our congregation. She never refused a simple request that was asked of her. She was quick to lend a generous helping hand without fail. She will be truly missed every Sunday morning. One thing I know for sure is that we will see her again in the Kingdom of Heaven. If we could put forth half the effort as our sister, April, then we, too, will surely make it there. Let us all sing a special hymn of praise."

As the pastor put his hands together, Maggie noticed that he had a white bandage on the fleshy part of his hand. She almost snickered at the thought of him karate-chopping walnuts with his bare hand. As she and Missy thumbed through the pages of the hymnal, she had a flashback to a memory of when she was in Junior Girl Scouts and her mother was the co-leader of her troop. Maggie was in the fourth grade and she remembers it was her first day of an exciting, week-long, activity-packed adventure of day camp at Pierson Park. She was so excited!

"Maggie, get the twins in the car while I grab the rest of my gear," shouted April from the kitchen.

Maggie loaded her brothers into the car and accidentally slammed Kenneth's fingers in the car door. Luckily, his little fingers were pinched between the plastic of the inside of the car door and not the metal. He let out a scream while Maggie quickly opened the door to help her brother.

"I'm sorry, Kenny! I'm so sorry! Shh! It's okay! I'll take care of you. Don't cry Kenny because Mom will hear you. Shh, it's okay," said Maggie desperately.

"*Sorry* doesn't make the pain go away, Maggie!" growled April as she crept behind her terrified daughter.

Maggie was quick to jump out of April's way so that she could carry Kenneth into the house. Maggie followed desperately behind April, hoping to be able to help her little brother. April soaked his tiny hand in a large bowl of ice water. Kenneth complained about the water being too cold opposed to saying anything about the pain. Maggie was glad to see that there was no blood, swelling, or bruising. She was just thankful to see that Kenneth was going to be fine.

"I am really sorry, Kenneth," said Maggie with the utmost sincerity.

"We are going to be late for sure and it's your fault, Maggie! Maybe I should make you stay here at home while we go without you," said April coldly.

"Maddie isn't home to watch over her, Mom," said Kobe.

"Hush now and get in the car."

Kenneth survived, but Maggie felt as if April accused her of trying to kill her little brother. Maggie would *never* do anything to harm anyone in her family. She loved and cared for her brothers deeply. She had always enjoyed helping out with the twins as often as possible and she never complained about doing so. She worried about her mother never trusting her to care for the twins in the future. She liked being asked to watch over them because it meant that she was growing up like Maddie. She desperately wanted to be just like her big sister.

On Friday, the last day of camp, the family was rushing out of the house again. This time Kenneth accidentally caught Maggie's hand in the car door. She was helping him into the car when he closed the door before she was expecting it. Her hand was on the top of the doorjamb as the metal part of the door trapped the fleshy part of her hand between the metal casings. Maggie screamed in pain as her mother stood at the driver's door staring at her. Kenneth was terrified by the sight of his sister screaming in pain that he began to cry. Not one person opened the door for her. Maggie's painful and frantic state resulted in her ripping her hand out of the door to free herself. Blood was everywhere!

"Well, it looks like paybacks to me," said April with a sneer. Kenneth was still screaming inside the car as Maggie tearfully grasped her bloody hand. April tossed the house key over the roof of the car so Maggie could dress her wound. As Maggie ran towards the house she heard April say, "Hurry up! We are running late enough as it is!"

Maggie was a mess. Blood was all over her camp T-shirt and it was running down her arm. She ran her hand under cold water from the kitchen faucet and would occasionally peak at the wound, which was gaping. Michael kept a spray bottle in the cupboard filled with peroxide for such occasions and it was marked with a white cross from bandage tape. She then wrapped her hand in wet paper towels because there were no bandages. Michael taught his daughters about compressing wounds. Maggie took the time to rid the floor and counter of her bloody trail. She was about to run upstairs to her bedroom to change her bloodstained shirt, but April was laying on the horn to hurry Maggie along.

"I'm sorry, Maggie," said Kenneth quietly from the back seat.

"There! Did that make the pain go away?" snapped April. "We're late!" she growled as she sped away from the curb.

After April raced off to the station where she was assisting, Maggie snuck off to the first aid tent for a bandage. The nurse was alarmed that Maggie needed stitches, four she was guessing, and she was getting ready to write a report for the child's injury at camp. She was stunned when Maggie told her that she did it at home and her mother knew about it. After she realized that April was the scout's mother, she put on a butterfly bandage and told Maggie to keep it clean and dry. She even gave Maggie a few extra bandages to get her through the weekend. Maggie found it uncanny that the scar was in the shape of a teardrop.

Maggie was looking around the church and she spotted her favorite cousins, Trent and Ron, who were sitting next to Aunt Kathleen and Aunt Ginny. She was so happy that they came. She found Kobe and his family sitting in front of them. Angie was stroking little Jessica's hair as the child was nestled in her mother's arms while she was seated comfortably on her mother's lap. The child looked as if she were ready for a nap. It was a precious sight. Maggie could feel her eyes burn as she found herself stare her way into another memory.

"I'm going to shave you bald if you don't learn how to brush that rat's nest on your head!" warned April to a three-year-old Maggie.

Maddie stood close by her sister for moral support every time April would fuss with Maggie's hair. Maddie's hair was thin and could handle the soft bristles of the hairbrush with ease while Maggie was cursed with long, thick, curly hair. Maggie would attempt to fix her own hair to the best of her ability while Maddie assisted when she could. The girls feared when April would inspect their work. Maggie would fail inspection every time!

"You've had your chance to do it your way, now it's *my* turn!" she said as she threw the brush across the room.

She would use a fine-toothed metal comb on Maggie. The little girl would scream in pain with each vicious stroke of the comb, ripping and pulling her hair out of her head. The more Maggie cried the harder April would pull. Maddie usually had to run off to her bedroom because she could not stand to watch it. The child's head would snap back with each stroke, which would make April even more furious. Michael was never around when she would use the metal comb. Hair-detangler spray was in reach, but only Michael used that on his daughter. The top of Maggie's little head was always tender.

Maggie shook off that thought and looked over at Alec. Her eyes were bloodshot. He smiled tenderly at her. Allie was fumbling through her purse for a piece of gum with Mark and Missy being quick to extend an open hand. The pastor kept speaking, but Maggie could not focus on his sermon to save her life. Her mind raced from one memory to the next.

Her mind was flooded with thoughts of the past that she forgot about. It was as if the death of her mother was the key that unlocked the repressed memories of her childhood. Maggie had endured so much pain in the past that when her boyfriend Bryce was buried, she felt that she buried Maggie Getman right along with him. He represented a large hurt in her childhood, but he was just one of many in her life. He just happened to finish off what was left of her childhood, which made her feel dead inside at the young age of sixteen.

Michael once told Maggie that she was missing for a couple of hours when she was a toddler. The child wandered into the doghouse in her back yard and took a nap. Maybe in reality she was locked out of the house. Michael had to come home from work to help April find her. He could never understand why April didn't call the sheriff to report a missing child. He didn't question his wife's story of Maggie wandering off because he was just glad to have his little girl back safe and sound.

She remembered living in that little house in Perrysburg as if it were yesterday. She remembered seeing her mother cry often and she slept all the time. Maggie was an early riser, but April would insist that she go back to bed and sleep in a while longer. One morning Maggie decided to get her own breakfast so her mother could sleep. She pulled the kitchen chair over to the cabinet and climbed onto the countertop. As she went to open the door to the cereal cupboard, she walked right off the counter and landed flat on her back. Maggie remembered being in the doctor's office after the fall and wondering how she got there.

Maggie sighed aloud. She leaned over and kissed her son on the top of his head. Mark leaned in to his mother for a little cuddle. He would only do that when his friends weren't around to witness such affection. Missy sat on the bench, which her timing was excellent because Maggie's legs had started to fall asleep.

Maggie leaned over to Alec and whispered, "The first time my dad came here to check out Mom's new church, he said that they pride themselves on being a non-denominational Christian church. He told me that after they passed the collection plate around the congregation, they said they were going to send it around again for a second collection because they invited the rabbi from the synagogue as a guest that morning. I suppose it was a contribution for him. Dad didn't know what to think!" laughed Maggie.

"I would have loved to have seen his expression after that," chuckled Alec.

She remembered that when they went to church as a family, she and Maddie could never sit next to one another because they would always get a bad case of the giggles. Michael usually sat between his young daughters to keep them in line. Maddie would *always* make Maggie laugh without saying a word. Michael usually pinched Maggie's leg to keep her from laughing out loud in church or, when he was really desperate to silence his youngest daughter, he would punch her in the thigh. Maggie remembered when she was younger she associated church with charley horses because, for her, they fell in the same category.

"...and to April's husband, children, and grandchildren, you should be so blessed to have had her in your lives. She was a true joy to all who knew her," said the pastor.

Maddie whipped around in her seat and looked over to her sister with one of those hilarious facial expressions that would *always* get

Maggie in trouble. Today was no exception! Maggie let out a loud laugh, which interrupted the pastor. The whole congregation turned to look at Maggie. Alec was going into shock knowing that his wife's inner child was alive and well. She recovered by burying her face into her hands, trying desperately to stifle her laughter. Many people thought she was moved to tears by the pastor's words and a few other people began to sob, which made her laugh out loud even harder.

By the time Maggie was ready to conduct herself in an adult manner, she lowered her hands to her lap as she saw five people offer her a tissue. She had a sneaking suspicion that her makeup was a mess from the tears that streamed down her cheeks. She collected the tissues with a modest thank you. She refused to look over at the other side of the church for the remainder of the ceremony. Maddie had to feel proud of herself for making her sister react better than expected. She even knew not to look at Alec because she was still in an unstable state of self-control.

"This is the time when we would like to give friends and family the opportunity to come forward to the microphone to offer a story or kind word about April," said the pastor.

Maddie's mind automatically went to a memory when she and April got into a fistfight. April was drunk and Maddie was frosting a chocolate cake. Her mother, obviously looking for a fight, poured a dustpan filled with dirt from the kitchen floor onto Maddie's cake.

"Why do you insist on acting like a bitch?" growled Maddie.

"Don't call me a bitch!" April yelled as she slapped her daughter across the face, which knocked Maddie out of her chair.

Maddie lunged at her mother while April grabbed her by the hair. They knocked the dining room chairs to the floor as Maddie fought with everything she had. April had a fist full of Maddie's hair as she was getting ready to drag her claws, from her other hand, across Maddie's face.

"Go ahead, Mom. Let's mark the occasion with pictures, shall we?" said Maddie. "I have my senior pictures in the morning and scratches on my face will be a wonderful memory, don't you think?"

April thought about what Maddie had just said to her as she had her daughter's flesh at her fingertips. April had Maddie pinned on the floor with her legs thrown around Maddie's waist. She had a handful of hair in one hand while the other hand was eager to leave war wounds on her daughter's face. April was quick to push her daughter away from her as she tried to justify her violent rage.

"You called me a bitch! No one gets away with that!" cried April.

"I said you were *acting* like one. You thought I called you one because that's what you wanted to hear! I hope that you feel better now because I know that I do," she said as she started heading towards the door. "I'll be at Jenny's house. By the way," she said as she looked over her shoulder, "I hope that your coworkers enjoy the cake at your company picnic tomorrow!"

Kenneth's memory took him to when he was four and he had his first fight with a neighbor kid down the street. The little boy was the same age, but came from a family who cussed a lot and lived in a house that was eventually condemned. He was the kid who taught Kenneth to say the word bitch, which he said aloud in the middle of mass just as the priest came to a pause in his prayer. April refused to let Kenneth play with that child again. Chad did not take the news too well because he cussed Kenneth out and pulled his hair. The little guy ran home crying to April.

"Who did this to you?" she demanded.

"Chad Michaels," he said. "He called me a bitch and he pulled my hair," sniffled Kenneth.

"No one pulls my son's hair and gets away with it!" she growled while baring her bridgework.

April marched down the street with Kenneth to pay Chad Michaels a little visit. His parents were not home, but the sixteen-year-old drug-dealing prostitute had been hired to baby-sit. She stomped onto the porch and knocked on the side of the house because the kids removed the front door and destroyed it. It was plain to see that April was furious.

"What the hell do you want?" asked the sitter with Chad standing behind her.

"I want to teach this young man a lesson!" she said as she reached around the sitter and grabbed the child with her claws buried deep in his arm.

"You can't touch him, you psycho bitch!" yelled the girl.

"Go on, Kenneth," she said as glared at the girl as if daring her to try and stop a mother on a mission. "You pull his hair like he did to yours!" she insisted as Kenneth cowered with fear. "I said do it!"

Kenneth just touched Chad's head hoping that April would have thought he pulled his hair. She continued to hold Chad tight in her grasp. The baby-sitter threatened to call the police, but the phone was turned off along with their gas.

"No, Kenneth. Like this!" she said as she yanked hard on a tuft of the little boy's hair.

"Ouch!" cried Chad. He was crying the whole time April had a hold of him.

"How does it feel? You remember what will happen the next time you try to pull his hair! I will be watching you!" she said as she pushed him back inside the house.

Meanwhile, Kobe was reminiscing of the time when he got suspended from junior high for spitting out the school bus window. He just happened to spit through a man's sunroof, which almost landed on his head. He followed the bus to school and approached the bus driver before the students got off the bus. The man was quick to identify Kobe. April came to the school ready to kill the boy. The dean of the school said that he received a five-day suspension.

"I hope that is an in-school suspension because I will kill him otherwise!"

"Sorry, Mrs. Getman, but this punishment requires that your son be *outside* of school for the duration of his suspension."

Kobe thought that he was a dead man. He remembered the rumbling of The Old Gray Mare's heavy footsteps and the blinding glare of her bridgework as she crashed through the office door. He had always felt like the son who never shone as often as his brother anyway, so he was another child who was no stranger to rebellion.

He was the child who needed orthodontic treatment the most, but April refused for any of her kids to have something that she was never privileged to as a child. Michael's insurance covered a portion of orthodontics, but not enough for her liking. April had suffered from an under-bite, which made her extremely self-conscious of her smile. As her wedding day neared, she insisted that her dentist extract her lower front teeth and replace them with a removable bridge, which, in reality, was a partial denture. He argued that he did not want to pull healthy teeth and that orthodontics would correct the problem.

"I can always pay someone else to pull these teeth. I want to smile for my wedding day!" she growled at the man. That sealed the deal and she got exactly what she wanted.

Michael remembered the time when he and the twins were having a pillow fight in his bedroom. He and April were still sharing a room then and the twins were about six or seven. Laughter filled the room and so did foam and feathers. Michael's pillow ripped and it looked like it was snowing in his bedroom. The twins thought it was the greatest experience ever! Maggie watched from the stairway and said, "Oh, wow!" with her best impersonation of April. Michael about had a heart attack from fear as he and his boys hid under the covers on the bed. He still giggled when he recollected that memory.

Angie remembered walking out of a funeral home of an elderly uncle when April announced out loud, "I couldn't imagine dating at this stage of the game. I mean I've worked very hard to have my man right where I want him. It took years for me to break him in!" Angie could not believe her ears. April then turned to her and said, "You know *exactly* what I mean because you have one at home, too!"

Alec reminisced the time when Michael was painting the exterior of the house. That was early into his and Maggie's courtship. Alec wanted to make a good impression with Michael by offering to help paint on that weekend he came to visit Maggie. Alec's intentions were to get to know Michael a bit better by working side by side with the man. A few of the neighbor guys came to help too because they have always enjoyed Michael's jokes throughout the years while growing up with his girls. April was working alone, on the other side of the house, which was how she preferred it.

When Alec asked how he could be of more help, Michael said, "Maybe it would be best for you to help April on the other side of the house."

Without hesitation, he said, "I'm *not* going over there! Are you crazy?"

There was a huge roar of laughter from the neighbors. They had complimented Maggie on finally finding a smart boyfriend. They applauded him on being a quick learner. Alec had all he could handle by hearing April say, "Get out of my face," to Michael about a hundred times that afternoon. For all the years Alec had been in the family, the insults between April and Michael seemed to get harsher with each passing year.

Chase's memory was far from humorous. He was thinking about the tears that Maddie shed, all the years he had known her, because of April. He would never forget how his heart broke when Maddie asked him for a divorce because she feared that she was turning into the same person as her mother.

"Chase, I love you and this is why I have to let you go. I refuse to punish you like my mother did to my father. You don't deserve such cruelty and neither did he," she cried.

"First off, you aren't going anywhere! Secondly, you are my wife and I love *you*, not your mother! There will be no more talk of divorce in our house ever again," he said as he tried to comfort his wife.

"I feel her inside of me. It is *her* face I see when I look in the mirror, not mine. I struggle with this daily and I fear that one day she will overtake my spirit! Some days I don't know what to do to the point that it takes my breath away. She's suffocating me!"

All he could think of was how much he hated April for inflicting so much pain on his wife over the years. Maddie's world was once a delicate and fragile place until her mother destroyed everything beautiful in her life. She made a train wreck out of Maddie's life to where he didn't know where to begin to help her from the wreckage. It nearly killed him to learn that his wife did not see the beauty she possessed inside of herself like he could. He loved his wife and he blamed April for him nearly losing her. He was thankful for coming home early that one afternoon to stop her from packing her bags.

The crowd searched the room to find the brave souls willing to speak freely in front of such a large group of people. Most people suffered from great anxiety when dealing with public speaking. A few elders walked to the podium, waiting patiently for their turn to speak. They all said basically the same things such as they thought of April as an angel for all she had done for the church. The social worker she worked with said that April was not afraid to get control of the children when others exhibited hesitation. She added that April was perfect for that job. Then a pregnant woman waddled up to share her story.

"I've known April since I became a member of this church five years ago. She was such a blessing for me during my lowest and darkest days after my miscarriage. I do not know where I would be today if it wasn't for April. She visited me in the hospital, she held my hand when I was scared, and she even cried with me. She reminded me that my child is with our Lord and Savior, which is better than any place here on Earth. She told me to think of my child as being too special for this world and God decided it was better for my little one to be with Him…"

Maggie squirmed in her seat and she could feel her stomach start to turn. She looked over at Alec with tears in her eyes. He reached over to rub her back, but Maggie refused his touch. Allie looked at her mother with concern because she could only imagine what was going through her mother's mind. Maggie could feel her blood pressure begin to soar as she plummeted deep into the saddest corner of her heart.

On Maggie's twenty-fifth birthday she discovered that she was pregnant, but the doctor warned that she could not keep the baby. She had experienced pain and heavy bleeding while dining at a restaurant earlier that day. She nearly passed out at the table because the pain was so intense. A blood test proved that she was pregnant. She was forced to have ultrasounds and blood tests before they would perform any surgery, which an ectopic pregnancy was confirmed. Maggie suffered with pain and bleeding for nine days before her surgery because the incompetent doctor told her that she was hoping that the baby would die all on its own. Those harsh words never left Maggie's memory.

The day came when Maggie was doubled over and she could not stand upright. Alec took her straight to the hospital. Allie, nearly two years old at the time, was at daycare until April could get to Indianapolis to pick her up. Alec told Maggie that her mother was happy to watch Allie for them during their little emergency. Even though Maggie was apprehensive about such an arrangement, she was touched by such kindness that her mother would drop everything and drive five hours just for Allie.

Surgery was backed up that afternoon, which pushed Maggie's surgery back for almost eight hours. She was nervous because she never had surgery before and she did not know what to expect. She insisted for Alec to grab something to eat from the cafeteria while she remained in her room. She had a private moment alone with her unborn baby. She rubbed her belly tenderly and closed her eyes. She could feel her heart open as if the words she was about to say to her second child flowed from her chest.

"I am so sorry, little one. I am sorry that I will never touch you or hold you here on Earth, but you will never leave my heart. Please know that your mommy loves you very, very much and that you will be my little shining star waiting for me in Heaven. On that special day, my little one, I promise you that we *will* meet again."

As Maggie sat on the edge of her bed, she felt her heart begin to sink. She had been consumed with such physical pain and concern for her not being able to care for Allie that she did not realize that she was going to lose the child that she was carrying. All that went through her mind most recently was that she wanted the pain to stop and she was willing to do anything to make it go away. She felt her lip start to quiver as her eyes began to fill with tears. She did not want to cry because she feared that she might not be able to stop. She thought it would be best that she ignore the situation all together.

She needed a distraction to take her mind off of her baby so she thought about little Allie. Maggie asked the nurse what time she was scheduled for surgery, but she said that it was looking more like late evening. She was relieved that she had time to phone home to check on Allie and April. She was hoping that April would have given some much-needed motherly advice about surgery or words of comfort on losing a child. Maggie's heart was overwhelmed at the very thought of her mother doing something so nice for her during her crisis. The phone rang and April answered it on the first ring.

"Hi, Mom!" she said, trying to remain upbeat and pleasant.

"Are you done with surgery yet?" said April, sounding hurried.

"No. They're really busy here and I have to wait my turn. How's Allie? May I speak with my little princess, please?"

"Well," she said with hesitation, "you're actually holding us up because I wanted to take her to the park. We are losing our daylight and we *don't* have time to talk to you right now. I'll see you tomorrow," she said just before she hung up the phone.

Feeling as if she was just slapped across the face, the nurse walked by and thought Maggie was in tremendous pain. She came in to check on her patient.

"Are you in pain, Maggie?" she asked sympathetically.

"No more than what I am used to dealing with," said Maggie softly as she crawled back into her bed.

After Maggie's surgery, she awoke to having her face being shoved into an emesis basin with her hair entangled in the tight grasp of a nurse's fist. A second nurse was standing at the foot of the gurney with a pan in her hand, too. The surgery was a success, but Maggie vomited during her recovery process. She aspirated a little and it was the cause of the terrible cough she suffered with for a week. The surgeon spoke with Maggie after the nurses left the room.

"Sorry about the nasty side effects of anesthesia, Maggie. We had to change your gown twice. How do you feel?"

"My lungs feel as if I were sucking on a garden hose."

"You should after what you went through," she giggled. "Maggie, I wanted to tell you that we did find the little guy. He was in the very entrance of your fallopian tube, which is why we were able to save your tube, not the baby. The hospital will be calling you tomorrow to check on you. They will also invite you to a support group that the hospital hosts. I strongly recommend that you do attend."

"Why? I feel really good."

"Physically you feel good, but emotionally you will be a wreck. You did lose a child tonight, Maggie. Believe me when I say that your heart will soon catch up to this evening's event."

Alec was able to take his wife home and he put her to bed. The hospital tried to have Maggie spend the night since it was so late, but she worried about Alec driving home alone while he was so exhausted. She worried about drunk drivers on the road at the midnight hour and she thought she could help keep him alert. The next morning the hospital called as expected. Alec went to work and April answered the phone. Maggie was still in bed and she could hear her mother's conversation.

"No. That's all right. Don't bother wasting the stamp. My daughter is just fine. No, she's sleeping right now. Really, it's no big deal! It was *just* an embryo!"

Maggie lay there feeling hollow inside after hearing her mother's description of her deceased baby. April never checked on Maggie to know how she was feeling, which made her think her mother had no authority to speak for her in the first place. The hospital called back ten minutes later and the supervisor spoke with April, but the conversation was the same. Maggie did receive a large package in the mail from the hospital the following day. She knew it was stuffed with information about the support group that she wasn't ready to read. She decided to leave it on the counter until she was ready to look at it. After breakfast the next morning, April left without warning. Maggie immediately felt it was safe to open the package from the hospital.

The first thing she pulled out was a little pamphlet with a single green leaf floating on a puddle surround by the color black. The leaf had a tiny droplet of water on its edge, which represented a teardrop, with a caption that read: "Gone, but never forgotten." She saw that and the tears flowed for two weeks straight. She grieved heavily for ten years over her little embryo. Maggie never attended group therapy because April reminded her that it was for weak people. She later regretted listening to her mother.

Maggie had sold a house to a grief counselor during her first year in real estate. They had lunch one afternoon and Maggie told her about how she grieved over her miscarriage.

"Isn't it silly that I am still emotional over my miscarriage that happened years ago? I had two healthy children afterwards, but I was nervous and paranoid with both pregnancies!"

"Maggie, you never had closure with that child."

"How do you mean? It wasn't like we could have a funeral or anything. I didn't even know if it was a girl or a boy."

"Did you ever name it?"

"I told you I didn't know the sex of the child."

"Maggie, do yourself a favor and name the child. Give it a unisex name. I promise you will feel differently after you do that. Be sure to include Alec on naming the baby."

She thought it was strange, but she did tell Alec what her client suggested about the baby. She decided to choose the name for a girl, while he chose the name for a boy. They settled on the names Andrew-Paige. They told their children about the baby and their little secret was no more. Mark immediately decided that he *did* have a brother, but he was now an angel. He found comfort on not being the only male in the family. Allie was the emotional one with the news and did not talk about him. Missy searched for a special star that her sister may be living on, but they all knew about him, which might have been his sole purpose in his short life.

She had accepted long ago that she lost a child, but she was still having trouble with letting April's comment roll off her back. Maggie never got any sympathy from her mother, much less any comfort. She would forever be thankful that her mother took care of Allie during the surgery, but she could never forget the additional pain her mother had caused her. Andrew-Paige was talked about amongst the Graham family, which warmed Maggie's heart. She knew that she had a special little guy to hold when she arrived in Heaven. She often dreamed about a happy baby that she could not hold, but she enjoyed him just the same.

When Maggie became pregnant with Missy, April refused to believe that she was pregnant until she'd had a pelvic exam from a doctor. Maggie was absolutely disgusted by such a comment. She had had two home pregnancy tests that were positive and April treated her as if she didn't know how to read the results properly. It broke Maggie's heart that her mother would say such a thing to her. It delivered more of a blow when Michael supported April. Maggie was devastated by her parents' acts of cruelty.

Maddie told her sister about April telling the Getman family on Christmas Eve, "Mom said that you *thought* you were pregnant *again*, but you never had a pelvic to prove it! She then rolled her eyes and continued to say that was just Maggie's way of getting attention. You know how Maggie can be."

Maggie was furious by that statement because she *never* said that she was pregnant when she was not! She never claimed to be pregnant if she "thought" she was. Maggie began to think that her mother was accusing her of lying about Andrew-Paige to say such a thing. He was the only baby that was never brought home from the hospital. Maggie's heart was broken. Maddie insisted that she write the reaction of the grandparents in Missy's baby book. Maggie was good at journaling and she did take her sister's advice.

"...as you can see, I'm pregnant today and feeling wonderful! I found out that I am having a boy, which if it were a girl, I would have named her after April. That might have to wait for the next time around," she smiled as she rubbed her protruding belly.

Alec leaned over to his wife and said, "Breathe, Maggie! Breathe."

A powerful feeling washed over her like a wave in a cesspool. Maggie's body was numb as her body kicked into automatic pilot. She found that she could no longer sit quietly like she had her whole life. She sprang from her seat while Alec tried to grab her hand.

She pulled her hand away from his and said under her breath, "I am *not* a child, Alec! I know what I'm doing."

Maggie walked down the aisle as she passed the pregnant woman heading back to her seat. All eyes were on Maggie. She felt as if she were floating toward the altar like in a dream. Her body felt as light as a balloon dancing in the sky. The sounds of her footsteps echoed within her ears. She walked past her mother's casket, which she noticed that Michael had put the memory quilt on top of it again as if he were desperate on shouting to the congregation that they were the family that April rarely mentioned. She might not have been proud of them, but he was.

With each step she took, as she approached the red carpeted alter, she asked for God to hold her by the hand while she spoke. The pastor was astonished by Maggie's bravery as he stepped away from the microphone surprised that a family member would be strong enough to speak on such a day of sorrow. She looked over at her mother's casket and had not one thought in her mind. She had no idea of what she was about to say, but there was something definitely dying to come out and be heard.

She stood before the church as everyone stared at her with guarded anticipation. Maddie had a look of surprise upon her face. Michael was puzzled. He sat there looking at his other children as if they knew what Maggie was doing up there. Maggie looked at her husband for some encouragement, while he sat there with a smile on his face giving his wife the thumbs-up sign. She took a deep breath and smiled. She looked at her children and winked. She lowered the microphone so that everyone would hear her loud and clear.

"First of all, I would like to thank each and every one of you for coming today. To actually put my emotions into words and expressing my gratitude would be an impossible task. So, please know that on behalf of my family and myself, we thank you all for sharing your love and respect for our mother is heartfelt and sincere. I would also like to thank the church for this opportunity to speak to you about my mother."

The pastor stood back and looked at his watch. Maggie had everyone's undivided attention. She looked over at her mother's casket and stared at the memory quilt for a moment before she began to speak. She thought it was so sad to see pictures of her family draped across her mother's casket knowing that she never cared for her family like one would expect. Maggie felt the whole funeral was getting to be one big lie.

"I need my support group to stand here with me because I would not be living and breathing today if it weren't for them."

She called on Michael, Maddie, the twins, Alec, her children, all of her in-laws, nieces and nephews to join her on the altar. The twins were apprehensive at first, but they saw Michael bolt up to the altar with no hesitation and they all followed his lead. There were about twenty-five people surrounding Maggie at the podium and the words that needed to be said suddenly surfaced.

"I wanted all of you to meet the family members that my mother may or may not have spoken to you about. I want you all to know that we are *not* tyrants, burdens, or rebels. We are living, breathing beings that were shut out of her life years ago," she said while watching the congregation whisper anxiously amongst themselves.

"Oh, that must be the troublemaker daughter!" said an elderly woman to her neighbor.

"I believe she is the child that April just could not rescue. I've heard that she is the ungrateful child of that poor woman. From what I heard, April was cursed with that one. It's a shame that a pretty little girl like that will be going to hell," said the other woman.

After a moment passed, a silence fell about the church. Maggie calmly stated, "You are the family she chose over us. In a way, we are like children of divorced parents trying to adjust to our new life with a step-family. For whatever reasons, my mother kept us from you, her new family, which really hurts me. Now that the two families have finally met, I would like to say a few words to you about my mother, the other side of April that you've never known."

APRIL SHOWERS

The congregation was stunned by what Maggie had said. A few people conversed amongst themselves trying to make sense of why Maggie was being disrespectful to the memory of her mother. Maggie could feel the pastor fidget nervously behind her, but somehow she felt at peace with what she had to say.

"Someone important in our lives once said that flowers are for the living. Today we say farewell to April Getman, to some a wife, mother, sister, grandmother, and so on. Today is a celebration, of sorts, of her life. A life cannot be measured by money or possessions—it is measured by memories that one leaves behind."

Maggie had everyone's undivided attention. Family, friends, and total strangers listened to the heartfelt message coming from April's daughter. The congregation studied the Getman family as they crowded around the altar. Maggie glanced over at her mother's casket and continued to speak.

"Memories could be viewed as a flower garden, in which no two beds are exactly alike. April left something behind today for each and every one who knew her. Today, some of you will walk away with a single flower or an entire bushel, depending on how well she tended her garden. Others might not be so privileged today to sport that sort of beauty. Some of us continue to carry our flowerpots filled with barren soil that was starved and neglected. When desperate times call for desperate measures, some of us had mixed our soils together. We found that each pot contributed a different element, when combined, it made the soil rich. These flowerpots could not survive alone, but they found their strength in unity."

Maggie's strength was that of a miracle. She looked out at the congregation with such poise and confidence that her speech sounded well rehearsed. She continued to say, "The seeds that thrived in our community pot were the new memories of our own children's lives and adventures while April remained disconnected and cold. We were forced to bloom without her. The sunshine represented the emotional support we were quick to share with one another, which offered more than just warmth to help our seeds grow; its rays warmed us with peace and the reassurance of a new beginning. God's love guided us on the path of survival. We stand before you today as living proof!"

Maggie had to pause for a moment because she heard Kobe clear his throat. She noticed that he was struggling with the ceremony. For a moment, the very thought of her being the cause of any tears of sorrow made her feel guilty for giving such a speech, but the moment quickly passed when she realized that through the tears was when healing could really begin. As she glanced at the crowd, she was relieved to see that they did not appear to be as uptight and judgmental as before. She smiled warmly at her mother's guests and she continued to speak from her heart. Her eyes were now fixed on her family members standing beside her.

"Our flowers may not be plush like yours, her church family, but we are present and accounted for. I look at our little garden and I thank God for the strength, love, and support He blessed us with through the years. His love was the umbrella that shielded us from drowning in the torrential rains of April showers! Let April's legacy be to you all this, live life with one question in mind—how will *you* be remembered?"

The family nodded in agreement with her statement. Maggie felt comfortable with her afternoon of public speaking and in her heart she wanted the real April Getman to be remembered. She offered the congregation one final thought before she stepped down from the podium.

"Remember to tend your gardens, folks. One day we, too, will be deceased. What will you leave behind? I hope to leave flowers, lots of flowers because my mother said that flowers are for the living. After saying that, I now understand and agree with her logic. What memories will *you* leave behind that can proudly be displayed and shared? Thank you for your time and may God bless you all."

As Maggie looked up from the podium, she got a shiver by the ghostly silence of the congregation. Despite the strangers' blank expressions, she felt that in her heart she had no regrets by announcing her dark, heartfelt, and long-overdue speech. A small part of her wished that she had the courage to say those words to her mother years ago. The pastor hastily shook Maggie's hand and thanked her for sharing such enlightenment for his congregation. It was obvious that the funeral was falling behind schedule as he continued the ceremony while the family was in the middle of clearing the altar.

Michael looked too choked up for words as he quietly stood along the wall. His silence made Maggie nervous that she had spoken out of turn. Alec grabbed his wife and hugged her tightly.

"I am so proud of you! I cannot believe you said that," he whispered in her ear.

"Thanks, hon. I believe that God himself was with me as the words poured from my heart. I felt so strong and confident," she said with surprise.

The family followed Michael's lead from the altar and stood along the wall of the church while the pastor said a closing prayer. The pallbearers escorted April out to the hearse while the people followed her casket outside. The family witnessed Michael desperately race through the crowd before they carried her down the steps. He grabbed the memory quilt and walked back inside the church to speak to his family with a perplexed look upon his face.

"Uh, Dad? Shouldn't we be getting into our cars?" asked Kenneth.

Michael then looked over at Maggie with such a look of respect and admiration. He smiled at her and said, "No. Today we are going to celebrate life! I think that today will be a perfect day to celebrate Maggie's birthday!"

"Dad! No, really, it wouldn't be right," said Maggie.

"Yeah, Grandpa! My mom is so old that she doesn't have birthdays anymore, she has anniversaries!" said Missy innocently revealing a private family joke.

"April always had the last word. Our family always did what she expected of us despite our feelings. Today, I say that we are going to break tradition and have a birthday celebration for my daughter. What do you say about burgers at Chet's Restaurant? It's my treat and I refuse to take no for an answer!"

As the funeral procession pulled away from the church, the family watched April from the curb take her final ride. The moment reflected how April wanted nothing to do with them in life. As the hearse drove out of sight, they were painfully reminded that in death, their connection with April remained the same as in life. They were all silent for a moment until Kobe yelled, "Burgers at Chet's and then a case or two at the house!"

"Amen to that!" said Chase and Maddie in unison.

"I'll have a cheeseburger without the cheese!" giggled Allie.

"What's Chet's?" asked Alec.

"It's a small family restaurant where the employees are friendly, the food is homemade and it's delicious. I've never heard of *anyone* being disappointed at Chet's," said Maggie.

"But they recently changed their name to New Chet's," said Kenneth. "I was in there a few weeks ago and had a nice conversation with the owners. They said that people who moved away from Toledo years ago have come back to visit Chet's Restaurant to treat their children to real home cooking. They pride themselves on that."

"How long have they been in business?" asked Alec.

"They've been around about as long as we've lived in Toledo," said Maddie.

"It's my favorite place to be! The owners are very personable and friendly. Where else can you find such warm service at affordable prices? We'll have a good time and there will be no one there to chase you all away from me," said Michael.

Chapter 21

After the family devoured their spectacular lunch at New Chet's, they caravanned back to the house. Maddie and Chase were the last ones to arrive because they snuck off to the store to purchase a birthday cake for Maggie. She was surprised by Maddie's thoughtfulness.

"Maggie, just for you..." said Maddie with a grin as she presented the cake.

"What flavor is it?" she asked with delight.

Maddie grinned and said, "Chocolate, of course."

"Lovely! Mom's favorite," said Maggie with a forced smile.

Everyone laughed because chocolate cake had become a crude family joke for Maggie. On April's sixtieth birthday, Allie baked her first cake and wanted to give it to her grandmother. Maggie thought the gesture was sweet. Besides, Maggie felt guilty for not planning a surprise party for her mother like she and Maddie had done for their father. She confessed her guilt to Michael, but he reassured her not to worry about it because he had more of a relationship with his kids than what April did. Maggie thought maybe a chocolate cake would be the perfect cure for any ill feelings.

The Graham family made the long-distance drive to deliver the chocolate birthday cake. When they were about a half-hour from Toledo, Maggie phoned her father on her cell phone to ask him if there were anything he might need before they arrived to the house. She told him that Allie had made a cake for her grandmother. Judging from the noise in the background, she could hear that the twins were visiting with their families and she thought that would make the birthday surprise even more special.

"Uh, I hope it isn't chocolate," he said nervously.

"It just so happens to be chocolate. Why? What's the problem? Mom loves chocolate."

"She gave it up for Lent."

"What? I thought she attends a non-denominational church and she no longer practices Catholic traditions."

"I don't know what to say," said Michael.

"I'm at a loss for words, Dad."

"There are other Christian religions that observe Lent, you know."

"Yeah, I know," she said sarcastically.

"When I asked your mother to define her religion and explain to me why she was doing it, she nearly bit my head off. She told me that she wasn't doing it for me, she was doing it for herself!"

"Wow!" she uttered without hesitation. "I thought Lent was for God. Anyway," she said as she was trying to regain her self-control, "all I can say is that Allie is going to be disappointed. Maybe we should just pitch the cake before we get to the house."

"I'm really sorry, Maggie. Do what you have to do. I know you'll do the right thing."

Maggie ended her conversation with her father. She was furious about the birthday cake, but she respected her mother's religious decision. She phoned her father back and came up with a solution to the problem.

"Is Tessa at the house?" inquired Maggie about her youngest goddaughter.

"Yes she is," he said with excitement, "why?"

"Well, if I remember correctly, she has a birthday next Saturday. We will give the cake to her since Mom's birthday is in two weeks anyway. I'm sure we can all put our heads together and come up with something special for Mom by then."

"That sounds perfect! We'll see you soon," he said with delight.

April was furious when she saw the chocolate cake come into her house. As expected, she was getting annoyed with all the bodies under her roof. There were too many people for her to dominate at one time. Maddie and Chase showed up because Michael invited them over, too. Little Tessa was so excited when she learned that the chocolate cake was just for her.

"Oh! Thank you, Aunt Maggie!" she said blissfully as she clasped her hands together as if being thankful that a personal wish had been granted. Maggie knelt down to look into the child's sparkling eyes as Tessa said sincerely, "I will never, *never* be mean to you ever again."

"You're welcome, baby girl! We love you and happy birthday!" she said as she kissed her niece on the top of her little, curly-topped head.

Angie was furious about the birthday cake because she knew that it was initially for April. She had six children of her own and her living space in her house was very limited. Birthday parties only consist of grandparents and her brother. No one else had ever been invited for birthday parties at Angie and Kobe's house. It was best not to add any unnecessary stress to an already existing tension.

"Is it my birthday, Mommy?" asked Tessa with excitement.

"No! It's next week!" snapped Angie. After realizing that she sounded a bit harsh, she did her best to change her tone and said, "You turn five *next* week, not today," through her tightly clenched teeth.

April confronted Maggie about her not being allowed to have chocolate because she gave it up for Lent. She was upset and looked as if she could cry about it. April's childish whining alarmed Maggie to where she could identify the warning signs that her mother was a ticking time bomb. The family cleared a spot at the dining room table and sang the Happy Birthday song to Tessa. She was so excited because the whole Getman family, for the first time, sang just for her. Maggie was delighted by the look of enthusiasm on the little girl's face, which made her feel that the trip was definitely worthwhile.

"Blow out the candles and don't forget to make a wish!" said Maddie.

"Mommy, am I five now?" Tessa asked with an optimistic tone.

"*Next* week, Tessa," Angie replied as she openly rolled her eyes with a sigh.

"Yeah, Tessa. Today is a practice birthday so you can be ready for your real party next week," said Maggie with a reassuring smile.

The little girl blew out her candles and everyone cheered. Maddie helped her young niece cut the first piece of cake while Maggie grabbed plates and forks. There was no ice cream, but no one seemed to mind. Mark asked his mother if he could sit in the living room with his cake, which Maggie was quick to deny his request. She stood at the sink washing plates and forks as they would come to the kitchen. She could see that April was getting ready to blow her top and Maggie tried to avoid triggers at all costs. Maddie came into the kitchen to catch up on conversation with her nervous sister. Allie raced into the kitchen with a look of panic on her face.

"Well, Mom, it wasn't Mark you had to worry about," Allie said as she pointed to the chocolate square high up on her thigh.

"You've got to be kidding me, Allie! *Please* don't tell me that you were sitting in the living room with your cake," said Maggie as she could feel a sense of panic override her best attempts at maintaining a calm disposition.

Maggie knew not to show fear because her mother could smell panic, no matter how small, in a hundred yard radius. That would certainly mean that there was little or no hope of recovery for those in a weakened state. Maggie quickly wrung out a washcloth to clean the brown sculpted, twenty-five-year-old, carpeting before April could discover the mess. Much to Maggie's horror and by the sounds of April's thunderous footsteps, she knew it was too late. April maneuvered her way around the little people standing in the kitchen to confront Maggie. There was such a look of rage fixed upon her face, which made Maggie gasp.

"Look what *I've* got!" growled April as she shoved her chocolaty fingers into Maggie's face.

Maggie reacted by pushing April's hand away from her face and said, "I'm really sorry, Mom. Where's the cake? I am on my way to clean it now."

Maggie was embarrassed and walked away, half-expecting to be grabbed by her enraged mother like when she was a child, while April continued to scream at her. April followed Maggie out to the living room searching for the tiniest morsel to complain about. The whole family stood silent as they witnessed April's little tirade.

"It's all over *my* house! I've got chocolate cake all over *my* house!" she shouted as the glare from her bridgework nearly blinded her daughter.

The tension in that house was so thick that it left one to believe that they could not breathe. No one could save Maggie now. April was in a full-blown tantrum. Maggie felt as if she were a child again as she glanced at Maddie with a look of total dread. Maddie smiled at her sister as she did her best to ease the tension created by April's personality known as The Basher!

"Allie! You ruined Grandma's brand-new carpeting. How dare you!" teased Maddie of the worn out old carpeting.

Maddie's little comment made everyone laugh out loud. She thought it was best to make light of the situation to snap April out of her dark mood. Maggie was relieved that her torture ended abruptly. She will always be grateful to her sister for thinking quick on her feet like she did; even though it later occurred to Maggie that her sister was just glad that it wasn't one of her own kids provoking Grandma for a change.

After Maggie cleaned three small crumbs of cake off the floor, she grabbed her family and left the house. She vowed to herself that her family would never walk into that house ever again. She was in shock that a chocolate cake was the landmine that created such heavy damage to one family. Maddie walked Maggie to the car and told her that she would have been a character witness if she would have punched that woman in the face. Maddie was a little disappointed in Maggie for passing up an opportunity to do so.

"I saw her shove her messy fingers in your face. No one else would have been expected to exercise such restraint in the eyes of the court! Just be thankful that was chocolate on her fingers," said Maddie lightly.

Alec drove away from the curb while Maggie tried to find the humor in what had just transpired. She clung on to the hope of one day laughing about the stupid chocolate cake, but she just could not see that ever happening any time soon. She apologized to her three children and Alec for having them witness such an atrocity. Maggie was angry at herself the most because she left the house brokenhearted. There were no apologies with April. Trying desperately to find a positive thought during such a negative situation, Maggie clung on to the idea that she was just happy that April took her aggressions out on her rather than Allie. Maggie would have reacted much differently if that had been the case.

Michael phoned Maggie two days later to do his usual damage control.

"Dad, I'm sorry if I got you in trouble over the chocolate cake incident," she said sincerely.

"She *won't* shut up about it! I've been hearing about it morning, noon, and night!"

"I'm really sorry, Dad."

"It will be a long time before we are all together in this house again," he said.

Maggie's heart was broken to hear such words fall from her father's mouth. She was devastated. She was irritated about Allie sneaking out into the living room in the first place, but the little incident just snowballed. Michael was unaware that Allie was the one who dropped her cake. April had told him that it was Trina who dropped her cake shortly after Maggie's family left the house. From that point on, Maddie always joked about everyone bringing their mother a chocolate cake every year. It was obvious to Maggie that her sister took great pleasure in that very thought.

"Why couldn't she give up being a bitch for Lent?" Maddie said half-joking to her father as she was cutting Maggie's birthday cake. "That way it would have benefited everyone!"

"For Lent, you are supposed to give up something you enjoy doing, which the purpose for the sacrifice is to feel the pains of doing without something you enjoy for God. That is a time for penance, not the time to be asking for miracles!" scoffed Michael.

The family celebrated Maggie's birthday with laughter. The cousins all paired off and had a wonderful time. The adults enjoyed a few beers and really began to feel relaxed. It was starting to get late and Maggie was ready to go home. All that she could think about was soaking in a nice hot bath and sleeping in her own bed. Michael tried to get her to stay one more night, but Alec agreed with his wife that it was time to head home. Alec rounded up his children as Maddie approached Maggie.

"Hey, sis, could I speak to you for a moment?"

"Sure. What's up, Maddie?"

"Let's go outside to the back porch where it's more private."

Maggie followed her sister outside as she was getting nervous about what her sister might possibly spring on her just before going back home to Indiana. She was feeling that she could not handle another nerve rattling surprise at that point in time. Maggie found her stomach begin to knot up again. As they approached a secluded corner of the patio, Maggie was studying her sister's body English. She was relieved to see that Maddie looked calm and relaxed. Maybe it was because of the twelve-pack that she polished off that afternoon, but Maggie could not be too sure.

"What's up, Maddie?"

"I just wanted to say that I appreciated our conversations over the past two days."

"I enjoyed catching up with you, too," said Maggie with apprehension.

"No. I mean that I *really* appreciated our conversations over the past few days," she said with a wide-eyed grin.

"Maddie, I don't believe that I'm following you. What are you talking about?"

"I just want to thank you, that's all."

"There is no need to thank me. I think that communication is the key to a healthy relationship. Sisters are supposed to lean on one another from time to time, right?"

"Yeah, but I realized that *you* set *me* free. You," she said as she pointed to Maggie, "of all people," and then she pointed to herself, "set me free, Maggie."

"What are you talking about, Maddie? How could I set you free? Free from what?"

"My whole life I thought of myself as the black sheep of the family. After hearing your stories about your life with our mother, I realized that my life wasn't that bad after all," she scoffed.

"How do you mean?" asked Maggie.

"What I mean is that it sucks to be you!" she laughed out loud.

Maggie stood in disbelief by her sister's harsh words. She felt her whole body go numb as if Maddie had slapped her across the face. Maggie was devastated. This blow was worse than anything Maddie had done to Maggie in the past. Maddie finally succeeded in crushing her sister. For Maggie, it left her with the familiar sting of disappointment and betrayal for which was a longstanding family tradition by nearly every woman in the Connolly family. Maggie could feel the rage build up inside of her, like it did as a kid, just before the first punch was thrown. Those familiar feelings are what had clearly marked the beginning of their many fistfights. Maggie closed her eyes and took a deep breath rather than taking a swing at her sister.

"How could you say something like that to me? Are you drunk?" Maggie asked, trying to justify or make sense of such an unprovoked attack.

"It's so obvious to me now. You have done everything right in your life. I mean that you have done *everything* that was expected of you! Looking at you now, I see that you are no better than me. I was blind not to see that *I* was the lucky one after all. I mean, I thought of you as Mom's favorite daughter for years, but I see that you are not. Mom *always* had to know where I was, but she never checked in on you. That proves to me that she *did* love me. If she didn't care, then she would have ignored me, too."

"I am happy to lift your spirits, Maddie," said Maggie softly as she looked away from her sister. Maggie was digesting the words that Maddie had just thrown at her. She was more upset at the fact that Maddie actually believed what she was saying. She found the courage to look Maddie in the eye with a combination of hurt and anger burning inside as she growled, "I wasn't a rebellious teen because I didn't have the time! I could *never* bring myself to abandon Kenneth and Kobe. *Someone* had to watch over those little boys!"

"That's what I'm talking about. You got nowhere by being an ass-kisser to Mom."

"I wouldn't call it ass-kissing. I see it as doing what I had to do. I realized early on that life wasn't all about me. I suppose that I chose to be a protector for the twins. Someone had to be there for them. Where were you, Maddie?"

"I don't mean any disrespect, but I don't know how else to thank you for making me feel so much better about myself," said Maddie with a grin.

Maggie closed her eyes briefly, which felt like an eternity. She took another deep breath and desperately fought back the urge to strike her sister across the face. But that little voice in her head screamed that Maddie might be exerting nervous tension and that she might be clinging on to any hope of having good memories of her relationship with April. Maggie opened her eyes and looked at her sister with a smile. Maddie stood in front of her anticipating a hostile retaliation. Maggie refused to give Maddie the fight she was looking for. Maggie reached inside of her purse as Maddie stood staring in wonder.

"Here," said Maggie as she placed April's wedding ring in the palm of Maddie's hand. "I do believe that since you were the favorite daughter, I suppose this belongs to you. I hope that you wear it in good health and good cheer. Each time you should gaze down at the ring, I hope that you remember all the wonderful memories you and our mother had shared. I believe that Dad gave it to me by mistake. Besides, I believe that you have a better use for it than me. I love you, Maddie, and I'd love to chat longer, but I need to get my family home."

Maddie stood as if she were frozen in time. Maggie kissed her sister on the cheek while Maddie continued to stare expressionless at the diamond ring resting in the palm of her hand. Maggie walked inside the house to collect her family. She had mastered the poker face because no one had noticed that she was upset in the slightest. It had been an incredibly long few days for Maggie, which felt more like a millennium. She was relieved to see that Alec had loaded up both vehicles. They said their good-byes to the rest of the family. Michael walked them to their vehicles.

"I'll never forget how you stood up for our family today. Maggie, it meant more to me than you'll ever know," said Michael.

"I meant every word of it, Dad. We underdogs need to stick together," she said as her voice cracked.

"You know something, Maggie? I believe that we are all going to be okay," he said with a reassuring smile.

Maggie looked Michael in the eye while reciprocating his comforting smile and said, "I *know* that we are okay, Dad."

"I love you guys and please drive safely."

"We love you, too, Dad. Welcome home!" she said as she hugged him tight.

"Yes, I *am* home," he said with a smile as he looked over Maggie's shoulder at the house.

Allie rode with Maggie because she knew they would listen to her CDs without arguments. Allie's favorite artists of the week were My Chemical Romance and Green Day, but she understood that they would not be heard before Maggie's favorite CD of Evanescence.

Maggie always found music as a way of alleviating her tension, which she felt that she had recently acquired more than her fair share. Mark and Missy share the same taste in music as their father, which would make for a more pleasant drive for them listening to the comedic tunes of Da Yoopers.

The kids eventually fell asleep, which made it easier for Alec and Maggie to drive straight through. The drive went smoothly and the construction was minimal in Fort Wayne because of the traffic being thinner in the evenings. It was also a dry experience, which was a real treat for Maggie. With each passing mile marker on the interstate, Maggie was happy to be putting more and more miles between her and the undeserved stress from her sister in Toledo.

The closer they got to Indianapolis Maggie saw a few real-estate billboards with her picture of sales person of the year. She always laughed when she saw them because she was too modest of a person to be so vane. It felt good for her to laugh out loud again. She was anxious to get home to her safe haven. Alec was ahead of her the whole ride home. She silently cheered when she saw him signal for their street. Maggie was so happy to be pulling into her own driveway. She could honestly say that she was never so happy to be home!

Chapter 22

The Graham family was anxious to settle into their own beds that evening and decided to tend to their luggage in the morning. Maggie had them all brush their teeth and hit the sheets. She was surprised that she got no arguments. Maggie snuggled up to Alec and instantly fell asleep. Alec thought she was joking at first, but he soon realized that she was down for the count. He had to get up to turn off the overhead light because Maggie still needed to replace her bedside lamp. As he made it back to the bed, he saw his wife twitch as she fell deeper into her sleep. She quickly fell into a dream, which was about her Aunt Paula.

Paula appeared to Maggie looking as beautiful as an angel in a painting. Her lips and cheeks were rosy and she looked so healthy. Her appearance was far different from what Maggie was accustomed to when seeing Paula in pictures or images etched in her memory. Maggie felt at peace with her great-aunt's visit. Somehow Maggie knew that this was more than just a dream. Not one word was spoken verbally between the two women, but a full conversation took place within Maggie's heart. She magically knew what it was that the woman had to say during their brief encounter.

The elderly woman handed her niece a small black box. She became insistent that Maggie accept the box as a gift from her. Maggie did not focus on the box because she was mesmerized by the angelic vision of her aunt. With Paula being persistent, Maggie finally realized that the gift must be important somehow and she extended an open hand to collect her gift. Paula, being agitated because she was running short on time, pressured Maggie to look inside the box. She smiled and looked relieved as Maggie began to open the box, but just as the hinged lid of the jeweler's box creaked, she awoke from the dream. She was consumed with disappointment because she never saw what Aunt Paula was trying so desperately to show her.

Maggie's disappointment quickly dissipated when she realized that Alec was cooking a nice Sunday breakfast downstairs. Above all else, she could smell the heavenly aroma of fresh brewed coffee coming from the kitchen. She sprang out of bed and raced down the stairs with a smile upon her face like a child on Christmas morning. She was so happy to be home with her family, her safe haven in Central Indiana.

"Good morning, handsome," she said to her husband with a kiss.

"Hello, gorgeous! Did I make too much noise this morning?"

"No, but the coffee sure did," she smiled.

"Did you have sweet dreams, my darling?" he asked sweetly as he handed her a fresh, steamy cup of inspiration.

"I had a weird dream this morning about my Aunt Paula. It's strange because I haven't dreamed of her in years."

"Yeah?" he asked with interest because he knew his wife experiences psychic dreams when she was stressed. "What did the old gal have to say?" he said with a smile.

"She gave me a present and she seemed to be anxious about it. She looked so beautiful! The dream was short, but I swear that it touched my heart as if I saw her for real."

"It sounds to me like you were in bed too long. Your dreams always get weird when you sleep in," he said, trying to keep the conversation light. "Now eat your eggs before they get cold."

The couple enjoyed their breakfast while the kids were doing their usual activities on a carefree day. Mark was playing his video games while Missy played with her dolls. Allie was on the phone already, which Maggie swore was a permanent apparatus attached to the side of that child's head. It was the kind of morning that felt like no one was getting dressed before noon. After breakfast, Maggie helped herself to a second cup of coffee. Alec was reading the *Indianapolis Star* while Maggie's mind drifted.

Being deep in thought, Maggie stumbled across a time when April came from Uncle Doug's house after one of her many weekly visits.

She told Maggie that she had stolen a small safe of jewelry off of his buffet. April discovered her grandmother's wedding band, from Ruby's father, within the broken safe. There were many rings inside with the stones removed. One ring was left in its original black jeweler's box that looked like a dark amethyst. It was a stone that Maggie thought looked a bit gaudy, but beautiful when held in different light. It would turn colors from a reddish purple to a greenish blue.

April was really drunk when she insisted that Maggie take the small box home with her by saying, "Here, take it! I just *know* that your Aunt Paula would want you to have it. Besides, the ring is too small for me. I swear that I was *meant* to take that jewelry because it spoke to me," she said boldly while trying to justifying her criminal actions.

That was the last time April was inside that little green house. Douglas Carr knew that she stole from him and he retaliated by changing his locks and phone number. He hired a full-time caregiver to help him with his affairs while April was out of the loop. He had April's name removed as sole beneficiary of his will and estate. When he died, the state took possession of the property. Because the house was vandalized so badly, it was leveled and the property remains vacant.

Maggie shuttered at that thought after learning what her father did. As she rinsed out her coffee mug, she had a nagging urge to search for the ring her mother gave her years ago. Maggie thought it might be in her small jewelry box in the back of her closet, which was a gift for her ninth birthday from her Grandma Getman just before she passed away. She had not looked inside of the little white ballerina jewelry box in years and she was starting to doubt that she would find what she was searching for in it. She thought it was strange how she had not thought about that ring, once she put it away, until her dream.

Maggie felt her hands tremble as she slowly pulled the white box off the top shelf. Her heart about leaped out of her chest when she saw the little black box inside of the jewelry box. It looked identical to the box in her dream. Maggie opened the box and immediately slid the ring on her finger. She was amazed that it fit her well. As she stared at the ring for a moment, she was taken by the little jewelry box ballerina dancing in front of her little triangle mirror after all those years. The music box took her back to her childhood, which made her feel giddy like a schoolgirl.

"Heck yeah-yah!" she squealed.

She was instantly inspired to get dressed and head over to the jewelry store with the ring. Out of curiosity, Alec was interested in hearing what a jewelry expert might have to say about it, too. He believed that his wife's dreams held some sort of psychic potential and this time he was hoping that it could mean collecting money, lots of money. Allie was all too happy to stay home to watch the kids because that would give her more time to catch-up with her friends on the phone. Maggie and Alec threw on their most comfortable jogging suits and tennis shoes for their little adventure. Maggie threw on some makeup and pulled her hair into a ponytail while Alec was being lazy and chose not to shave that morning.

When they arrived at the mall, they entered the first jewelry store they came across. They walked into the store and were greeted by the manager. Maggie pulled her little black box from her purse and asked the woman if she happened to know what type of ring it was. Maggie explained that it was an inheritance and it was an old ring from her great-aunt. The woman never saw a ring like that before, but she was very interested on finding out exactly what it was.

"Well, what do you suggest?" asked Alec impatiently.

"I suggest that you have a gemologist test this stone for you because it may be worth more than you realize."

"What do you think it is? Do you have a clue?" asked Maggie.

"Like I said, you really need to have someone more qualified to check this out because you may need to have this insured."

Alec looked over at Maggie with surprise, while Maggie continued to maintain her famous poker face. She thanked the woman for her time and they went across the hall to another store. They got the same reaction there, too. The ring was passed to each employee, but no one knew for sure what he or she was looking at. Alec was becoming anxious about the ring to the point where he felt it was best for him to carry the ring in the mall for safekeeping. Maggie did not know what to think. They finally walked into the last jewelry store.

They proudly walked up to the register to ask an older gentleman for some assistance. He was winding his pocket watch as he glanced up at the couple. He saw that they were grossly underdressed for walking into the expensive store and he snubbed them. He went back to winding his watch. Maggie smiled at Alec and winked. She was used to dealing with all walks of life in her profession. She was not offended because she found this to be quite amusing. She could only imagine what the man was thinking of them.

"Excuse me, sir. I need an *expert* opinion on what type of ring I had inherited recently from my great-aunt. Do you have two seconds to take a peek? Please?" she asked as she slid the opened black box across the counter.

The man let out a sigh and grabbed the box with a huff. He rolled his eyes as he gazed down at the ring. Alec and Maggie just stood back and observed the man's expressions. He looked at the ring and nearly choked. He looked at the couple with excitement.

"Good afternoon, my name is Benton. And yours?" he said as he extended his hand to greet the couple properly.

"Graham," said Maggie with a smile. She could not help notice that he shook her hand first. She's been in many situations where Alec got all the greetings before she did.

"Mrs. Graham, may I remove this ring from the box?"

She looked over at Alec with a grin. "Sure, why not," she said.

He removed the ring as gently as his trembling hands would allow him. His breathing became more and more labored while he broke out into a cold sweat before the couple's eyes. He was a heavyset man who appeared not to be in the best of health. Maggie began to grow concerned about the well-being of the gentleman. Other customers noticed his reactions and stood by the Grahams out of curiosity. Benton held the ring up to the light and then took it to the back of the office into a dark room. Maggie and Alec had no idea what that man was doing because he was not saying much. As the man walked out of the store, Alec thought he was trying to steal the ring.

"Where are you going?" he asked excitedly.

"I'll be right back," was all he could mutter without ever looking up from the ring.

The manager came out from the office and asked another employee where Benton was going with a customer's merchandise.

She had been watching him from the security cameras in the back and thought he was acting a bit strange. Alec stood at the entrance of the jewelry store and watched the man walk into a hippy store across the hall.

"Sir, don't worry about Benton. He's a bit eccentric, but he does know his jewelry," said the manager.

Benton walked back into the store and the collar on his shirt was wet with sweat. He handed the ring to Maggie with very sweaty palms. He was still shaking as perspiration rolled down his red glowing face. There were about fifteen people huddled around the desk, including the manager and a few employees.

"Are you all right, sir?" asked Maggie with concern.

"Mrs. Graham, do you realize what you have here?"

"No, I don't. I am not much of a jewelry person," she admitted sheepishly.

"You need to have a gemologist test this stone to be certain, but I believe that you have an Alexandrite!" he said eagerly.

"Okay. So, what does that mean?" she calmly asked.

"Russia stopped exporting these decades ago. This stone is very rare!"

"How can you be certain it is an Alexandrite?" asked Alec.

"Mr. Graham, I held this stone over a black light and I saw a distinct color of red! I have waited my entire career to see an authentic Russian Alexandrite! Make sure that you have a gemologist perform the test in front of you so no one steals it. These are extremely rare, which means they are worth lots of money!"

"Do you sell Alexandrite gems in your store?"

"We sell synthetics, which are lab created. Look at your ring and then compare it to what we sell. Look at the price tags. Your ring could be worth *thousands* more than our finest synthetics!"

Maggie could feel her heart begin to pound! She looked over at Alec. He took the ring from his wife and carefully put it back into the box. Customers were looking over their shoulders to get a glimpse of the ring, which made Alec nervous. Maggie was praying that they wouldn't get mugged in the parking lot.

"Thank you, Benton, for your time. You have been more than helpful," said Maggie as she shook the man's hand.

"Thank *you*, Mrs. Graham, for giving me the privilege of viewing such a rare stone! I apologize if I was rude in the beginning," he said humbly as he kept shaking Maggie's hand all the way out of the store.

Maggie and Alec found themselves laughing like school children as they ran across the parking lot to the truck. They jumped inside the truck with a quick hit of the button to lock the doors. They continued to laugh out loud.

"Wow! Now *that* was enjoyable, don't you think?" said Maggie.

"I thought that guy was going to have a heart attack for sure!"

"I though *you* were going to have a coronary yourself when he left the store with the ring!" she laughed.

"I didn't know what to think. I didn't expect him to go into the mall with it."

"I guess he was desperate to find a black light for a stone like that."

"Yeah, and what a better place to find a black light than in a hippy store?" said Alec.

The couple made it back home and locked the ring in their safe. Maggie did not touch it for two weeks. She confided in a friend about their little excitement. She used to be a manager for a department store jeweler years ago. Maggie showed her the ring, but she was no jewelry expert. Her jewelry experience consisted of assisting with a few sales, but she mainly concentrated on the books. When Maggie told her the name of the gentleman at the jewelry store, she became excited.

"Benton? His name was Benton?" asked Karris.

"Yes."

"Oh, my gosh, Megan! That man was a jewelry expert. I used to work with him until he got fired. He was an ass, but he did know his jewelry!"

"Why did he get fired?" asked Maggie with her best attempts at being clueless.

"He snubbed the customers and his arrogance clouded his judgment. He did not have a professional demeanor with the public."

"I don't understand," Maggie teased, "maybe you can come back to the jewelry store with me to see Benton. He made me feel at home as if I were a member of his family," she giggled.

"Uh, that's not possible, Megan."

"Why not?"

"I read his obituary last week and it said that he died of a heart attack."

Maggie was not surprised that he passed away, but it did come as a shock that it happened so close to when they saw him at the store. She felt bad for the man and she hoped that her Alexandrite did not push him over the edge.

"Do you know of a trustworthy gemologist?" asked Maggie remembering Benton insisting that she find one.

"Yes I do. His name is Lou Gazardi and I've got his number at home. He is wonderful!"

"Lou Gazardi? Why does that name sound familiar?"

"Maybe you sold him a house."

"No, but I know that I've heard that name before."

Karris phoned Maggie as soon as she got home to pass on the phone number of the gemologist. Maggie could not get the name Lou Gazardi out of her head and it was driving her nutty trying to place where she had heard that name. She went for a jog in her neighborhood that evening to ease some anxieties. Afterwards, she went home to soak in a nice bubble bath with hopes to free her mind of her inner monolog, which seemed to sound like a broken record from events of the day that would replay over and over again.

As she found herself beginning to relax in the tub, she slid under the water to saturate her hair. The elevated temperature of her bathwater was heavenly. She stayed under water until she could no longer hold her breath. As she came up for air, the name Lou Gazardi fell into place as if someone flicked on a switch. Her clear and quiet mind, she had struggled to achieve, was now flooded with the memory of that man's name.

She remembered having the dream of the angel in white. She remembered the woman saving her from the man in black. She searched her mind for the name of the woman.

"Tosconda! That was her name," she said aloud.

She mentioned the name Lou Gazardi just before Maggie woke up, but it was so distant and unclear that she thought it was something Gazarri. Maggie had no idea why, but now the mystery must revolve around the ring. Maggie's nerve endings felt fully charged from her recent discovery. She felt that her adrenaline awoke each and every nerve in her body. She placed the warm washcloth over her face to try to calm her mind. She lay back in the tub trying to relax her mind with hopes that her body would soon follow.

Maggie added hot water to her bath to help soothe her tense muscles. She concentrated on the sounds of the running water while enjoying its warmth surrounding her with comfort. She tried to empty her mind, but it wandered to the woman in white. Her bath was at a comfortable temperature and she turned off the faucet. She lay back in the tub and closed her eyes. She could picture the woman's face clearly and she wondered how she knew her as a child. Maggie finally drifted off to a state of relaxation that bordered between consciousness and sleep.

She stumbled into a memory of when she was a young child. Maggie looked to be around six or seven. She could see herself playing in the back bedroom, at Aunt Paula's house, in front of the large mirror next to the bed. She had no one to play with at that house since Maddie started to skate every weekend with Aunt Cami. Little Maggie created an imaginary friend she discovered living in the mirror. She was a gentle soul and she was a young woman. Maggie remembered how her imagination ran wild when her new friend told her that her name was Tosconda, as if saying the number two.

Every time Maggie would walk into that bedroom, she could see Tosconda waving at her with a gentle smile. When Maddie would visit on rare occasions, Maggie would try to introduce her friend to her sister, but only Maggie could see her. This woman was as real to the little girl as any other human being. She played with her friend in the mirror for hours. She remembered wishing that she could live on Tosconda's side of the mirror because it looked happier over there. She thought about the joy and comfort her friend in the mirror brought to such an unhappy child. Maggie wondered how she could possibly forget such a compassionate friend. She studied the woman's friendly face in the mirror with great admiration until Uncle Doug's lascivious face appeared suddenly over the woman's shoulder. Maggie felt as if he were peering into the very depths of her soul.

Maggie gasped and quickly sat up in the bathtub with a start! She found herself staring wildly around the bathroom as she tried to catch her breath. She felt spooked to the point that she felt an unwanted presence watching her in the bathroom.

"Go away! Get out of my home," she yelled as she grabbed the towel to conceal her naked body.

Alec ran to check on his wife. He found her trembling with fear. As their eyes met, she was embarrassed by her reaction and she claimed that she fell asleep in the tub and had a nightmare. She attributed her uncontrollable shivering to being cold. As she darted past Alec to get to her bedroom, she decided to put Lou Gazardi's phone number into the safe with her ring and forget about them both. She did not want to think about that silly ring anymore. She just wanted things to go back to normal. She wanted to concentrate on her family and her job, like usual.

Months had gone by and one evening Maggie received a phone call from a Mr. Gazardi. Allie had taken the call earlier when Maggie was at the office. Allie wrote down his name and number by the phone. As Maggie was reading the message, the phone rang and it was the gemologist she desperately tried to avoid.

"Hello, Maggie. My name is Lou Gazardi. I saw your friend, Karris, the other day and she told me about a ring you inherited."

Maggie was surprised that the man was calling her at home, much less him calling her Maggie. Everyone outside of the family knows her as Megan, not Maggie. She remained pleasant on the phone with Mr. Gazardi, but she was hesitant to discuss the subject at hand.

"She had no right to trouble you with such nonsense. I apologize for her making you call me. I'm sure you're a very busy man."

"Actually, I got your number from your husband. He brought your ring to me last week. I'm just getting around to phoning you about the results. I ran into Karris and her husband coincidently at the symphony the other night."

Maggie was in disbelief that she was having this conversation. She could not believe that her husband would take her ring behind her back like that. She was appalled by Alec's actions and embarrassed by her sounding clueless over the phone. Maggie was angry. She wished that the ring had never fallen into her possession because it had brought her nothing but grief and misery.

"Well, Lou, what do you have to report? Is it costume jewelry or what?" she said sarcastically with a sigh while still feeling the sting of betrayal by her husband.

"Actually, you have a treasure chest in this little black box of yours. Most people don't know what they're looking at when they see an Alexandrite. It is a very rare stone."

"Are you telling me that it's authentic?" she asked enthusiastically.

"Yes. It's a Russian Alexandrite. There is a history behind it. It was discovered in the early eighteen hundreds and named after the Russian Tsar Alexander II. The mines became depleted years ago and the gems were no longer allowed to be exported. The chemical composition makes the color change, which is also what makes these gems rare."

"What does this mean exactly?"

"Collectors would pay a fortune to have this four carat ring. I could bore you with the details of the tests I preformed if you like," he said.

"I appreciate your trouble, but I wouldn't understand your jargon if my life depended on it. Please forgive me for cutting to the chase, but how much value does this ring hold exactly?"

"I know a group of collectors that are eager to look at your ring here in my store. I keep it locked up tight in my safe. If you are interested in selling, I will personally see that you get a handsome price. You are welcome to be present if you wish. I'm anticipating this event to be a blast!"

"As tempting as that sounds, my schedule at the office is tight. How much of a cut are you asking?"

"It would be my pleasure and there is no charge to you at all. This would be a bragging right for me to sell a genuine Alexandrite. It's said that an Alexandrite brings a good omen to all who own it. It is also said to enhance creativity and imagination for those who wear it. Like I said, this stone has a history to it."

"What is it they are looking for specifically?"

"They look for vivid color change, clarity, and so forth. Like anyone who shops around, it all depends on the individual's personal taste. Your ring puts on quite a show of color. That's what makes it more valuable. I'm guessing that the starting bid might be $25,000."

"Really?"

"Yes. Russia is not the only place to have Alexandrite gems. They have been found in other countries, but the color is a little different."

"This sounds like quite an adventure," said Maggie. "I give you my permission to have your meeting with your group of collectors. Please call me and keep me posted on what they think. Thank you, Lou, for your time."

Alec walked in the back door from his golf tournament. Maggie met him in the kitchen to discuss the ring. He was embarrassed that she found out about the ring like she had, but that quickly diminished when he heard that big money could be involved. Alec assured his wife that it would be strictly her decision on what she wants to do with the ring.

"It all depends on how much we can get for it," she said.

"Look at it this way; does it have any sentimental value to you?"

Maggie thought about that question long and hard. She knew that her mother stole it from a criminal. She also knew that Doug's second wife was probably the one who picked out the other stones from the old jewelry before his arrest. Luckily, she did not know that the ring in the little black box was of any value.

"Something good has to come out of this ring, right?" she said, trying to analyze the whole situation.

"Think about the dream you had of Aunt Paula. Maybe she really wanted you to have the ring," said Alec.

"But then again, maybe there is something more that I should be doing with it."

"How do you mean?" he asked nervously.

"If the price is right, then I might want to use the money to start a crisis hotline for dysfunctional families or for people having trouble suppressing urges to hurt children. I would like to have advertisements with little messages of encouragement along with the phone number to my center. This could be big, Alec!" she said with great enthusiasm.

"Are you serious?"

"There are so many daily pressures that some individuals cannot handle on their own and this is how children become punching bags and so forth. I want the money from this ring to pay professionals to offer support groups at no cost to those in need. We will offer help to *anyone* who asks for it."

"If you want to start a business, you should be *making* money, not giving it away!" he said.

"Alec, it all depends on how much we can get for the ring. I would love to put aside money for our children's college funds, but I would also like to help individuals receive the help they need to function in life. Maybe the ring will get us started enough to see how well the idea of the center is received by the community."

"I don't understand."

"It's becoming clearer to me now," she said as she stared off in the distance. "Tosconda! The angel in my dream saved me from death. She became the rope that swung me to safety. I want to be the one to throw a rope to rescue those in need. I want to help mend the bridge of broken dreams and help guide families to a brighter future."

"How do you mean?"

"I eventually want to offer short-term counseling from professionals, depending on how far we can go with the finances. I want to bridge the gap for those who need help through child services. Maybe I can be the voice for those who are not heard. I would like to offer a referral service for the care needed for individuals who need more intensive therapy. Our hotline would be open to everyone and place people where they can receive the help they need."

"Whoa! Slow down, Maggie. What would you gain by doing all of this?"

"Alec, by helping others is a way of helping me. It is time to stop ignoring my past and face it head on. Maybe I can heal my pain by helping others through theirs."

Alec noticed the tears welling in Maggie's eyes. He had never heard her so excited about any project before during the whole time he's known her. How could he say "no" to such ambition and sincerity? He loved his wife and he knew that it was his responsibility to support her, whether he was fully invested in the idea or not. What he did want for his wife was for her to finally find peace. He knew that helping others in need was in her nature and that he would forever be devoted to her and her needs.

He strived on being that one person she could trust and count on to never let her down. Maggie hadn't had very many heroes in her life, but Alec was her knight in shining armor. He understood that his wife believed that everything that happened in her life was for a specific reason. He knew that she would find comfort in knowing that her painful past happened so that she could help others. That was how she would be able to find the peace she so desperately deserved. She always strived to find the positive in any dark situation. That was what he loved most about his wife.

"Okay, Maggie, I see your point of view."

"Do you really?" she asked.

"Sure. A dirty old man once owned the ring, which so happens to be the same ring, according to your mother, that was stolen for you. In a round about way, his money will be helping those in need. Am I right?"

"That's *exactly* what I mean. Besides, Lou said that the Alexandrite is said to bring a good omen to those who own it. How could we argue with that?" she said with a smile.

"Only you, Maggie, would think of something like that," he said with a half-hearted smile.

"It's what's in my heart, Alec. It's like a calling. I've never felt this adamant about anything else before in my life. This is really strange to be making plans for something so big when I don't have the finances in my possession, but it feels so right."

"Well, all we can do now is wait for the phone call," said Alec with a sigh.

Maggie just smiled as she watched Alec plop down into the kitchen chair. She walked over to her husband and massaged his shoulder because she could see that he was disappointed with her decision, which made her feel slightly sorry for him. She straddled his lap and embraced him in her arms tenderly. She looked him in the eye and smiled. She could see him start to melt. She kissed him passionately as she ran her fingers through his hair. She always got a frisky response when she touched him like that.

As she pulled away from him slightly, she whispered in his ear, "I promise to make it worth your while, Sir Alec; my knight in shining armor," as her lips softly brushed his earlobe.

"You're damn straight you will, me lady!" he said with a mischievous grin as he scooped his wife up into his muscular arms and carried her upstairs.

"Did you remember to grab the key?" she teased as she was kissing his neck.

He paused on the step for a moment. He looked into his wife's eyes and replied, "Don't you fret, me lady. I conquered that lock on your chastity belt long ago." Maggie just smiled at her handsome man with excitement as he swiftly carried his woman up the stairs.

Later that evening, Maggie had a dream about walking through a crowded room filled with strangers. This particular dream looked familiar with its colorless atmosphere. It possessed the sense of ordinary with individuals all looking the same while a white fog encircled the room. She realized that she was having a recurring dream. She quickly headed towards the door because she did not want to see Uncle Doug again. As she was about to exit the room, she noticed someone standing in the corner. This time it was not her Uncle Doug. It was April.

Maggie hardly recognized her mother. April stood cowering in the corner like a frightened child. She looked thin, dirty, and she was wearing old rags for clothes. Maggie ran to assist and comfort her mother without hesitation. Maggie was also sad to see that her mother had become a shadow like Uncle Doug.

Maggie gently lifted April's chin to look her in the eyes and said, "Mom? What are you doing here? You don't belong in a place like this."

She was surprised to see April crying real tears. She reacted as if Maggie was a stranger when she was approached. April was backed into a corner and she had nowhere to turn. April said desperately, "I'm lost. I don't know where I belong. Can you help me? No one here seems to care. I don't know where else to go," she cried.

Maggie's heart was broken to see her mother so miserable. It was obvious to Maggie that her mother did not recognize her. Maggie was beside herself with grief. She took her mother by the hand and guided her to the door. April was apprehensive at first, but she followed Maggie as if she were a small child who was lost in a department store.

"Don't be afraid, Mom. I don't know what is beyond this door, but what I do know is that you do *not* belong in a place like this. Stay close to me, Mom. I will keep you safe," promised Maggie.

Just as Maggie stepped through the open door, she turned to see that her mother would not walk beyond the doorway. Maggie tried to have her mother walk with her, but she refused to take another step. Maggie knew that there was no way of talking her mother into something she did not want to do. By the look on April's face, Maggie knew she would walk no further with her. Maggie felt helpless and weak. Such a feeling of sadness and desperation filled Maggie's heart. All she could do was embrace her mother tightly, knowing that she would never see her again.

Maggie held no resentment in her heart towards her mother. All that was available was the love she always held for the woman. She cried on her mother's shoulder so hard that Maggie began to feel as if she had just grown down into the body of a small five-year-old child. She was now hugging April at the waist. Maggie could not recall ever holding her mother like that in her whole life. It was an innate emotion between mother and child, which somehow felt comforting to her.

"Shhh, there, there. Don't cry, Maggie," April said as she was gently stroking her daughter's hair.

Maggie looked up at her mother with surprise. She saw that her mother was bright in color just like Aunt Paula was in her dream. She was beautiful. April slowly backed away from Maggie as the door began to close, separating them forever. She was staring at her daughter with admiration. She smiled sweetly at Maggie and said, "I had to see you one more time before I had to go. I just wanted to be sure that you loved me as much as I love you. I'm very proud of the person you are, Maggie. I absolutely love everything about you. You have a good heart, Maggie. Never forget that, please," said April as she about disappeared behind the door.

"Mom! Don't go! *Please*, stay here with me! You don't belong in there with that crowd," cried Maggie as she tried to keep the door from closing.

"It's all good, Maggie," she said with a gentle smile. "Come take a peek inside and you will see for yourself. This is the place we will meet together once more when it's your time to come home."

Maggie walked towards the door as it swung open wide. She was amazed to see every color of the rainbow light up the room. There was life within what was once a dark and lifeless room. Her heart felt that it was about to burst with the sudden rush of warm and compassionate emotion. She possessed such an overpowering feeling of love and peace that was never before experienced in such a way. She looked back at her mother with a smile. Maggie was happy for her to be in such a place. She could see her grandparents through the door along with other people who passed away in the past. Maggie was glad to see that Douglas Carr was not among the many faces in the crowd.

"Maggie, I've got to go. I love you so much, honey."

"I love you, too, Mom," she said with tears streaming down her cheeks.

"Just remember that all is good, Maggie," she said with a smile as the door slowly began to close. "All is good," April said just as the door shut.

Maggie was beside herself with an overwhelming sense of happiness mixed with sorrow. "All is good," were the last words that Maggie heard from her mother in a glorious dream.

As soon as April closed the dingy door, Maggie awoke feeling exhausted. She felt as if it were impossible to lift her head off of her pillow. Her whole body felt like it weighed a ton. Just as she wondered if that were a dream or if it were real, she fell fast asleep. She never again dreamed of that place. Since April's funeral, Maggie had never experienced nightmares of the man in black and there were no more dreams of falling from broken bridges. It was as if April took all those horrors with her and locked them away behind that door. Maggie finally felt at peace with herself for the first time in her life.

Chapter 23

The years passed by quickly and Maggie could not believe that it was the fifth anniversary of April's death. Maggie was sitting at a traffic light in Indianapolis after a long day at the office. She had a million things on her mind. She reflected on her conversation with Aunt Kathleen a few weeks prior. Kathleen was passing through Indianapolis and she invited Maggie to meet her for lunch.

They met in a quiet restaurant in the heart of the city. Kathleen was thrilled to meet with her niece, but Maggie was quick to notice that her aunt seemed a bit melancholy. Besides exchanging Christmas cards every year, Maggie had not seen or heard from her aunt since the funeral. Their little rendezvous was accredited to Kathleen traveling back home to Ohio after visiting her grandson in St. Louis, Missouri. After the ladies received their drinks, Kathleen was quick to blurt out that April had problems that reached deeper than anyone could possibly imagine.

Maggie remained quiet and expressionless as not to offend her aunt, even though she wanted to ask Kathleen what she meant by such a statement. Michael had instilled upon his children the understanding that it was better to keep one's mouth shut in order to gain information from someone just by listening rather than flapping their lips in the wind. It was obvious to Maggie that Kathleen was struggling with elaborating on that remark by the way she avoided eye contact with her. After she finished her cocktail, Kathleen confessed that she told April, weeks before her death, that she knew why Katherine hated her.

The credibility of Kathleen's story was honest and trustworthy to April since her eldest sister was their grandmother's favorite. April's lifelong obsession of finding the answer to "why did Grandma hate me so much?" was finally coming to an end. It was unfortunate for April that it was a double-edged sword. It had been a family secret amongst April's sisters for years that Ruby had an affair with Bo's father, Herbert Connolly, not Bo's brother Ed, whom April had suspected for years. Maggie was stunned by such a statement, which made her wonder how her mother reacted to such an accusation.

Kathleen went on to say that Bo had been away at boot camp while she, just an infant at the time, and Ruby resided with the in-laws. Herbert was twenty years Ruby's senior and Katherine cut the man off from having maritals because she preferred being sexually pleasured by women. Katherine dropped that bombshell on Herbert after Ed, their second child, was born. She told him that she had the doctor sew it up down there because she was done using it. Herbert was a man with sexual needs and Ruby was more than happy to oblige him. She just did not plan on getting pregnant. No one would ever know if the sex was consensual or not, but Ruby's reputation would make one suspect that it was.

Kathleen felt bad for saying something so terrible to April, but she felt that she could no longer keep the ten year secret that she and her sisters swore to never tell. On Bo's deathbed, he confessed to Kathleen that April was not his daughter, but she was his half-sister. He told her that after the affair, Paula learned of it and the pregnancy that followed; harsh words were said during a confrontation between the Connolly couple and Paula. Ruby's big sister defended her honor and accused Herbert of raping her sister as his way of collecting rent. That was the day when the hatred between Katherine and Paula was born.

Bo said that they attempted to cover up the affair by shipping Ruby to meet him while he was finished with boot camp, which was obvious that the couple would be having intercourse. He told Kathleen that April was born early, but he could not understand why her birth weight was that of a full-term baby. When Ginny was going through her divorce, her soon-to-be ex-husband was the one who told Bo about the affair just to create strife for Ginny. It was said that

Ruby confessed the affair to Ginny shortly before she died. Ginny, thinking that she could confide such an emotional upset with her husband, never dreamed he would use it against her and the secret would get back to April or Bo.

The news was a shock to Bo and it landed him in the hospital. He had a bad heart, which was a condition that ran deep in their family history. Kathleen happened to be the one person he felt comfortable telling such a tale, which Ginny had confided in her also. He told her that he counted back nine months from when he and Ruby were together, but he came up short on the gestational timeline. He told Kathleen that he did not ever want April to find out the truth. He also told her that April might not be his by birth, but she was definitely his by choice. That heartfelt statement in itself was why Kathleen eventually told April the painful truth since April lived her life thinking that Bo never loved her like a father should love a child.

Maggie felt bad to hear that her mother had endured such hardships. April lived her life not knowing where she fit in with her family by looking so different and having a grandmother hate her so much. It was painfully obvious to her sisters. April died knowing that Bo was not her father, but her half-brother. Her sisters became half-sisters and the other half were April's nieces. She lived her life suspecting that it was a strong possibility that Ed was her biological father, but she never dreamed that it would be her Grandpa Herbert. She learned the painful truth that her whole life was a sham. Everything she ever believed in was far from the truth.

Kathleen offered to pay for the DNA testing if April wanted scientific proof of such a rumor. April was brave and she challenged her sister to put her money where her mouth was. Kathleen was surprised that April accepted her generosity. Bo had been dead for years, but Kathleen saved clippings of her father's hair, which was easy for her to do since she was the one who cut his hair. Kathleen even offered to partake in the DNA testing to help build up a parental profile. She volunteered a salvia sample to aid in accuracy for the test. The results were mailed to Kathleen and she opened them at April's house. The tests proved that Bo was not April's father. They did a sibling DNA on April and Bo, which proved to be a match by isolating their father's DNA.

The news was sad to Maggie because no one knew of such a tragedy. Her mother died days after she learned the truth. Kathleen felt responsible for her sister's death, but Maggie was quick to tell her aunt that her mother died knowing the truth. Maggie pondered that thought for a moment. She thought it was an uncanny statement since her mother repeatedly stated throughout the years just how much she hated liars when in reality, her whole life was noting but a lie.

April lived her life believing that she was the outcast in her family. Maggie understood then why Aunt Paula was so close to April. It was all out of pity. She thought it was sad that April had no intentions on sharing such news with her family. Maggie figured that her mother was ashamed of the truth, but in reality April was the innocent victim. It was surprising to Maggie that even Kenneth did not hear of such a story. Maybe the truth was too much for April to bear, but April wanted the truth and the truth is exactly what she got. It was sad to Maggie that her mother chose to keep it to herself. Maggie thanked her Aunt Kathleen for being brave enough to uncover the truth. She also reassured her aunt that she did not kill her mother.

As Maggie remained at, what seemed to be, the longest light in town, she just shook her head in disbelief. She thought that her own screwed up childhood came from a woman born into this world from lies and deceit. Maggie pitied her Grandpa Bo for being a victim, too. It was bad enough that his wife cheated on him, but the real gut-wrenching truth of cheating with his own father was far more than anyone could possibly bear. She then thought about how Herbert paid for his affair for the rest of his life. Katherine rode that man to his grave. He died a broken shell of a man.

Maggie's attention was diverted to a city bus as it drove through the intersection. It displayed an advertisement that read: "How will *you* be remembered? Call 1-CAN-HELP YOU. Tell them Maggie sent you." She smiled feeling as if she had won the lottery. Her advertisements have been seen all around the city. She had made many friends in the business world who were more than eager to help her get started with her hotline. Her real-estate company started a fund raising campaign for her cause, which was really catching on with the locals. They'd get calls from various large businesses offering to donate generous sums of money. Her center was called

April Showers Family Crisis Center with the slogan "Let us shield you through the storm," with a large umbrella being their logo.

Many families benefited from its group therapy sessions at no charge and professional help through their twenty-four hour hotline. Maggie's ring paid-off big! She put some money aside for college for her children and had enough money left over to get her little project started. The facility was funded mostly by various sponsors, who sought help through Maggie's center for their employees as a fringe benefit. Alec created a professional website for the center and he managed the advertising, which was attracting attention from other states. Eventually, Alec hoped to expand the April Showers Family Crisis Center nationwide. Maggie was elated to know that people were willing to help make this world a better and brighter place to live. She understood that everyone had a tale of tragedy to share and that it took a lot of courage asking for help. She wanted people to feel that it was safe to be able to do so at her center.

Maggie continued to sell houses part-time because of her love of interacting with people in her community. She encouraged her coworkers to earn their title as sales person of the year while she concentrated on her new path in life, which was helping people just like herself. She had learned that by helping those in need was a way of her dealing with her own tragedies. She could not change things in her past, but she could certainly focus on a more stable future by helping people along the way. She had learned to embrace her personal tragedies and share them with others. By freeing such sadness and pain was her first step towards gaining her emotional freedom.

For a brief second, Maggie's mind visited a memory of the last time she saw April in a dream. She remembered her mother saying in a most comforting and reassuring voice, "All is good, Maggie," she said, accompanied with the sweetest smile that never before touched Maggie's heart so deeply. Maggie's traffic light finally turned green and she said aloud with confidence and a heartfelt smile, "Yes, all *is* good."

Printed in the United States
92213LV00007B/15/A